D0938234

The Suspense Is Killing Me

By Thomas Maxwell

KISS ME ONCE
THE SABERDENE VARIATIONS
KISS ME TWICE

THOMAS MAXWELL

The Suspense Is Killing Me

THE MYSTERIOUS PRESS
New York • Tokyo • Sweden • Milan
Published by Warner Books

 A Time Warner Company

Copyright © 1990 by Thomas Maxwell
All rights reserved.

 Mysterious Press books are published by
Warner Books, Inc., 666 Fifth Avenue, New York, NY 10103

 A Time Warner Company

Printed in the United States of America
First Printing: October 1990

10 9 8 7 6 5 4 3 2 1

Library of Congress Cataloging-in-Publication Data

Maxwell, Thomas.
    The suspense is killing me / Thomas Maxwell.
        p.   cm.
    ISBN 0-89296-167-8
    I. Title.
PS3563.A926S87   1990
813'.54—dc20   90-33640
                                                                  CIP

For Rachel and Tom

The Suspense Is Killing Me

Ah, for the days
That set our hearts ablaze.
                    —Rimbaud

My god, how the time slips away.
                    —JC Tripper

Author's Note

Any writer of fiction is bound to be asked the sources of his characters. Are they real? Are they composites of people he has known? Are they entirely fictional? And if so, how is that possible? Writers spend a certain amount of time wriggling away from being too specific, frequently because they can't really pin down a character's birth.

But not always.

A character I find particularly interesting and appealing in this novel, Annie DeWinter, doesn't appear until fairly late in the proceedings. She is, however, a pivotal character. You don't have to ask me about her because I'm taking this opportunity to tell you from whence she came.

I found her in Greenwich Village, working in a bookstore about three blocks from where I live. Initially I noticed, as chaps will, that she was strikingly—indeed, almost alarmingly—beautiful. Tall, slender, square-shouldered, her skin very pale, her hair dramatically black. In time I noticed her earrings. They were new ones on me and they were perfect for Annie DeWinter. She was perfect for Annie DeWinter. Her name was Michelle.

Annie was a blank until then. And then she took over Michelle's body. I asked her for the use of her earrings and she told me how she'd come to get them—also incorporated into the story, at least in outline. Annie became Michelle. And that is how this writer found a crucial character.

Needless to say, Annie's personality is entirely her own; her experiences and her generation and her life have nothing whatever to do with Michelle. But she wouldn't be Annie if I hadn't met Michelle. So, my thanks to Michelle a thousand times over.

This writing gig. Nothing to it.

—Thomas Maxwell
New York City
February 1990

Greetings . . .

I've just come back from visiting my attorney and my banker. I tell them I see them on Visiting Day, not because they are actually in prison but—let's face it—they might very well be, only a couple more deals down the road. Morris and Harold, to give them names, find me something of a joker, but that's not to be confused with thinking I'm funny. They seldom smile when I'm around, and even if they had once, they wouldn't have been smiling much today. They were wearing what you might call their openmouthed, dying-fish looks when I got through with them. I signed a hand-written statement while they looked on and then we made use of a safe-deposit box. Harold Berger looked as if he might be doing something criminal without quite being sure. I was indeed the only one doing any laughing. I handed my key to the box to Morris Dicker. He frowned. It was the look of a man who has just been videotaped accepting the Baggie bulging with cocaine. "Everything be fine," I said, "everything be cool. Ax me no questions, relax, my man."

Morris looked at Harold. Harold looked at me and said, "I hate you, Lee."

1

Morris nodded. "You're an absolute charlie, Lee. There's no other word for it. For you, I mean."

"Don't give me that crapola," I explained. Then I smilingly outlined his place in the great scheme of things. I told him about the lawyer who fell into the school of feeding sharks but went untouched, climbed back into the boat, and said to his astonished companions, "Professional courtesy." It is not uncommon for lawyers to forget their place in the g. s. and then they must be reminded. Ditto for investment bankers who are frequently too young to have learned their place. Harold was not an investment banker. He was just a banker banker.

The hell with all this. It's always a mistake for me to get started on lawyers and bankers. Morris and Harold are okay guys. Slow but okay. And I've never actually caught either of them molesting a child.

I felt better having taken care of business because I'm trying to save myself a lot of heartache and grief and unnecessary confusion later on when the shit hits the f. I'm not sure anything's going to happen, mind you, but it might, and better safe than sorry. Pay attention to Granny's samplers and you can never go far wrong. That's my advice. A fool and his money are soon parted, too.

Now you'd better sort of brace yourself for this story because, let me be absolutely frank with you, it's full to the brim with deceit and treachery and violence and the occasional laugh to break the tension, and plain, outright, bald-faced lies. I'm going to tell it as it happened, lies and all, and good luck to you. Don't trust a goddamn thing anybody says and never return by the way you came.

My name is Lee Tripper.

And I wouldn't lie to you.

Unless I absolutely had to.

Prologue

The package arrived by UPS. It was signed for and delivered up to my condominium by one of the smartly attired doormen whose cheery, helpful disposition indicated he knew on which side his croissants were buttered. He all but saluted once he'd handed it over and adroitly stepped away when I reached into my pocket for a tip. "Part of the job, Mr. Tripper," he said, as he almost always did. He knew the payoff was in the end much larger when he hadn't nickeled-and-dimed everybody to death all year.

I took it to the terrace, where the afternoon shadows had cooled off one of the summer's first hot days. The breeze rustling the trees in Central Park below felt good and clean and pure. Summer hadn't yet beaten Manhattan to its grubby knees.

The return address meant nothing to me. A street somewhere in Seattle, the initials ABM. I slit the twine and tape with the old Swiss Army knife I used for a letter opener and peeled the wrapping paper away, then unfolded the top of a cardboard box somewhat larger than a shoe box.

It contained a letter, an old envelope marked HARRIGAN'S DELUXE PHOTO FINISHING, and a largish, heavy oilskin package with several thick rubber bands tightly enclosing it. The letter was short. It was signed by someone I'd never met.

Dear Mr. Tripper,

My father, Martin Bjorklund, with whom you were once acquainted, died recently. Among his possessions we found the contents of this box with the instructions that upon his death it all be sent to you. I have no idea what either item is but be assured they have not been opened and are exactly as Father left them. Perhaps they are keepsakes with some particular significance to the two of you.

Sincerely,
Anita Bjorklund Montgomery

For God's sake . . . Marty Bjorklund. I hadn't seen him in twenty years, not since that last meeting in Tangier.

I opened the envelope first.

There were four cracked photographs, each of the same subject. They were Polaroid shots. Harrigan had had nothing to do with them beyond providing an envelope of the right size. They were pictures of a dead man.

I tried unwrapping the rubber bands but they were old and brittle and snapped at my touch. Some of the strands of rubber were embedded in the oilskin, which was itself cracked, dried out. Slowly I unfolded the flaps, it slowly dawning on me what I'd find. When the oilskin was entirely pried away, the heavy oily thing, so redolent of what it was, lay on the table before me.

A Mauser Parabellum nine-millimeter automatic. The four-inch barrel gave it a slender elegance. It was built on the Swiss Luger model.

Pictures and a gun.

It looked like the evidence in a murder case . . .

One

This story gets so hairy so fast I vote for a nice calm beginning, saxophones and some strings and your overall Nelson Riddle arrangement. Because soon enough we get to the Death's Head Rangers and the Traveling Executioner's Band and there'll be times when all you can do is put your hands over your ears and wait for it to be over. So, nice and easy does it every time. Incidentally, did you know that the publisher of this tale is giving a very large reward for the longest list of song titles any reader finds embedded in the text? Cheggidout.

The first time you meet me—well, let's begin with the day I found my first corpse. That put a real crimp in my general state of mind, which was too bad because I'd started the day without a care to my name. It had been a long time since I'd felt so good about things. In fact, now I think about it, I'd never felt so good about things, not once in my entire life, and that was saying something because I'm known for my sunny dispozish. Naturally it couldn't last, this feeling of well-being. No sane person would expect it to. But a corpse? How often does a corpse louse up your momentary euphoric glimpse of true, unencumbered contentment? Not very damned often, would be my guess.

5

I was lingering over my coffee and the morning's papers, sitting on the spacious terrace of my recently acquired home, a condo in a gravely imposing temple to money and the vague New Yorky status that goes with it. Central Park West. Looking out across the topless towers of Ilium or something, looking down on the lakes and meadows of the Park, the Delacorte Theater, Tavern on the Green, all baking under the summer sun. The Metropolitan Museum and the cliffs of Fifth Avenue across the Park. Mia and all the kids lived not far away and Woody was over on the other side cutting his new movie and I could practically hear the Gershwin from *Manhattan*. Actually I could hear the music from *Manhattan* because it was playing on the stereo while I breakfasted and enjoyed the view. This, you may already have predicted, was too good to last; but I hadn't, I admit, seen the inevitability of disaster. I was a silly fellow who thought he'd at last achieved what he'd always deserved. Well, I was just about to, as it turned out.

The striped, fringed awning over the French doors flapped as it caught the morning breeze. My potted palms stood swaying like languid, leftover guests who couldn't bear the idea of going home. I felt so robust and healthy and happy I was within a hair's breadth of bellowing and whacking my chest. I had my reasons.

My heavy doping days were behind me. I never thought about all that anymore. If you, gentle reader, peruse these pp. in hope of zeroing in on lurid dramatic reconstructions, you are out of luck. As Katharine Hepburn once said to me and my brother JC on another occasion, "You are barking up a tree you can't climb." No recollections of druggy days. Well, maybe the odd reminiscence of my famous brother's exploits is inevitable, but none of mine. Or damn little of mine, anyway.

This happy, Mary Poppins–like state of mind was of recent origin. Let me tell you how I'd lost touch with reality and found myself in such a good mood.

A couple of years before, I was scraping along as a sort of ragtag journalist, trying to live off my late brother's reputation and having fairly hard going of it. I was treated in some quarters as a kind of fourth-rate Rock Icon, having you know like been there and all with JC himself—which is just the way these nitwits talk. I was caught between a James Dean Rock Fantasy and the Nostalgia Wave. I was a man with a sketchy-looking future at best and a very messy Rock Generation Gone Sour past, and forgive the capitalizations, but that's the way the poor jerks who *think* about those days like their prose. It was all incredibly humbling, having been on top of the pile, no matter if it had been a pretty rubbishy pile. As I sank lower and lower in the pecking order of Post–Modern Rock personages, I didn't complain: I had my reasons for preferring anonymity. And the truth was, those had been the days, hadn't they? At least some of them.

Anyway, I'd kicked around Europe and a few other less well-known and certainly less promising continents for more than a decade, lying doggo, like a lost ball in the high weeds, as Robert Ryan says to Dean Jagger in *Bad Day at Black Rock*. I had a lot of time for movies and books and staring into space, mistakenly looking for my soul because I was trying to recover from the rock days, all those weird rock dreams everybody always used to talk about so long ago. I was getting older, my hair was flecking with gray and I was losing a lot of it. I got used to my face without a beard and it got a good bit fuller. I raised a perfectly respectable crop of jowls. People I'd known for years would see me on the street in Paris or Brisbane or Asunción— that was when I picked up a fair piece of change acting as the radio man on a team trying to locate Martin Bormann but that is most definitely another story—and brush past, not a clue as to who I was. I lived in Paris for a time, did some hiking in the Dordogne and in Tuscany, even went through a misguided attempt at fitness training involving jogging in the Bois de Boulogne. I ran afoul of unpleasant, uncouth scoundrels during what I think of as the Christ of the Andes Blunder. But mainly I let the years pass me by. I watched the river of Time wash away the old days, wash away many of my sins, wash away JC Tripper and his Traveling Executioner's Band and the huge electric-chair gizmo and JC's endless girlfriends—they had ends, to be sure, but there were a lot of them, is what I meant to say there—and yes, wash away even the chap who had spent all those years being the brother at JC's side—me. I enjoyed being washed away. All the memories became blurred; the memory of the person I'd been was one of those memories, and it fared no better than all the others. I was like a snapshot left in the sun on a window ledge, growing dimmer and dimmer as the time passed. Fine. It was better that way and, believe me, no great loss. And eventually it was time to come home.

When I finally got back from the great out-of-touch-ness called abroad, I ran across a woman called Sally Feinman, who was a magazine writer. Once she realized who I was she behaved as if she'd struck the mother lode. After a month of heavy talking on her part and a fair amount of heavy breathing on mine, she wrote her famous piece for *New York* magazine, "The Traveling Executioner's Last Trip."

Sally was the rare sort of person who felt no need to keep all the good things for herself. When the publishers Hawthorne & Hedrick approached her about doing a book on the final days of JC Tripper, she demurred, insisting to them that I was the man they wanted.

An editor by the name of Tony Fleming gave me a call and set things in motion, primarily by waving a contract and an advance of $50,000 at me. Not princely, perhaps, but I liked the cut of his jib and the fact that there would be no wait for the first twenty-five grand. The check was in hand. And all reasonable expenses. If I would tell the true story of JC's death in Tangier all those years ago. Well, there was the money and I'd been there, an eyewitness. More or less. Unconscious during many of the crucial events, perhaps, but there was no point in going into all that trivia with hopeful, generous Tony. His confidence might reasonably have been expected to flag and I wanted none of that.

The thing was, my brother had surely died back there in Tangier, but you know how it is with the icons of rock and roll. He died of a drug overdose and a liver that had drowned in bourbon and cataclysmic bouts of depression—or "black dog," as he called it, after Churchill. He also died of excessive adulation, unceasing sexual hysteria, and worrying too much about all of it. He just ceased to exist, only the idea of him remained, and in the end it wasn't such a hot idea, if you ask me. He died after running through the better part of thirty or forty million bucks. He died of a bloated, infected ego, like a punchy old fighter who thinks he's got another title shot coming.

These guys like JC and Jim Morrison and Joplin and the biggest tuna of them all, Elvis, the thing is nobody wants them to be really and truly *dead*. Truly gone, never to come twanging and throbbing and gyrating and sweating and screaming back into the spotlight. Dead, these guys become the death of youth and hope, the death of whatever they have become in the tiny, unformed, adolescent and utterly hormone-drowned minds of their fans. God damn it, they were supposed to be immortal . . . when in fact most of them were self-destructive, self-indulgent assholes who bit the big weenie just about on schedule. At least some of them.

The rumors of JC Tripper's survival, the faked death in a remote part of the world where officialdom was thought to be open to persuasion, his subsequent disappearance into the landscape, a victim of pressure and whatnot . . . Was any of that true? Or was he dead? There were all these people sitting around The Four Seasons or Mortimer's or Area in its fleeting day who reflexively gave a knowing wink at the mention of JC's name. Everybody knew there was a book in it somewhere. Tony Fleming was paying me to write it.

I did what any man in my pozish would have done. I took the money. And I traipsed hither and yon on my expense account, from Tangier to the old Moon Club in Zurich, this way and that, checking things out in my old diaries, trying to do the job, or at least trying to look like I was doing the job. I told Fleming that I'd replayed the final frenzied years of JC's life and that, yes, beyond a reasonable doubt, my brother was dead just as I'd told him, his ashes scattered over the Moroccan desert at least a thousand years ago.

JC was, in the opinion of many, one of the era's greatest figures. Or he wasn't. What possible difference could it make? I don't know. But I wrote the book, took the reader back through the finale of rock's first great age. Tony Fleming got his money's worth.

While I was writing back in New York, Sally Feinman did another story, this one for the *Sunday Times Magazine*, about my search for the truth. It made a wonderful promo for my book, which Tony Fleming entitled *Rocking Death: The Tangier Days of JC Tripper.* The book sold something over a hundred thousand copies in hardcover; the paperback rights brought $700,000 and escalators at auction; and MagnaFilms bought the film rights for $450,000. They also paid Sally Feinmann $100,000 for the rights to her two stories, just to cover all the bases and because I told them that my deal hinged on the deal with her. There was a small JC Tripper industry all of a sudden.

And MagnaDisc released his recordings with very snazzy matching artwork in all three formats. As JC's sole heir, I was cleaning up on that front, too. *Fried Psychos* and *Defective Wiring*, the first two albums released in CD form, hit the top of the charts. Big money, my friends. And there were thirteen more albums on the way. Recycling, the wave of the future.

Of course, as Somerset Maugham observed, it wasn't all cakes and ale. Let me give you a for instance. *Time*'s critic reviewed my book in a couple of brief, dismissive paragraphs and trained his Bofors gun on your hmbl servt. He called me "a pathetic remnant of a drugged-out, sex-obsessed subculture without which an entire generation might have stood some slight chance of developing into conscientious, responsible adults." That sounded to me as if he'd been paying attention and pretty much got my drift. I was a pathetic twerp feeding off the iconic remains of my brother, etcetera, etcetera. Well, our generation made an inviting target, didn't it? Who were the survivors? A bunch of gray-bearded ex-hippies who hadn't quite noticed the parade passing them by. And the rest had been pretty well absorbed into the vast body politic, occasionally squeezing into tie-dyed jeans and shirts and remembering the old days. When you get right down to it, however, I'm not altogether sure a bunch of snot-nosed, post-adolescent, ethically stunted Masters of the Universe, practitioners of corporate raiding and lever-aged buyouts and hawkers of junk bonds—greedy little shits who'd sell their grandmothers to make another month's nut on the condo and the BMW—I can't really see how they represent some big step upward on the evolutionary ladder. But don't get me going on all that. Who cares, right? I haven't got anything original to say about it. Viewed in the proper glare, whose generation can withstand careful scrutiny? We're all only befuddled travelers on the Circle Line, yesterday, today, and tomorrow, going round and round and round.

So, back to the day it began.

What happened is that I met this woman, Heidi Dillinger. One of the oldest and most devoutly adhered-to rules in the history of movie-making is what was dubbed a very long time ago "the cute meet." Well, Heidi and I should have been in a movie because we definitely met cute. It didn't last but it was cute.

I left my place about noon with nothing more important on my mind than hitting Dunhill and J & R for cigars, Scribner's for some book browsing—checking on the supply of my book, which was still selling nine months after publication, testament to old JC, and then maybe a call at Paul Stuart for a gander at the new duds. I could make all that last until mid-afternoon, at which time I'd set off on the shady side of Fifth Avenue for an hour or so of strolling, fetching up at Sally's loft in SoHo. Cocktails in her sun room, maybe some dinner at an irritating joint called Raoul's where we'd probably be the only people in the room not gabbling on in French. People thought Raoul's was still the center of the Eurotrash chow line, but in fact most of them had already begun oiling their way up toward Indochine across the street from Joe Papp's place. As it turned out, Sally and I never made it to Raoul's for dinner, but I'm getting ahead of myself here. Nothing turned out the way it was supposed to, not from the time I ran into Mellow Yellow on Fifth Avenue near the entrance to Number 666, beside the B. Dalton Bookstore.

Mellow Yellow was a nimble young fellow of the black persuasion, about six and a half feet high by four feet wide, weighing in at roughly 350, and the operative word would be "roughly." He habitually wore a yellow T-shirt with MELLOW YELLOW printed in black across his pecs, which looked like sacks of wet cement. He and five of his colleagues operated a three-card monte game on Fifth, Sixth, and down on Forty-second between Sixth and Broadway. He was in his own way a tourist attraction, like the Statue of Liberty, only larger. He had an agreement with the cops on the beat, who only rousted him once a day per location. So Mellow and his merry band were raking in $2500 a day. When I stopped to watch the show he was just getting into it, sucking the tourists in with his patter, with his extraordinary manual dexterity. It was a show, and the price for the wary was right. I figured Mellow may have been the only man in America who was being paid exactly what he was worth, to the penny.

I once knew a man in Zurich who said that the simplest cons were best and the simplest cons were those based on nothing but elementary psychology and pure skill. The con man could attain a level of skill that enabled him to bet on himself with nearly absolute certainty. The rest of it was knowing how to sucker the rubes into insisting that you take their money. Mellow had a benign faith in himself and, since he never lost, I assumed he'd found an inner peace that others could only envy.

Watching him work was a little like watching Art Tatum play the piano. Those big black fingers moved with a kind of effortless Zen concentration, as if they were operating out of a genetic muscle-memory inherited from practitioners on the Mississippi riverboats in the years preceding the Civil War. He used two spades and one diamond drawn from a pinochle deck. He shuffled the three cards back and forth, using a fluid cross-handed motion. Each card was bent in exactly the same way as the others, except that for the moment the diamond carried an extra crease at the corner, making it easily identifiable by even the slowest students. Only a blind man could fail to see it, which is, of course, the point.

Mellow was playing to a crowd of twenty or thirty passersby, several of whom actually worked for him. It was hot and he'd set up just inside the shade of the arcade. Some days he'd have had somebody dispensing free lemonade; he was a hell of a businessman, a Donald Trump of the street. Same street, after all. Fifth Avenue.

I'd been watching for five or ten minutes when I noticed the woman who'd come to stand beside me. She was tall and was craning her neck to get a good view. She wasn't paying the slightest attention to me, so I gave her a practiced once-over. Five-nine or -ten; short, close-cropped blond hair revealing tiny, perfectly shaped ears and a long, slender neck, with the hair cut to a geometric point on the nape. Her face was oval with a faint roundness at the cheekbones, pale eyebrows, a short, straight nose, a flat forehead, unusually pale tan eyes, a wide mouth with thin, precise lips and a bemused, quirky smile. She was wearing a navy-blue summer dress, sleeveless with white piping, a necklace of white balls that looked like wood and emphasized her tan. Blue-and-white spectator pumps. Bracelet matching the necklace. She carried a two-tone brown-and-black briefcase I recognized as a Madler, about $1200. She was clearly all business, no nods to current fashion; a paragon of efficiency who, I'd have guessed, had forgotten what it was like to have a personal life or an emotional attachment to another human being. She was very pretty, but in that first summing-up I saw no particular allure in her looks. Everything about her said *I dare you, just try something, make my day* . . . Everything about her was a gauntlet flung down, a challenge. Maybe if she had a weakness, it was gambling. She was a born victim for a guy like Mellow. One look and he'd be licking his lips: she was money in the bank. She thought she was the smartest kid in the class, the smartest thing since Hattie Carnegie's hat.

Mellow's game was progressing by the script.

Three sticks working with Mellow picked the wrong card three successive times when it was perfectly obvious to everyone in the crowd where the diamond was. The sticks were of Tony Award caliber. One guy, a white yuppie in a three-piece suit, about twenty-five, a Vuitton briefcase under his arm, looked as if he were lunching at Prunelle or "21" before heading back down to Wall Street. Another guy was the classic rube tourist— terry-cloth polo shirt, snappy plaid Bermudas, black socks and thong sandals. The female stick was Hispanic: a bright-eyed, intelligent face, cotton blouse, designer jeans from Fourteenth Street sprayed on, bright red toenails in medium heels, a big leather shoulder bag. Among them they *lost* a couple hundred bucks in five minutes, while the rest of the crowd felt superior and groaned each time they picked the wrong card. Finally Mellow rapped out some patter about taking candy from babies and allowed someone else into the game. Now the con began in

13

earnest, the shuffling faster and smoother, the cards fluttering to the surface of the upturned cardboard box. There was the telltale crease in the red diamond.

Forty bucks on the table.

But the red diamond was a spade.

Eighty bucks on the table.

But the red diamond had become the other spade.

That was the problem. Nothing was what it seemed.

The woman standing beside me chuckled, turned to me, shaking that fine small head. Not a hair out of place. "These people are morons." Her voice was deep and throaty.

"Well, Mellow is a considerable artist. A genius in his own way."

"You're cheapening the language," she said.

"It's an unimportant art, but an art nonetheless."

"You're a romantic. He's a creep who is proficient at a creepy job. Anybody with half a brain could clean him out." She was impatient with the stupidity of it all.

"I have an entire brain," I said, "the full complement of brain. And I wouldn't have a chance with Mellow here." I flashed my timeworn boyish grin. "And neither, let me add, would you."

She caught my eye with those odd pale tan numbers of hers, a quizzical expression on her face. "You can't be serious."

"I'll tell you what I would bet on. I'll bet you lunch you can't beat him once."

She looked at her gold Rolex, then back up at me. "You look familiar. Are you a well-known loser about town?"

I shrugged. "It'll cost you lunch to find out."

She checked her watch again, then fished a couple of twenties from the green alligator Filofax. She pushed her way to the front of the crowd and waved the bills in front of Mellow, who grinned broadly, lots of gold bridgework showing. The shuffling began, the cards dropped. She cocked her head, calmly watching his hands, a tiny smile tugging at the corners of her mouth. There was a faint patina of perspiration on her upper lip. Now *that* was alluring.

The cards dropped. Instantaneously, almost as if she weren't looking at them, had lost interest in them, she pointed at one of

14

them. Just the hint of surprise registered on Mellow's massive face.

He turned it over. The diamond.

"Let's do it again," she said. "I wouldn't want to think you were letting me win. I'd love to see how mellow you really are, Mellow. I'm a test, the person you prayed you'd never meet."

He grinned and she won a second time, then a third, collected the money, and stuffed it into the Filofax. Mellow just stared at her impassively, neither angry nor beaten, just relieved to see the last of her. In the end I'm sure it was good for business. Everybody standing around Mellow figured they could do it if this hot-shit broad could do it, but of course they couldn't.

She looked at her watch again.

"There ought to be a law against me," she said. "It's your treat. A fool and his money . . . and you have no excuse. Mellow didn't know I was going to whip his fat black ass but you, my friend, did."

"I did?"

"Well, I told you I would. And I never lie."

"Gambling interests me," she said. "In all its forms." She sipped at a tall glass of iced tea. The yellow table umbrellas flapped overhead. There were flowers everywhere, water splashing beneath the golden sculpture of Prometheus overlooking the outdoor café at Rock Center. Music tinkled from loudspeakers. Hundreds of tourists leaned on the railings staring down into the sea of yellow canvas, a field of dandelions. "For instance, today's the hundredth-and-something anniversary of Wild Bill Hickock's death. He was playing poker in Deadwood, South Dakota, fella shot him in the back. He was holding two pairs, aces and eights. That's why they call it the Dead Man's Hand." She smiled at me but her eyes were still remote and cool and appraising. "You look like a man whose hope blooms eternal. You'll always try to fill an inside straight and you'll be lucky if you pull it off five times in your life."

"How did you do that to Mellow?"

"I know the con. Obviously it's not really gambling. Mellow isn't supposed to run any risk of losing. It's not sport, it's

Mellow's business. When I engage in a game of chance I try to remove the element of chance. Like Mellow. It's a business investment. I hate losing. I mean, what's the point?"

"So how'd you beat Mellow?"

"It's the right hand. He can drop the top card or the bottom card. When he's setting you up he works the top card out first, then the bottom. The two cards in his right hand, the diamond and one of the spades, get dropped bottom-to-top when he's setting it up, then he goes top-to-bottom when it's for money—"

"But what about the crease in the diamond?" I said innocently. She seemed to know what she was talking about.

"Oh, Mellow was good enough at his job. He uncreased the diamond and creased a spade, no way you could see him do it. But when he dropped the cards, one thing you knew for sure—the diamond wouldn't have a crease." She let the tip of her tongue slowly circle her lips. "Look, people get excited, they want to win, they forget to give the dealer credit for skill and brains. I never get excited and I never underestimate."

It was *hot*. We ordered lunch and I shifted around in my sweaty linen suit that was wrinkling just the way it was supposed to, about eighty-five bucks per wrinkle. Lavender-striped shirt, a big floppy lime-green bow tie, a lavender silk pocket square, chocolate-brown reverse calf wing tips. And all of it felt wet. She was, of course, supernaturally cool and dry, perfect. That drove me crazy.

"What's your name?" I said, cutting to the chase.

"Dillinger." That smile, a little one, a tease.

"The blood of the late Public Enemy Number One flows in your veins?"

"Quite possibly. I have made my pilgrimage to Greencastle, Indiana."

"Oh, good!"

"That's the jail John Dillinger broke out of with a gun he carved from a bar of soap and blackened with shoe polish. I like that in a man."

"What?"

"Audacity. Fuck the odds."

"But you always stack the odds in your favor."

"I'm not talking about me. I'm talking about men. Audacity

16

in a man is good. Brains don't much matter. I've got the brains. My first name is Heidi. You have one, too, right?"

"Lee Tripper."

"Ahhh," she said softly. "Tripper. You do look familiar, don't you—I read your book about that brother of yours. What an asshole! I can see his face in you. Is he really dead?" She shook her head, laughing. "No, scratch that. You must get that all the time. So you're a professional brother and—"

"Tactless, Miss Dillinger. You wound me."

"Oh, buck up. You're made of sterner stuff than that. Mustn't crumble in the face of little Heidi's chitchat."

"What is it a person like you does?"

She daintily chewed a forkful of chicken salad and dabbed at her mouth with the napkin. "I'm an adjunct to the writing business, actually. A wholly owned subsidiary specializing in research."

"Owned by whom?"

"ABC. No, not that ABC. Mine is the Allan Bechtol Corporation."

Everything she said seemed to get my attention. Allan Bechtol was one of the world's best-selling novelists—unreadable in my view, but he didn't notice that I no longer bought his books. He was a highly reclusive writer of gigantic thrillers that might just as well have been sold by the pound. Each book contained a great deal of information, so when you finished reading one of the damn things—while the plot may have made no sense—you sort of felt like you'd learned something. He'd written one about the world of computer hackers and viruses, and that literary weekly *People* ran a piece telling how the book had dramatically goosed the sales of some new personal computer. He'd written another one set in a national park, dealing with the search for a Russian mole who had taken refuge among diseased killer bears. That one had really worn your polish off after 750 pages. And the country had gone nuts about bears. Research was what set his books apart. Heidi Dillinger's contribution. It was reported in the press that Bechtol's advance for a novel was approaching five million dollars.

"You must be very well compensated," I said. "Without the

fruits of your labors, he'd have to pay people to read that crap."

"I do all right, but of course you see the truth of things. So I'm not doing as well as I should be. My owning him would be a better arrangement. I'm nothing if not candid."

"Behind Bechtol's back, however."

She laughed at me. "You think I haven't told him the same thing? Don't kid yourself. Of course you're a romantic. Kidding yourself is your style."

"Did you just spring full-grown from Bechtol's brow, or did you do something before Bechtol?"

"Well, he didn't invent me. I was a yup computer whiz after Cal Tech and suddenly I realized I was surrounded by major nerds and I was only making a couple hundred thousand a year. My analyst at the time told me I was a 'people person.' Two things happened. I realized I could not tell my innermost thoughts, fears, hopes, and dreams to a woman who let the words 'people person' escape her lips. And I saw that in a way she was right. Computers were not my life and I didn't mind dealing with people . . . if they bathed regularly and so on. So I quit the computer business, quit my analyst, got an angle on Bechtol and blindsided him with my brains and—relatively speaking—my looks. Four years ago. I'm thirty-one." She looked at her watch again. "Look, I really have to run. Have you enjoyed our little talk, Mr. Tripper?"

"I think so."

"The judicious approach. Not exactly timid. I make people timid sometimes. Well, I've enjoyed it, too. You're a good listener—I like that in a man. You won't believe me, but I very seldom want to talk about myself. Today was the day, I guess. Maybe it has something to do with my period. Would it be nice to meet again and then maybe you could decide for sure if you enjoy my company? What about dinner tomorrow?"

"Shouldn't you check your Filofax? It might be your body-waxing night."

"I already have. Give me your number and I'll call you with time and place. My treat. You have a machine?"

"A car? A plane? A lawn mower?" I scribbled my number on a napkin.

"That's pitiful, and—"

"Don't say it. You like that in a man."

"An answering machine."

"Yes, I do. I'm hip."

"That I doubt." She pushed her chair back and stood up before I could move. "Mr. Tripper, you're easy, very easy, and . . ." She waited.

"You like that in a man."

She patted my arm. "I'll call you tomorrow. Don't get up. Finish your lunch. You look like a member of the Clean Plate Club."

She was gone. A very cute meet.

I began to wonder. Had I picked her up? Or had it been the other way around?

Two

The temperature hit ninety-six later that afternoon. Even on the shady side of Fifth it was too hot to live, let alone walk around, but the chances of getting an air-conditioned cab were too low to make the effort. So I walked and tried to catch every breeze. I walked down through Washington Square where the arch baked in the direct sunlight and gave off heat waves you could actually feel. It was like watching one of those scary movies of an atomic explosion. A one-man steel band was clanging away, tolling the end of civilization as we knew it, and a few roller skaters moseyed listlessly around the basin. That was it. Everybody else had lost consciousness.

The radiator cap had blown off a T-bird on Houston and gone halfway through the hood, where it remained looking like a groundhog checking for its shadow. I saw it happen. Thwang—bang-thunk. The driver just pulled over to the curb, slid to a stop by a young entrepreneur engaged in purveying crack to the masses, and slumped slowly across his steering wheel. A broken man who might never see his split-level rambler in Jersey again. I had my jacket slung over my shoulder by then and my shoes were doing that unhealthy thing where they stick to the streets and sidewalk. It was a struggle. The nice thing, what kept me going, was the knowledge that Sally kept two industrial-strength air conditioners going in her Prince Street loft. I liked that in a woman.

I was still thinking about Heidi Dillinger. She'd told me more about herself than would have seemed likely, given her type, but as she'd said, she'd felt like talking and maybe it was, after all, her period. Still, her face—particularly those pale, coffee-with-cream eyes—was one that gave nothing away, continually insisted on tabulating a running score and calculated each and every angle. She wasn't the sort of creature who would allow herself to get picked up. Unless, of course, that was the point.

She couldn't have been less like Sally Feinman, who was Brooklyn-born and -raised, who was the daughter of respectable fellow travelers destroyed in the Red Scare of the fifties, who'd been a teenager in the sixties and never got over it. Her consciousness had been raised on cut-rate campus grass, the assassinations, the Beatles and the Stones, Vietnam body counts, burning bras and draft cards, Mayor Daley and Chicago in the summer of 1968, civil rights marches in Alabama, police brutality, sexual intercourse as the basic grammar of your communication. Sally always looked intense and committed and funny and ironic and serious. She saw two Establishment politicians together and she saw yet another lethal conspiracy. She looked as if she'd gotten a frizzy permanent in the sixties and never been able to wash it out. She was short and stocky and sexy, and though we'd never had what anyone might call an affair, we'd certainly had a great deal of what any right-thinker would call sex. Sally was at home with sex. Comfortable with it, confident, sure that everybody was going to wind up wearing a smile. The first day we knew each other we did indeed go to sleep with smiles on our faces. But it wasn't an affair and we weren't in love. I wasn't committed enough to anything, didn't take anything seriously enough for her. I told her how I felt about the Yankees and she said baseball didn't count. But we loved each other. It was all very sixties. We couldn't help it. It was in our genes.

Heidi Dillinger wouldn't have understood. She'd have

21

thought we were morons who weren't maximizing our various potentials. But we were all products of our times, Heidi in her cool remote-distancing just as much as laid-back, ex-druggy me and weight-of-the-world-on-her-shoulders Sally. We were what we were. And the gulf between me on one side and Heidi on the other seemed wider and more unbridgeable than ever. Perhaps I was about to learn whether or not we could make sense of one another. Some things never changed, not even for the Heidi Dillingers of this world.

I had to get her out of my mind. I was already thinking about her too much. That's a cute meet for you. Everything is suddenly out of proportion, all because it was cute. A Heidi Dillinger got hold of you with her cute little personality, all decked out with alluring contradictions, and the real people, like Sal, got bumped from the next flight.

Well, not tonight.

I knew who my friends were.

The street-level door was a half-assed affair of chipped green paint, protective wire mesh over a glass panel, iron bars bolted on top of the mesh. As usual, it stood open about an inch, so much for space-age security. Any random homicidal maniac could enter unannounced and work off his frustrations about the cost of condos with a meat cleaver. The stairway was dark, lit only by a smudged, begrimed skylight five stories above. The freight elevator was padlocked. The building housed a couple of painters, a sculptor who worked in neon tubing, a couple who operated a jewelry-making concern, and Sally. Sally often carried a flashlight in her bag for illuminating the stairway at night, along with Mace and a brass whistle and a spring-loaded knife big enough to geld a water buffalo. And this was SoHo, not a slum, not Alphabet City, not Bed-Stuy. This was a loft for which she'd paid several hundred thousand dollars. And so it goes.

I was halfway up the second flight of stairs when I heard something in the gloom above me. I looked up just in time to catch the full impact of a man's shoulder in my chest. He'd come hurtling around the landing, head down, a blur of motion, I thought a dark suit maybe or a blazer, a necktie flapping, then the shoulder and the grunting sound—me or him—and I was slammed to my right against the blistered wall where I hit hard, the blows to front and back knocking the wind out of me and shooting a rocket through my kidneys. He stumbled going past me, reached out with a fist or elbow and clipped my knee. I heard him hit the landing below me, turn without looking back and head down the steps sounding like a man and a piano in the middle of a bad mistake. I was collapsing from the dig to my knee, skidding forward, hands out trying to grab the banister, failing, jamming my wrist against a step, then pitching six or seven more steps down to the landing, where I lay on my side, doubled up, wondering whether my forehead, wrist, knee, chest, or kidney needed attention first. My one clear thought was that—since people were stacked up in New York City emergency rooms for twenty-four to thirty-six hours waiting to see doctors—the hospital was clearly the last place I wanted to go. Better to die where I was. All this in four or five seconds. I'd been reduced to a bedraggled bag of blood and pain and bruises, a hit-and-run victim with a tear in his linen Paul Stuart suit pants, a split seam in the coat which I'd put on before entering the building, a bloody nose from cleverly using it to break my fall. I strained to see the judges' scorecards. 2-2-1-2-1-1-1 . . .

My breathing apparatus slowly returned to the fray; I could stop gagging and gasping and rely primarily on moaning. I held on to the wall like a drunk grappling with a lamppost and gingerly drew myself into a sagging upright squat. I reminded myself of one of the schoolroom posters depicting the evolution of the species. From the looks of things I'd just crawled out of the slime and didn't quite know what to make of dry land. I held my handkerchief to my nose. My suit, shirt, tie, and sense of irony were in ruins. Five seconds without the blow of a fist. God help me if I ever found myself in a fight. I wished I had a steering wheel across which I could slump. But instead I dragged myself the rest of the way up and climbed, panting, bleeding, trying to rearrange my kidneys, until I stood outside Sally's door. It too stood slightly ajar.

I pushed it open and shouted her name, deciding I should prepare her for the spectacle she was about to confront.

23

"Sally, I am a wounded man, a thing of shreds and patches! I have become a statistic!"

At the very least I could retain my good humor and make a New York story out of my disaster. Left for dead by speeding man in blazer. "Sally?"

There was no answer.

And there was something very wrong with this picture. But what?

Everything seemed in order. Her huge desk was relatively neat. The computer sat ready to go, the couches and chairs and palm trees and paintings and throw rugs were all as they always were.

I stood still, sweating like Doc Gooden in a ninth-inning jam with Kirk Gibson coming to bat. I let my eyes roam slowly across the huge space. It was like being the Pillsbury Doughboy in the oven, the heat finishing me off.

That was what was wrong.

The air conditioners weren't running.

The windows were closed tight. The loft was still and humid and quiet. It must have been 120 degrees in that room and Sally was the sort of person who ran the air conditioners even when she wasn't home. She couldn't stand the heat, refused to deal with it. But the air conditioners were silent.

My nose had stopped bleeding. I pushed the stained handkerchief up my sleeve. I went to the desk and flipped the switch on the long-necked black lamp. Nothing. I turned the computer on. Nothing. There was no power. Something had blown the fuses and Sally had gone in search of the super. Logical.

I went to the bathroom to wash the blood from my face and hands.

Sally was in the bathroom.

She was in the tub. One leg up over the edge of the white porcelain, the foot dangling awkwardly. Her toenails were painted orange. The stench in the bathroom was ghastly. There was vomit down the side of the tub and puddled on the floor. There was an unidentifiable smell, as if something had been scorched. And I smelled a strong scent of cherries, like certain kinds of cough syrup. I leaned over the toilet just in time. My knees buckled from the smell. Reflexively I lost my lunch. I wasn't thinking about Heidi Dillinger anymore.

I made myself go back to the bathtub and look at her.

Terrible things had been done to Sally Feinman. I looked at the scars and I felt skewered, as if I'd been caught in the worst kind of rock and roll nightmare. For an instant, longer, I felt as if I'd stumbled into a ritual killing by some gory band of Satanists who'd feasted on Sally.

Her eyes were open and fixed on the ceiling. Her face was contorted in a rictus of pain and agony and surprise and pleading. Her eyes had just glimpsed evil and then death had protected her, taken her. Her hands were trussed tight before her, bound with wire that had split the skin. Her wrists had bled profusely. The water in the tub was pink. Her body bore a dozen raw and blistered burns. Stuck in one of the wounds was a curler from an electric hot-curler set. At the bottom of the tub, wavering through the water like lost treasure, an apparition, was the rest of the hot-curler set, box, electrodes, the works. It was still plugged into the wall socket just below the medicine cabinet and above the sink. She was badly burned and I couldn't look anymore. There wasn't any more to see anyway.

It didn't take a genius to pose some questions, contemplate some conclusions. It was involuntary.

Having been tortured, she'd been killed, electrocuted, when the curler set had been dropped or thrown into the tub. Dropped or thrown: that was somehow relevant, the way my mind was working. The only reason you torture someone—if you write off the madman who does it for the simple joy it gives him, or the revenge, or the expiation of guilt, whatever—is to force them to tell you something. Torture was invented and has been improved on with alarming regularity and determination to elicit a desired response. I wondered if she'd told her killer what he wanted to know. If she had, he might have casually dropped the curler set into the tub to put her out of her misery. If she'd withheld the information, he could have hurled it into the water in frustration, hatred, punishing her. Or—my mind was racing ahead—maybe she'd still be alive if she'd held out . . . Or maybe she'd have survived if she'd told . . . What? Told what? What did she know that she had to die for?

What did it matter to me? All that mattered to me was that Sally was horribly dead, as if a monster had wanted to prove a point.

I went back to the other room and sat down at her desk. My stomach felt as if it were about to do another half-gainer. The smell, the sight of her eyes . . . I closed mine tight, squeezing them against the image of death and agony in the face of someone I loved . . . But the tighter I shut them, the clearer another image became: I saw my brother stretched out dead as a carp on a dock, mouth gaping, eyes empty and lonely in Tangier . . .

My nose had begun bleeding again. It was dripping onto her desk, big red circles. I held my handkerchief against the flow and thought about the man who had flattened me on the stairway. I had smelled the cherry cough syrup or the cough drops in the collision, the sweet sickly smell—had he killed Sally? It seemed like the logical place to start.

A man who smelled like that would be capable of anything.

I opened the windows above Prince Street. The curler set hitting the water must have blown out the fuses. The moment the windows were open, the city attacked: horns honking, people yelling, sirens screeching. There wasn't any new air out there. It was all used air and hot out there, but it moved, which was better than the air in the loft. I called the police. I'd been in the loft for ten or twelve minutes. I was still dripping with sweat. I was aching and bruised and my mouth was full of the metallic taste of blood. I seemed to be able to smell the mess in the bathroom no matter where I went in the loft.

I wondered if I was afraid.

But afraid of what?

It had nothing to do with me.

When the police arrived, a smallish detective with a smallish mustache fringing a small, puckered mouth listened while I told him the story. William Powell would have liked the mustache and looked good in it. On the detective it was iffy. He smoked Camels and nodded sympathetically and was interested in the man on the stairway. He was the least threatening man imaginable. He told me he understood how I didn't have too much in the way of a description, not with that dark a stairwell.

I told him about Sally, what she did for a living, how we'd met and why I'd come on down on such an ungodly hot day. He was fascinated by my relationship to JC Tripper. He wanted to know if JC had *really* died in Tangier . . .

I left the loft in the faded light of early evening. It looked cooler even if the appearance was an illusion. I ignored the rips and tears and bloodstains for a couple of blocks, but the onset of aches and pains—look, I'm not a fellow who knocks himself out with heavy exercise—wore me down at the corner of Houston. The T-bird was still there, but the driver was nowhere to be seen.

I hailed a cab. It might have been simpler just to let him run me down. The driver had apparently just arrived on Earth, and to him Central Park West was *terra incognita* and then some. I thought of him as Abdul Abulbul Amir, and the ride with the windows open wasn't bad at all. When I got home I took six Advils and a shower, sat on my terrace alone watching the Yankees on television, trying to work up some enthusiasm for a tuna-salad sandwich.

But I felt tears on my face. A good person had died like someone in a concentration camp.

I hated it. I hated her dying and I hated my pathetic impotence in doing anything about it. A smallish man with a smallish mustache was handling all that.

All I'd done was find her body.

Now I was out of it, alone with my memories of a particularly loving and lively friend.

And the day had begun *so* well.

Three

Heidi Dillinger's call woke me up at nine o'clock and I let the machine take it. I was faintly surprised that she'd called at all. Our meeting seemed an unlikely part of an altogether unreal day, the promise to call the sort of thing that seems a less good idea once slept on. But there she was, 9 A.M. and sounding as if she'd been up for hours. She left an address on Fifth Avenue across the Park, a little south of the Metropolitan. A very pricey line of country. She hadn't been kidding when she said she was well compensated by her novelist boss. The appointed hour was eight o'clock.

I took a shower while my mind came to grips with the full horror of what I'd stumbled into the day before. It seemed even crazier in the morning light, like something you remember from a disreputable movie, but of course it was real. I was standing out on the terrace, having felt the morning's heat hammer me like a fist, listening to Gershwin, when the telephone rang again. It was the homicide detective from the night before. He wondered if he could stop by around noon and run through a couple more questions with me. I said sure and called The Ginger Man for a lunch reservation in case I had a hungry cop on my hands. Then Tony Fleming called to tell me that Sally Feinman's murder was on the front page of the *Post*.

HOT WRITER GETS BURNED!
MURDER IN LUXURY SOHO LOFT!

Sally and I had once agreed that the greatest *Post* murder headline had been the immortal HEADLESS BODY IN TOPLESS BAR, and while the morning's attempt didn't challenge that, Sal would have gotten a smile out of being called a "hot writer." Tony said my name was indeed mentioned as a friend of Miss Feinman's who found the body. Naturally I was identified as JC's brother, and Tony suggested I might want to screen my calls. He certainly wouldn't give out my number, but newspapermen and TV reporters had ways of getting numbers. I told him that in my case all they had to do was check the phone book.

The cop did turn out to be hungry and I insisted on taking him to The Ginger Man. I tried to be helpful, but I knew nothing about enemies Sally might have had or what projects she was working on. We wound up talking about JC Tripper. My fate, it would seem.

The elevator in my building was pleasantly Art Deco: the elevator in Heidi Dillinger's building might have been on loan from the Istanbul Museum. It looked as if all the craftsmen of the Sultan had slaved over the wood and the grillwork and the marble flooring until it was something fit for carrying the master to the side of Allah, where he might sit and eat figs and peel grapes throughout eternity. It was apparent that we were dealing with profoundly heavy money here, which made me wonder further about Ms. Dillinger and her resources.

I stepped off into a foyer of inlaid parquetry, polished wood paneling, bowls of rust and lavender flowers, and Heidi in a lavender-and-beige filmy, flowing, graceful bit of summer dress, underneath which she was moving with athletic ease and grace. Her long tanned arm was extended as she came toward me and the hand at the end of it took mine. She was so glad I could come. She led me past delicately arching date palms that swayed slightly in the breeze of the air conditioners. We passed down a wide carpeted hallway and into a long room that resembled the smoking room of a venerable and well-funded men's club. Leather furniture with brass studs, a Persian carpet properly threadbare in spots, bellpulls for summoning the staff, a vast refectory table that smelled faintly of lemon polish, several tables with chess pieces deployed at various battle stations. Subtle lighting from large, squat lamps with cream-colored fabric shades made every surface glow.

There was something weird about the room and it wasn't just that there was a blazing fire in the huge fireplace complete with lion-head andirons and logs the thickness of telephone poles. The fire crackled and snapped, heedless of the ninety-three degrees of sopping-wet heat prevailing when I'd left my place. It was cooled well down into the sixties in the room and the heat emanating from the fireplace felt good. Heidi Dillinger threw a soft cashmere cardigan around her shoulders as we entered the room. But there was something else. She was regarding me with a smile and I cocked my head, trying to pin it down.

"It's the weather," I said at last. "I'm hearing a storm with lots of wind and rain and some distant thunder. All because you enjoy the fire. Rather conspicuous eccentricity. All on tape, I assume."

She lowered herself onto one end of a long leather chester-field couch, near a table covered with drink mixings. She sat on the edge of the cushion and dug ice out of a sterling bucket with sterling tongs. "Here it is always a dark and stormy night. A small conceit. Does it bother you? Does illusion bother you?" She'd taken the stopper from a bottle of Edradour Scotch and was drizzling it over the ice.

"Only insofar as this reminds me of President Nixon in the White House with the air conditioners blowing like the billtails of hell in a Washington summer so he could have a nice log fire. While he set things up with the plumbers and bagmen. You and he will be joined in my mind now and ever after. I can stand it if you can. I'll take soda with that."

She sprayed it from a siphon, the kind with metal mesh

30

around it. Mine never works, but hers was right on the money. "Nixon never had this kind of money at his disposal, of course. And this tape system is obviously superior to his." She handed me my glass and lifted her own, which she'd been nursing along since before I'd arrived. "May we ride out the night's storms in safety."

"And confusion to our enemies," I said.

We drank and she grinned at me without indicating any desire to speak.

"This," I said, nodding at the room, "is the cat's pajamas. It must have cost a fortune."

"About six million, as I recall. I guess that's a fortune."

"You guess? Well, it's a good guess. Whither comes this attitude about money, Miss Dillinger? Downright cavalier."

"Call me Heidi."

"Not until I know you better."

"Call me Heidi. You'll never know me any better."

"About the cavalier way with a dollar?"

The sound of rain lashed at windows that didn't exist. It sounded like the storm that raised such hell in *Key Largo*. "You probably drew the inference from my invitation to dinner that this was my place."

"Silly me," I said.

"It isn't mine. I only work here. This is Allan Bechtol's home. Allan Bechtol's money, Allan Bechtol's never-ending dark and stormy night." She sipped her drink, leaned back and crossed her legs, sank into the leather corner, awesomely aware of her body and in absolute control. My sweat-dampened suit clung clammily to my ditto self.

"What are you telling me? Is this the old story about the mice playing while the cat's away?"

"Not at all. Mr. Bechtol is in the galley preparing our dinner even now. Nothing elaborate, but it will be perfect. He loves to cook."

"And you hate to cook?"

"Never tried. Mr. Bechtol does it because he likes to, not to fend off starvation. The staff can do that."

"This Bechtol—is he crazy? Never grants interviews, his

photograph never appears on the dust jackets of his books, he won't promote the books, he lives in this phony storm . . . It seems to me he has a serious problem."

"He likes it this way. He does what he likes."

"And what do you do because you like to?"

"I play chess. That's one thing." She waved vaguely at the games arrayed about the room. "Please don't tell me that you play."

"I won't. I played as a kid. It took more concentration than I could muster once I grew up."

"Good. I never play against people. When I did, they invariably ended up hating me. Now I play only against computers. It's good for my character."

"Do you ever beat them?"

"I always beat them. Losing does nothing for one's character, surely. Winning is very helpful. I have lost two matches in the last three hundred, and I always play it out to the end. Artificial intelligence has . . . a lot to learn."

"I thought machines could be made that would always win."

"I'm sure one *could* be made." She sighed. "I always feel a little pang of sorrow for the machine, the computer, the pure mind. If it can't outthink me, then what can it do? The intelligence is trapped in the box and it is so prosaic, so pedestrian. It can't write a poem. It can't go to Harry Winston to reward itself . . . it's trapped, and in this instance all it can do is play chess. If it can't win at that, it might as well pull the plug on itself. But someone would just come along and plug it back in, I suppose."

"You speak as if there's a soul in the machine," I said.

"Silly, isn't it? But I do feel sorry for them, all the creatures of artificial intelligence. We create them, we teach them to do the things we find the most difficult to do—consider all the options, retrieve data, find one needle in a million haystacks, analyze thousands upon thousands of chess moves . . . But try to teach a robotic to reach out and move a poor little pawn—there's where you've got a problem, I'm afraid. And I can beat them, anyway. It's a dog's life, Mr. Tripper. Take a robot for a walk around the block and you'll spend the whole time picking him up and getting him walking again. My, you were thirsty."

Allan Bechtol came in from the hallway wearing an apron bearing some fresh stains, a plaid shirt, tan corduroy slacks, beat-up old penny loafers, white sweat socks. He was a burly man of medium height, just under six feet tall. His crop of thinning red hair had gone mostly gray. His beard matched. Definitely grizzled. His small, slightly bulbous nose wore a couple of broken veins accenting the tip. His eyes grabbed your attention: small, clear blue, intense, intelligent, with a tendency to fix on you and stay there. He stood watching me, a kitchen towel in one hand, a can of Diet Cherry Coke in the other, smiling at me so his uneven gray teeth appeared like smudges behind the scruffy facial hair that had encroached raggedly on his mouth.

"Soup's on, more or less." His voice had a resonant, moist quality, deep and metallic like a great baseball announcer, a voice that could mesmerize, hypnotize, convince. I couldn't tell all that from those five words. But I'd heard him say a lot more in my time.

I'd known him long ago, and his name sure as hell hadn't been Allan Bechtol. He just kept smiling at me, waiting for me to catch on. Heidi Dillinger was looking from one of us to the other. When she started to break the silence Bechtol shook his head at her and she swallowed whatever she might have said.

Everything in the room, in his world, for all I knew, was some kind of illusion. The computerized chess players who couldn't beat the girl. The weather was rough and it had begun to thunder, but it was all on tape and bore no relationship to reality. And the host was passing himself off under an alias. I was beginning to have serious doubts about the role of fate in bringing me together with Heidi Dillinger on Fifth Avenue.

"Sam," I said. "You wanted to see me, you could have just called me."

"Heidi needed a workout on the street. You know how it is with skills, use 'em or lose 'em." The hairy face kept grinning at me. "You've changed, Lee. Took off some weight. You remind me of JC now. Rest his soul. You're looking good." He hadn't moved. Then he took a sip of the Coke.

"You haven't changed much," I said. "You still look like a bucket of shit."

"Hey, remember we used to think we'd open a chain of burger joints? Chili, burgers, tacos. The Bucket o' Shit. And the first one was going to be in Harvard Square. Dammit, Lee, it was more than a quarter of a century ago. We even had a slogan, right?"

"Right," I said.

"*Just Throw It in the Toilet . . . Cut Out the Middleman!*"

"We were scintillating wits in those days. Why am I here, Sam?"

"Come on, follow me, we'll chow down. I'll tell you all about it. And don't get all shirty with me and pissed off at little Heidi here. She was just doing her job. I've gotten a little strange over the years, Lee. Gotta make a game out of everything. Only way I can stay interested." He hung his arm around my shoulders. It felt just as it had hundreds of years ago when we'd gone down to the Cape on September weekends and got drunk together, got laid together, and talked a lot of collegiate bullshit together. We were always draping an arm over the next guy's shoulders, sucking on something in a can, wearing our madras Bermudas and loafers. JC had called us all the sad young men, drinking in the bars, but he had a poetic soul in those days. We were a good threesome. JC and me and Sam Innis. Now JC was dead, Sam Innis had become somebody else, and I was something of a changed man myself. Nothing ever stayed the same and everybody was always telling lies.

"I'm not pissed off," I said. "But soon I'll want to twist somebody's head off. When JC went, his legacy to me was his short fuse."

"You *have* changed, pal."

"Everybody's changed. It's been a helluva long time."

"Whatever happened to the Law of Immutability?"

"Shut up, Sam. Let's just get on with the game."

Heidi Dillinger said, "Am I going to have to listen to dumb repartee all evening?"

"You work for this man," I said. "You ought to be used to it."

The dining room was as spare and antiseptic and minimal as the other room—library, study, whatever it was—had been traditional, cluttered, and maximalist. The table was gleaming black lacquer with chairs to match in an Art Deco mode, there were a black-and-white carpet, a gold Japanese screen painting covering one wall, high windows looking out over the Park to the lights of the West Side, a Jasper Johns target filling another wall above a black-lacquered sideboard, and in the middle of the table was an unusual centerpiece—a large model of an Afrika Korps tank set atop a mound of loose sand. The long barrel of the gun was pointing out toward Central Park. A black lacquer bowl shone on the sideboard, full of bright scarlet flowers.

Dinner was simple and superb. Black squid-ink pasta with bright green broccoli buds, slivers of red and yellow peppers, oil and garlic and coarsely ground black pepper and capers, with individual pots of Parmesan beside each plain white plate; followed by delicate scallopine of veal sautéed with butter, lemon, and capers; then a simple salad of arugula, endive, walnuts, and crumbled Gorgonzola; concluding with rich, high Italian cheesecake, lemony and crumbs everywhere. The wines were cold and smooth and not at all intimidating. Sam Innis knew his way around the kitchen. While he ate he kept coming at me from every angle, dazzling me with his footwork, all the time taking a reading on me while giving me only what he wanted me to have.

"The tank sits there to keep me in mind of the book I'm writing. It's a little departure for me, just off the scary edge of science fiction. Time-warp kind of thing. A lost tank, one of Rommel's, wanders aimlessly in the desert, losing track of time and space and finally slipping through one of eternity's cracks . . . they crest this big fucking dune and who do they find? T. E. Lawrence. Lawrence of Arabia. Who is their only hope of being saved. Lawrence discovers the English are once

35

again at war with the Germans, just as they'd been twenty-five years before, when he had rallied the Arabs against the Turks. Now he must decide to save these doomed Germans or not . . ." He looked up at me, tucking black pasta into the corners of his mouth. "That's the setup, anyway. How does it sound?"

"A helluva lot better than your other stuff," I said. "You need an editor, somebody to cut your stuff. That's your big problem."

"You're probably right." He paid no attention to the aspersions I was casting. "Anyway, the tank keeps me centered, as the shrinks say."

"I know more about the Afrika Korps," Heidi Dillinger said, "than Rommel did."

"Look, what is behind the Allan Bechtol routine? What am I doing here, Sam?"

"I must tell you I'm a little disappointed at the cool reception," he said, trying to look hurt. "You seem to have forgotten how close the three of us were—"

"I haven't heard a word from you in twenty years. Somewhere along the way you lost your grip on my affections. Now you're somebody else and you get me here under false pretenses—"

"False pretenses! Jesus, Lee—"

"And I've had an absolute bitch of a time ever since this Dillinger character slithered across my path. So, in general terms, why not just cut the shit and tell me what's going on?"

"I did not slither! What is your problem, anyway? Is it just that you can't take a joke, or what?" She was vastly amused.

"I know you've had a lousy twenty-four hours, pal. And I want to talk to you about that. But really I just wanted to renew our friendship. A fella gets older, he wants to reconnect with his past. Continuity. We're middle-aged men; all of a sudden we aren't going to live forever. So now that JC's gone, I thought about you—"

"He's been gone a long time," I said. "You just hear about it, Sam?"

"No, no, I've known about it just like everybody else, no need to get snotty. There's a time for things. This was the time to get together, that's all, Lee." He finished off the last of his salad, put his fork aside and leaned back, staring at me again as if lost in deepest, darkest thought.

Heidi Dillinger stood up, went to the sideboard and pressed a small black button recessed in the wood. A Japanese gentleman wearing an alpaca jacket over a white shirt came in soundlessly within half a minute and cleared the table. Then he was back with a Melior infusion coffee maker, a steaming teakettle, and a grinder full of beans. He set it all in front of Sam Innis and was gone, as if Mellow Yellow had made him disappear.

Sam made the coffee grinder pulverize the beans, then transferred them to the glass cylinder. He poured the boiling water in on top of them, inserted the press and left it at the top of the cylinder while the coffee brewed.

"I'm something of a fake, Lee," he said at last. The aroma of the rich coffee filled the room. "I wrote some books after we left Harvard, terrible stuff, I suppose. I didn't think of myself as a writer, didn't think I was really capable. I was just a guy who hated working and couldn't act or sing like JC or play a goddamn guitar and I didn't have much money. So I kicked around some radio stations here and there, staff announcing jobs, sold some time for the ad guys, did a little sports announcing . . . that was Sam Innis. But all the time I was wondering what it took to *write*. So I read and read and read, mostly the old serial writers from *Saturday Evening Post* in the forties, and I kept notebooks on how I'd update the stories— not just the details but the tone. The tone was everything. I rewrote the serials. Actually rewrote them. I learned structure, but I had to invent the new tone. And I had to figure out how the readers' values had changed, I had to plug into the tone and values that would attract the masses of readers now . . . then I had to make it simple and flashy and bright. While I was making headway at that, I set about creating a character who'd be a writer, *the* writer I'd become, not just Sam Innis scraping along picking up the scraps. Thus Allan Bechtol, writer, was born. I didn't write the books. I became Allan Bechtol, and *he* wrote them. And he was a rather mysterious fellow, reclusive, impossible to pin down. Sam Innis just sort of wasted away and I became Allan Bechtol. And it worked, you see. As Bechtol I am hugely successful. Sam Innis would never have been so successful. Believe me." He plunged the press down through the dark coffee, forcing the grounds to the bottom of the cylinder. "I became someone else and . . ." He shrugged. "I went into the darkness a failure called Sam Innis and when I came out I was Allan Bechtol, and by God I was rich and famous!" He began pouring the coffee into our cups. "I didn't want to explain the transformation to my old friends. Maybe you can understand why. The whole thing needed time. Now I can face it. At least with you, Lee. You're the first person from the past who knows. I just want to be friends again. That's all."

The cool little eyes never strayed from my face.

"I'm sorry, Sam," I said.

He reached across the mirrorlike surface of the table and put out his hand. I took it. It was a good thing to do. It was good to be straight with Sam again.

"Pals?" he said.

"Pals."

Late in the evening Sam Innis decided he'd had enough of the wind and the rain inside, so we went out onto the terrace, into the thick wetness and deadening heat broken only by the infrequent limp breeze staggering through the tops of the trees in the Park. The terrace wrapped around the corner of the building and featured a nautical theme. Jazz played through the kind of speakers you found on cruise ships. The flooring was a polished deck and the chairs were elegant things that came from a defunct ocean liner, the *Titanic* for all I knew. There was a wet bar with a fridge under a green-and-white awning. There was a stairway that led up to the bedrooms of the second floor of the duplex. There was a greenhouse with rounded corners. Everything but a shuffleboard court and the ladies outnumbering the men. Apparently wherever Sam was, he liked to pretend he was somewhere else. I didn't know whether to feel sorry for him or wish I could trade places with him. But the fact was when I was at my place across the Park, I was exactly where I wanted to be.

The three of us leaned on the brass railing embedded in the terrace wall and looked out over the city, down Fifth Avenue to the fountain and the Plaza and the Trump Tower and way on down to the glow of Little Italy and Chinatown.

"Land ho!" I said.

"Been said before," Heidi remarked. "Very witty."

Sam slapped the *Post* on the railing. The picture of Sally Feinman stared up at me. "Came across your name in the paper, Lee. This is just a damn tragedy. Poor, poor girl. What's the story?"

I must have been holding it in because I let it go, the tale of Sally and me and how it ended a couple of hours after my lunch with Heidi Dillinger. Innis came to life as I laid out the story line, all the stuff about the search for JC and how Sal had helped me with putting my life back together when I'd finally returned to New York. Then he wanted to know all the details of my finding the body, the guy knocking me down on the stairway, the terrible heat in the loft, the stench in the bathroom, the smell of burning, the condition of the body. In the end I saw that it was the violence, the viciousness in Sally's fate, the horror that had been waiting for her around the last corner, the fact that I'd come so close to barging in while the work was in progress—all that was what he was after. It was the darkest side of life that drew him like a bagful of iron filings to a magnet: the darkness lay just below the surface of the man, like a beckoning pool that might claim him, or someone near him, at any moment. I saw it all in his face—the cool eyes, the way he wet his lips and tugged at his beard as he listened. Sam Innis might be dead after all. And it occurred to me that Allan Bechtol might be a dangerous man.

Heidi Dillinger's interest was less visceral, as you might expect, and more analytical. Why did they torture her? What could she have come across that was so important? Wasn't her Tripper story the last really big thing she'd done? I didn't think it could have anything to do with me, did I? I had to give Heidi credit for that one later on: she was the first person who suggested any kind of connection between yours truly and the murder of Sally Feinman. The thought simply hadn't crossed my mind before that moment. Then she slid on past it, observing how lucky I'd been not to have arrived earlier. She took credit for using up enough time at lunch to save my life.

When she excused herself and went indoors, Sam and I stood awhile longer leaning on the railing, with all the beauty of New York's light show on a sultry summer night spread out before us. Ships were moving slowly on the East River, lights twinkling. I recognized the sound of the Mary Lou Williams Quartet with little Don Byas on sax playing "Moonglow." I commented on it and Sam said, "With all respect to JC, I stopped listening to most of the post-1964 music long ago. Rock, anyway. Oh, the Beatles and Dylan, but they're different, they exist outside of time. But mainly I'm stuck in the forties and fifties."

"Mary Lou and Byas recorded this at the City of Light in Paris in the early seventies. Not long before he died."

"Hey, I know that. But it's not seventies' music, pal."

"I know, I know." It surely wasn't. I didn't even enjoy listening to JC and the Traveling Executioner's Band anymore. The moment had passed for me.

"So what do you think of Heidi?" he asked.

"I'm not sure. She's a beautiful girl. Of a kind."

"Your kind?"

"I'll never find out."

"Ah, don't be so sure. She's brilliant, Lee, a genius in a way. She's a whiz with computers. A bulldog when it comes to research—I mean the hard kind, stuff people don't want to let you know. At chess, well, it's scary. She's a tactician, a strategist—she's a plotter, second to none. How much do you think I pay her?"

"I have no idea."

"Base salary a quarter of a mil, with an override on my royalties. I have no choice. She could better what I pay her before you could say 'Frank Lorenzo' or 'Carl Icahn.' Maybe even before you could say 'poison pill'—"

"How about before you say 'federal prison' or 'Ivan Boesky'?"

"She's a great one for setting goals, planning, then improvising within the overall scope of the plan. She's also a security expert."

"And," I said, "I'll bet you could stick her heart in a thimble and have room left over for her code of ethics."

40

He chuckled and shook his head. "You do her a grave injustice. I adore her. I'd be lost without her."

"Isn't adoration a little strong?"

He looked startled for a moment, then relaxed. "Look, this is a purely nonsexual adoration. More like the adoration of Saint Heidi. Without whom my make-believe worlds would go down in flames or up in smoke or some damn thing. As far as sex goes, Heidi's life is a mystery to me. But since she has her own suite in my place here, and since I seem to require her at all sorts of odd hours, I'd say she pretty well sublimates all that."

"What about you? Girlfriend?"

"Oh, now we come to the secret of my success—the formula that made me what I am today. I am completely impotent." He laughed at my expression. "No kidding. It's been my salvation. I haven't had a hard-on in fifteen years. Can you imagine the time that has freed up? The energy? I recommend it, Lee, it's the answer to the world's ills. I guess it's some psychological problem, but if I'm ever cured it's curtains for Allan Bechtol. I was a slave to sex for so damn long . . . it was like having an eight-hundred-pound man stop standing on my face. Then, suddenly, I was free. I live in fear I'll unexpectedly get horny and sprout a woody again. The time saved in not whacking off, waxing the old otter, amounts to months, years of life I wouldn't have had."

"I wonder if you're telling me the truth. Maybe you're just playing another tape for me. Sucking me into another game."

"Would I kid you about a thing like this?" He looked at his watch. "Listen, I've got six or eight hours of work ahead of me. Always work at night. Like a ballplayer. Which reminds me, we've gotta get up to the Stadium together, Lee. But now, I must work. I'll have Heidi see you home."

We went back inside and he gave me a hug and said he'd see me soon and disappeared down the hall.

Heidi said, "Feel like a slow walk? We could walk down around the Park if you feel like it."

I told her that would be fine.

"Well, that certainly warmed the cockles of this old heart."

Heidi Dillinger was being ironic on the subject of Sam and

41

me and I was being hot and sticky. That's the way with New York. When the heat and humidity hit, they just won't let go. Day or night, it just goes on and on, banging your head with a manhole cover until you think you can't take any more. Then it gets really hot. That's the kind of a summer it was turning into. Of course, Heidi Dillinger took no notice. No sweat, no complaining. She liked it. We were walking past the Strand's outdoor book cabinets near the Plaza, and the Park was still and oppressively humid. The muggers and killers and rapists waited in the dark, you could almost hear them breathing, almost hear their eyeballs clicking as they peered after the unwary. But we were a few feet away from all that. We were safe from damn near everything but irony.

"Women are frequently irritated by male bonding," I said. "There's no female equivalent. The best the poor things can do is something they call networking. Not my view particularly. I'm quoting Sally Feinman. She used to tell me that a woman with a best female friend also knows she has a lifelong enemy, somebody to dance on her grave. Personally I hold women in higher regard than that."

"How about male bonding, then—do you trust Allan?"

"Call him Sam. He's Sam." I said it but I wasn't sure.

"No, he's Allan," she insisted. "He used to be this Sam person. But forget Sam. Call him Allan."

"All right. Do I trust Allan? How should I know? I've only known him a few hours."

"He has plans for you, you know."

"No, I didn't know. And I don't really care about what he has—"

"Oh, but you will. He's very persuasive. He wants something from you." We were strolling along Central Park South. The horse-drawn carriages were still for hire, and across the street in front of the hotels the sidewalk was crowded. On nights this hot, New York never really goes to sleep.

"So he's persuasive. What does he want?"

"He wants you to come for dinner again tomorrow."

"Okay, fine by me. That was easy, wasn't it?"

"That's not all he wants."

"But you're not going to tell me the rest."

"That's right. I'm not."

"How is he going to persuade me?"

"Allan firmly believes that everyone has his price. I believe it myself, for that matter."

"Just because he met yours?"

"Is that a way of saying you're made of finer stuff? That you're above all that?"

"You've got to be kidding. I'm a man well known to have a price. And not too bloody high, at that."

"Sometimes you take me off guard," she said.

"Try not to kid a kidder. The last time someone took you off guard, Lefty Gomez was on the hill at the Stadium."

"Who on earth is Lefty Gomez?"

"You're the researcher. Go look him up."

"Simple curiosity—what have you got against me?" She glanced up sharply. "What are you laughing at? I don't much like being laughed at."

"Don't worry. You don't seem to do funny things. I'm just thinking of an old joke."

"I suppose it has something to do with Mr. Gomez—"

"No, no. It's old and it's dumb. Like Ronald Reagan."

"Are you going to tell me or are you intent on just being irritating?"

"If I told you you have a beautiful body, would you hold it against me?"

"I beg your pardon?"

"That's the joke. Old and dumb. I know a lot of them like that. For instance, a page is always a page, but once a knight—"

"Is enough. Even I've heard that one."

"Look, you don't like being laughed at. And I don't like being conned. As in the way you did that little number on me yesterday. You and good old Allan can play all the stupid little games you like, but leave me out of 'em. No games with Lee Tripper. My tolerance level is lower than Joel Skinner's batting average."

"Who is Joel Skinner?" She made a face and sighed. "Don't say it. I'm the researcher. Well, I'm sorry if yesterday upset you—"

"No, I thought I was a pretty nifty guy yesterday. You are

43

very, very beautiful and getting more so with each passing minute. Picking you up was a small but meaningful triumph. Finding out that my charm, wit, and good tailoring had nothing to do with it—well, my hopes were dashed. Made me unhappy. Put me in a funk. I may not come out of it until tomorrow."

"What hopes?"

"Oh, you know. Probably base animal hopes . . ."

"I might have known."

"I suppose you're made of finer stuff, you're above all that. Fine. It's your life, and welcome to it."

This lively patter, true to the traditions of the earlier cute meet, got us to the big statue of Columbus at the southwest corner of the Park. Which seemed to me just about as far as it was ever likely to get us.

"I can get home safely from here," I said. I hailed a cab but she pulled my hand out of the air.

"My instructions were to get you home." She slid her arm through mine and we headed uptown on Central Park West.

I couldn't get any more out of her about Bechtol, and when we got to my building we stopped and I couldn't stop smiling at her. "Want to come up and spend the night?"

"You are truly absurd."

"It's nothing, really."

"I like that in a man."

"Well, I take it back."

"Take what back?"

"What I said. You *are* sort of funny."

"If you do what Allan wants, if you let him persuade you"—her tan eyes fastened on mine, I was conscious of the cut of her hair and the shape of her head—"you and I will be seeing more of each other."

"Oh, I don't mind. I might do it anyway."

She kissed my cheek and I felt her wide mouth grinning against me. "What a gallant guy."

"I never kiss on the first date."

"Your reputation is safe, Tripper. This wasn't a date. This was business." She was moving back toward the curb. A taxi was waiting. "Make it eight o'clock. We'll be waiting for you."

I had no doubt about that. I saw the dark pool beneath the surface of Allan Bechtol's life, the pool that beckoned so seductively, and I wondered if it was beckoning not to Bechtol but to his old friend. Me.

Four

The next night the plot, as the man said,
thickened. The pool of darkness deepened and I heard what
passed for the siren song. In a way it was one of JC's songs
haunting me, the past reaching out, like Noel Coward's obser-
vation on the powers of what he called cheap music. Strolling
through the Park with the sun setting down long shadow lines
past the towers of the West Side, I was feeling somewhat less
sprightly than is normal. The bruiser on the stairway was taking
his toll. My back was aching where my kidneys were supposed
to be. I'd hit hard on the edges of several steps. I was feeling
pretty punk. But curious.

The mood at Bechtol's was entirely different from the previous night. The audio storm persisted, but we three ate by
candlelight on the terrace. A couple of strategically placed
oscillating fans created an artificial breeze, the candles gut-
tered, the sweat eventually dried on my face. Bechtol had left
the cooking to the Japanese couple, and the result was grilled
swordfish with a biting jalapeño sauce, hot and crusty rolls,
fresh green beans steamed to crunchy perfection with a hint of
ginger about them, a dry Australian white wine—I mention this

not because I aspire to Gael Greene's station in life but rather to indicate the way my old pal Sam Innis (who could survive on cold anchovy pizza and chili sandwiches and plan a chain of horror-show restaurants) had changed as he metamorphosed into Allan Bechtol. He might have been a different man, not old Sam at all. Now he lived like a king, and the king who came most readily to mind was mad Ludwig of Bavaria.

The connection seemed even more appropriate once I heard my old friend's proposal, but when he got to the part about the persuasion he proved that he had my number. It was a rather large number, as it turned out, but that will come in due course. Over the cocktails I asked him what the hell he was up to that took two nights to get through. I suggested that he remember what fantastically close pals we'd been once and now were once more. I told him it was time for the con to stop.

He began talking, selling his idea hard, and with my occasional interruptions the pitch lasted all the way through dinner, which concluded with strawberries in clotted cream, coffee, and cognac, and finally came the demand for an answer from me. Watching and listening, I would hardly have thought him the man I'd seen the night before. He was wearing an immaculate, virginal white suit, a pearl gray shirt by Paul Smith of lower Fifth, a pale green tie, and a gold Patek Philippe that made a Ritz cracker look like a tractor tire. His beard was neatly groomed, his hair trimmed and combed. Heidi Dillinger was dressed to kill, simply turned out in a drop-dead black cocktail dress with spaghetti straps. It clung to her like a naughty reputation. She wore pearls: a necklace, earrings, and a large ring. Thank God I'd at least thrown on a beat-up old safari jacket I'd carried over my shoulder across the Park. The way they looked made me wonder how I smelled.

"I'll get right to the heart of it, pal," he said. He was wearing slightly tinted glasses with tortoiseshell frames. The candlelight was reflected in the lenses. "I have the sneaking suspicion that old JC is still alive." He paused, waited for me to roll over with all four paws in the air.

"So do several million of his fans. Their brains have been

47

turned into Doggie Treats by LSD, hash, grass, cocaine, and who cares what else. What's your excuse?"

"Just a hunch, a rumor or two, things I've heard. None of that really matters. The point is I think JC's out there someplace in the tall grass. I want you to find him if he is . . . if he's not, if he's dead, well, we'll know once and for all."

"Listen, this is where I came in. I've been all through this once before. JC is dead, ashes scattered across the desert."

He smiled at me with an expression of infinite patience. "This will be different. This time you've got Allan Bechtol behind you. I'm prepared to put unlimited financial resources behind this search. For however long it takes. I'm also prepared to give you certain pieces of information I've collected, stuff that wasn't available two years ago when you went looking for him."

"Why not just hire a private detective? Or better yet, one of the huge outfits with hundreds of agents all over the world? What's it got to do with me? Maybe I don't want him found— I'm living off him, remember? I'm his beneficiary . . . this is crazy, it's a lousy idea—"

"Now you're being glib and irrelevant. You have your own life now." This from Heidi Dillinger.

"I do? Not without the ghost of JC, I don't!"

"Of course you do. You're a writer now."

"All I've ever written about is my brother—"

She leaned forward, the shadows flickering across her face. She and Bechtol made a good team. "That's the point," she said softly. "You were his brother. It would be just the job for you. What more could it have to do with you?"

"And it could make you financially secure, pal." Bechtol had picked up the ball again.

"How do you figure that?"

"We'll come to that. But the point is you were with him all those years. You understood him, Lee. He always trusted you. Didn't he, Lee? Weren't you always the one he turned to for help and advice?"

"Who remembers?" I said. "Who cares?"

"Of course you were. You know damn well you were. What it

48

comes down to is this—if he's alive, you're the one person he won't be able to elude. That's what I'm counting on."

"One question," I said. "You haven't told me your excuse for such a harebrained idea. What's in it for you, Sam?"

I caught sight of our reflections in the sliding glass doors. We looked like characters in a movie, conspirators, which is what we were, give or take. Sam—Allan, of course—leaning back in his chair, slowly munching on a strawberry, his dark glasses sinister in the evening, in the candlelight. Heidi looking elegant and haughty, head back, looking down her nose, listening, toying with her cognac, circling the rim with the tip of her finger. Then there was me. My headache didn't show, but Ali and Liston had been going at it between my ears ever since that guy knocked me down the stairs. That was when I'd split the bridge of my nose and why I had the little Band-Aid that I couldn't avoid seeing no matter where I looked. No one had made jokes about the Band-Aid, which was nice of them. We fit our roles in the movie perfectly. Mr. Big and his gorgeous tootsie and the dumb jerk they were manipulating. Guess who was going to take over the heavy lifting and finally take the fall. Guess who was going up the river. For some reason I'd gotten the Elisha Cook role. I sensed something wrong with this picture. It was me. But my old pal lit up a ten-dollar cigar and I lit one, too, and I kept right on listening, a willing accomplice in my own downfall. My old pal Sam sure knew his man.

"I take it you've read my books," he said.

"I'm afraid not. At least not all the way through."

"Jeez, you can be disagreeable, Lee. You used to be such a nice guy. Wouldn't hurt a fly. You left all the fly hurting to JC. Now you do it."

"Well, a spade's a spade," I said.

"But you said my present book—the tank and all, with Lawrence of Arabia—you said it sounded better than my usual thing. I naturally thought . . . well, how the hell do you know?"

"I've read the reviews," I said. "This one sounded better. That's all."

"Graffiti on a subway car would sound better! Reviews . . . Christ. Critics!" He spat the word, and considering his reviews I didn't blame him. Still, why should he care? "Critics! You know what they are. The critics come in after the battle's over, after the smoke has cleared, and shoot the wounded. Pretenders . . . poltroons . . . a swinish lot—no, they give swine a bad name . . ."

Heidi Dillinger said, "Allan holds them in low esteem. He takes them too seriously, Mr. Tripper. His readership is so huge, the critics are quite powerless to hurt him—"

"The fuckers wound my soul," he shouted.

"Perhaps you should try one of the books yourself, keep an open mind." She smiled at me. I wondered what she thought of them.

"Okay, okay. But right now we're trying to find out what he sees in JC—"

"Well," he said, refusing to calm down, "let me tell you a thing or three about my books. They may be trash, I can understand that, but they're what I do, and I do the best I can. They may well be quite forgotten in twenty years, I see that. But the little fartbrains who write about them, who are so quick to piss all over them, well, the little fartbrains are forgotten *the next day*. They're insects. I resent them. And if I weren't such a highly controlled man, I might kill a couple just for fucking sport."

"Look, if you're going to babble on about critics, I'm bailing out and going home to bed. I'm as willing to be bored by a windy novelist worth multimillions as the next man, but the next man wouldn't put up with this gratuitous bullshit either. You're rich, they're poor, to hell with them."

He waved his cigar at me, the ash falling into his cognac. "Shit! You see? The critics again!" He stared me back down into my chair. "All right, enough." He sighed and pushed the snifter away. He poured cognac into his coffee cup. "The trademark of my books is their verisimilitude. To one degree or another, they are always related to actual events. I overlay them with a dense layer of fiction—intrigue, sex, inside dope, violence, fairly one-dimensional characters drawn with a broad brush and

50

tangentially based on the kind of dimwits you see in the supermarket tabloids . . . but that structure, the steel skeleton of my story, the basis of truth, it always shines through, it carries the weight of the story. For instance, I found an Afrika Korps tank out there in the northern desert, the real skeletons still inside the damn thing . . . Friend of mine told me he'd heard rumors about it, I went all the way over there and found it . . . It must've been like an oven in that tank . . . forty years and more it sat there and when I found it, it was mostly buried in sand, the cannon barrel sticking up as if it were giving the world the finger! That was my truth. I found out everything I could about the tank, quite a big job for young Dillinger here, and then I began laying the rest of it on . . . That tank could bear a hell of a lot of weight, you follow me?

"Well, JC Tripper is the underpinning of my next book. Now is the time to get cracking on the research, so it'll all be in place when I'm done with Rommel's tank and dear old Lawrence . . . he was a great man, a very great man."

"JC? You're kidding, you've got to be kidding!"

"Lawrence. I was speaking of T.E. Lawrence. JC? No. Not a great man. But an interesting man, for all his faults and failings. JC was a prototype. Dramatic, girls fancied him, bit of a satyr—I can't even imagine some of the stuff he must have got up to, wicked reputation . . . as I say, a prototype. Your book was fine, but it was superficial—let's face it, Lee—at least by the standards I bring to this sort of thing. But now you've got the chance to find out if he's really alive! I have to know the truth before I proceed . . . and you were there, Lee. You more than anyone know what it was like at the end. You saw all the gory details, you must have your own deep, dark, secret ideas . . . You can't look me in the eye and tell me you haven't doubted the official story, the story you backed up with your book . . . hell, Lee, given the chance and the time, you're the one person who's bound to be able to recognize the truth."

My old pal was getting on my nerves. Two days ago someone I cared about had been murdered, but her death had been brushed aside by Allan Bechtol and Heidi Dillinger. They were like movie people I'd known. Nothing mattered but their plans.

Lost your leg and your baby was kidnapped by skinheads and your sister murdered and eaten by cannibals? Listen, man, that's heavy, but we're shooting the scene where the top of the girl's bikini comes off . . . They mattered. Not Sally Feinman, not the manner of her death, not my sorrow. They mattered and they were all that mattered, and I'd better get used to the idea if I let them buy me.

I pushed my chair back and stood up. The lights were winking in the darkness and the night sky glowed pink, as if the city had been torched by General Sherman. I tasted the cigar; too mild for me—a fine Havana. They were both staring at me, unwilling to let me slip away. They had no idea what I was thinking, which was all right with me.

I was trying to hear a voice, Sally's. I wanted to hear what she had to say to me. She was someone in whom I had placed complete trust. Her advice would have convinced me about almost anything. The decency and integrity that were the coin of her realm were beyond price in the easy corruption of our lives and times.

"You're overestimating me, I'm afraid." I was sweating again. The smell of nighttime summer rain was in the air like a hint of relief, a tinge of madness. There was a real breeze loitering in the Park and I could almost feel it. There was a soft peal of thunder somewhere off across the Hudson. "Think about it. I wasn't much good to anyone, not to JC and not to myself, not by the time our little caravan got the wagons into a circle in Tangier. I had a dope problem, a very big dope problem—you name it, I was on it. And the dope was made worse by the booze and all of it was complicated and compounded by all the wrong women. Including JC's hand-me-downs, and their name was legion. Then, when everything started turning Tangier to shit, your faithful servant here went entirely to pieces. I mean like one of those all-red jigsaw puzzles . . . lots of pieces and it looked like they were never going to get it put back together. The next time I knew my name was in a Swiss hospital. Sanatorium, I guess. I'm not the authority you seem to think I am, that's what I'm telling you."

Bechtol was shaking his head, being patient with me again.

"You gotta give me some credit, Lee." One of the candles had burned down and gone out. The other was flickering low in the stick, the fan threatening it with extinction any moment. His cigar's tip glowed like a stoplight, a warning. "I'm into details. Obsessive. Ask Heidi. Or trust me on it, it's true. I know how sloppy that mess at the end was—"

"Hardly anybody left alive knows how sloppy," I said.

"I know about the strange disappearance of the grief-stricken brother. Namely, you. Hell, Lee, one of the main scenarios the fans and the rock magazines used to put out was that maybe you were part of the cover-up surrounding the cause of death, the famous three-day delay . . . there were people who said you made sure JC got away safe . . ."

"Right, that's it," I said. "We killed a drunken stranger, cremated the body to give it that little extra touch of realism, then I went bananas to draw attention away from JC. Who then sneaked away wearing a burnoose and riding a camel . . . damn, we didn't think anyone would notice."

There was a long silence and then Bechtol said, "I've heard crazier stories in my time."

Heidi Dillinger looked at me, her tan eyes wide. I hadn't noticed before how they seemed to slant upward slightly, giving her an almost Asian look. "Are you sure that this is absolutely the right time for irony?"

I shrugged.

She went on, "There are even those people who have suggested that *you* killed JC . . . that you couldn't live in his shadow anymore, that you were tired of his leftovers—"

"Let me assure you," Bechtol said hastily, "we don't believe that for a moment. Not a moment." He glanced at her with a look of surprise and irritation.

"Well, that's a weight off my shoulders," I said. "I've also heard the cannibal story—it was the best. Clive and Annie and I and assorted guests were supposed to have sort of barbecued JC and dined on him. Giving whole worlds of new meaning to the idea of having lived off someone—"

"Self-protection through irony again."

"Ah, Dr. Dillinger, how good of you to join us. Why shouldn't

I be ironic? I always respond to psychodrama with irony. I don't like being surprised with truth-game crap and I can't abide bullshit." They kept staring at me as if everything I said could be taken down and used against me in a pinch. Or maybe they were just thinking how everything depended on me. I didn't know it then but I figured it out in due time. Everything had always depended on me. But of course there were things I knew that they didn't. In a way we each had a private agenda, a private loyalty. Maybe that was the way it always was. "Look, what do you want me to say? I was in the bin, wasn't I? I was in and out of clinics for a year. More than a year. Not just because of drugs. Psychological refurbishment as well. A head case. Do you hear me?"

"We hear you, pal. We know all that."

"Surviving wasn't easy," I said. "It was Clive Taillor—he was JC's driver—and Annie DeWinter, they pretty much handled things in Tangier. They were pumping out money like blood from a ruptured aorta, paying people off, trying to keep JC's death from becoming a goddamn carnival. They paid for the three-day delay you're talking about. They cremated old JC—"

"You didn't put all this into your book," he said.

"I wasn't trying to remake the world with that book," I said. "I was trying to make some money and shut people up." I was praying for rain. I patted my forehead with my handkerchief. "I never even found the place where they let the wind take the ashes."

But none of that mattered to Allan Bechtol, of course, because he'd made up his mind and everything had to conform. He knew what he wanted and he was a very persuasive fellow.

"Now I've gotta tell you some harsh facts of life, Lee." The smoke drifted into the candle's dying flame, was sucked upward into the night. Heidi Dillinger was watching him now, as if it were the most interesting example of harsh facts she'd ever heard. "I think JC is tucked away in his own jolly corner with good reason. I think we're not the only people looking for him. There are other people who are very serious about finding him. Or—try to follow this very closely, old son—or JC himself is going to considerable extremes to stay hidden." He sighed. "Or . . . both."

"What he's saying," she said quietly, "is that there is a certain element of danger in all this. Risk."

"Risk," I said, "sounds like something you'd manage."

"I'd try. Probably." She smiled.

"What makes you think there's danger? Maybe your imagination is working overtime."

"I don't think so," Allan said. He got up from the table and came to stand beside me. He slipped the tinted specs off and put them in his breast pocket. His face bore an expression of heartbreaking sincerity. "A disc jockey in Los Angeles who was very, very close to JC—"

"You must mean Shadow Flicker," I interrupted. "They were buddies, that's true."

"He's the one. Somebody murdered him just a few days ago."

It hit me hard. Flicker had been all right. He'd never betrayed JC, never used him. It was always a two-way street with Shadow. "If we can't use each other," he'd say, "we'll skip it. There'll always be another time, my man," he'd say. Well, there wouldn't be another time now. My stomach had felt a whole lot better in its time and my eyes filled up, thinking about Flicker. It must have been a drug deal. Or maybe he'd been porking a record exec's wife. Or daughter. It had to be something like that. Flicker was a little wild and not the type who would mellow, who would chill out with age.

"There's more, Lee. I'm sorry to break this stuff to you. But I gotta tell you, gotta be fair—I've got a feeling that the murder of Sally Feinman is connected, too. Too much coincidence for it to be any other way. Flicker was JC's friend and Sally was a reporter, she'd written too much about JC, and she was, y'know, very close to you."

"You might say," Heidi Dillinger said softly, "that she was Tripper-Intensive."

"*You* might say it," I said and dropped it. I turned to Bechtol. "You think JC might be having people killed to maintain his privacy? Maybe Elvis and Marilyn are in it with him. And Jack Kennedy, too."

55

"It ain't funny, Lee. If JC's alive, who knows what he's like now? Maybe he's got a reason we can't imagine. And maybe he's got nothing to do with it. Maybe people looking for JC are just very determined to find him. The point is, I don't know. But there sure as hell is something scary going on."

"What if you just scared me all the way off?"

"I figure half a million dollars might bring you back."

"You're serious?"

"Seems like serious money to me. I'm always serious about money. Half of it now, tonight, and the rest when it's over. When we mutually agree it's over. It's a lot of money, Lee."

"You are serious," I said. "Which means you're one of the people wanting to find JC. Which means you might have killed Shadow and Sally, and because you struck out with them you turn to me with a somewhat altered approach—how's that? Sound like a novel for Allan Bechtol?"

"Lee, I'm not going to take umbrage at that. But it's not worthy of you."

"Okay, okay. I'm trying to cope here . . ." I looked up slowly to give them the benefit of my radiant smile, what little they could see of it in the night. "Let's get serious, then. Let's say the half million is an advance against ten percent of world royalties, print and film and TV, if you ever write the novel. If you don't, the half million is mine for combat pay. You have a problem with that?"

Bechtol's mouth dropped open on that one.

Heidi Dillinger laughed, a surprising, rather musical sound. "And he thinks we're the cold-blooded cynics! You're a rogue, Lee. A real rogue and a scoundrel!"

"And I'll bet you like that in a man," I said.

Bechtol and I shook hands on the deal. Heidi Dillinger jotted the primary elements of the deal on a piece of Bechtol's stationery and we signed it. She was a notary public. She got out her stamp and notarized it. She gave it to me to hold on to. "You've got to trust Mr. Bechtol," she said. "This will help."

So we were partners.

Bechtol gave me a bank draft for a quarter of a million dollars.

How the hell could I say no?

Heidi Dillinger shook hands with me too, and handed me an envelope with a couple of sheets of paper in it. She also gave me an airline paper wallet.

"We're going to Los Angeles in the morning."

We drank a toast and I gathered up my knotted stomach and went home. The rain finally began on the way.

Five

Did any of Bechtol's story make sense?

Shadow Flicker and Sally Feinman had been murdered in the space of a few days. But were the murders connected by anything other than the time frame? Did anything else tie them together? The answer to that, of course, was JC Tripper. But did it matter? Did it mean there was an effective connection?

I could see how it would appeal to a man like Bechtol whose business was plotting novels. And in the old days when he was just plain Sam Innis he'd been fond of JC, and maybe that counted for something. But was his view skewed by the needs of his new personality and his peculiar career? Maybe all of his books were about conspiracies.

I had my doubts.

Still, there were two dead folks, both of whom I had known, and both had been involved in the life of JC Tripper—one by knowing him, one by researching him, writing about him. Hmmm. And they had both known me . . .

I had my doubts, but I also had a chill skittering along my spine. The past was always reaching out, threatening you.

Why was Bechtol so obsessed with writing a novel based on

the death, or faked death, of JC Tripper? Was it that JC was still that hot? It hardly seemed possible. But he was: I had my income, my book to prove it.

But was he the only goddamned thing Bechtol/Innis could find to write about?

Who knew how a novelist's mind worked?

If Bechtol was an accurate example of the writer-at-work, I could do with never knowing another. The more I thought about him, the crazier I thought he was.

But that didn't mean he wasn't right about the murders of Flicker and Sally.

It was raining hard by the time I got home, gurgling in the gutters and turning the potholes into small, deadly lakes. The temperature wasn't going down much, so the feel was tropical, malarial. The thunder was loud and nervous, cracking like gunfire, and lightning was snapping to the west, turning the clouds stark white at fretful intervals. You could smell the rain.

When I opened the door from the carpeted, mirrored hallway with its Japanese Kabuki paintings, I saw a dim light seeping out of the living room.

I stood in the doorway, the key in my hand, waiting, wondering, my mind flashing back on Sally and what had happened to her. Maybe she'd walked into her loft without a care in the world and maybe somebody had been waiting for her.

It was quiet and otherwise dark. The French doors to the terrace were open, as the rain bounced hard on the concrete floor. It dripped thickly from the awning. The light from the living room threw most of its illumination out the window onto the terrace, but it was still soft and dim. I swallowed back the first creeping fear. I told myself to lighten up, for God's sake.

I closed the door quietly and crossed the foyer, stared into the living room. A table lamp was turned on. Beside its base lay a novel by Howard Browne. Thunder exploded and the rain drummed and the curtains swayed slightly in the wind. I *must* have left the light on. I checked out the study, the bedroom, the kitchen. I didn't want to look in the bathroom. It was silly, but I kept seeing Sally in the water, her dead eyes staring, her teeth sunk into the pulpy, protruding tongue. I was acting like a nitwit. I reached in and flicked on the light. There was no one, dead or alive, in the bathroom. I yanked the shower curtain back. Nobody in the tub.

When I walked back down the hall I thought I smelled something funny. When I stood looking out at the rain on the terrace I felt the flush of breeze and I smelled it again. Just a whiff, then it was gone. Something from childhood, something I should have recognized.

I dropped the safari jacket over the back of the couch and went into the kitchen. I looked at the contents of the refrigerator. Lime Jell-O with bananas cut up in it. A couple cans of Tecate. I wasn't quite in the mood for the Jell-O, so I took one of the beers, popped it, and took a big gulp. I went through a big box of Jell-O every day. Lime today, yesterday cherry.

Cherry.

I was headed for the terrace when I remembered what it was I was smelling. From childhood, all right. Cherry soda. Cherry cough syrup. That sweet, sickly smell. Cherries.

I'd smelled it in Sally Feinman's loft, mixing in my nostrils with the horrible stench of burned flesh coming from the bathroom.

Now I was home and I was smelling cherries. And the light had been on but I hadn't left it on. And I was standing in the doorway watching the rain bounce and my knees were beginning to sound like the tap-dancing feet of Astaire.

There was a man sitting in one of my deck chairs. Most of him was protected by the awning from the rain. He was wearing what seemed to be a venerable seersucker suit, rumpled, wrinkled, shapeless, baggy. A Panama hat with a brightly colored band sat on the little table beside the chair next to a can of Tecate. His trousers had cuffs and they weren't covered by the awning. Neither were his cream-colored leather shoes with crepe soles. These bottom extremities were very wet. He didn't seem to mind. There was a snub-nosed Smith & Wesson in his lap. In one hand he held a corncob pipe. It was the tobacco I smelled. A cherry-flavored drugstore brand. His eyes were closed. His face was square, heavy-jowled, thin-lipped, and looked as if it were composed primarily of freshly poured concrete. There were several strands of damp gray hair plastered across the top of his balding head. There was also a large red stain on his blue shirt below a plaid bow tie that looked like it might be a clip-on.

"Hi, there," I ventured. I didn't sound like a man whose native tongue was English. Or any other known earth language.

He didn't move.

I had a dead man on my terrace.

I took another man-size hit of Tecate. "Shit," I said, meaning every word of it. I bent down and peered fleetingly at the gory stain, obviously lethal even in the dim light on the terrace. In a lightning flash it really looked god-awful. I inspected the dead gray face. "So who the hell are you, anyway," I mused. I hated this.

"Morris Fleury," the corpse said in a raspy voice thick with weariness and what turned into a Texas drawl or twang or whatever it was. "And you, son, are talking in my sleep."

If you've never seen a man actually levitate, you've really missed something. I've never seen it happen either, but I have Morris Fleury's word for it. He says he figures the only thing that would outright beat it would be spontaneous human combustion, and there we're talking *rare*.

When I settled back onto the terrace, grabbing for the doorframe to keep from falling down, Morris Fleury, the un-dead, surveyed me with scrunched-up sleepy eyes and dropped his pipe. When he reached down to get it, his revolver fell on the floor. He grunted and retrieved both items, held one in each hand, stared at me with a perplexed look on the cement face, as if he were trying to recall just where he was and who I might be.

"Jesus, your chest—are you all right?"

"My chest? My chest?"

"Yes, your chest, there, your chest. You're wounded."

He ducked his chin, trying to see the wound.

"Ketchup and mayonnaise," he said. "Double cheeseburger with the works, fries, chocolate malt. Two people I respect have told me to lay off the ketchup." He yawned mightily, covered his mouth with the hand holding the Smith & Wesson. He looked like he was about to eat it.

"Two," I said.

61

"My doctor and my dry cleaner." He made a noise that was a laugh of sorts. "You'll have to excuse me," he grumbled, "but I'm bushed. I suppose you're Lee Tripper."

"I suppose."

"He supposes," he said to an invisible audience. "That's a good one."

"Please don't point the gun at me."

"Look, you could jump me, overpower me or something. Morris Fleury wasn't born yesterday." He didn't actually say "wasn't"; he said "wun't." If he was ever called upon to say "'Throw' me the ball," he'd say "Tho"; he'd say "bidness," not "business," "hep" instead of "help." You get the idea. But you do the dialect yo'sef, podna, because I'll go nuts if I try to write it all down phonetically. We'll both go nuts, for that matter. Back to the story: he decided to put the gun away. He dropped it into the pocket of his baggy jacket. He stared up at me while he stuck the corncob pipe in his mouth and lit it with a Bic lighter. Suddenly the smell of cherries was overwhelming, nauseating.

"My God, that smells awful. How can you stand it?"

"If you smoke it, you can't smell it."

I drank some beer. "Sally's loft reeked of that smell."

"I'm not surprised." He struggled to a standing position. About five-eight, about one-ninety, but mostly gut. His seersucker trousers were belted with a slab of leather two inches wide with a flat heavy buckle featuring the head of a longhorn steer inlaid in bone. His legs were spindly and bowed. I couldn't imagine why he was wearing crepe soles and not cowboy boots unless crepe soles were quieter. He looked at his soaked trouser cuffs and shoes. "You'd think a man would know enough to come in out of the rain. But I slept through it. I coulda slept in the saddle." He flinched at a whacking great clap of thunder. "Bad coupla days, chumley. Nerves shot. Trigger finger itchy. Morris Fleury's not the man he once was."

"Why are you napping on my terrace?"

He stared at me, tapping the pipe stem against his teeth.

"Did you kill Sally Feinman? Look, I don't know my lines . . . aren't you supposed to tell me what's going on here? Before I pass out from sheer excitement . . ." I figured he'd put the gun away and that was a good sign. Without the gun he wasn't a scary guy. I wondered how quick he was on the draw. The Texas drawl made me think twice.

"Me? Kill Sally Feinman? What the hell you talkin' about, boy? Snuff my meal ticket? Use your head, Tripper."

"Listen, Furry, I don't know you or anything about you—"

"Come on, let's have some respect here. It's not Furry. It's Fleury. Morris Fleury." He jumped again at an avalanche of thunder and lightning. "Can I have another beer?" He nodded toward the kitchen. "Then we can siddown, clear a coupla things up." Sweat was running down his face. I pointed to the fridge and told him to make it two beers.

I went into the living room and sank down into the deep gray sofa. Another faint breeze weaseled its way damply through the open window. Morris Fleury came back, handed me a can, and slumped down on the other couch, facing me. He pulled a red bandanna from his back pocket and mopped his face. "This kinda night . . . reminds me of the worst time of my life . . . runnin' guns to some bandidos through Belize . . . talk about the asshole of the known universe . . .."

"We weren't. We were talking about Sally Feinman. And the smell your tobacco left behind . . . Now tell me why I should believe you didn't kill her."

"You should believe it because I'm the one with the gun, smartmouth." He made a lot of noise sucking his beer. "You shoulda been in Belize, smartmouth."

"You're not going to shoot me. We're having a beer, we're getting to know each other. Establishing a little trust, Morris. Why were you in her loft? Are you the guy who knocked me down the stairs?" I blithered on while I got back to breathing normally. I kept telling myself there was nothing to be afraid of, not with this guy.

"I didn't kill her but you might have. You're a damn sight better bet than me." He licked his lips. "She was paying me, why would I kill her? You—you had a motive. Maybe I oughta have me a little confab with the coppers. How would you like that, amigo?" He smirked without much success. "Explain a coupla things to the fuzz." He coughed up an oily little laugh. He gave the impression that he might have spent a lifetime blackmailing people who couldn't afford to pay him off.

63

"You were working for Sally? Doing what?"

"Well, you might call it research."

"About what? And what the hell was my motive? I loved that woman. I wasn't in love with her but I loved her. Are these sentiments at all familiar to you?"

"Don't be such a jerk, okay? I've forgotten more about love than you'll ever know. Trust me." As the protestation of a noble nature, it was unconvincing.

"Talk to me, Morris. Tell me your story."

"So you loved Sally Feinman! Well, ain't that a good one!" He grinned, tilted the can to his mouth, shook his head at the wonder of it all. "Just goes to show you, don't it?"

I wasn't going to ask him any more questions. He could talk or not. He was wearing me out.

"She hired me to do some legwork, see. She said she was on to the biggest story of her life . . . You know how writers are, the story's the thing, I guess. So go figure. It was a big deal to her. You know what it was? This'll kill ya—it was your brother again! No shit, amigo. She was on to JC Tripper again!" He was sweating again. He pressed the cold beer can to his forehead, rolled it back and forth.

"That doesn't make any sense," I said. "She knew JC's dead."

"You think so, do you? Well, not to hear her tell it, my friend. She told me she knew damn well that JC Tripper was alive—"

"No, that's nuts. She'd have talked to me about it before anyone else. It was *our* project, we'd been all through it together—"

"Exactly. That's why she didn't tell you, get it?"

"No, I don't get it." What the hell was going on? Suddenly everybody had decided that my long-dead brother was doing an encore.

"She smelled a rat, Lee. Bottom line, the girl had a nose for news. A nose for news!" He seemed to like the sound of that. "So she hired Morris Fleury to check up on a coupla things. 'Discretion with Reasonable Rates, Fleury's the Man.' Lemme throw some names at you . . . a fella by the name of Clive Taillor, he was JC's driver, boozin' buddy . . ."

"I'm aware of who Clive Taillor is," I said.

"Damn right you are. Clive Taillor, now resident in Zurich.

And there was this other fella Feinman was interested in, fella by the name of Flicker . . . he's had some bad luck lately, though, along the lines of Sally Feinman's bad luck. You hear the one about this Flicker? My friend Flicker? Old pal of JC's, disc jockey in LA. You hear about him?" His small eyes, shiny and close together, were suddenly very alert. "No? Well, he's no longer with us. Died. He wound up looking like the Death of a Thousand Cuts. He only lived through the first hundred or so, that's my guess. They found him clogging up a cistern in some place called Pacoima. I'm told he was all shriveled up. Looked like one of them dancin' California raisins, that's what I hear. Then she said there's a strange report or two outta London about Annie DeWinter, who was JC's old girlfriend . . . Whattaya make of this?" He laughed. I was getting tired of his laugh. "Well, I got one more name for you—gonna blow your cotton-pickin' mind. Ready?"

"Amaze me, Mr. Fleury."

"Lee Tripper."

"What's that mean? Lee Tripper?"

"You. Don't you get it? This woman you loved so much! I told you—you're the one with the motive, not me. She was just about to turn me loose on you. Deep research. She was gonna give me a file she'd been collecting, all about Lee Tripper—"

"This is insane," I said. "Sally wouldn't—"

"She thought you'd lied to her. She thought you'd written your book to cover your tracks, chumley." He grinned, not a winning sight. "She wanted your ass. True, as God is my witness. You love her now?"

"My faith in human nature is, I admit, badly shaken." I swallowed hard. The trick was to stay cool. I didn't want to show Fleury any weakness. He'd never let you forget it. That was *his* nature.

"She thought you had something to do with whatever happened to JC. His death . . . or his disappearing, willing or otherwise. Maybe you murdered him. Maybe you got him to wherever the dickens he wanted to go. Whichever—she figured that keeping it secret was pretty important to you. Now she's dead . . . Was it that important to you, amigo? I told you, you're the one with the motive, see."

I was trying to keep track of all the things I could say in my defense, but what was the point in wasting them on him? Sally had never let on a word to me. But I wasn't an idiot, appearances to the contrary. Fleury might be telling me the truth, and if he was, then I'd badly misunderstood Sally. I'd truly thought we were square with one another. More or less. Well, you live and learn, la-di-da.

"So what brought you here? Your employer is dead, you're out of a job."

He shrugged. "She'd paid me and I thought I owed it to her. I've always made that my rule, good value for money. Ask around. You'll find out."

"What a bullshitter! You'd probably like to put the squeeze on me. Get me to fall for your story about Sally investigating me and you'd have a perfect pigeon for a little blackmail. Except you don't know what she thought she had on me—if anything. So you're a brick shy of a load. I'll bet that's the story of your life."

"You have a cow pie for a mind, my friend. I went to see her, she was gonna give me this file she had—"

"On me?"

"On the whole business. You included, I suppose. Even if you didn't kill her, you were there, you know what I found. I did a pretty thorough search, like lookin' for a tick on an old black hound. But there wasn't anything. She was a helluva mess, though. Well, I don't know what to think, so I go back down to the street. I'm thinking I don't know what's goin' on . . . so I go stand in the shade down the block a ways. I get me a Sabrett's, put a lotta mustard on it . . . you shoulda seen *that* shit by the time I got done . . . and then you show up, all dewy-eyed and in love, heh, heh . . . And then a little while later we got curb-to-curb cops, a field of blue . . . and I think to myself, dear old Lee Tripper is Johnny-on-the-spot—"

"How'd you recognize me?"

"She gave me a picture, of course. Cut from the back of your book."

"So I dropped in to see her. But you yourself know she was already dead. Me as the murderer doesn't compute."

"Details, details. Give me motive every time, dammit. Once

you find the chumley with the motive you can make the details fit. We know you coulda had the motive . . . the hell with the details. You found out she was on to you, you gave her a good going-over to find out what she knew about you and your brother, and once she told you, you dropped the hot curlers into the tub. You grabbed the folder, sneaked out, and then came back a little later to find the body and call the cops. That's what I was thinkin'."

"If you were watching the building, you must have seen someone else . . . if not going in, then coming out for sure. There was a man who ran over me on the stairway. I went in, he came out a minute later. You had to see him."

"Sorry, pal. Nobody else came out." The smile slowly faded from Fleury's gray face. "Jeez. You think the killer was in there while I went through the loft? Oh, Christ. Glad I didn't know about that. Life's hazardous enough without that kinda crap."

"Somebody beat hell out of me on the stairs—well, that's overstating it, I guess. But, well—"

"Sure, sure." He gave me one of his stagey smirks and I stood up and went to the window. The thunder and lightning seemed to have stopped. The rain had settled into a steady throbbing downpour. The palm trees on my terrace soaked it up, loving it. "I suppose you've never heard of guys wounding themselves to prove they were victims, too. Well, believe me, it happens. Hell, I've done it myself. All you'd a had to do was fall down the stairs."

I looked at him. He was wet and hot and his face was still ashen and the thin gray hair was plastered across his skull and his shirt had that big gob of ketchup on it and his bow tie had worked itself loose and now hung from one collar point by its clip. He was such a wreck it was hard to be too angry with him.

"Fleury, you're too much for me. No point in arguing."

"Aw, hell, I don't suppose you did it. And if you did . . . well, you probably had your reasons. Lotta murderers in my experience damn nice fellas. She was gonna louse up your life, the way it sounded." He sighed. "I'm bushed."

The beer was gone, but I got my weary guest into gin and tonic. I told him I had a few things to do around the house. He nodded and turned on the television. Maybe he was thinking

67

about moving in. I didn't quite have the heart to throw him out into the rain. I went to the bedroom and packed a suitcase for Los Angeles.

How could you judge the information provided by a Morris Fleury? Did he have some peculiar private agenda? Had Sally really harbored suspicions about me? I'd been so close to her, I'd slept with her and worked with her, I'd even wondered at one time if I was falling in love with her. Whatever she'd thought she had on me—had it led to her death? If it had, that made me a part of it.

And somebody had the file she'd collected.

The file on Lee Tripper.

Morris Fleury was asleep the next time I saw him. I went to bed myself and got up a few hours later, showered, and put on a spiffy seersucker suit of my own, praying I'd never wind up looking like Morris Fleury in his. When I went into the living room he was gone. He'd gone out to the terrace and resumed sleeping in the deck chair. The sun was coming up. Soon it would be shining across Fifth Avenue, peeking between the buildings, across the Park, and into Morris Fleury's eyes.

But by then I'd be boarding the plane for LA.

Six

There was a message waiting for me at the check-in desk at LaGuardia. Heidi Dillinger had to take care of some business matters and would be taking a flight a couple of hours later. She'd meet me in Los Angeles at the hotel. Before boarding I called my banker, Harold Berger, and told him that my building concierge was holding an envelope containing a bank draft for a quarter of a million dollars payable to me. After he finished saying "Oh God, oh God, what have you done now?" I told him I thought it was worth his personally picking it up at his earliest convenience. I told him to relax, money was not necessarily the root of all evil. He replied that as a banker he was surely better equipped to comment authoritatively on anything related to money and it certainly was the root of all evil and the root of everything else, too, for that matter. Sometimes Harold gets philosophical and I have to hang up on him.

Settling back in my first-class seat, I was confronted with fruit and champagne and several varieties of Danish and scrambled eggs with smoked salmon and steaming coffee.

While eating I opened the envelope from the night before.

Reservations had been made and confirmed at the Bel Air Hotel. A car from Rent-A-Wreck, bit of humor, that, would be waiting for me. And there were the names of two men with whom I should speak. I knew both names but neither of the men personally. I'd seen the names on letters and contracts relating to my becoming the legal heir to JC's interests and to the rights of the book I'd written.

Manny Stryker was the producer preparing the film about the last days of JC Tripper's life. Freddie Rosen was the record producer who now headed MagnaDisc.

Allan Bechtol suggested in his accompanying note that these men might well know more than had previously been suspected about the secret fate of JC Tripper.

I'd only had a couple of hours of not very satisfactory sleep after my chat with Morris Fleury. Consequently I dozed off shortly after my five-thousand-calorie breakfast and came back to life somewhere approaching the Rockies. I poured fresh coffee into the bottomless pit and began to think things over.

My first thoughts turned to Heidi Dillinger. I didn't know what was going on in her mind any more than I did Bechtol's, but I'd been around enough highbinders in the old days not to trust either one of them. Not yet. Highbinders. That had been one of JC's favorite words, an archaism whose meaning seemed clear without resorting to the Unabridged. Ms. Dillinger and Bechtol were or were not highbinders, but I was bound to find out. In the meantime I had to figure out just how much I could tell her if I was going to be working with her.

Was there any point in telling her about Morris Fleury?

Was there any point in telling her about the suspicions he said Sally Feinman had had about me?

How far could I trust her?

Not far enough. Not yet.

If somebody was out to tie me into some nutty plot to kill my brother or hide him, then I had no allies. Not until I'd made sure. Not until they'd proved themselves.

She showed up at the Bel Air two hours after I checked in. She found me outside on one of the picturesque bridges looking down on the swans. It was hard to take my eyes off the black one, who was the star of the show and seemed to know it.

We went back to the shady veranda and sat down at a table giving an enchanting view of the grounds, emerald green from steady watering beneath the thick stands of trees. She was in what I took for California dress, splashes of color and not at all buisnessy. "What's your plan?" There was just a hint of mockery in the tone and the smile, as if she were kidding both of us. I could see it in her mouth and her eyes: she felt that we were skipping school. I doubted that she ever looked quite this way in New York. Maybe her guard was slipping. Maybe she was falling for my boyish charm. Maybe she liked that in a man.

"I'm going to start with Stryker."

"*We* are going to—"

"No," I said, heading her off at the pass. "There's no point in duplicating our efforts. I want you to do some checking on exactly what happened to Shadow Flicker. What do the cops say? They can't just ignore it. I want the story—talk to people at the radio station, find a reporter who covered the story. Flicker may have been killed for reasons that have nothing whatever to do with our investigation. Maybe he was still a big doper. Maybe he had violent friends . . . getting stuffed into a cistern may be a message for other dopers who aren't paying their bills. He could have been an informer for the narcs. He used to spend a lot of time out at the track. Maybe he had gambling debts. We don't know a damned thing about what happened to him."

She didn't look overly enthused. "I thought we were going to work together. That was the point. That's why I came out here. Two heads are better than one." Well, either she was falling for me or was supposed to keep me on Bechtol's leash.

"Look, leave all that out. If you're going to hang around, you're going to do it my way."

"Next you'll tell me you work alone and keep a bottle in the desk drawer."

"I do work alone. Particularly when people are getting killed." I was fighting against the impulse to feel like Bogart. I was much too large, for one thing. And I sure as hell wasn't a private eye. Everything I knew about how to act I'd learned

71

from books and movies. I was pathetic, but maybe I could keep everybody else from finding out the truth.

She actually batted her baby browns at me. At least we seemed to be in the same story. "You don't trust me, do you?"

"Not much farther than Gallivan," I said.

"Who's Gallivan?"

"Man I used to know. Pray you never meet him."

"What did he do to you?"

"Let's just say he was a lowlife."

"How low?"

"Low enough to sit on a dime and kick his heels. Thanks for asking."

"Why don't you trust me?"

"You suckered me. Anybody can get suckered once. But if I let you do it to me again, then it's my fault. It's like an inside straight. Anybody can try to fill it at first. But if you keep doing it, then you're just not learning. I hate being a chump."

"Chump? I don't believe I've ever heard anyone actually use that word before."

"If you stick around, who knows what you might hear. I may call you 'sister' soon or tell you you've got great stems that go all the way to the floor."

"You mean you're capable of almost any enormity."

"Almost."

"You might just say 'Follow that cab!' without warning."

I stood up. "You're catching on. Now let's get to work."

"Shall we meet back here for dinner or something?"

"Let's just wait and see."

"You're suddenly awfully mysterious and–"

"Don't say it."

"—and I like that in a man."

The car from Rent-A-Wreck was a white '58 Cadillac convertible with tires that reminded me of Yul Brynner, one broken taillight, and the smell of stale cigar smoke clinging to the black leather. The huge engine sounded as if it had been tuned yesterday. You could probably have seen the tips of the tail fins with a good pair of binoculars. From behind the steering wheel you really should have sent word by messenger to the front end before you hung a left, which is what I did once I passed through the huge Bel Air gates onto Sunset Boulevard.

I wondered if the car was Heidi's touch. Maybe there were depths of humor among the shallows and reefs of ambition, greed, and calculation. Were those qualities I liked in a woman? I'd have to give it some thought. I wouldn't have to think much about her eyes and her mouth and the willowy length of her arms and legs. I wondered where she kept her tan up-to-date. On Bechtol's penthouse deck? Or did he have a place in the Hamptons? And what the hell difference did it make to me? She was growing on me, that was the difference.

What I really wanted to know was her place in the equation Bechtol had worked out. Was she helping me or spying on me for her master? Wouldn't it be a good one on me if the Great-Author-and-possible-psychopath was among those who believed I was the one who needed investigating?

I'd called Stryker from the hotel to get directions to his home. It turned out Bechtol had called him and such was Bechtol's influence that Stryker had made time for me. He said, "I'm throwing Katz here and I've got Lamas on the way. But sure, sure, come on. Things can't get any more fucked up than they are." He told me how to get to his place up on Mulholland. "If the gate's locked, just honk your horn until that moron lets you in. Christ." He sounded like a man who was letting things wear him down. I didn't know who Katz was or why he was throwing him around. Or where. And Fernando Lamas was dead. In the back of my mind I had the idea that Lamas had a son who passed for an actor. Maybe he'd be there. Unfortunately I'd left my autograph book in New York.

The gate was, of course, locked. I honked the horn and in the fullness of time a young man appeared wearing cut-off jeans and a maroon-and-gold University of Southern California sweatshirt with the sleeves chopped jaggedly off. He was tall and tan and young and lovely, like someone from Ipanema. He also looked strong enough to take the gate off the hinges with his bare hands. He had a sweatband holding in place yellow hair, short back and sides and long on top. He was carrying a tennis racket and waved it at me. I nodded, he did something to the gate, and it swung back.

He looked down at me. He was probably twenty. He leaned on the doorsill. I hoped he wasn't going to pick up the car with me in it. "You're not the man," he said, "to fix the tennis-court fence."

"How true."

"Huge hole in the fence. It was just there one morning. The ball usually stops rolling between Sunset and Santa Monica. What can I do for you?"

"Point me at Manny Stryker. He's expecting me."

"Well, I'm the son and heir. William Randolph. The poor man's Harry Cohn is out back throwing Katz off the deck."

"So I keep hearing."

"It's an experiment."

A teenage girl the color of honey strolled up the driveway from the tennis court. She was, from twenty feet away, so beautiful you wanted to die for her. Then, like so many California girls, she diminished with each step closer until she was just another kid by the time you could reach out and grab a handful. It was the Great California Illusion.

"We're out of balls, Bill," she pouted.

The big kid looked at me. "Wouldn't you know," he said, "out of balls." He pointed to a spot where I could leave the car. "Great wheels," he said.

I nodded. "One at each corner. Standard on these older models."

They went off to look for more balls and I set off around the corner of a house that was made of some sort of stone and looked flat, like an elongated gun emplacement defending the spine of the hills. It lived out the back, as the real estate agents love to say. I stood at the corner and watched a man in sweatpants and a loose-fitting blue shirt holding a ball of black fur at arm's length before him. He was above me on a balcony, a story and a half above my head, leaning out over the grassy slope. A girl in a bikini waited below, aiming a video camera at the ball of fur. "Okay," she called. "Fire one!"

The man released the ball of fur, which turned into a cat. The girl in the bikini shot the process as the cat performed a blindingly quick series of acrobatic maneuvers and landed lightly on its feet. It shook itself, gave the girl's bare feet a look

74

that implied it was thinking of using them as a box of kitty litter, then strolled off with massive insouciance.

Manny Stryker wasn't throwing Katz. He was dropping cats. Hurray for Hollywood. You just never knew, that was the lesson.

He launched a couple more feline conscripts, saw me, and dropped a third without bothering to watch its landing. He called my name and came down the stairway barefoot. "Hey, nice to meet you, pal. Nice to know who you're doing business with. Listen, Shirl, that's enough for now. Take a look at the tape and we'll talk and get it over to the costumer. That's the girl." The girl in the bikini went away, one of the cats grumbling along beside her. Stryker led the way to a large round table sitting out on a promontory of stone, and looking down on the neighbors scattered on the hillside among the blue, shimmering disks of swimming pools. Stryker's pool was being attended to by a pair of men in coveralls. They were trolling with large nets. Below us Los Angeles seemed to be burning beneath a scary brown haze of smoke. Through the brown murk it seemed to be a city sacked and left to smolder by vandals.

Stryker motioned me into a canvas chair as a small Mexican woman arrived with a tray containing a pitcher of iced tea, a plate of lemon wedges, and two glasses also full of ice. The day wasn't nearly as hot as it had been in New York City. "Funny thing about cats," he said. "The higher up they are, as a general rule, the safer they're likely to be when they fall or jump. They're very different from people. No matter how far a cat falls, it never falls faster than sixty miles per hour. People, see, have a much lower ratio of body surface to mass, ergo less air resistance. So people reach a velocity of a hundred and twenty miles per hour when they fall. And of course your cat is your natural acrobat, having descended over several million years from your tree leapers. But—tell me if I'm boring you, 'kay?—it takes the cat about five stories of falling, or more accurately five stories of accelerating to reach its top speed . . . and it's only then that the little bugger really relaxes and splays out its legs and begins a kind of floating. Like a flying squirrel. Thus the drag's increased and the impact of landing is spread out over a larger area. Results are incredible—there's the case of a cat in

New York who fell thirty-two stories onto a sidewalk . . . What do you think happened?" He waited patiently for an answer. Here was a man with a hobby.

To prove I was paying attention, I said, "Sidewalk splattered with cat as far as the eye could see." I knew my cue. His research report was giving me a chance to look him over. His dark curly hair was cut close to his head, his nose looked as if it had repeatedly fallen thirty-two stories to the sidewalk and been considerably broadened by the experience. His eyes were dark and quiet while the rest of him tended to fidget. He was pouring iced tea, dropping lemon wedges in our glasses.

"Cat chipped a tooth." He sighed. "Thus, the cat's nine lives. I've gotta find a taller building. I might kill one of the little bastards here. They don't have the time to spread out and increase drag and get the landing gear down properly."

"Are you crazy or is there some point to this?"

"I've got a screenplay about a cat burglar. Almost a comic-book figure but not quite. He escapes by turning himself into a cat. Literally, figuratively speaking. Concept's a little hazy, but it's easy to catch on to, y'know. So who can say? We could have a hit, we could have a fart in a space suit. No way to tell. But you didn't come here to listen to me rave on about cats—"

"You could have fooled me," I said.

"Bechtol said something about your brother. Well, hell, I bought the rights to your book, we've got the screenplay in development. The writer's a turd, but what can you do, he's a *writer*. Bane of my fucking existence. So what's Bechtol's problem?"

"You know. He thinks JC is alive. He seems to think you're of the same mind. Why does he think that?"

"What do you think?" He gave me a look so shifty it had to be a joke. "Is he alive?"

"Look, I'm just glad we're off cats."

"Listen, pal, I've got an interest in JC. Obviously. We've all got an interest in JC. If he's alive, well, hell . . . I don't want to have fifteen, twenty million in a picture that has the wrong ending. Not if I can help it. I don't want to picture him dead as a lox and suddenly he's on the front page of every paper in the world, making me look like a total asshole. Only makes sense, 'kay? Who knows what it could mean for the picture, plus or minus? Nobody, that's who. But I'd like some warning if he's gonna pop up on *Entertainment Tonight*. Maybe it would give the picture a real boost, maybe it would sink it for all time. I'm not saying I know. But I'd like to have the time to lay out a campaign for any eventuality . . . so, sure, I've got some inquiries out, some of my people looking around, trying to pick up a piece of information here and there. No crime in that. For instance, I'm going to Paris tomorrow, I've got a lead there, some A-rab camel driver or some goddamn thing, says he knew JC in Casablanca a couple of weeks before he died . . ."

There was an explosion of honking from up above the house. Another visitor. Fernando Lamas's son, perhaps.

"Lamas," he said, sensing my curiosity. "Been waiting three days."

"Camel driver," I said. "Sounds weak to me."

"Maybe yes, maybe no. Thing is, this guy says your brother talked to him about some crazy escape route he'd laid out, told the A-rab it was foolproof. He says your brother wanted to hide away and spend the rest of his days writing poetry."

"Not exactly the brother I remember so well. Pornographic limericks, maybe."

"Well, wait a minute. He wrote a lot of lyrics, 'kay? Some are pretty bloody marvelous, 'kay? I don't think the A-rab's story is so farfetched. Listen to some of his stuff again—"

"Please," I said.

"Anyway, this A-rab says JC was pretty sexed out in Casablanca. Says he was providing JC with some very young girls—"

"So he was a pimp, not a camel driver. You and he have credibility problems, my friend."

"Very, very young girls and boys of all ages. Sort of burning his candle at both ends, as they say."

"What utter bullshit!"

"Well, you'd naturally protect his reputation, wouldn't you? He's your brother—"

"Look, I was there. Girls maybe, but JC was not into boys, young or old. If you're paying this Arab anything, you're dumber than your cats."

I looked up. Something funny was being led around the

corner of the house. It had four legs and looked as if it had started out to be a horse and run into design difficulties. Another one followed the first.

"I'm not impressed," Stryker said. And he wasn't even looking at the recent arrivals. "Not with your indignation and your outrage. What's it to you, anyway? You've made your pile off your brother . . . Maybe you're afraid he'll come back and the record royalties will go to him—is that it?"

"I believe my brother is dead. I want it to stay that way. I don't want him, the memory of him, dragged through the slime just to hype your movie. He's dead. I don't want to look up at the screen and see him turned into some crazy Arab procurer's idea of a sex-crazed rocker, not when he's not here to defend himself. That isn't why I sold you the rights to my book."

Stryker stood up. His back was still to the three—count 'em, three—creatures being led past the pool in our general direction.

"Why did you sell the movie rights? 'Cause you wanted the money. Don't kid yourself about that. Look, why not just keep your shirt on, Sunny Lee. We're talking about show business here. Which is the money business. A money business which to a very large extent depends on the total, brainless crap the twelve-year-old mind clamors for. Leave us have no illusions. I'm in this for the money. MagnaFilms is sure as hell in it for the money. So don't be a sanctimonious asshole while you're still getting your cut, 'kay? There's plenty for everybody. If you don't like it, find him yourself . . . or prove he's dead. Do you hear me saying that maybe you killed him yourself and then pulled that disappearing act in Switzerland? No, you do not. But there are people who believe that. They're around, my friend. So don't make an enemy out of somebody who's got nothing against you, 'kay?"

One of the creatures made a peculiar sound and Stryker's face broke into a broad smile. He was fifty or so but his teeth were clearly about a year old. He spun around to face the animals and their two attendants.

"My llamas! My llamas are here! You little fuckers, come to Poppa!"

I hadn't needed my autograph book after all.

No one took much notice of my departures except for William Randolph Stryker, who was poking around in the shrubbery looking for a ball. I slowed the Caddy and he looked up, grinned. "Lost two just since you were here. It's Ellen, no sense of direction."

I gave him an address and asked him how to get there from here. He said, "Hey, that's Freddie Rosen's place. Silver Lake. It's a lot closer to downtown. Freddie's a good man. I work for him sometimes. Y'know, little stuff. He gives me free CDs." He told me how to get there.

Seven

I finally got to the right part of town—I had no idea which town or city I was in, Los Angeles itself or one of the towns that hug a lower-middle-class neighborhood with kids playing catch and hanging out looking teenage-shifty. I asked directions again and began to climb through increasingly narrow streets of aging bungalows and cars parked at curbside rather than hidden in garages. The sidewalks were old and cracked but the palm trees swayed above and seemed to make everything else okay.

I felt the stinging in my eyes. My face felt as if I'd stuck it into a bag of hot coffee grounds. Los Angeles was a mystery to me. Geographically, climatologically, and zoologically. Katz and Lamas. I was still thinking of how cute movie people could be when they got serious about it, then suddenly realized I could breathe without coughing. I'd fumbled out of the worst of the smog and was looking down on it again past the tops of palm trees and some towering oaks.

Rosen's house was hidden behind a wall and gate at the top of the hill in a cul-de-sac. Was it a hill or a mountain? How the hell should I know? I was a stranger there myself, as the man said.

I parked the Caddy and walked across the shady street to the gate, which was a showstopper. It was about ten feet tall and solid wood, no peek-a-boo grille. And it was carved. All over, like something conceived and executed by the English genius Grinling Gibbons. It's not often that the old chap comes to mind, but when he does there's no alternative to him. Staring at that gate, what else could a fellow think? Grinling Gibbons. Of course Gibbons didn't specialize in countless anthropomorphic mice, ducks, squirrels, kitties, bunnies, hound dogs, teddy bears, chipmunks, beavers, knights in armor, maidens leaning from tower windows, dragons with great elongated tails and talons, serpents with flicking tongues twisting around tree trunks featuring owls on branches and more gnarls than you could count. It all resembled a Disney animator's worst hangover. But there was a nutty magnificence to it as well; it might have been a metaphor for the whole place. That's one of the problems about Los Angeles, Hollywood, whatever you want to call it. You've got to keep fighting the impulse to find metaphors everywhere. It's all a result of the movies, which are themselves merely metaphors for reality . . . you see, there I go again. Anyway, it was late afternoon and the sun was casting long shadows. As the light lowered, the carved animals seemed almost alive. Maybe when night fell they left the gate and went to town.

If they could find it . . .

I pushed the gate and slowly it swung back on its massive hinges. The driveway curled around a small pond with a very large fountain in the middle, lily pads below. Mermaids sat on the edge of the fountain feeling the gentle spray of three cherubs peeing. There were no actual human beings in sight, peeing or otherwise, but I could hear a hellish din coming from inside the big house, which was, I supposed, vaguely hacienda-like. There were stucco or adobe and terra-cotta tiles and pots and big dark beams that appeared to be poking through the walls. A very classy-looking old Mercedes convertible sat up near the porch, the kind of car Reichsmarschall Göring would have liked. I stopped to look at the car and found someone in the backseat. The noise from the house was getting louder. It was—if you were willing to stretch a point or two—a rock band.

"Hello, there," I said, but the little boy on the black leather upholstery was engrossed in a picture book about dinosaurs. "That's a stegosaurus," I said.

He looked up. He was three, maybe three and a half. "No way, José," he said confidently, patient with adult idocy. "Dimetrodon. They're very different." He pointed to the spine fin. "Very different," he said again for the slower students.

"What's that?"

"What?" He looked up, round-eyed. Maybe he was four. I've never had kids of my own. How should I know how old he was? But definitely not five. He was wearing a Brooklyn Dodgers baseball shirt, blue jeans with plaid cuffs, and red sneakers the size of my thumb.

"That Baggie. What's in it?" I prayed I was wrong.

"Daddy's coke, I guess."

"Ah." The baggie was open and some of the white powder had sifted out onto the black leather. There was a smudge of it on one of his fingers. "Would you like me to take it to your daddy?"

"No way, José. I'm guarding it." He folded the top of the Baggie tight and moved it closer to his thigh with a proprietary gesture.

"Right. I get it. Now that's a brontosaurus, I'm sure about that."

"Nope. Seismosaurus. It's bigger. Biggest of all."

"Man, you really know your stuff."

"Yeah." He nodded.

"Is your daddy in the house?"

"I guess. Sleeping, I bet."

"I'll go see. Say, how do you like the music?"

He made a face.

"You got that right," I said.

It was dim and gloomy inside the house and the noise was overpoweringly awful. A blonde in a seersucker skirt and jacket with blue-and-white spectator pumps was standing in the hallway. A gold-and-platinum Rolex sliding on her wrist like a bracelet. Brownish-red nails approximating the color of dried blood. Her hair was cut in a page boy that swirled around her face when she noticed me standing in the open doorway. She looked at me with sharp, distrustful eyes, and wasn't over-whelmed. She had a Vuitton bag hung over one shoulder. She was speaking into empty space and her voice cut like a saber through the concrete wall of sound. She was shouting about the plans for the evening, names and places and hours. The recitation sounded like the day's marching orders at Fort Zinderneuf. Sort of the march-or-die approach to social en-gagements. She concluded on a grace note.

"And if you didn't hear me over this shit and you fail to keep your appointed rounds, my dear little dickhead, you are dead meat." She looked at me as if she had some suggestions for my social calendar that I probably wouldn't much like, then stuck a ruthless smile on her pretty face. She reminded me of Doris Day in the old days. "And who the hell are you? No, on second thought, no. You're not the vet and the only man on earth I want to see right now is the vet. I've got a Bouvier des Flandres who's been upchucking into the swimming pool all morning. Not pretty, believe me. Do dogs get hair balls? No, I suppose not. You want Freddie, well, miraculously he is risen. In the music room." She speared the air with one of the nails. A Masai warrior would have thought twice about going up against her. "I've always said Freddie needed a damn good thrashing." She showed her teeth. "And now he's got one." She brushed past me on a cloud of Giorgio and I went into the room she'd pointed out.

The biggest, rattiest speakers I'd ever seen were standing in the corners of a room that half-shook with the noise. You could feel the sound coming from the floor, like snakes up your pant leg. A man with a bald head sat in what looked to me like the Barcalounger my grandfather had acquired in his sunset years. He wore a faded blue terry-cloth robe and watched me through a cloud of cigarette smoke. His mouth moved but I couldn't hear a word. I shrugged. A cheap turntable played an unla-beled disc. A forty-five. His mouth moved some more and I shrugged some more. His mouth went on and on and I saw he was swearing. It was like watching the manager run out onto the field to engage the umpire in dialogue. He reached over, flipped a switch, and the sudden silence made my ears sting.

"I suppose," he said, still shouting, "you're the guy Bechtol called me about."

"I'm not some guy, birdbrain. I'm Lee Tripper. You send me very large royalty checks. I could take JC and go to another label anytime I choose. *Guy*. Jesus." I looked at the stereo equipment. "Nice rig you got here."

"Basic rule. You gotta listen to shit if you're gonna play shit. The worse the rig, the better it sounds. Mick the J taught me that. You must know that, your background."

"I've heard the theory. And I didn't mean to bust in on you here—you could have taken me for a narc and blown me away."

"What's that supposed to mean? I just got up, got my cup of Yuban Instant, I'm not thinking clearly. You giving me shit or what?"

"You're a sleaze farm and I've known you thirty seconds and already I feel like I'm up to my heinie in manure. I met your son in the back of that little Mercedes out front. He was guarding your cocaine for you. Very classy touch. If I were half a man I'd rip your head off and stuff it down the hole."

"Jeez, man, you get outta bed on the wrong side, or what?" He stood up and slipped out of the robe. He was about a size forty-eight, portly, deeply tanned, and looked oily. There were gold chains and medallions around his thick neck. He was about fifteen years out of date, but this was the record business, this was LA. Maybe he looked exactly right but it was hard to believe. Maybe time had stood still for Freddie Rosen. "We're off to a bad start, my man. Let's just chill out a minute here. Damned good thrashing always puts me in a lousy mood."

"Leave your sex life out of this."

He picked up a hand-painted shirt and slipped it on. I just knew it would be too tight. Somewhere there was a Too Tight Shop and all the Freddie Rosens were steadies. He buttoned the shirt and he looked like he'd just won the Wet T-Shirt Contest the first night of his Club Med vacation. He stuck out a hand with four rings on it, all set with diamonds that looked like zircons on him. This guy was head of MagnaDisc. I shook his hand. A man's gotta do what a man's gotta do.

"Come on, it's time for Freddie Deuce's computer class." He led the way back outside. Late afternoon shadows were length-

84

ening. "Then I'll buy you breakfast. We gonna get along just fahn." He leaned into the back of his Mercedes where his son was playing with little plastic dinosaurs. "Hey, Deuce, you want to play with the computers?"

"You gotta be kidding," the little boy said. "Sure."

"Gimme five, man," Rosen said, slapping palms with his son. "And gimme that Baggie. Nasty stuff. Bad." His son handed him the Baggie. We got into the elegant little car and set off down the driveway, through the gate where the animals still gamboled, and down the hill.

"My car's back there," I said. "Can you find your way back?"

"Do it every day."

"It's the breadcrumbs," his son said from the backseat and broke into maniacal laughter.

"So what about a damned good thrashing?"

"No, thanks, never indulge."

He laughed, stroked his bandido mustache. "That's the name of the new band. We're about to blanket the earth with 'em. A Damned Good Thrashing. ADGT. That's their name. A return to pure Heavy Metal. Gonna be a monster. Hey, Deuce? Here, take the Baggie." He handed the bag of cocaine back to his son. "It's bad. You got that? Coke is bad. Okay, now open the bag and dump it over the side."

I watched the grinning kid as the wind took the white powder and blew it away down the street.

"Showing off for me?" I asked.

He laughed again. "I could care less what you think. Gotta set the Deuce here an example." He sighed. "The joys of fatherhood. I gotta kick it, man. Always said I could if I wanted to. The Deuce makes me want to. Freddie Rosen the Second. Now we'll see if I was right." He pulled over to the curb beside a grammar school. His son was already out of the car, impatient to get at the computers. Freddie Rosen said he'd be back in a minute. I watched them walk across the grass and through the front door. By then the little boy was already talking to another kid and Freddie Rosen was chatting with a woman who'd brought her daughter.

When he came back he said, "Breakfast time." It was five o'clock, but apparently it was morning for Freddie Rosen. We drove forever and found a place called Nate and Al's in Beverly Hills. It turned out to be a big New York deli. He led the way to a booth far from the door. I ordered a toasted bagel and coffee. He had a lox-and-onion omelet, potatoes, bagels, a knish on the side, an order of cole slaw. He looked at me. "I gotta go on a diet. I'm a mess, man. I need an image transplant. I need a really good rug. I need a really first-rate trainer, guy comes to the house, sculpts my body into a thing of beauty, into the temple it's meant to be . . . What have I got now? Body by fuckin' Sara Lee. What can I say?" He shoveled in about two hundred calories, one forkload, and looked miserable.

"You could tell me what you know about my brother. Bechtol thinks he might still be alive. He said you're one of the people I should talk to about that."

He didn't seem to hear me. "You think I like lookin' like this? for Chrissakes, what am I, crazy? Fuckin' gold chains make me look like a fuckin' bondage freak from Keokuk. Shirts too tight make me look fat—hell, I am fat. And that miserable cunt of a wife, Samantha, Sammy she likes to be called, Sammy Shit I call her—what did I do to deserve her? What sins were so terrible? You think I want to raise the kid in a sandbox full of cocaine? My problem is an occupational hazard. I'm forty-eight, I'm a carryover from the Stone Age. The stoned age, right? I mean I got no fuckin' guts, right? They bought me a long time ago . . ." Sweat was beading up on his swarthy bald head. "You know how much money I made last year? Way over a million bucks. Now I spend my life dealing with what? The second, third generation of these freaked-out little bastards with all their whining and butt-fucking and electric guitars and key-boards and plug-in MTV brains, the deejays on the take as much as ever. I'm selling this crap and calling it entertainment and music and fun . . . It's disgusting. I'm underpaid, my soul is in limbo." He kept on eating and talking like an old-time speed freak. "Now JC Tripper, he was different, one of the greats, the American Joe Cocker, a legitimate legend, y'know, Joseph Christian Tripper, a Harvard man . . . a Renaissance man, fuckin' A, we're not gonna see his like again . . . The dope, of course, did him in, more or less . . ."

"Did you ever meet my brother?"

"Coupla parties, shook hands, award ceremonies. He was a pretty private guy—well, hell, what am I telling you for? But I didn't like *know* him." He probed at the knish, cut it in half, and opened wide. You had to hand it to him, the man could put it away.

"So what's with you and Bechtol?" I asked. "Why am I here? Not that I'm not fascinated by your list of complaints—"

"Admit it," he said. "You didn't like me at the start."

"You noticed that?"

"I had to win you over." He smiled as winsomely as possible. "I'm sensitive to that kind of thing. Vibes, y'know. Bad karma. You like me better now, would you say?"

"Sure," I said. "I like you better."

"Thanks, pal. It's important to me. So what's on Bechtol's mind . . . what's on Bechtol's mind . . . well, who knows? The man's a genius, a great writer, am I right?" One of the greats. A giant—"

"All right already."

"We're very simpatico, Bechtol and me. So, Lee—you don't mind if I call you Lee, right?—so, Lee, we were talking about your brother, Bechtol's running all these stories past me, and I'm getting into it, telling him things I've heard . . ." He shrugged. "You know."

"No time to be coy and demure, Freddie. I don't know, that's the point."

"The murder stuff." He sniffled and busied himself with the last of the knish and the cole slaw. "It's hard to talk about this stuff with, y'know, *you*."

"And why is that, Freddie?"

"Well, I keep hearing about what happened in Tangier and it always comes back to murder. Somebody got murdered back there in Tangier . . . now, was it your brother? Or some other poor asshole who got it in the back so your brother could do a fade? And maybe you, the faithful brother, were the, ah, well, the hit man . . . your brother's keeper . . . and they hustled you off to the nuthatch in Switzerland and papered over the whole thing . . . heh, heh . . ."

"All so JC could disappear." I shook my head.

"Listen, people high in the Magna Group were scared shitless

87

about all of it for a long time. Serious anxiety." He had begun to squirm and look at his watch.

"What were they afraid of?"

"Afraid of? Afraid of?"

"That's right, Freddie. That's the question."

"Don't you think the idea of murder is just a little scary? Murder scares me. You? Maybe not. But put it together: JC Tripper is dead . . . the brother disappears . . . secret cremation . . . The whole thing is covered up but there are rumors right away . . . is JC really dead? Did somebody off him for reasons unknown? Or did he just die? And why in some utterly half-assed place like Tangier? It's like an old Claude Rains movie. Turns out they're not such hot record-keepers over there in Tangier, everything's a little hazy in Tangier . . . Sounds like a great JC Tripper song, right?" He laughed softly, suddenly comfortable with himself.

"It was a JC Tripper song," I said. "I watched him working on it. The last song he ever wrote. The famous lost valedictory of JC Tripper . . . it's a legend because nobody ever knew what happened to it." I felt a chill along my spine and it wasn't the air-conditioning.

"That was the whole story all right." He smiled and pushed his plate away. "'Everything's Hazy in Tangier.' Imagine what it would be worth if it ever turned up . . ."

"Imagine," I said.

"Everything's hazy in Tangier," he said, reciting the words slowly, "or is it really clear . . . in Tangier . . . maybe all the haze and smoke and fog . . . exists in here . . . in my mind, in the daze and the smoke and the fog . . . of a mind on fire . . . in Tangier . . .

"How do you know those words? Nobody knows those words—"

"*You* know them," Rosen said.

"*I* was there. You weren't. How, Freddie?"

"It came in the mail, my friend."

"When did it come in the mail, Freddie?"

"About a month ago. Sucker just came in the mail."

"What makes you think it's real?"

"Oh, it was JC's handwriting. No doubt of it. We had all that checked out."

"Where was it posted?" My heart was down to about three beats a minute. I wasn't ready for this. Who'd had it all these years?"

"One of the secretaries opened it. Put it on my desk. I was out of town, up in Vegas, some damn place. I got back, fuckin' girl never even put a flag on it. I got to it a couple days later. The envelope was long gone. There was no covering letter, nothing. Just some handwritten sheet music. Oh, it's a mystery, pal."

"You told Bechtol?"

"Listen, I'm a good soldier."

"What's that supposed to mean?"

"A good soldier gets his marching orders, he marches."

"Why Bechtol?"

"Marching orders, my man."

"Who gives you your orders?"

"Who do I work for?" He signaled for the check.

"What is this cagey thing you're doing?"

"I'm just someone in the middle. I keep thinking about murder . . . rumors of murder." He shrugged. "It all scares me. It all comes out of the past and yells 'boo' at me and I'm scared. People dyin' around here . . . dig?"

"'Rumors of Murder.' Another JC Tripper platinum hit."

"He recorded that one, Lee. Man, I don't like the look in your eyes."

"'The Look in Your Eyes.' What are we doing, Freddie? Carrying on a whole damn conversation in JC's titles? Y'know, Fred—you don't mind if I call you just plain Fred, do you?— some of the murders are more than rumors . . . some are absolutely real—"

"I *know* that. The real murders, those are the scariest of all . . ."

"Sally Feinman was tortured before she was killed. Do you know why, Fred?"

"Come *on*, Lee."

"It couldn't have been much fun in that cistern out in Pacoima . . . what if he was still just barely alive when they stuffed him in the cistern? Poor old Shadow."

"That's the understatement of the eighties, Lee. And it's exactly why I am staying as cagey as I can while still being a good little soldier—"

"I'm getting tired of the soldier shtick, okay?"

"Sorry. But it's fitting as a metaphor. Or I could call myself a pawn. How's that?"

"We're talking about my late brother," I said. "I don't like any of this—"

"Look on the bright side. Maybe he's not so late. Maybe JC himself sent the song . . . maybe he's gonna come out of hiding after all these years—why not? Crazy dude, JC."

"JC's dead," I said. "Anybody hanging around in those days could have grabbed that song . . . it was a mess back then."

"Listen, if that works for you, go with it. I gotta haul ass, man. We gotta pick up the Deuce and get you back to your jalopy." He eased his bulk along the booth, the buttons of his shirt screaming for mercy.

We picked up Freddie II and listened to his chatter about computers. Neither one of us knew what the hell he was talking about.

When he pulled up next to the old Caddy, Freddie turned to me, put his hand on my shoulder.

"You're okay, Lee. Really okay. You listened to all my shit, you were very patient with me."

"Talk about understatement," I said.

"So I'm gonna give you a little present."

"No coke, no thanks."

"Bad stuff," came from the backseat. "Throw away."

"Just a name," Rosen said. "Save you some digging. Cotter Whitney the Third. I'm only a soldier. Cotter Whitney is the commander in chief, you might say."

Freddie the Deuce was waving to me as they disappeared through the carved gate toward home, toward Sammy the Shit.

Eight

I drove back to the Bel Air Hotel with the cool breeze in my face and the shadows creeping across Sunset Boulevard. The traffic moved smoothly on the undulating surface and I let the Caddy drive itself. I figured it knew the way. It gave me time to think about Stryker and his A-rab in Paris who'd said he knew JC's escape route, Morris Fleury and the file on me that Sally Feinman had been going to give him but which was now we-knew-not-where, and Freddie Rosen who'd found JC's last song in the mail a month ago . . . twenty years after JC died.

It was a heavy load of thinking because it was so laden with implications, all of which seemed to involve me. Did anyone really think I'd killed my brother? Or killed someone else so my brother could take a powder? And who was killing people now? Why? Sally Feinman and Shadow Flicker—was there going to be a next? Was it going to be me?

What exactly had Bechtol gotten me into when he dispatched Heidi Dillinger to bring me back alive? Was I supposed to find JC per our agreement? Or was there some other role I was playing but didn't know about? Was half a million, assuming I lived long enough to collect the second half, enough?

The shadows were deep on the grounds of the hotel. The smell of flowers and vegetation was heady and thick. It was a far better example of hacienda building than Freddie Rosen's place. The black swan, haughty as all get-out, hadn't yet knocked off for the day. I wondered who represented the swan. Mike Ovitz, if I knew my swans. The swan had a deal you were bound to respect. I cross the little bridge, checked for messages, and was given an envelope. My name was handwritten in microscopic letters and the stationery bore the hotel's imprint. Who else but Heidi Dillinger?

I went to my room, ordered some ice and a bottle of Scotch, and took a quick shower. When I came out there was a knock at the door, room service with the goods. I avoided looking at the bill, which I signed, then I poured myself a drink and called Heidi Dillinger's room. There was no answer, so I rang the desk to see if she'd left word as to when she might be returning.

The guy told me that he'd *already* given me the envelope she'd left for me. I said I hadn't looked at it yet. He explained in a tone appropriate for explaining the details of toilet training to a moron that Ms. Dillinger had suddenly checked out an hour ago. It was business, she'd said, and she'd left the envelope. He was sure there was something more pertinent if I'd only open the envelope and peruse the contents. He sounded as if the strains of his occupation had him very near the abyss. He was still talking to me when I hung up on him.

I'd been looking forward to spending the evening with her and now she was gone and I felt sorry for myself. I was also very, very tired. I'd lost three hours during the flight and Morris Fleury had used up most of the previous night. I opened the envelope and read the note while I lay stretched out on the big bed. I could hear the little night sounds outside as darkness fell.

Tripper
Sorry to leave you in the lurch like this but the siren call of Herr Doktor Bechtol was heard in the land. So, I'm off. What

can I say after I say I'm sorry? But I'll be popping up when you least expect me. I guarantee it.

I found out what I could about the fate of your friend Flicker. Didn't amount to much. Someone cut his throat. Etc., etc.

There is an open investigation but the feeling I got was that it was all drug-related and not of any great interest to the cops. I mean, they are trying but they are not knocking themselves out. A newspaper reporter told me that the cops are shy of digging too deep because "the guy was a music-business parasite, had mob connections, was a druggie, and nobody wants to open all those cans of worms." You get the idea?

But I do have a lead for you, proving once again that research is my middle name. Donna Kordova is Flicker's widow. They split up a month ago but they stayed close. She's bound to know things we don't and some of it might be useful. Shouldn't be too tough for a guy like you—that charm, that smile. Her address is on the enclosed sheet.

Keep digging. Be trustworthy, loyal, helpful, friendly, courteous, kind, obedient, cheerful, thrifty, brave, clean, and reverent.

I like that in a man.

> *Yours till Niagara Falls*
> *Dillinger*

She had the tiniest handwriting I'd ever seen, each stroke straight up and down, utterly precise. I wondered what that meant. She'd have been excellent, say, at inscribing The Lord's Prayer on the heads of pins.

There was something about her. She was growing on me.

I liked that in a woman. Whatever it was.

I know how ridiculous it sounds but it took me three hours to find the Marina City Club. Don't laugh if you haven't tried it yourself. It was a jungle out there. There was a thick, wet, chilly morning fog inching its way across the Malibu beach when I got to the very end of Sunset. I looked around for Jim Rockford's beat-up old trailer but couldn't find it. He was just the guy I could have used, too. I headed south following the directions

I'd squeezed out of the guy at the desk. He'd intimated with a grin that it would be quite a drive with a maze waiting for me at the end.

There was the Santa Monica Pier pointing like an accusing finger into the fog where the Japanese fleet might be waiting. Reality had gone to hide in the hills. I wondered how people dealt with the fog on a regular basis. It was like taking a nap and waking up on Mars. There was Venice, and Marina del Rey, and I felt as if I must be closing in on San Diego. I smelled oil. On the side of the road a truck was burning like a huge flare guiding us on our way. Christ, get me out of here!

With a sigh of relief I finally saw a promising road sign and staggered off the freeway and plunged into the maze. I stopped at two liquor stores and a gas station asking directions. In time I drove through yet another set of gates, these manned by an elderly gunslinger who wasn't looking for any trouble and wanted only my name and the name of the resident I was visiting. I told him I was Chevy Chase and he didn't bat an eye, didn't put a warning shot across my bow, just wrote it down. It turned out that Donna Kordova had only arrived the day before yesterday. I was her first visitor.

The maze and the fog inside the boundaries of the Marina City Club kept me at bay for awhile. I was a bulldog that morning, however. And I really wanted a break before having to find my way back onto the freeway. So I stuck with it and finally found her. I rang the doorbell and while I waited I looked out across the marina at the masts of the sailboats and the various antennas of the cabin cruisers. I heard the ghostly lap of the water sucking at the piers, the hulls softly bumping. Sea gulls squawked, swept in and out of the billowing fog.

The door opened behind me. I turned around and saw a thin, rather pale woman with mousy light-brown hair cut short and gray eyes the size of silver dollars. She was wearing a T-shirt with something I hadn't seen before spread across the front of it. It was the stylized logo of A Damned Good Thrashing. It must have been a very new T-shirt. The logo was a smiling, trusting face. With a bullet hole between the eyes. She folded her thin white arms across the bottom of the logo. Any expert on body language would have told me I was in for tough sledding.

"Who and what are you?" Her voice was high and cracked like a dry stick. She licked her lips. Her mouth was very dry. "If you're a reporter, you're in the wrong place. If you're not a reporter, you're in the wrong place. I am not expecting guests." She stepped back and began to close the door.

"Please, I'm not a reporter. I was a friend of your husband's. A long time ago. My name's Tripper. Lee Tripper." I smiled as bashfully as I could. "You know . . . the brother. I'll bet you even knew JC back then—"

"Wait. Let me get this straight. You're JC Tripper's brother and you knew Shadow?"

"That's right. I just thought I'd stop by and pay my respects. I was awfully sorry to hear about Shadow—"

"And you're not a reporter? This isn't some sleazy trick?"

"No, no, take a look at my driver's license."

She actually waited for me to get it out. Then she looked at it. Then she looked up at me and squinted.

"It *is* me," I said.

"Come on in," she said, having decided that maybe I was who I said I was. She was wearing Guess? jeans that were way too loose on her. She was a bony little thing. She looked like a little girl who had by some caprice of fate found herself in her forties. At least she wasn't poor. I'd checked the *Los Angeles Times* real estate classifieds at breakfast and the condos in the Marina City Club kicked in at $350,000 and then took off like Saturn rockets. "I'm just moving in, getting furniture delivered from the stores, everything is a mess. I found the coffee maker yesterday, thank God, you want a cup?" I nodded at her and as she picked her way through the boxes and wadded-up packing paper she looked over her shoulder and said, "We've met, you know. You and I. You danced with me once. About twenty years ago. Oh, God, maybe more. I hate realizing things like that—it all seems like yesterday. Twenty-three or twenty-four years ago. Yes, we danced. You and I." She went on into the kitchen. "Your famous brother didn't have time to dance with me."

"I'm sorry, but I don't remember very much from those days. Where did all this happen?"

"The Grammies, I guess. Some big awards thing. JC won for best single and best album. Grace Slick got to dance with JC. I got the brother. You were nice, though. But, let's face it, kind of a consolation prize. You've changed." She poured two cups of coffee. "We've all changed. Sob, sob."

"Some of us have changed more than others. JC and Shadow have changed even more than we have."

"Black or light? Sugar? Sweet 'n Low?"

"Black's fine."

"Don't lean there. Painters just finished some custom trim. It's wet."

She handed me the cup and I followed her back into the two-story living room.

"Pull up a box, Tripper."

There was a good-sized aquarium that she'd obviously set up and connected first thing. The bubbles were rising in a steady column. The fish were purple and blue and yellow and red and black and pampered. She sipped her coffee and said, "Why did you really come here?" The fog at the window was seeping into the room.

"Do you have any idea why Shadow was killed?" It was hard to look away from the fish.

"I've been told not to talk about it."

"That's absurd. Your husband gets murdered, it's in all the papers, he's a prominent show-biz figure in LA, and you're not supposed to talk about it? Was there ever such a controlled person? You know I'm not a reporter—"

"And I also know you've dropped in out of nowhere. Shadow didn't talk about you. You weren't old pals or anything." She shrugged. "Don't try to convince me that you came here all grief-stricken over poor Shadow."

"So who told you not to talk about it?"

"What do you care? Why are you here? Really?"

"Did Shadow ever talk about my brother?"

"I don't remember—"

"Did he ever say he thought my brother might still be alive? I'm not kidding, Donna. It's not just Shadow who got murdered. There was another murder just a few days ago in New York. There's a real possibility that JC was the link between the victims . . . A lot of people seem to think JC is alive and worth looking for—"

"Oh," she gasped, "that song came in the mail!" Before she could go on, her hand flew to her mouth. Her eyes were round with surprise at her own indiscretion.

"So that's where you got the T-shirt," I said. I was developing detective instincts. It was fun. It was like playing chess and knowing you've outthought the other person.

"Where?" she asked defensively.

"Freddie Rosen. Relax, Donna . . . Was Freddie the one who told you not to talk about the murder?"

She grinned and nodded. "All right, but will you promise not to tell him I blew it? Do you even know him?"

"Of course. I'm Lee Tripper, Donna. I spent yesterday afternoon with him. And Freddie the Deuce, too. Just saw Sam for a minute, but a minute's usually enough. Sure, Freddie and I go way back." It wasn't a lie; it was encouragement for Donna Kordova. "He didn't come right out and say anything, but I got the feeling you two are . . . well, you know . . . close." Well, that was a lie, okay?

"Freddie told you where to find me," she said.

"Who else?"

"Well, you should have said so. Freddie's been very good to me since Shadow's death. He and Shadow, they were real close. Shadow's show was the place Freddie debuted MagnaDisc's new stuff. Shadow's the only jock in the world who's played these guys." She pointed to the logo on her shirt.

"Freddie thinks JC's alive," I said. "He told you about the song coming in the mail—"

"Isn't that something? I was just floored. So was Freddie. He wasn't as happy as I thought he'd be—I mean, think of the publicity a new Tripper song could generate. I thought he'd be in heaven . . . but he seemed stunned, almost unhappy—"

"Or afraid? Worried?"

"Maybe. Worried. He said he was going directly to the top with it. To MagnaGroup . . . that guy who runs the whole show. The one out in some apolis or other—"

"Apolis?"

"You know, Minneapolis or Indianapolis, like that."

97

"Which guy is this?"

"The one with the hotsy-totsy name. Cotter Whitney the Third. The big chief."

"Freddie mentioned him . . ." She was up now, sprinkling food into the aquarium.

"Donna, let me ask you again . . . and think about it—why might somebody have killed Shadow? Who could have had a reason? You and Freddie must have talked it over . . . there must have been something Freddie meant when he told you not to talk about it to anyone . . ."

She was staring into the fish tank, watching the bits of bright color darting and flashing as if they hadn't a care in the world. Little did they know. I'd once had some fish. The air-pump motor overheated one night. I flushed the tiny bloated corpses down the toilet. Very delicate, tropical fish, and they don't do well in hot water.

"Shadow was in very deep with MagnaDisc." She had lowered her voice into a conspiratorial whisper. "It went back to the sixties. Sometimes he served as the middleman between the company and the artists . . . you know what I mean, Tripper. It was your world as much as your brother's. Say something!"

"You're doing fine. Keep talking."

She put her hands on her bony hips. More body language. "Jesus," she sighed. "He *delivered* things. He performed services. It was good for him to maintain a special relationship with MagnaDisc. So he delivered *things* . . . girls, boys, drugs . . . he wasn't an angel. It's not a business for angels."

"What it boils down to is this," I said. "Shadow may have known too much and somebody got worried. Is that an old story or what? But if what he knew got him killed—well, it makes you wonder what was suddenly so important . . . or how did things suddenly change, what new element was introduced?"

"I really don't know. And now I've talked way too much. Freddie's been so good to me." She looked around the room as if it were the evidence of Freddie's goodness. "Don't let him know I went on and on, please?"

"Freddie and you, you're a thing, I take it."

"A very quiet thing. But he's a sweet guy in his way and I love the way he is with his son and, heaven help us, you should get to know that wife of his sometime. Spend some time with her." She made a face. "Freddie felt responsible for me . . . no, don't ask, I don't know why. But we'd been lovers for a long time—"

"Did that bother Shadow?"

She laughed, not particularly bitterly. "Not Shadow. Shadow led his own life. When he died, Freddie came in and did everything for me." She shrugged helplessly. Her lower lip was trembling. "Nobody had done things for me in a long time."

I didn't want to be there when the tears came. If they came. I got off my box and told her I appreciated the chance to talk with her. I assured her that my lips were sealed.

Standing in the doorway she watched me watching the fog. "It's usually burned off by now. I guess it's just one of those days."

"One last thing," I said. "Shadow. Did Freddie ever tell *him* about getting 'Everything's Hazy in Tangier'? Did Shadow ever mention it?"

"He never mentioned it to me, but, look, they were always talking, always on the phone, having lunch—Freddie must have told him. He was always after Shadow's opinions about anything to do with the business."

"Thanks, Donna."

"Tripper?"

"Yes?"

"Save the last dance for me, okay?"

Nine

There must have been fifty weeping willows lining the long drive that led to the imposing Italianate villa west of Minneapolis in what a gas station attendant called "the lake country." The private road was straight as Pat Boone. Some of the willows' drooping branches swished at the top of the car, which was now a rented Chrysler Fifth Avenue. Or was it a New Yorker? It was white with red leather upholstery and a little compass overhead that indicated I was heading due south. Great little gadget. Set out for Charleston and wind up in Albany.

It was hot in Minneapolis, pushing past ninety, as I drove out Highway 12. The towns had names like Wayzata and Minnetonka and I expected a ravishing Indian maiden to appear around each bend in the road. So much for expectations. Once off the main road I found the lakes, wound my way among them, watching the sailboats in the bright sunshine. More sailboats than I'd ever imagined could be gathered in a single place. More little blond girls with deep tans and headbands holding their straight yellow hair in place. More Volvo and Mercedes station wagons and super Jeeps that ran over twenty grand. If this wasn't the good life, deep in the kingdom of the robust preppies, then I didn't know what the hell it was.

But the road up toward the Whitney estate was somehow apart from all that. This was orderly and old-seeming, like a comparable road in certain parts of France, and when I'd passed beneath the arch made by the willows I got the full impact of the château or villa: architecture has never been my strong suit but I knew right away it wasn't as big as Versailles. The forecourt was surrounded by large statues of VIPs from Bulfinch's *Mythology*. The air was still and hot, and dust hung in the air marking my arrival. That little summer squeaking sound, crickets or locusts or something, filled the world. Thirty cars were parked at the edges of the fine gray gravel, each nosing into puddles of shade left by the oaks and evergreens and sycamores and maples. When I cut the engine and stepped out into the heat my knees buckled slightly. I didn't think Minnesota was supposed to be so hot. Another miscalculation. Walking toward the front of the house I heard, in addition to the insects squeaking, faint music from somewhere. Someone who had the air of staff appeared at the front door, waited for me with a faint welcoming smile.

"You would be Mr. Tripper, sir?"

"I would indeed."

"I'm Dobson, sir. I took your call. The directions were accurate, I hope."

"I'm here, Dobson."

"Very gratifying, sir. Mrs. Whitney wonders if you might join her on the sun porch before you meet the others. This way, sir."

He was white-haired and fit, looked like a man who relaxed with a sprightly forty miles of cross-country skiing on subzero weekends. I followed him inside, where it was cool and dim and preposterously spacious. A knight in armor stood at the bottom of a ten-ton carved wood stairway and the only light came from the sun glowing behind a stained glass window one landing up. Unless I was missing something, the window seemed to depict a wooded glade bordering a lake where a very manly and solemn brave was paddling a canoe. Fish leapt in the water. There may have been more to it—settlers with muskets in ambush, maybe?—but I was too busy following Dobson to fill in the details. I'd spoken with Dobson the day before, after I'd left Donna Kordova, and then with Cotter Whitney's private secretary, who'd informed me that Whitney would be pleased to have me drop by the house when I got to town. Then I'd called Dobson again a couple of hours before from the Twin Cities International Airport to get the directions. Most of what I knew about Minneapolis came via *The Mary Tyler Moore Show*, but I did remember a bit of trivia about the airport. It was where they'd made the original film *Airport*. You could win a lot of saloon bets with that one. The mind is a swamp of such irrelevant information, but I can't help that.

The sun porch was enclosed and effectively cooled but gave the impression of being part of the outdoors. The furniture was old wicker in dark brown, the colors were all pale, blue and beige and lime and lavender. There were lots of plants, big green leafy affairs, and there was a pretty woman in a wheelchair that was also wicker and very old. Dobson announced me and, like Jeeves, shimmered away. Beyond the expanse of windows there were what looked like hundreds of people scattered across a long sloping lawn that led down to a lake. It was a large lake by my humble standards. You could just barely see the rim of fir trees low on the horizon marking the opposite shore. There were some brightly colored sails on the blue water and a motorboat sent up a plume of white foam and a cabin cruiser sat at anchor. The lake must have been connected by a channel to other lakes and waterways. People were swatting a shuttlecock or playing croquet, others stretched in the sun, and some were standing around a couple of cooking fires munching huge sandwiches and drinking gin and sangria and having a hell of a good time. They all managed to look like the largest advertisement ever created for the good folks at Orvis.

"I'm Eleanor Whitney." She held out her hand. It was tan and the Piaget on her wrist was gold with diamonds and emeralds. "I don't mean to keep you from my husband, but I wanted so much to meet you and I am a bit isolated in here." She pushed herself away from the table where she'd been writing letters. There was also a black plate with some exquisitely arranged bits of food on it. Something that had been shaved into delicate curls. She had a wonderful wide smile. The tan was almost too good to be true. Her hair was streaked blond and worn in a soft page boy. She asked me to sit down. "My husband and I fell in love to the music of your brother, you see. Cotter was working in the family business here in the Twin Cities then, just a trainee, but"—she smiled again—"you might say his prospects were good. His father and grandfather wanted him to work his way up, even if it only took a year. The accident of birth—there's nothing quite like it, is there? In any case, we loved your brother's music and we saw him both times he played here . . . at the Guthrie and then at the old Met Stadium." She looked out the window at the crowd of friends swarming across her lawn. I figured she wasn't seeing them just then but rather something that had happened long ago. I wondered which one was her husband. "I used to love to dance . . . Cotter was never much for dancing. Now that my dancing days are behind me, he's discovered he really doesn't mind dancing so much after all. One of life's little ironies. We loved your brother's music . . . and the thought never crossed our minds that someday Cotter would be operating the company that brought JC Tripper to the world. Milling and lumber, that's what our families had always done. But times change, diversification became the rule of the day, and we swallowed the Magna Group . . . quite a digestive trick." She gave me that big smile. "No, we'd never thought such a thing would happen, nor Cotter's father passing away and Cotter taking over—and we couldn't have imagined JC Tripper dying. It was easier to imagine our own deaths in those days than to contemplate the deaths of people like Tripper and Joplin and Hendrix and Lennon. We were a remarkably silly generation for all our great causes. No sense of proportion about anything. But I mustn't bore you with the fruits of my solitary reflections."

"You're not boring me," I said. "I never imagined my brother's death either. Some people seem to be doomed to immortality—"

"Doomed? That's an odd word to use. Like doomed to good health . . . doomed to have the use of your legs."

"Well, immortality wouldn't be much of a bargain," I said. "People get tired, they long for the big sleep."

"I suppose you're right, Mr. Tripper. But still—when your

brother died, there it was, front pages, all that mystery, the exotic setting . . . it must have been very difficult for you."

"I wish I could dramatize it for you, but I was such a mess—well, I didn't distinguish myself. I hardly remember any of it. I was having a very bad year."

"I had rather a bad year myself," she said. "I thought it was important to be young and pretty and rich and daring. I should have settled for young and pretty and rich. The young and pretty would go soon enough anyway—"

"If you don't mind my saying so, it looks like they're all still pretty much intact."

"Mmm. Well, I'm a thirty-nine-year-old cripple with good bones and a nice tan."

"And you're rich. Surely that's a comfort."

"Of course. But I don't really appreciate it. Rich people seldom do in my experience because the rich people I know—I really don't know anyone else, actually—have always been rich. The thought of being poor is a kind of unimaginable abstraction to them. And to me. Our grandparents, they understood poor."

"Nothing's ever perfect."

"You're making fun of me for being rich."

"Just a little."

"But you can't make fun of me for being a cripple."

"No, I can't. But at least what cripples you is visible. You can see it, others can see it, you get credit for it. A lot of cripples I've known were crippled in other ways. Worse ways, I'm afraid."

"That may be easier for you to say since you're walking around on two good legs."

"Let's leave my legs out of this."

She laughed. "If you insist. But I was about to tell you about my bad year. You don't mind my rattling on? It always seems so much easier to talk with a stranger. Probably because one's old stories are new to them. Do you mind? I could send you off to find the lord of the Manor—really, would you rather?"

"No, I wouldn't. I'm probably falling in love with you."

"For the money?"

"It couldn't hurt."

"Candor can be so irritating. But back to my bad year and my theory about daring. Those were daring days, whether it was drugs or fast cars or going without a bra or burning your draft card or running for Canada or going south for civil-rights marches and risking the redneck ambushes. It was important to be daring. I didn't really have the nerve to be daring. So I was foolhardy and managed to cripple myself in the most prosaic way imaginable. I dived from some stupid boat in some stupid lake and hit a shelf of rock and that was that. I've been in a wheelchair since the year your brother died. And I've been starved for daring and/or foolhardiness ever since. Are you hungry, by the way? Why don't you try some of my sushi? We have a Japanese cook who is simply wonderful . . . go ahead, please, be my guest. This is my second plate and I'm stuffed. Here, I'll pour the last of this wine. Treat it as an appetizer. Cotter's roasting pigs, so you'll be having a pig sandwich for the main course. Barbecue sauce. You'll taste it for a week. So now I've told you why I wanted to meet you. I must say that we were terribly upset by your brother's death . . . I was pretty depressed myself, crying a lot, wanting to die, and then JC Tripper actually did die and the result was that I came back to reality and began to deal with it—JC died and it made me realize I wanted or needed to live . . . I had a young child, a loving husband, the best care—"

"And very good prospects," I said.

"And very good prospects. I owe some of my life to your brother's music and his death. I never got to thank him, now I'm at least telling you. How do you like the sushi?"

"Delicious. Different from any other I've ever tasted."

"I can almost guarantee that," she said. "It's fugu. My chef smuggles it into the United States. He goes home to visit his family in Japan and somehow brings it back with him. Fugu."

"Would it screw up your sense of gratitude if you found out my brother was still alive?"

She stared at me for a moment, then said, "Is that purely hypothetical?"

"Maybe, maybe not."

"You mean he may be alive?"

I nodded.

"And that's why you're here to talk to Cotter. Well, good luck

105

to you. He's not really into the performers but he's into money . . . I wonder if JC Tripper is worth more to the MagnaGroup balance sheet dead or alive? Well, I'm sure Cotter will be interested. If not himself very interesting to you—"

"Well, maybe it's a wild-goose chase, but I want to know if my brother is still alive. You can't blame me."

"Did you love him? Were you close to him?"

"We were close. I've got a lot of reasons to love him and few to hate him. But more than anything else I want to get it settled, once and for all. He's dead or alive—which is it?"

"Finish your lunch, Mr. Tripper."

I finished the delicately curled shavings of raw fish and the pungent sauce.

"I told you how hard up I am for daring these days. Well, you and I have both just done something rather daring. Fugu is the most dangerous fish on earth to eat. It's also known as puffer or blowfish. You've seen the translucent flesh, really exquisite in taste and color. But the guts, the ovaries, and the liver and whatnot are full of something called tetrodotoxin, which is a pretty good bet to kill you if you eat it. The cleaning is a bit of an art. A hundred fatalities a year in Japan from eating fugu." She took a deep breath and clasped her hands in her lap. "How are you feeling?"

"Okay, I guess."

"Well, it's probably the most dangerous thing that will happen to you all day."

"Don't forget the pig sandwich."

"That's why I said probably. Well, I've taken up enough of your time. If your brother's alive, I hope you find him. It'll be considerably easier to find Cotter. He's the least daring-*looking* man out there, but don't underestimate him—he can be an utter devil. He's short, stocky, not much hair. And there are the pants. He's wearing a pair of pants made of patches of different fabrics and colors. A Brooks Brothers fashion statement. You can go out through this door."

She held out her hand and I kissed it. I didn't know why exactly. Maybe because daring was important to her.

I liked that in a woman.

* * *

106

Cotter Whitney was standing alone beneath the vast crown of a huge, towering oak tree not far from the water's edge. His hands were jammed down in his trouser pockets. The trousers and the man wearing them were exactly as advertised. He wore a white shirt with the sleeves rolled up. He wasn't at all tan. He was an indoors type of guy. Plump, unassuming, a little sweaty but very, very clean. The top of his head, with a few strands of dark hair drawn across it, was red with sunburn.

He saw me closing in on him and waved a small plump hand at me. "Mr. Tripper, how very good of you to come all the way out here to the boonies. Dobson told me you'd arrived." His eyes slid past me, back up toward the house, to the windows of the porch looking out across the party, the lawn of milling brightly clad guests and the yellow canvas tent where a dance floor had been set up. "I wish Ellie would come out and join the party." He sighed. "She won't do it; I've tried everything. Did she mention that this is part of her birthday weekend? This shebang here, she insisted we do it. I just don't understand her sometimes . . . tomorrow night's the formal dinner party, a few close friends, she'll be fine for that. But these people, they'd love to see her, pay their respects. She's known many of them all her life, but she won't come down in her chair . . ." He looked at me inquisitively. "Do you understand women, Mr. Tripper?"

He shook my hand. The soft white hand clamped on mine like a vise. I had the feeling he could win a lot of money arm wrestling if anybody arm-wrestled where he hung out.

"Your wife and I shared a lunch of fugu. Beyond what that tells me I'm not qualified to discuss her psychology. As far as women go, I'm with the man who said a woman's mind is a treacherous swamp."

"Fugu. Gosh, I wish she wouldn't eat that stuff. I mean, what's the point?" He shifted gears. "Let's go for a walk. These folks don't need me. They're having a fine time." He smiled at me, putting on a new face. With his moon face and horn-rimmed glasses he looked about twenty, presiding over a frat party. "I wondered when you were going to show up. I've been looking forward to meeting you."

"I think I'm on the wrong page here. You were expecting me?"

107

He leaned down and picked up an errant croquet ball and pitched it back in the general direction of the players. Somebody suggested to Mary that next time she not hit the damned thing quite so hard. "It's not like baseball, darling," the voice said and there was a spasm of girlish laughter.

"Well, I thought you were bound to show up sooner or later." He wore old penny loafers, kicked them through the long grass. "I assumed Allan Bechtol would send you out here."

"You know Bechtol?" I was sounding like an idiot even to myself, but things kept popping up out of nowhere. People were always telling me things, but they never told me everything.

"Know him? Sure I know him. Heck, he's the main reason we're trying to take over his publisher. I'm a great fan of Allan Bechtol's work. You may not know it, but we're great readers out in this part of the world. We've produced lots of writers, too, some of the big ones. Sinclair Lewis, Scott Fitzgerald; Tom Heggen wrote *Mister Roberts;* Max Shulman wrote *Barefoot Boy with Cheek* and created Dobie Gillis, that Tom Gifford fellow wrote *The Wind Chill Factor* and Judy Guest wrote *Ordinary People,* there's that Rebecca Hill up in St. Cloud, there's Jon Hassler, and Garrison Keillor, though frankly he gets on my nerves . . . I mean we read *and* write out here. So my mind turned to publishing and Allan Bechtol. Well, he's not one of us exactly, but he worked for WCCO radio a million years ago and when it comes to writing he's a honey, better than Ludlum for my money. So, anyway, I got to know Bechtol, put him on the board of the MagnaGroup, got to know him as a man. MagnaFilms has got two of his novels in development right now. So, yes, I know Bechtol. I figured he must have sent you to talk to me, brief me, whatever." He looked up at me expectantly. I couldn't see his eyes behind the dark glasses. We passed a bunch of youngsters in the care of a couple of teenagers in swimming suits who were shepherding them into canoes. Much splashing and laughter. Cotter Whitney was looking past my shoulder. I turned. An airplane was turning over the trees, banking far across the lake. Pontoons hung from the wings. At the distance it looked like a great rare bird with very big feet.

"Brief you about what?"

"Look, it sounds to me like Allan didn't put you all the way into the picture. But you can level with me. We at Magna are up to our ears in the JC Tripper industry . . . heck, we *are* the JC Tripper industry, everything about JC Tripper is of surpassing interest to us. When Allan told me he was going to write a novel about a dead rock star who turns up alive—well, he hit the jackpot with me. Allan and I are now in this together, you might call it a joint venture."

The airplane—or seaplane, I should say—was slowly circling the lake, wobbling a bit like a fat bee trying to get his gyrocompass in working order. Both Whitney and I were watching it, hearing the shouts of the kids splashing around with the canoes. Whitney muttered something under his breath and waved at the teenagers in charge of the kids. "Get those canoes out of there," he said just loud enough for me to hear. Then he turned his attention back to me.

"Joint venture?" Everything I said sounded sort of simple-minded to me. I felt like a dummy who had lost his ventriloquist.

"You're getting half a million, correct? Seems like a lot to me, if you don't mind my saying so, but I'm new to all this. And in the light of Allan's sales, well, half a million may be fair, if he gets a big book out of it. Anyway, half of it is Magna's money. So"—he ducked his head a trifle sheepishly as if he weren't altogether comfortable saying such things—"you might say you're working for me, heh, heh."

"What do you know about this idea that JC's alive somewhere? Who starts this kind of rumor? Are there things I'm not being told? Everyone's so committed to the idea that he's out there . . . all this money being thrown around—"

"Know? I don't *know* a darn thing. That's why I'm putting up a quarter of a million dollars—to find out if he's alive or not. It'll turn out that the whole half million comes out of my hide sooner or later, as an advance or something, if I know Allan Bechtol."

"How do the murders fit into your scheme of things?"

He favored me with a blank stare.

"The murders," I repeated. "The woman in New York, friend

of mine, worked with me on the first JC pieces . . . then Shadow Flicker, the disc jockey in LA—"

"Oh my gosh, the *murders*, yes, sure, where do they fit in? Well, beats me. Heck, this is Minnesota. I don't know much about murders. In New York and LA, they're pretty standard equipment, right? But here? Murders? Out of my league. Do they have anything to do with finding JC Tripper?" He shrugged, pushing his hands deep into the pockets of his spectacularly weird trousers. "You're the man who's going to find out." The thought seemed to comfort him. Sally Feinman would have loved the whole scene.

"And what if I find him? Just what if . . . what then?"

"Now you're talking, Mr. Tripper. This is what I like to hear. Positive thinking. Did you ever read Hubbard?"

The name meant nothing to me. "Hubbard?"

"L. Ron Hubbard. Scientology. Oh, it's all a bunch of garbage, as Ellie keeps reminding me, but still . . . I've read him. There's *something* there. Give it a quick read. Life problems. Positive thinking. It's that kind of thing—"

"All I know about L. Ron Hubbard is that there was a place on Melrose, I think it was, long time ago, may not be there anymore, they sold plaster fawns and mythological gods and golden gnomes and stuff for your yard—they used to sell these big plaster busts of L. Ron Hubbard in that stupid little hat he wore—"

"I know the place." He smiled. "You may have noticed the various deities surrounding my forecourt out front—got those at the place you're talking about. It's a small world, isn't it, Mr. Tripper?"

"I guess so," I said.

"Now, if JC's found alive . . . JC Tripper back from the Other Side. Not a bad title for his return album, *Back from the Other Side*. He would be a considerable asset to MagnaDisc, would he not? Money, Mr. Tripper, it all comes down to money, just as my father and grandfather always told me. And, of course, it would, I'm afraid, impact on Freddie Rosen. Can we be frank . . ." His eyes wandered up to the seaplane, which was circling away from us again, its wings at an angle, banking. "Freddie is, to be brutally honest, past it. We have to face it."

"It's no problem for me," I said. But suddenly I was thinking of Sammy the Shit and Freddie Deuce and Donna Kordova out at the marina in her new condo, all Freddie's people.

"MagnaDisc is in big trouble. Freddie is a relic of another age, an age of gold chains and bell-bottoms and, heaven help us, Carnaby Street. An age gone by, in short. Did you ever see the man? It's embarrassing. He's a rusted golden oldie, he's pretty creepy—"

"I get the idea," I said. "He wouldn't fit in here today. Is that what you're saying? You've really got it all over him when it comes to pants."

"And Freddie has run MagnaDisc into the ground. We just can't have that, can we? We are all answerable to our boards, our shareholder. So, if we find JC and pension Freddie off, we can get MagnaDisc back with the program, back where the Magna name belongs. On top."

"All this planning and thinking based on a bit of fiction," I said. "My brother is dead. It's crazy, my friend."

"Crazy? Well, we shall see. But *somebody* sent that song . . . Somebody trying to prove a point. Now . . . we can't help wondering, *who?* And what is the point?" His gaze moved away from me again, back up into the sky over the lake. "Well, look at that . . . Jesus-fucking-Christ!"

I saw his point.

The seaplane was shuddering as it came closer and closer to where we stood, sinking toward the lake past a couple of sailboats, the plane looking older and older the closer it came, the wings struggling, seeming to bend and flex as the pilot fought to level off. The single cyclopean engine was choking to death. The nose pushed upward, a final spasm, then dipped toward the water, the wings at a thirty-degree angle. And then it hit.

The tip of one wing caught the water. The plane began to spin slowly like the Tilt-a-Whirl at the carnival. One fat pontoon, looking like a big sausage, slid deep into the water and broke off, but by then it had skewed the plane, slowing and then stopping the spinning motion. The plane wobbled irresolutely forward and began to settle as it edged closer to the dock. The spray it had sent up was settling across the fuselage, twinkling in the glare of the sun. The thick snubbed nose with the big propeller was nosing down. The pilot was pushing the hatch open before the water pressure sealed him inside. He struggled out, trying to get a foothold on the strut and the remaining pontoon. He was a big kid and looked vaguely familiar behind the big lenses of his sunglasses. He wore a blue denim work shirt and chino slacks and Reeboks. He was clutching three green seat cushions.

The canoes were coming in closer now, the pilot shouting to the teenagers guiding them. The crowd, exclaiming in a single voice as crowds often do, had moved down across the grass to watch the unexpected entertainment. The danger, for a few moments so very possible, had passed and people were laughing, kidding Whitney about the flyover, asking where the parachutists would be landing. Whitney stood still, watching, as the pilot threw the seat cushions into the canoes. The plane was going down fast, the lake sucking it toward the deep mud at the bottom.

The pilot had a deep tan and wore a headband. He was laughing now, exchanging shouts with the kids in the canoes. He was about thirty yards from shore. With tremendous elan he stepped off into the water and began swimming toward the dock. The canoes accompanied him and a welcoming committee of party guests moved down toward the weather-beaten old dock.

Whitney looked at me and heaved an enormous sigh of relief. "What next, I ask you?" he said. "Will you excuse me? All these folks could make the dock go . . . I don't want this party to become a legend." He scuttled off toward the dock, calling to his friends, trying to wave them off the old wooden structure.

I'd seen it all but I was running it back in slo-mo, trying to differentiate one moment from another in my mind. There was no point in my going down to get a close-up. The swimmer reached the dock and was hoisted up. No one seemed to be concerned at what had happened, how narrowly something horrible had been avoided. All that remained of the plane now was the tip of one wing and the tail, and as I watched the lake got them, too.

The canoes reached the dock and the seat cushions were

handed up to the pilot, who took them. He was smiling and talking to Cotter Whitney as others crowded around him, clapping him on the back as if he were a local hero. Finally Whitney led him through the jostling guests and on up across the lawn. The pilot had suffered a cut above one eye. He was still holding those valuable cushions.

I waited near the bank until the crowd had filtered back up across the sweep of green acreage. I watched one pontoon floating quietly on the still surface of the lake. I went down to the dock and found the spot I was looking for, knelt down, and peered at the rutted wooden planks. I wetted my finger and placed it in the dusting of fine white powder. It had all but been ground away by the passage of so many feet. I recognized the taste, of course, but it had been a long time. It wasn't just a guess on my part. I'd seen a white smudge on one of the cushions as the pilot had passed me, walking with Cotter Whitney.

William Randolph Stryker, Manny's son, was the pilot.

I remembered his telling me he occasionally did some jobs for Freddie Rosen.

Was this one of them?

Did Cotter Whitney know what was going on?

Whitney, hell . . . did *I* have any idea what was going on?

Murder. Drugs. And the widespread belief that a dead rock star was still alive. But how did it fit together? Or didn't it . . . ?

Ten

It struck me that an airplane crash in the middle of a party might throw things into a bit of a tizzy, or indeed cast a pall over the proceedings generally, but not so with these determined Minnesotans. They seemed almost to lose interest in the phenomenon about half an hour after the old seaplane had sunk beneath the surface of the lake. The kids were back in the canoes poking at the pontoon and laughing, and the help was at work down at the boathouse. Another bunch of diligent workers were stringing Japanese lanterns around the dance floor and all around the edges of the boathouse. Things were beginning to look like Jay Gatsby's summer place at East Egg must have looked to young Nick Carraway in the dim long ago. Or was it West Egg? Well, one of those Eggs.

I didn't know anyone, so I lurked hither and yon trying to appear like a man who belonged. While I lurked I wrestled with all the demons the whole business kept producing every time I met someone new. It was as if each of my informants had added a new layer of paint on the canvas, so that now the original sketch—what Allan Bechtol had given me—was pretty well obliterated, gone beneath a covering of new story elements. Nothing was what it appeared, and nothing had been since I thought I'd picked Heidi Dillinger up on Fifth Avenue . . . since Allan Bechtol had turned out to be Sam Innis from Harvard. The surprises began to wear you down eventually, made you wonder if you'd ever get any of it straight.

I was thinking about Bill Stryker and the cushions packed with cocaine when I saw Cotter Whitney coming toward me across the lawn. He was smiling broadly and shaking his head rather ruefully. "Well, what can I say? We always try to provide a show out here . . . Chalk up one beat-up old plane. I guess this party will become a legend. At least in our little circle."

"Lucky nobody was hurt," I said. "Do you report the crash to anybody?"

He shrugged, indifferent. "I hadn't thought about it. It's a private lake . . . my lake, that is. Plane wasn't worth much, nobody hurt. To whom would I report it? Well, I'll ask around."

"Now you're stuck for an encore."

He shook his head again. "That's about as much excitement as I can take. Where were we, anyway?"

Before he could return to another crack at our conversation I said, "Seems to me I recognized the pilot. Bill Stryker, wasn't it? I met him at Manny Stryker's place the other day."

"Why, yes, that was young Bill. He's a fine specimen, isn't he? Cool in a crisis, grace under pressure. And a mighty fine boy. Aren't kids amazing these days? It's another era, Tripper. They're so much more—what's the word I want? Accomplished, I guess."

"Those who can read," I said. "The rest?" I shrugged.

"But those who can—my God, they can *do* so many things. Take Bill—he's a licensed pilot, quite a talented documentary filmmaker. USC, y'know. Ellie and I think we're mighty lucky." He positively beamed at me, his round little eyes shiny without the sunglasses.

"Lucky?"

"Well, you know how it is. Bill and our Amanda are sweethearts. I've got the idea that it's pretty serious. Lovely young couple. Manny's got a lodge right up on the Canadian border and Bill flies that old heap down here to see Mandy in the

115

summer. She's going to be getting her MA at USC, special education for handicapped kids. In the summer she works in a center for those kids here in the Twin Cities. Two fine young people."

He seemed so overcome with a sense of well-being that I couldn't think of anything much worse than making some vulgar comment about the cocaine. I wasn't there to wreck the party. But the questions were crowding everything else out of my mind. Was young Bill in business for himself? Or for Magna in some way I couldn't quite pin down? Or for Freddie Rosen? Had he brought it in from Canada? Did it have anything at all to do with me and my digging around . . . or had I just stumbled onto something ugly?

On a great flat sweep of lawn beyond the greenhouse and the stables a softball game was forming of its own will, as if it had a mind of its own. Whitney leaned against the rough trunk of a mighty oak, crossed his arms like the village smithy, and surveyed his domain. From the look on his round face it was clear that he found it good. On the seventh day he would probably rest. "The dance floor," he said, "you recognize it?" I looked properly stupefied. *"Picnic,"* he said. "Kim Novak, Bill Holden . . . my God, they made movies in those days, didn't they? I'm thinking about pushing a remake—what do you think of that?"

"Why? They'll only desecrate a masterpiece. Madonna and Sean Penn, maybe? It's going to be tough finding another Kim Novak. There was just the one."

"Melanie Griffith and Don Johnson," he said matter-of-factly. "There's always another Kim Novak." He was either very stupid or very smart. "Freddie Rosen wants to feature that new rock band from St. Paul, A Damned Good Thrashing. No matter what anybody says, any idea at all about anything, Freddie coughs up A Damned Good Thrashing. Or DGT, as he intends to call them. He wants to build the darned picnic itself around these guys, this band . . . One-Track-Mind Freddie. OTMF." He rolled his eyes in exaggerated disgust.

"He must have known what he was talking about once," I said.

Whitney shrugged. "I suppose. He *must* have."

"Somebody," I said slowly, "thought enough of him to send him JC's song . . ."

He shrugged again. "Somebody," he repeated, then focused on me, dismissing Freddie Rosen to the outer limits. "I'm not an entertainment genius. Or if I am, they don't know it yet. I'm a guy who goes to the movies. I read when I have the time. I am a businessman—not a genius, not by a long shot—just a kid who got to run the family store. But there are a couple things I know . . . Now let's face it, what we're talking about—when we talk about this JC Tripper thing—is big. The recording and movie divisions of Magna are very visible, very high-profile aspects of Magna Group. We've got fast-food franchises, we've got frozen food, we're going through the roof on microwaveable crap I wouldn't feed my worst enemy, we've got the paper-products division, we've got the motel chain, but records and movies—little-nothing businesses, three, four percent of our gross revenues, really *nothing*—they're what people know about. That's what Magna means to most people. It's crazy. And the fact is they are at best very erratic profit centers . . . up, down, up, down, all worth in a good year about one moderately large hill of beans—which would cost a heck of a lot less to produce and which we could freeze and which we'd know ahead of time people would buy. Not with movies and records. But if you do this JC Tripper thing right, we could have *something* . . . a mixture of *Midnight Express* and Prince and The Mad Dogs and Englishmen Tour and Lord Byron and everything else you've ever seen about a doomed romantic hero . . . I think of JC Tripper that way, the Lord Byron of Rock—"

"You're talking about the same fella I am," I said, "Joseph Christian Tripper? My brother?" I didn't know whether to laugh or cry.

"The Lord Byron of Rock," he repeated.

"Stop saying that."

"Why shouldn't I? I like it. That's what he was, the—"

"Stop."

"—Lord Byron—"

"Why do you keep saying this?"

117

"—of Rock. Why? Because it works for me. Because it spells very, very big money. More than a hill of beans."

"Show biz has you in its magical grip," I said.

"We make the film about JC's last days—"

"I thought he's supposed to be alive."

"—with some kid like the young Peter O'Toole—"

"I suppose there's always another Peter O'Toole around. Probably on the same island as the young Kim Novak."

"—and we push, push, push—all the old records, the new sound track, we re-package, we put videos together, we push and we push—"

"And huff and puff, I'll bet, and blow the house down."

"No, no, we go right off the charts is what we do, and I go to my board and to the stockholders and you know what happens? In the words of the late great Harry Pebble, I look like a genius-boy. It's a scene I'd like to play, Mr. Tripper. And your brother, late or otherwise, can help me play it."

"Well, you've got it bad," I said.

"But," he cautioned, finger raised, "we cannot get caught with our pants down on this is-he-alive-or-is-he-dead flimflam. We have got to know the truth. No two ways about it. This is not frozen peas or beans or fast-food burritos. Any mistake is too visible, another *Heaven's Gate*, God forbid. As an entity, Magna could absorb the loss of a *Heaven's Gate*—a hundred fifty, two hundred million—and barely notice it. You'd have a tough time finding it on the balance sheet. Magna is big, Mr. Tripper . . . B-I-G. But it would *look* terrible in the papers. So I don't want to go forward unless your brother is all cut-and-dried, pardon the expression, because as far as I'm concerned we've gone as far with the uncertainty thing as we can." He slapped me shyly on the shoulder. "Which is your cue, my fine-feathered friend."

A representative of the softball game was trotting toward us. He was a middle-aged man, gaunt, with a long face and more hair than was good for him. "Come on, Piggers," he said with the snotty good humor you found between chaps who'd given each other the occasional hand job at Choate in their salad days. "We need an umpire." He stood before us perspiring heavily, half out of breath. "You're the man. We tried to get Hugo, but he's such an old fruit . . . claimed he knew nothing of the game. So it's you."

Whitney nodded. "In a minute," he said. The fellow grinned and jogged away. Just watching him sweat was exhausting work. My host turned back to me, wiping his forehead with his handkerchief. "If I were you—in your shoes, so to speak—I'd start all over again in Tangier. If he's alive, that must be the spot where the hoax began. As I understand it, you were there when it was all coming to an end . . . but I also understand that you were in pretty rocky condition. Go back with fresh, clear eyes—who knows what you might shake loose with all the money you've got to throw around now."

"It was a hell of a long time ago," I said dubiously.

"Well, it's just a thought. I leave it up to you and Bechtol. You must suit yourselves, of course."

As the sun drifted lower, slowly easing itself down behind the trees and out of the day, the humidity increased and the crowd seemed to grow larger until it furled like the sea across the shadowy green expanses of lawn. The softball game went on and on into the deepening twilight. Shouts and screams, the soft thunk of bat on ball, the blur as it flew through the gathering dark, runners lumbering around the bases, girls throwing the ball in that fetching, ungainly way they have.

I stood on the edges of the game, drinking gin and tonic, feeling the humidity condense on the cold glass, making it slippery. A brace of Dalmatians added to the confusion by scampering in and out among the players, chasing the ball. Bill Stryker was pitching for one of the teams, and his girlfriend, Amanda Whitney, was playing an enthusiastic second base. The expenditure of energy was frightening. I felt as if I were watching a sacrificial rite of some kind. I'd once read some-where that the Aztecs or Mayans had played something like football in something like our stadia, but it was all rather more in earnest than our games. The losers were slaughtered. Cotter Whitney, umpiring in the old-fashioned way from behind the pitcher, would have been some kind of high priest. I suppose that in a way he was.

My eyes were beginning to glaze over. The game was taking

on the tempo of something that would go on forever, something by which we could measure the remainder of our lives. I
was tired and hot, and some kind of bug was making an
appearance with the growing darkness. They flitted about,
bumping into one another in their haste to get to my face.
There couldn't have been more than ten or twenty million of
them in my immediate vicinity.

Then, as I stood there batting the air—apparently a gesture
that attracted rather than discouraged the little bastards—I
thought I saw someone I recognized across the ball field, over
behind the third-base bag. It was too dark to be sure. A shape,
perhaps looking across at me. Perhaps not.

I tried to react casually, taking some time to think. What
would my quarry of the moment be doing here? It was a long
way from home. But then, where was home?

I slowly moved around the edges of the cheering players and
their advocates. Every so often I'd look across toward where I'd
seen the face, but I couldn't be sure if it was still there. By the
time I got there, all that remained was a scent in the air. But
that was enough.

The figure was moving ahead of me through the shadows,
drifting in and out of view, past the dance floor where the
Japanese lanterns in red and green and blue and yellow were lit
and a dance band from another era was setting up. It wasn't A
Damned Good Thrashing. This was a bunch of guys with gray
hair and one of them was blowing the melodic line of "Blue
Moon" on a saxophone.

He slipped out of sight past the bandstand and I'd begun to
think I was following a figment of my imagination. I'd had a
long day. I was probably just losing my mind.

But there he was again.

Standing by the boathouse, slowly looking back in my general
direction. At me? I didn't know. Then he was disappearing
again, through the doorway and into the boathouse.

Along the dock some of the staff were lining up a flotilla of
rowboats, fitting them out with candles in more Japanese
lanterns in the bows. The bright colors glowed softly, reflecting
in the water.

I reached the boathouse, stood watching the boats, which bobbed gently, glowing, enchanting.

Morris Fleury had been there. There was no mistaking the ripe smell of the cherry pipe tobacco, the round-shouldered shape, the rumpled seersucker suit that was so right for him.

What was he doing at Cotter Whitney's party?

I was pondering that one when I heard a voice behind me.

"Are you going to dance with me? Will you take me out in a rowboat and play your banjo?"

I turned and saw Heidi Dillinger regarding me with a big soft smile. The remote, brittle ironist seemed to have been sent packing, replaced by a very pretty girl.

I thought that maybe she was the prettiest girl I'd ever seen.

Eleven

No, actually, she wasn't the prettiest girl I'd ever seen. She wasn't as pretty as Julie Christie or Natalie Wood or Jean Seberg or Inger Stevens, all of whom at one time or another I'd seen at close range. But three of them are dead, and in the battle for the top spot among the live beauties Heidi Dillinger, that night, was a very serious contender. Maybe it was partly the setting, maybe my mood. Maybe the scales had fallen from my eyes. Maybe the fairies had sprinkled moon dust on our heads. That was probably it. Fairies. Moon dust. It fit.

"You're looking at me," she said, "like you're about to turn into Mr. Hyde."

"I always look like that when I'm happy."

"Great. Just great."

She was wearing a loose-fitting dress with a dropped waist that rested rakishly on her hips. The material looked like an African print—dancing figures, masks, shields, spears. I thought I'd seen the dress in the window at Putumayo on Lexington. I watched her moving inside the dress, her breasts and her thighs occasionally stretching the fabric, and every few seconds the dress would grab at her hips and cling for dear life. Airplanes falling out of the sky?

Seat cushions full of cocaine? Two people tortured and snuffed? Lee Tripper could handle all that. But this woman moving around inside that dress—now we're talking dangerous.

Her arms and legs were golden. Her legs were bare and she was wearing sandals and her toenails were bright red. She did a girlish pirouette and stood looking out at the lake, at the bobbing brightly colored lights in the rowboats. The band was playing "Moon over Miami." Lots of saxophones. The evening breeze caressed the trees as I knew it would. "What a heavenly night," she said. "I'm glad you're here but—well, what exactly brings you here?"

"A nose for news. Too bad I have to find everything out for myself, but . . ." I shrugged philosophically. "Did you see the guy who was just standing here?"

"What guy?" She was still looking at the lights on the water.

"Can you smell it? Cherry pipe tobacco?"

"Smells like cough syrup."

"Funny guy, rumpled seersucker suit that looks like he's had it on since last summer. Panama hat with a loud band."

"Loud as A Damned Good Thrashing?"

I ignored her. Better she should leave the jokes to me. "Smoking a corncob pipe. I followed him down here. He went into the boathouse." Shadows dropped across us, willows swaying.

She went to the door and opened it. It was dark inside, but the far end was open to the lake and kids were finishing up putting the candles in the boats. The water slushed and lapped at the hulls of a couple of motorboats. I peered into the corners. He wasn't there.

"The little man," she murmured, "who wasn't there."

"He's the kind of guy who's probably good at disappearing."

"Friend of yours?"

"No. A guy named Morris Fleury. Does that mean anything to you?"

"Should it?" She was shaking her head no.

"He knew Sally Feinman. I was just surprised to see him here."

"It's dark. It was probably somebody else." She was standing

123

in the doorway. Behind her, up the sloping lawn, some people had begun dancing. She held out her hand. "Come on."

She led me up toward the dance floor. I was soaked with sweat. She was calm and shimmery and cool. "I'll bet you've mastered the box step."

"I might as well tell you now . . ."

"What?"

"I don't dip under any circumstances. It's a question of dignity."

"Your dignity is safe with me," she said.

I hadn't danced with anyone in a long time, not since I'd danced one night at The Ritz with Annie DeWinter. Heidi Dillinger made dancing very easy. I hated dancing, but Heidi Dillinger fixed it so I wasn't really aware of what I was doing. She put her hand around the back of my neck and smiled while I looked at her face. Her lips were shiny and there was a faint dewiness on her upper lip.

She said, "So, why are you here?"

I told her how I'd found out about Whitney, via Freddie Rosen and Donna Kordova. I ran over the talk I'd had with Cotter Whitney but I left some of it out. What was the point of dragging Bill Stryker and the cocaine into it? She'd heard about the plane crash but had arrived too late actually to see it. I told her it had been well worth the price of admission. The band segued into "You Do Something to Me," a slow, romantic arrangement that kept us on the floor. I held her loosely against me. Maybe dancing wasn't really so bad after all. However, before I began composing rhyming couplets to love and the night, I asked her what had brought her to Minnesota.

"Allan and Whitney have business. Book business. Magna wants to acquire Purvis and Ledbetter, Allan's publisher. I'm serving as the messenger." She moved closer. The dance floor was filling up. She slowly rested her head on my shoulder and sighed. "Hugo Ledbetter is here this weekend. A confederacy of dunces." She sighed again.

"I like it when your mask slips."

"My Ms. Invincible mask?"

I nodded.

"You can't imagine how glad I was to see you here. Allan is

terribly curious about what you're learning. When he called the Bel Air Hotel this morning he discovered you'd gone. He was disconcerted, how were we to find you, could you be trusted, why hadn't you reported to him before leaving Los Angeles . . . but here you are. We'll bring him up-to-date. Tomorrow. Tonight . . . we dance."

The band played "Blue Moon" every third number while I tried to make a connection between the Heidi I'd met on Fifth Avenue and the one in my arms. She might have been two entirely different women. She might have been an actress, not a computer whiz and aide-de-camp to Bechtol. Maybe she *was* an actress. Maybe all women were actresses. Or maybe she had fallen victim to my comparatively devilish charm. In a night full of fairies and moonbeams I decided it must have been my charm.

"You know," I whispered in her ear, "some men will believe anything."

"I know," she whispered back. "That's the nicest thing about men."

"One might almost say that men are gullible."

She nodded and looked up into my eyes.

"I like that in a man."

"Romance," I said, "couldn't exist without the gullibility of men."

"La Rochefoucauld?"

"Lee Tripper."

"Well, very few men realize the truth of what you say. My hat's off to you, Tripper."

"You're not wearing a hat. Try something else."

"Details," she said. "You must rise above them when the night is full of romance." She stopped dancing, led me off the floor. "Do you row?" Her dress clung to her breasts. Row? I'd have walked through fire.

The music floated out across the water, and occasionally something leapt and splashed in the darkness. A saving breeze moved across the surface of the lake. The immense house was illuminated by some floodlights arranged in the shrubbery. The colored Japanese lanterns shimmered in the humid evening. The candle in our boat was green, the flame flickered. We sat on cushions in the bottom of the boat, leaning back, seeing the stars and the moon above us. Somewhere off to my left an airplane had sunk a few hours before.

I was not altogether sure about what was going on. To be specific, was this business or pleasure?

Letting nature take its course, following my impulses, I touched her chin to turn her head toward me, but she was already turning and tilting her face up, and we kissed for quite a long time.

This was definitely pleasure. Any fool could see that. She made me feel like a kid again. Shortness of breath, a ping or two in my engine, the vague feeling that the wheels might come off at any moment. When we parted I was panting like the winner of the Boston Marathon. She looked into my eyes and smiled as if congratulating at least one of us on a job well done. She made me feel as if I'd passed a test.

She lay back again, looking at the stars. Heidi Dillinger probably looked dreamy and relaxed as seldom as any woman on earth. It didn't come naturally to her. I knew that much. But caught in the grip of the moment, she was giving it a try.

"Well," she whispered at last, "is he?"

I drifted back, feeling her words like little fingers tugging at my mooring ropes. "Is who what?"

"Is JC alive?" she murmured.

"Not so far as I know." I looked down at her. The dress was molded against her long thighs and stomach. The fabric rose and fell as she breathed. JC was far from my thoughts, which extended only about as far as the tips of her bright red toenails. "But what if he's alive? What's it to you, really?"

"He's a corporate asset. Please don't think I'm cold. I understand, he's your brother. But to me he's part of my job . . . if he's out there, I'm responsible for seeing that we get him back." She sighed. "That's what JC means to me."

"JC—the Corporate Asset. Times change."

"We'll find him, Tripper."

"Don't kid yourself," I said.

"Somebody sent that song to Rosen." She was trailing her

fingers in the water. "Somebody killed those people. When we find out who . . . then we'll be almost home. I can feel it."

I kissed her again.

"You're an irresponsible fellow. We're supposed to be working."

"Not my idea of work."

"It's late. You're going to have to spend the night."

"I'll have to talk to Whitney."

"Why bother him? I've got a room. Third floor in the West Wing. I think it's the Lincoln Bedroom." She giggled.

"Still leaves me without a room."

"So incredibly dense. I'm making you an offer."

"In that case, I say let's turn in."

"Row, row, row your boat."

Half an hour later I'd showered and padded back down the hallway to her room. She was in bed, the sheet pulled up under her chin. The windows were open. The band was still playing and the floodlights cast shadows across the bedroom wall. Nobody missed us out there. The crowd had thinned but the party was far from over. It had settled into an easy rhythm, an endless supply of gin and tonic and ice, the low burble of conversation, the music floating on the night's breeze. The curtains moved slowly at the window. It was cooler, a delicious summer night.

We didn't say anything. I slid into bed and she turned toward me, her eyes closed, her mouth soft and open. We made love for a long time. Anyway, it seemed slow and languorous, a word I've seldom used. She proceeded deliberately, no giggling now, with a real respect for what she was doing, for what we were doing. At one point she whispered in my ear; "You'd laugh at me if I told you how long it has been since I did any of this . . ."

"Tell me."

"I couldn't bear it if you laughed. Let's not stop."

I couldn't figure her out. I didn't even try.

Later we lay on our backs, covered with sweat, feeling it dry as the breeze blew across us. Her eyes were closed. I watched the shadows of the tree limbs moving on the walls. The band was playing "String of Pearls." I inhaled her smell. She stroked her hand slowly along her thigh. I watched her fingertips against the flesh. She rested her palm on her flat belly. I had to have her again. I kissed her fingers and she pushed her hand lower and lower, breathing harder, and I kept kissing and lost track of everything else.

The next time I noticed the band, they were playing "A Fine Romance" and our heads were at opposite ends of the bed. I rested my hand on her knee.

"Are you awake?" she said.

"Just thinking."

"What about?"

"One thing was, would I die if we did all this again right away?"

"Probably. But it would be a good death."

"That's just what I was thinking, Hemingway."

"What else were you thinking?"

"Bechtol."

"Oh, no," she groaned. "Why? Now, of all times?"

"Are you sure that you and he aren't . . . you know?"

She was laughing softly. "Gee, let me think. Maybe I forgot something." She paused. "No, I'm sure we're not you-know, never have been you-know, and frankly, I've never known him to be you-know with anyone. But it's sweet that you asked. Anyway, he insists he's impotent and I'm omnipotent . . ."

"Well," I said, "I have another question about him."

"Uh-oh."

"Why didn't *he* tell me about JC's song arriving like it did? What was the point of making me stumble across that little shocker on my own?"

"Bechtol's whole life is a plot. He lives it like a novel-in-progress. He likes to have the plot unfold . . . he knew you'd discover things as you went along—and they'd have more impact if you found them out yourself."

"Well, that's cute. It's very nice for him, but it's less appealing to me, the guinea pig. What else does he know—and you, too, for that matter—that I'm going to find out for myself?"

"I don't know. Nothing so far as I'm concerned. God knows I can't answer for Bechtol."

"Well, I'm gonna start developing some secrets of my own. I don't like to be the one doing all the trusting."

"You are the only one being paid, my sweet."

"So fire me. I'll survive."

"Ahhh. You've figured that out—"

"The fact is I'm the only one Bechtol thinks can find JC. I keep telling myself in my noble way that he needs me more than I need his money."

"That *is* noble."

"It's the kind of guy I am."

"But you would like to find your brother."

"I can take it or leave it. I say he's dead."

"But you don't know."

"Oh, I know. I'm just humoring everyone by taking the money. Why didn't Bechtol tell me Whitney or Magna is putting up half the money? Part of the plot unfolding?"

"Well, why should he? What has that to do with you?"

"Somebody's lying to me." I was turning toward the top of the bed and had stopped to kiss the back of her right knee on the way back to the pillow.

"Somebody's always lying," she sighed.

"You want to go to Tangier with me?"

"You're going, then?"

"Why not? Whitney thinks it would be a good idea."

"You *do* think JC's alive, don't you?"

"My brother is dead as they come. It's not my fault no one will believe me."

"You're already starting to keep secrets!"

"I'll tell you what I really want—"

"Oh, God . . . I really am exhausted . . ."

"Relax. I've sated my lust for the moment."

"There is a God," she sighed.

"I want to know who sent that song to Freddie Rosen. That's what bothers hell out of me."

It was three o'clock in the morning and the band was gone and the guests had shuffled off and the floodlights were off and the Japanese lanterns were dark and the rowboats were bumping the dock and the moonlight lay in quiet liquid patches across the lawn, flowing and silver as if it had been poured from a pitcher. I stood at the bedroom window doing a reality check. Yes, it was all true—the airplane crash, Morris Fleury, Heidi Dillinger, the bed, all real. She was deeply asleep. I slid into my pants and shirt and shoes. The house was quiet and dark. I went outside. The doors stood open to the warmth. The hum of the crickets was loud and insistent, once you noticed it at all.

I stood in the shadows, felt the night all around me. I heard the sounds things made in the lake and in the foliage. Nothing was what it seemed. The quiet night was actually noisy and alive with activity. And there were people abroad in the night, as well. I felt like a spy.

I clung to the shadows for safety. There were so many imposing trees, it wasn't difficult. I made my way down toward the lake, but I was only halfway there when I heard the low murmur of the voices and a faint creaking sound. I stood near the trunk of an oak big around as a picnic table.

The creaking sound came from Eleanor Whitney's wheel-chair being pushed along a path of fine gravel. She was speaking very softly, the words indistinct to my ears. She was being pushed by a man who in outline resembled an ambulatory haystack. Very tall, vast in girth, and his voice box must have required an exceptional woofer. When he spoke it was as if there were giants in the earth, rumbling, shaking the crust on which we'd chosen to build a civilization. Hearing the rumble, I saw in my mind the needle bouncing on my idea of what a Richter Scale doohickey looked like. He seemed to be clad in an immense smock. There was a beard of impressive dimension. When they passed closest to me I made out a single word, her exclamation in reply to something scandalous he'd said. "Hugo!" Then their shared laughter.

Hugo Ledbetter, I assumed. Publisher. Soon to be part of the Magna Group?

I watched their stately procession on up the path toward the house. Before they got there they had disappeared in the shadows.

The night smelled of flowers, and of the clean wetness of the dew on the grass. I meandered on toward the lake, past the

130

boathouse toward the dock where Bill Stryker had climbed out of the lake.

I thought I smelled the cherry tobacco, but that was impossible. Hours had passed. My sense memory was working overtime.

And then I saw them. Two figures standing at the end of the dock, looking out at the lake in the moonlight. The smell of the pipe smoke wasn't a figment of my imagination. The breeze coming off the lake carried it like a hint of death, a rumor of murder.

Morris Fleury was back. Rounded shoulders, beat-up seersucker suit, corncob pipe, smoke curling from the bowl. He was talking, the other man listening. I leaned against the boathouse wall out of sight, watching.

Finally the two men turned and came back, strolling the length of the dock. I saw their faces in the moonlight.

Fleury had the pipe clamped in his mouth. The other man with his round, boyishly innocent face was doing the talking now.

Cotter Whitney.

I walked alone back up to the stone patio where the stone fireplace still smelled of roasted pig and gave off some leftover heat. I sank down into one of the striped deck chairs, clasped my hands behind my head, and looked up at the moon and the stars and the occasional cloud that drifted past.

The cricket-infested quiet reassured me that everything would be all right. Never believe nature's easy reassurances. It simply wants you to lower your guard before you are visited with a rain of toads.

But I didn't need to look as far as nature for duplicity. It was all around me, culminating in whatever connection existed between the New York detective Morris Fleury and the Magna chairman Cotter Whitney. I couldn't pretend to reach any sane conclusions, but I managed to sort out some questions that I felt were worth asking. The questions—even without an answer among them—made me feel for the first time that I was beginning to glimpse the outline, the great shadowy bulk of the elephant.

Maybe none of them had been telling me the truth, beyond the fact that they wanted JC found. Maybe I wasn't being told why. So, watching the heavens, trying not to wonder if Morris Fleury might be hiding in a bush watching me, I put a little spin on things.

Could it be that they wanted me to find JC because they were *afraid* he was alive?

Were they, then, afraid of JC because he was doing something to them? That would mean they weren't so excited about getting him back to recording again: they just wanted to find him . . . to make him stop whatever he was doing?

The song he sent; was the song "evidence" to prove to them that he was, is, alive and well? Could be. Why else would he send it? But what did it really prove? I knew the song had been written many years ago . . . so all it proved was that *somebody* sent it.

What could JC be doing to Magna? Maybe he knew something he shouldn't. Like Magna and drugs? Music business equaled drugs. A lot of drugs, or just enough for the talent under contract and the deejays? Would, therefore, JC be blackmailing Magna in some way? But I knew JC was dead. Still I had to admit it could be somebody pretending to be JC who was blackmailing them . . .

So, JC or the pretender will want to remain safe, secure, and hidden.

Which meant that somebody was bound to try to keep me from finding him.

How far was he prepared to stay hidden?

And was I the one sent to set him up to be killed by Magna? Maybe by Morris Fleury?

"I'd had enough questions for one night. And in the morning Heidi Dillinger and I would set out for Morocco.

Back, back to Tangier.

Twelve

Well, Tangier was a terrible idea. It was like having your feet held to the fire while somebody shaves your eyeballs away.

It had been a bad idea from the beginning, and maybe I should have known it. I should never have gone, there was nothing there for me but the poison from old wounds, the dregs of the old life, the razor wire I'd carefully strung around the past and now found myself blundering through like a dumb animal, panic-stricken and doomed. Psychologically speaking, as well as literally, it turned me into a bloody mess.

And there was poor Heidi caught in the trap I'd set myself so long ago. She had a madman on her hands all of a sudden and she was at the same time trying to do her job for Sam Innis. He was back to his old name in my mind. I know it's confusing when somebody has two names, the only similarity between this story and the great Russian novels. What can I tell you? He was Innis to me. But he was Bechtol to everybody else. And his wires and demands for reports and plans were a pain in the ass. From his point of view it was his money paying the bills, and two first-class tickets to Casablanca made for a considerable jolt to the American Express card Heidi wielded so deftly.

We drove on to Tangier, and the sights and smells and the desert wind and the sights of camels and robed figures moving like shadows among the palm trees—it all conspired to drag me unwillingly into the past. Twenty years ago, everything had come apart in Tangier and I'd never really dealt with it, though the doctors in Switzerland had pushed and led me as far as they could. I'd dodged and weaved and pretended and denied and lied: I'd been good at all that.

And many years later when I'd come back to do my own book with Sally Feinman's encouragement, I'd kept my head down, done a quick once-over so I could say I'd retraced the steps I'd once taken. Now, everything was different. This was serious. I wasn't in it on my own and Innis wasn't kidding.

Heidi didn't know what to make of my behavior, which would presumably have lumped her with the other nine-tenths of mankind. The remaining tenth were the outright crazies. And I was among them. For two days in Tangier I stayed drunk and wouldn't leave the room we were sharing. I didn't want to talk, I didn't want to make love, I wanted to sit and stare and try to keep the past from drowning me. Boy- and girl-wise it wasn't much of a romance. Maybe that hand just hadn't been dealt to Heidi and me.

She was discovering just how hard it was to make Tangier sit up and pay attention and behave. She was looking into the circumstances of a death and cremation that had taken place twenty years before. Beyond the official records she couldn't find any evidence to suggest that my brother was somehow still alive. The records were simply that, what they always were—the papering over life's messy details. The records of the death of Joseph Christian Tripper. She couldn't find the doctor who had signed the death certificate. She couldn't find anyone who had had a damn thing to do with any of us. And I kept yelling at her that I couldn't remember any of it, not a goddamn thing.

Then on the third day she found Will Sasser.

I could have killed her.

Heidi and I ran smack into the breaking point on the morning of the third day.

While she was asleep I'd kept drinking and gotten well into the heebie-jeebies. In my addled brain I was back in the past and it was god-awful. There's no point in going into it. But it was bad and I could hear this incredible metronomic banging. My whole body was trembling with the impact, the shock wave of the hammering, but it wouldn't stop, just kept banging away, and I kept trying to open my eyes but I couldn't see anything.

The pounding was no dream. It woke Heidi. I heard a little scream of surprise and felt her pulling at me, pushing me over onto the floor, where I assumed the fetal pozish.

For some reason I'd been on my hands and knees banging my head against the wall. I'd knocked a hole in the wall and ripped my scalp open. Just an average night in Bedlam. I couldn't see because I was covered with blood. The floor was slick with blood, I was babbling incoherently, trying to sing snatches of "Everything's Hazy in Tangier." Lovely. I don't know what the hell I thought I was doing. I wasn't human, I was sure of that once my attention was brought to what I was trying to do. If I'd wanted to go next door, there were easier ways than through the wall.

The time for Heidi to get tough had arrived, either that or just say the hell with it and go home. Or strike off on her own.

She got tough.

She cleaned me up, told me I was a complete shithead, got a doctor who put twenty-five stitches in the top of my head. She explained to me that it was time to shape up. Or she would finish the job on my head. It sounds simpler than it was, but it worked. The blood and the stitches had a considerable effect on me as well. And so did she. She took care of me and held my hand.

I finally collapsed and slept for a long time. It was evening when I woke up. She'd been busy all day, talking to Innis, asking questions in Tangier, digging at the rubble piled up on my past. And over dinner she told me she'd found Will Sasser. I groaned.

"You must remember Will," she said. "God knows he remembers you."

My headache was suddenly much worse.

She said, "We're seeing him tomorrow."

135

* * *

Will Sasser had grown gray and sallow and his long hair was still drawn back in a sixties ponytail. But now it was gray, like his bushy eyebrows and the long bandito mustache that draped damply down across his mouth. His eyes peered out from bags of wet cement and, honest to God, his long pointy nose was still straddled by a pair of granny glasses. He was probably wearing a Peter Max T-shirt. He squinted at me through the cigarette smoke as if he were trying to place me, figure out just exactly who I was. We sat in the dim hotel bar with big ceiling fans and potted palms and boys in mess jackets. It looked like Hollywood's idea of Tangier in the forties. I kept thinking Marta Toren should come in out of the heat clutching a purseful of family heirlooms she'd give Richard Conte in exchange for an exit visa.

"You look a mite better than when I last saw you, man," Sasser wheezed. He had the vestigial traces of a Southern drawl. He sucked smoke, feeding his emphysema. He'd been a loose-joined kid in his twenties when I'd last encountered him, writing for rock weeklies on the Continent and in England, full of enthusiasm and fervor and rock dreams. Rock was the gospel of the new world and he would be one of its prophets. Rock would show the way and he'd be a traffic cop. Maybe all that was so, but somehow he had missed the last bus. The band had left without him and now he'd been a long time in Tangier. Heidi Dillinger was nursing a Perrier, watching us the way you might eye a couple of dinosaurs lurching about among their memories, searching out the last bite of the last leaf. Except I didn't have any memories, just the blackness that grabbed me from time to time. We were working our way through Will Sasser's Tangier memories. Of me and others.

"I'm not very clear about all that," I murmured.

"No, I'm not surprised, man." He eyed me again, giving me that old hippie stare, real quiet, as if that should convince me there was heavy thinking going on inside. "Jesus, I'd have bet the ranch there was no coming back from where you were, no ladder high enough to get you out—I've seen some real bad, real strung-out cases, y'know, but you were as bad as any, man . . . you were yellow, man, hepatitis, bad needles, liver on the blink, you kept falling down, no sense of balance, you couldn't keep anything in your stomach, you couldn't remember where the hell you were, puking and shooting up and drinking two, three quarts a day, you wouldn't see the sawbones JC got for you . . . Jesus, man,"—his eyes blinked from behind the folds of solid, heavy bags—"and now here you are, big as life. You're a fucking miracle. I mean, you were *dying*, man, last time I saw you . . ."

"Let me get this straight," I said. "Your saying I wasn't feeling so well the last time we met—is that the essence of it?"

"Fuckin' A, man, you were done, *well* done, y'know what I—"

"I get your point," I said. "Well, fortunately I can't remember how bad it all was. Maybe we could just drop it. It's JC we're interested in—"

"I know, I know," he said, shaking his head, the ponytail swinging. He wore a blue shirt and a bow tie and a seersucker suit that seemed to be composed largely of cigarette burns. "But you come as quite a shock, Lee. You look so fit . . . except that head. Hurt your head, did you?"

"Accident. Fell down."

"Some fall," he said softly. He was drinking a glass of gin with the merest splash of tonic.

"JC," Heidi reminded him.

"Yes, well, JC, that was what I was just thinking about. It was you, Lee, you were the one everybody thought would die. Fact was, we all figured you were going to kill yourself . . . JC was okay, more or less, sort of burned out, kept saying he couldn't write anything anymore, didn't want to perform anymore. Rock Syndrome. That was what was eating him . . . couldn't work, couldn't concentrate . . . JC was trying to hold everything together at just the time when everything wanted to fly apart. Entropy. He wasn't sleeping, his voice was shot, said he had some nodes on his vocal cords . . . but he just didn't look or act like a man who was about to die." He kept giving me long hard stares, curious about how I'd survived while my comparatively healthy brother hadn't gotten out of Tangier alive. I was beginning to feel I owed him an apology for surviving. "Do you remember me?" he asked quickly.

"Sure, sure, vaguely." I tried out my ingratiating smile.

137

"Which is better than I remember most people from those days. Nothing personal. You saw the shape I was in."

"You remember the night you set yourself on fire?"

"Mainly I remember getting hosed down—"

"That was JC with the hose that night. He saved your life."

"Look, my friend, it's not my fault my brother died. You seem to hold me responsible and you're beginning to piss me off. I'm sorry I didn't die in his place, but we're stuck with it now. We can't change it, okay? Agreed?"

"Hey, relax, man, relax. Chill out. It was just a shock seeing you so healthy . . . I wouldn't have recognized you."

"Good God, I hope not!"

"Who all was there when JC died?" Heidi was growing impatient with us. She wanted to stick to business.

"Well, the party seemed to be over, y'know. The way a couple of people leave and it seems like thousands have walked out. Thumper Gordon—"

"The drummer," she interjected as if some of us might have forgotten MacDonald "Thumper" Gordon, who co-wrote some of JC's greatest hits and was just about peerless with the skins.

"Thumper had gone to Berlin," Sasser said, a long ash dribbling down the front of his coat, "to set up the next big date, the concert that never was. Christ. It would have been something, that one—maybe it was just too big ever to be pulled off. 'Brandenburg Rock' it was gonna be called." He sighed in awe at the idea.

Heidi looked at me for clarification and I said, "One of JC's more grandiose schemes. Would have happened, too, if things hadn't gone bad. They were going to build a model, same scale or, hell, maybe bigger, of the Brandenburg Gate, only on the west side of the Wall. And there was going to be a twenty-four -hour concert. Or open-ended maybe. I don't recall . . . any-way, it never happened, and besides, the chap is dead." Heidi had me on iced Coke and I wanted a real drink. It was hell, and Sasser just kept going on, reminding me of everything I didn't want to remember.

"So Thumper was gone," he resumed. "I took him to the airport in Casablanca. He said he was going to talk to JC about giving me the rights to do an inside book devoted solely to the

Berlin concert . . . lost worlds," he sighed. "It would have been the making of Will Sasser." He struck a bitter, brooding pose, staring at me again as if I might peel off my face and emerge as someone else entirely.

"Who else was there?" Heidi prodded, stroking her blond hair away from the corners of her eyes. Her features were so clear, so sharp, so alert to nuance and subtext. I wondered what she was thinking, but there were too many layers to get through. She'd been a child when JC died and we all went slightly crazy.

"There was Annie DeWinter, of course. She'd just left for London—Tangier hadn't really agreed with her, her stomach couldn't handle it . . . she was sick and tired of the doping and JC and the girls he kept around, it was like a movie, like that movie"—he snapped his fingers at his memory—"*Blow-Up*, David Hemmings playing the photographer, like what's his name, David Bailey, the birds always after him, I *loved* that movie. Anyway, that's the way it was with JC, birds coming out of the closets wanting to take their pants off for him. The Rock Life. I was going to write a play, *The Rock Life*, but I stayed mostly in Tangier and never got around to it."

"That *is* the rock life, my friend," I said. "Things slipping away."

"So Annie DeWinter was gone," Heidi said. "What was the story with JC and her?"

"Lovers," Sasser said with a shrug. "She was almost like a wife . . . but it was rock 'n' roll, y'know. She put up with JC being a star, she put up with the girls—"

"And she didn't go off on her own?" Heidi asked.

"Oh, you mean with other men? We wondered. But she wasn't the type. Very classy, very English, veddy veddy discreet. It was tough to get a line on her. And once JC died and all that was over, she just dropped out of sight. Amazing, when you think of it . . . she was bloody near as famous as he was." He snapped his fingers for another glass of gin and lit another cigarette, coughed like a jackhammer into his fist. His fingernails were long and chipped and there was a tremor in his hands that the gin had accentuated. The Rock Life playing itself out.

139

"So who was actually there?"

"Well, Lee here, of course, and Clive Taillor, he was the one who was with JC all the time. Valet, driver, confidant—he sort of took your place"—he nodded at me—"when you . . . when you got sick and weren't really up to much. Clive stepped in, he was the guy JC could talk to all through the night. He was a real four-in-the-morning kind of guy."

"Clive Taillor," I said, "was the best friend JC ever had. Loyal, honorable, never let him down. Everybody let JC down, one way or another, but not Clive."

Heidi looked at me expectantly. "And?"

I shrugged. "Just a testimonial to Clive, that's all."

"Where is he now?"

"I didn't keep up—"

"Zurich," Sasser said. "JC deeded the Moon Club in Zurich to him. A few weeks before he died. Almost as if he knew he wasn't long for this world."

"Or maybe he had completed his plan to disappear," Heidi said. "So . . . Clive, JC, and Lee, that was it?"

"Right. And then one night JC woke up dead, as they say. Would have been the devil of a mess if it hadn't been for Clive Taillor. He took care of things . . . Lee here collapsed when he heard the news, Clive got him into a private hospital until he had JC cremated—"

"What was the big hurry?" Heidi asked. "Lots of people have thought that was pretty fishy."

"Nothing fishy," Sasser said, wheezing. "Taillor didn't want it to turn into some festival of ghouls gathering in Tangier for some god-awful funeral orgy. By the time the news got out, JC was already scattered over the desert. It was all over. Thumper and Annie, they didn't even have time to get back to Tangier." He snapped his fingers. "Just like that, JC was a memory. A legend."

"Just like clockwork," Heidi said, catching my eye. I was fed up.

"Jesus, my brother died! Taillor acted out of love and respect and friendship. Rest in peace, for God's sake. He was devoted to JC. It's not some big mystery."

Sasser was determined to finish his recollections. "Lee

140

here . . . maybe the day after the cremation Taillor had him wrapped up and sent him off to the Feldstein Clinic outside of Geneva—"

"He didn't send me," I said. "He hand-delivered me. That's the kind of guy Taillor was."

He went on. "I heard Annie DeWinter had a nervous breakdown. Disappeared for a while there. Could have been a rumor, I have no way of knowing, do I? Thumper Gordon went off to Japan with his millions, then he was supposed to be in Martinique buying a hotel, then he was supposed to have bought a castle in Scotland . . ." He sighed, sucking by turns at the cigarette and the gin. "And JC and The Traveling Executioner's Band was a part of rock history. The . . . End."

I was feeling somewhat more like a human being. Heidi and I lay in bed with the hotel windows open to the cool night. We'd made love and I'd slept for a while and when I woke I realized I'd been dreaming about Annie DeWinter. You never forgot a woman like Annie DeWinter. In her own way she'd been as famous twenty years ago as JC. She was one of the great photographic models of the sixties, one of the symbols girls tried to look like. There were millions of little pretend Annies running around in those days wishing they were so tall and gangly and had such long legs and long straight hair and eyes as big and dark as ink bottles. She wore headbands and vests and skirts that didn't even reach halfway down her thighs. Her mouth was immensely wide, full of huge white teeth, and she wore that shiny pale pink lipstick and had long tan fingers and almost no chest. She was perfect for the times, an icon. She had arrived on the scene, the daughter of a London solicitor, at the age of eighteen in 1965. She had met JC Tripper in 1967 and had been with him off and on for two years when he died. I often wondered if such icons as they were ever really got to know one another, ever really fell in love, or if, as I suspected, it was more a meeting and mingling of two immense public images. Did they ever get past their public personae? Was it always a battle for the mirror, a struggle to look the parts they had played and finally become? Was it the ordeal of being all the time the couple the public wanted them to be?

141

When JC died it was as if Annie DeWinter had gone with him. Her huge contract with the cosmetics manufacturer was voided by her. She chose to disappear from the pages of *Vogue*. There were no answers to the movie offers. There were rumors that she lived in the south of France on a farm, or in the Cotswolds, or on an island somewhere. Then there weren't even the rumors anymore. I never saw her again. But neither did I ever get her out of my mind. I suppose I loved her. She was, however, part of the past I'd had to reject in order to survive.

Still, I woke up next to Heidi Dillinger in Tangier twenty years later and I was thinking about Annie DeWinter, the smell of her shampoo, the way she tapped her fingertips on her lips as she listened to you, the way she'd been one of the first to start collecting Egon Schiele's paintings. I woke up thinking about her face and seeing it before me. And in my mind she was wearing a pair of earrings I'd once given her. She loved them, made them one of her trademarks, partly, I'm sure, because I got them from a gum-ball machine.

We were having breakfast and Heidi was making notes and going on about how the doctor who had signed JC's death certificate had died ten years ago. She was saying that the way things were in Tangier when JC died, "just about anything could have happened. They could have cremated a camel driver who died of old age. They could have cremated the camel, nobody would have paid any attention. They might not have cremated anybody at all. Think about it, Lee," she insisted. "You were completely wasted, you don't remember anything. Will Sasser was just a journalist, and from the looks of him now I'd bet he was stoned for about a decade at the very least. It was just Clive Taillor and JC . . . JC felt used up, couldn't write, he was worn out, wanted a new life. Maybe he was tired of Annie DeWinter. And no offense, but he must have been pretty fed up with the state you were in. So he decided it was time to get out while he could—he might never have the chance again. He had more money than he could count, he set Taillor up with the Moon Club in Zurich, he packed you off to the clinic with Taillor to make sure you got there. And he was free. He and

Taillor had probably concocted a perfect plan—and it has been perfect, the world thinks he's dead . . ."

When she stopped to take a breath I put down my coffee cup and covered her hand with mine. "Heidi," I said patiently, "He's dead." I smiled at her. I pretended that my head wasn't aching and that I didn't want to pick at the stitches. I pretended that the idea of another six months in the Feldstein Clinic wasn't sounding better to me every day.

"You're just saying that and you know it. You know I'm right. You know tenacious Heidi Dillinger is on to something."

A call came through from Sam Innis shortly before noon when she and I were wrangling over our next destination. I was being an obstructionist in a hopeless cause while she was deciding we'd go to Zurich and catch up on old times with Clive Taillor. I was wishing I'd never gotten into any of it. I wanted to go home. But I also wanted the half million with more to come. And most of all I wanted to get the monkey called JC Tripper off my back.

The conversation was pretty one-sided once she took Innis's call. Heidi did most of the listening. I went into the bathroom and came out and stood at the window and flopped down in a chair and got up and paced. She was getting a word in edgewise every so often, telling him what he wanted to hear. Eventually she hung up and sat lost in thought.

"Well?" I said.

"We're going to Rome. Right now."

"What happened to Zurich?"

"Rome."

"Don't be irritating and obscure."

"Another party has been heard from."

"I refuse to guess."

"Thumper Gordon," she said.

And I thought I'd had a headache before.

The whole thing was out of control and we hadn't had lunch yet.

She went out to get the tickets. I stood at the hotel window staring out at the traffic, trying to get hold in my mind of Thumper and Annie and dreading everything. I wasn't thinking about the view in the street and square before me.

143

Then I saw Heidi walking through the crowds in that determined way of hers. She was going to pick up the tickets.

But then I saw someone scuttle up beside her, saw her turn and nod as he fell in beside her. They were talking hard, as if time were limited. They made what struck me as an unlikely pair. And the sight of them frightened me. I was being lied to. And I was doing my share of the lying. I was running out of people to trust.

Then I watched Heidi Dillinger and Morris Fleury lose themselves in the crowd.

Thirteen

Things could have been worse.

The flight to Rome could have been hijacked by the Libyans or the Iranians or the PLO and we could have been left to sit on a wasted corner of tarmac somewhere with the air-conditioning off and a bad-smelling guy shoving an attack rifle up our noses. Or a bomb could have blown us into bits scattering over the Mediterranean. Or we could have been forced to eat the in-flight lunch. None of these things happened, however, so in the larger sense, I was a pretty lucky guy. But you know how it is—it's always something. Now I had to face the fact that my sleeping companion, my fellow Hardy Boy, my partner in the enterprise was lying to me, playing yet another game, covering up yet another bundle of secrets. This particular bundle was the rumpled, dandruff-dusted creature of the darkness, Morris Fleury.

He seemed at times, in my analytical moments, to have been grafted onto the story, but most of the time I had the uneasy feeling that when it all played out he'd be somewhere near its center doing a Harry Lime on me. Everybody lied about this guy. Nobody admitted knowing him, as if he were the doubtful guest no one wanted to admit inviting. But there was Cotter Whitney, tycoon, communing with him on the dock in the moonlight. There he was in Sally Feinman's apartment keeping company with her burned and defiled corpse. There he was smoking his pipe, waiting for me in the darkness of my own apartment, waiting to tell me that Sally was betraying me, had a file on me . . . And now Heidi had lied to me about him. His very existence seemed to drive people to falsehood.

Why was Heidi lying to me? What did she know that I shouldn't? What kind of doofus guy was I? Weren't we on the same side, after all?

Who was Fleury working for? Why had he too gone from Cotter Whitney's estate in Minnesota to Tangier? Was he supposed to be keeping track of me? Or, if he worked for Whitney—which certainly seemed the best bet—maybe he was watching Heidi and me, since we were creatures of Sam Innis/Bechtol. But would Fleury be meeting on the sly with Heidi, then? Not if he was spying on her . . . unless he was double-crossing his employer . . .

You see where this kind of thinking can get a chap.

But my head was throbbing anyway. I decided never again to hit my head repeatedly against a wall. And the more I thought about Heidi Dillinger and Morris Fleury in the street below my window, the worse my headache got. It's always unnerving when you find out unpleasant truths about somebody with whom you're sleeping . . . about somebody you trust.

I was in a lousy mood and on my guard when we got to the Hassler in Rome and fell into Sam Innis's clutches. Heidi must have noticed what a churl I was being, but maybe she'd decided to attribute it to my overall performance in Tangier and the inevitable psychological hangover. There were messages waiting for us at the desk. There was a room reservation in my name, none for Heidi. Innis wanted her to report at once to his suite. I was to settle into my room. "Have a shower and a drink, pussycat," Innis's handwritten note suggested.

Easily led, as always, I did as I was told, only I didn't like showering on my stitches, which I couldn't quite ignore, though; in fact, they were pretty well hidden by my hair. So I sank into a tub and let the hot water soak out the aches and pains of my drunken Moroccan exploits. The sight of Sally Feinman in her tub, the smell of the scorched flesh flashed across my mind, but eventually that image gave way and my subconscious went ahead considering some of the elements of this entire JC Tripper affair. I found myself humming the plaintive, haunting tune to "Everything's Hazy in Tangier," wondering why it had been sent to Freddie Rosen and by whom—what did it *mean?* Why had Sally and Shadow had to die and how were they connected to the search for my brother? From behind closed eyes I saw the seaplane slowly and with a fine inevitability crashing into Cotter Whitney's lake . . . I saw Bill Stryker rescuing the seat cushions with the cocaine packed inside and I tried to square that with the kind of man Whitney seemed to be and it just wouldn't fit . . . I saw Heidi Dillinger picking me up so cleverly on Fifth Avenue with Mellow Yellow flicking the cards on the upturned cardboard box . . . I smelled the cherry tobacco in my darkened apartment, in the narrow stairway to Sally's, floating in the heat near the boat-house . . . I tried to plot out in my mind the role of the Magna Group in all of it but it was hopeless; Magna was every-where . . .

The telephone woke me up. Sam was ready to see me.

Three of them were waiting for me. I felt like a doctoral candidate about to screw up his orals. Sam Innis didn't have the tape-recorded dark and stormy night to comfort him, but otherwise he wasn't much different. He wore rumpled khaki pants and a short-sleeved bush shirt. The wiry hair on his heavy forearms matched the Brillo-pad beard. He wore Clark desert boots and his feet were crossed on the gilt coffee table. He spoke my name and waved me toward a gilt chair with a gold brocade cushion and back. It looked spindly. "You know Cotter," he said, and Whitney, his round choirboy face in place, stood up and shook my hand. He wore a gray summer-weight pinstripe and smelled of Royall Lyme. "And this big one is my publisher, Hugo Ledbetter." Ledbetter looked at least as large as he had the night I'd seen him pushing Eleanor Whitney's wheelchair up the garden path. He'd exchanged the volumi-nous smock for a dark blue suit. His head, a fullish salt-

and-pepper beard included, was about the size of a Rolls-Royce engine block. He was upwards of six and a half feet tall and must have gone well over three hundred pounds. When he stood, the room gave the illusion of lurching into a thirty-degree tilt. "Mr. Tripper," he rumbled. His voice reminded me of either Orson Welles or God, depending. It was like shaking hands with the business end of a twenty-ton earth scoop. Heidi Dillinger was nowhere to be seen.

Sam Innis pointed to a tray of Diet Cokes and a bucket of ice. "The comforts of home. Wet your whistle, Lee. Tangier is thirsty work, I hear."

"You have no idea how thirsty," I said.

"Yes, we do. Heidi related your adventures in some detail. How's your head, by the way?"

"Reminds me of the old days," I said.

"Sorry to hear that."

"I'll survive."

Innis nodded. "Well, what do you think, Lee? Is JC still alive?"

"I see no reason to think so. We certainly didn't learn anything in Tangier to change my mind."

Heidi had obviously told him something he wanted to hear—part of her job, I supposed, letting him down easily—and he insisted on nattering away about Tangier and Will Sasser and I kept watching his piercing little eyes that made me feel like I was being thumbtacked to a specimen board. So many years had passed between my sightings of Sam Innis, I had to keep remembering that I didn't know this guy at all. And he sure as hell wasn't my pal. The question now was whether or not he was my enemy. Heidi worked for Innis and she had lied to me, had known Morris Fleury after all. Did that mean Innis also knew Fleury? And if so, where did that put them when it came to the murder of Sally Feinman . . . which Morris Fleury knew all about? And may have committed, for all I knew. All my pent-up anxiety called for a Diet Coke.

I found myself in the preposterous situation of not daring to blurt out my questions for fear of what the answers might be. If the enemy—whatever that meant—was in the room, the worst thing I could do was alert him—or them—to the fact that I had peeked under the tent flap and had a glimpse of the freak show. Who was the enemy? Anybody lying to me? Or were they just trying to keep me out of extraneous matters? Why would anyone be my enemy, anyway? What had I done to them? At worst I was only the Judas goat intended to lure JC out somehow—and that was the worst scenario. But then there were JC's enemies. And JC's enemies were my enemies, weren't they? There may have been more ways, simpler ways, to look at it, but we were stuck with mine. And I was both scared and confused, trying to hide it all.

Cotter Whitney screwed his round have-a-nice-day face into a mask of adult concern and edged forward in his chair. "There is a new development, Lee, that could be important. We've got to bring you in on it."

I nodded, waited. Ledbetter was standing by the window, which looked out at the headquarters of the Order of the Sacred Heart and the Spanish Steps. He was humming, recognizably, the opening movement of the Elgar Cello Concerto.

Whitney continued in a slightly perplexed manner. "We seem to have heard from Mr. Thumper Gordon."

"Seem?" Innis said sourly. He was scratching his beard, flaking dandruff onto his bush shirt. "*Seem?* Don't be a pussy, Cotter—"

"Well, we can't prove it actually came from Gordon," Whitney said. He was all patience, which was undoubtedly his customary style in the face of crisis.

"We must proceed," Innis snapped, "as if it did. Period."

"Listen, the squabbling is fun," I said, "but you girls don't need me for it."

"Careful, laddie," Innis said, shaking a forefinger at me.

I stood. "Sam, old buddy, fuck yourself." I reached the door at the same time his voice caught me, brought me back with a forced laugh and an apology. "You guys have got to relax," I said. "It's all a game. You know damn well JC's dead. We're all running around chasing our tails. You're going to have to write a novel about a dead rock star, Sam."

"We'll see," he said.

"Sometimes," I said, coming back and sitting down, "I think none of this has anything to do with a novel. I think you've all been bullshitting me from Day One . . . I'm not complaining, it's your money. But I wish you were all better liars. We've got bodies everywhere, we know it's all connected to JC and Magna and who the hell knows what else . . . and you've got me out on the point. Frankly, though I think you're mighty swell fellas, I'm getting a wee bit anxious." They were all looking anywhere but at me. Not exactly forthcoming. I gave up. "So," I said heartily, "how's the old Thump?"

"He simply sent me a letter, postmarked London, asking me how Freddie Rosen and I like 'Everything's Hazy in Tangier.' Obviously he'd sent it to Freddie. This letter came from Thumper or someone who knew about the song, anyway." Whitney sighed wearily. "In other words, a player."

"It's a delicate kind of blackmail," Innis interrupted.

"Doesn't sound like Thump," I said.

"I don't give a shit what it sounds like to you."

"Careful, laddie," I said softly, waving a finger at him. "I'm right on the verge of shoving your money up your ass and taking a hike back to sanity."

"The hell you are," he said. He was smiling.

"Men, men," Whitney said, "let's stay calm. The point is, Lee, there is an element of blackmail, I'm afraid. Very discreet but—"

"If it walks like a duck," Innis said, "quacks like a duck, and looks like a duck—"

"—but still earmarked by a threat. Mr. Gordon says he has in his possession many unpublished, unheard songs from JC's final months. He sent us the one as evidence. Now he wants to make a deal with Magna for the songs—he incidentally claims co-authorship of many of them. He wants to make a publishing and recording deal with Magna . . . and he wants Magna to forgo all profits, instead forwarding the money to Thumper for music-therapy centers for disturbed children. I see you smile— may I ask why?"

"Because it's beautiful," I said. "He probably means it."

"He brings you into it, too. An aspect of his plan which you may find less amusing. Of course, since you are JC's legal heir, the royalties due JC would go to you . . . they would amount to a considerable sum. But Mr. Gordon guarantees that you would agree to contribute those royalties to his scheme . . . *guarantees it.*" Whitney paused, pursing his lips, giving me a long, liquid stare. "Tell us, Lee, has Mr. Gordon been in touch with you?" He looked as if someone he trusted had stolen his tricycle.

I was laughing, shaking my head no. "But I promise you, this guy is definitely Thumper. And you know what? He's right. I'll sign over the royalties to his project. No problem. Man, this is really sinister." I couldn't stop smiling.

"But may I ask you, speaking as a businessman," Whitney said softly, "what's in it for Magna?"

"I should think that's obvious. It would be humiliating if someone else, some other label, did a new collection of JC's stuff. Lousy for your image. And you can publicize what you're doing . . . contributing your share of the proceeds to this worthwhile cause. Very good for your image. And if Thumper forms a new group, comes out of retirement, you'd have him and you could cut some deals with him there . . . and don't try to make anybody believe that some twenty-five-year-old contract with JC is still in effect. Don't even *try* that one. So, why not bite the bullet, drop him a friendly line, say you'll throw him a party in LA the town will never forget—"

"Your sweet-natured innocence becomes you," Whitney said. "But I'm persuaded that there is rather more to this than meets the eye."

Innis was still digging for the mother lode in his beard. "You seriously believe this shit, Lee?"

"Why not?"

"Aw, Lee, gimme a break."

"I don't know why I should, actually. But, if you don't believe it, what are you going to do about it?"

Innis shrugged.

"You've got to talk to him," I said.

"Well, we can't actually do that," Whitney said. "He didn't give us any way to get in touch with him. And he's been out of sight for years."

The conversation dribbled on and I learned that Heidi was already off somewhere doing Innis's bidding and would meet me in Zurich, where we could have a chat with Clive Taillor.

Innis made it clear that he believed JC was alive and we'd drive him out of his hole at any moment. I told him it was his money and his brainless faith and I'd keep playing. Whitney discreetly chewed a fingernail. Hugo Ledbetter didn't say a damned thing.

There was, of course, something going on in that room about which I knew little or nothing. But it was thick and palpable and clung to all three of them as if they'd just waded through a lake of it up to their chins. I thought about it on the way back to my room and decided, all things considered, I didn't want to know. Well, that was a lie. I did want to know. I just figured it wouldn't bring me any peace of mind.

Propped up on the desk in my room was an envelope containing a ticket for Zurich and a hotel reservation. I lay down on the bed with all my unanswerable questions and spooky suspicions. I found myself wishing Heidi were there beside me and then I remembered I couldn't talk to her anymore. Not until I figured out what she and Morris Fleury had in common. Which looked like forever at the rate I was going.

I was remembering Annie DeWinter, her thick straight black hair held in place by a brightly colored headband, her tiny breasts loose inside a fringed vest, high boots . . . My God, that had all been a long time ago. I was wondering what she looked like now, what her frames of reference were, what she'd experienced and learned and cried over and laughed at as two decades had passed. She was taking hold of my mind, digging in and holding on, just the way she had in the old days, when the telephone rang. The voice at the other end was so deep that it sent funny little vibrations bouncing around my eardrums. It was Hugo Ledbetter and he wanted to have dinner with me. He gave me an address in the Trastevere section, told me which bridge to cross, and suggested I leave the taxi before I crossed it. "I want to see you alone, Mr. Tripper. Very much alone."

"You're not sending me a corsage or chocolates, are you?"

"I'm sure your sense of humor is all the rage in your circle, Mr. Tripper, but it palls very quickly with me."

"Then you're not after my body, that's definite?"

"You are nothing like my type, sir. This is business. You may discover that we have congruent interests. Be there at nine, Mr. Tripper, or I shall be put out with you."

"Cotter Whitney is a hopeless twat, that's the problem with the whole bloody thing. He knows frozen peas, he knows fast-food burgers, he knows a lot of things, but he hasn't any idea what the entertainment business is about. Lord knows, neither do I but for publishing . . . which is why it's so important that my new associate should know what he's doing. Well, that's what it boils down to, the residue, shall we say."

Hugo Ledbetter was putting away his second pound of linguine with clam sauce, occasionally dabbing at the chunks of clam lodged in his beard. We were sitting at a wooden table in the back room of a family groceria, candles flickering on tabletops, dripping onto the sauce-stained cloth. Ledbetter was wearing a straw hat Van Gogh would have admired, a lavender smock, old corduroys, and heavy sandals. His hands were huge but twirled the pasta with practiced care. He drank his dago red with gusto, enjoying it all out of proportion to its quality, as if it were water. He looked like something from another world and sounded a lot like Darth Vader.

"Somebody is blackmailing Magna," he said, "and it's putting me off my stroke. *Somebody.* Your late brother? Thumper Gordon? How the devil should I know? I'm a publisher. A *gentleman* publisher, more or less, within limits. But I am not an idiot. I can smell it when somebody farts and this deal has got fart all over it."

"Are you sure you're not a writer?"

He shoved a great deal of warm crusty bread into the hole in the middle of his beard. Then he reached over to the plate of antipasti, then looked up at me, perplexed. "You've eaten all the anchovies."

"Salty little bastards," I said.

"Very disappointing."

"It's just the way life works sometimes."

"Murder. Blackmail. What is going on? That's a very difficult question to answer, Mr. Tripper. But I'm only interested in one small aspect of it—how it concerns me. And it concerns me only to the extent that I'm involved with this Magna deal. My firm

153

has existed for more than a century without a huge parent company hovering hungrily over us. We can go on a while longer. Even if Allan Bechtol should leave us—say if Magna acquired a different publishing house, or simply started one— we would survive handsomely. Now there are certain advantages for us in merging, I don't deny that for a moment, but they are far from essential. So when people start getting murdered, and my author is obviously either using or being used in a game I don't understand, and then a dead rock star may or may not be dead but is certainly involved—then, Mr. Tripper, I smell a fart and when I smell a fart I grow lachrymose and peckish. I grow unhappy. I've officially told Whitney that I'm having second thoughts . . . and he's upset. He wanted to bag the famous publisher, put his head up on the wall—he doesn't want to fail, it's that simple. He doesn't like being told he's on the verge of failure . . . Mr. Tripper, what the fuck is going on?"

"Very bad things," I said.

"How perceptive," he said between bites.

"I simply don't know. But your instincts are probably pretty good. Somewhere in the maze we're going to find drugs—"

"Oh, shit! I hate that!"

"—and murder and . . . what else? Name it, it'll be there."

"Why don't you just bow out, then? Or do you want to find your brother?"

"I want to lay JC Tripper to rest once and for all. If I convince Innis—Bechtol—then I figure it's a wrap. That's why I'm in it. And for the money, of course. Not only for what Bechtol's paying me but can you imagine what all this will do for JC's record sales? I'm his heir . . . I can afford to give Thumper royalties on the new stuff. So mainly I want JC to die once and for all; I don't want to find him."

"You may have a problem, Mr. Tripper."

"What's that? On my own I can think of a handful, but what's on your mind?"

"I'm quite sure that JC Tripper is alive."

"Not bloody likely."

"Ah, hear me out, you impetuous fellow. It all comes back to JC, when you think about it. Do you really believe this is all some peculiar coincidence? Hardly. No, I think it began with Cotter Whitney . . . and JC Tripper. For whatever reason, JC faked his death twenty years ago, went off to live the life he wanted, and then decided—again for reasons of his own, his motivations hardly matter—to hold Magna hostage. JC knows enough about Magna, whether it's drugs or financial irregularities or something else, to scare them. He made contact with Whitney, he sent the song, he made his demands—and scared hell out of the little twat. But Whitney doesn't know if it's really JC or Thumper or just some nut. Or someone in between. So he goes to Bechtol with the idea for the novel about the phony death of the rock singer . . . Bechtol likes the idea, he went to school with you and JC, it all fits . . . and he makes contact with you, tells you about his idea for the novel, tells you enough about the background to get you interested. And . . . at the same time it all heats up around you, because real life, real murder, intrudes, and Sally Feinman is dead. It all comes together—JC, Bechtol, Sally Feinman, that disc jockey in Los Angeles, all of them have JC in common. And, lest we forget, they all have *you* in common, young sir . . ." He finished our second bottle of wine while I carved away at a giant veal chop. "My scenario answers the one relevant question—do you know what it is?" A third bottle of wine arrived and he poured both our glasses full.

"Which question is that?"

"Why are they so obsessed with finding JC? Why are they so desperate? Why not wait for him to find them? If they're going to pay off, what's the big hurry?" He grinned as if he were stashing secrets behind the heavy beard. "Because they're so scared of what he's holding over them—they can't wait, they've got to seal off the element of chance. He's toying with them and they can't stand it. Whitney is having what they'd call in the vernacular a shit fit. They want to make a deal—"

"Don't kid yourself," I said. "If you're right, they'll kill him."

"I'm not altogether sure that's true." He patted his mouth with his soiled napkin. You could have boiled it and made soup. "I'm not sure that they're doing the killing. What if JC is quite sensibly afraid they will kill him? He might well kill people to keep from being found—it follows, doesn't it? And he might kill the people with the best chance of finding him." He leered at me from beneath wild, hairy eyebrows. "I'm naming no names, mind."

"My brother is not a threat to my life."

"Very loyal of you to say so. But you may be the one most likely to find him, just as Allan says. And, thus, the greatest danger."

"My brother's dead."

"And regrettably so are others." He grinned. "Someone is a liar here, someone is a scoundrel. More likely there are several liars and scoundrels, dangerous people. They all make me want to be somewhere else. But I've had the use of your ear quite long enough, Mr. Tripper. You've been very patient with me and my theories . . . but I must say I wanted you to be aware of the situation among Whitney, Bechtol, and me. It may or may not be of interest to you, but Whitney is very worried that I'll forsake his deal because of all this unsavory what-not . . . and he really is being held hostage, if not by your brother then by someone else. The danger is real, Mr. Tripper. That's what I'm saying. Their motives are so baroque, so layered over with lies and denials and fear and greed, they no longer recognize what they were in the beginning. They have lost their way in a wilderness of fear, and such men are dangerous indeed. They have so much to lose. They want to protect what is theirs. And that applies to everyone." His eyebrows rose and an impish smile formed itself behind the beard. "Even to you, Mr. Tripper. I've looked at all of you and you are in some ways the most mysterious of all. Let me in on your secret, Mr. Tripper."

"I'm the only one telling the truth," I lied.

He began to shake with thunderous mirth, which struck me in the instant as genuine. "Well, you're all quite mad. What, I wonder, will happen next?"

I shrugged. "The suspense is killing me."

That set him off again, his belly shaking the table between us.

Fourteen

The Alitalia jet slipped down through the clouds of dusk like a tumbling coin, reflecting bits of setting sunshine along the silver wings, finally dropping through the darkest layer into the murky fog below the mountaintops. The stands of dark-green trees looked black on the mountainside and reminded me of fairy tales and ogres and pulling the covers over my head. I was still thinking of the mountain habitat of bearded trolls with gnarled clubs when the plane settled down on what had always struck me as a postage-stamp runway.

The Zurich airport echoed emptily, mausoleum-like, a kind of elephants' graveyard for pilgrims coming to visit their money before dying. Everything was neat and clean. The Mercedes taxi had apparently just rolled off the assembly line and been driven directly to the airport. Inside it I felt hermetically encapsulated. No conversation with the driver, no radio. Soundlessly we arrived at a new, surgically spotless hotel looking down on the city from one of the forested hillsides. From my balcony I could see the huge railway station and by the Limmat Quay the site where the old Central Hotel had once stood. The fog hung low and cool in the treetops and it didn't seem like summer anymore. The pavement was wet and a steady mist filled the air.

I took a bath and wondered if Heidi was on her way to meet me. Innis had said not to worry, she'd catch up with me. Well, as far as I was concerned he didn't know from worry, but I didn't go into it with him. I didn't need Heidi, although I might have been happier keeping my eye on her: when I couldn't see her I wondered if she might be off somewhere whispering with Morris Fleury. I tried not to think about her, concentrating instead on Clive Taillor. Innis had said that Clive was as likely as anyone to know where JC was and, if JC had been alive, Innis would have been right. They had been close, those two, JC and Clive. Clive had been willing to put up with him longer than anyone else.

I was going through the telephone book looking him up when there was a knock at the door. A bellhop stood there with an envelope resting on a little silver tray. I took it and tipped him and went to stand by the window, where the fog was lowering over the city. The lights below were lit and blurred the face of the city.

My name was typed on the envelope. I tore it open and there was a single piece of hotel stationery. The message was short and perfectly clear.

Taillor will meet you at his place. Nine o'clock. Don't be late.

An address followed. But for some reason it was unsigned. I called the front desk and they connected me with someone whose job involved messages. This one had come by telephone and been typed by someone at the desk. No, that someone was gone for the day. No, if it wasn't signed, there was really no way to know if it had been a man or woman, was there? Could the lack of a signature have been an oversight? Perhaps, sir, an oversight by the individual who had left the message.

I won't say it didn't bother me, but what was I supposed to do, run and hide? I'd come to Zurich specifically to see Clive Taillor. Someone had made the appointment for me. It must have been Heidi working to Innis's order. And if it was someone else, what harm could they do me at Clive Taillor's place that they couldn't do anywhere else? I felt like the old Indian chief. Sitting Duck.

I put on fresh clothing. How could anything happen to you in your good clothes? Gray slacks, a J. Press blazer, a blue shirt, a regimental-stripe tie and shell cordovans I could use for mirrors. Was I a keeper of the old traditions or a hopeless anachronism? Or a worn-out old rocker in disguise?

I got another Mercedes taxi in front of the hotel. The driver nodded reassuringly when I gave him the address. He popped a Vic Damone tape into the deck and I leaned back against the creaky leather, opened the window and felt the cool mist on my face. It was ten minutes to nine.

He dropped me at the corner of a steep little cul-de-sac, told me it would be the second or third house on my right. I got out and slipped into my trench coat. The streetlight cast long shadows up the narrow sidewalk. The trees were thick on every side and smelled like Christmas. The houses were hidden behind them, but the lights in the windows winked through the spaces.

There were no welcoming lights behind the trees at Clive Taillor's house. The fir trees encroached on the narrow width of the stone stairway winding up toward the house from the sidewalk. It was like stepping into a very dicey tunnel. The light behind me was being curtained off by the foliage. It was becoming a very wet night. A dog was yapping nearby and I heard laughter, a party, people having fun next door. Then I stepped out of the tunnel just a few feet from Taillor's front door. There was a dim little light burning beside the empty mailbox. The door was heavy and solid. The windows were dark. The house was a kind of mini-chalet with a balcony, not at all common in the area of Zurich. Weedy plants hung in pots dangling from hooks. The windows upstairs were shuttered. Not much of a welcome.

I lifted the heavy brass knocker—a fox's head, a very pointy nose real enough to twitch—and let it fall, but there was no answer. I knew there wouldn't be, but I was there, it was a time for observing the formalities. If for some reason a trap had been laid, I'd walked into it. The only thing lacking was the sudden whiff of cherry pipe tobacco, the scent of brimstone.

But there was only the smell of the mist on the trees. Somebody put a record on next door and it might have been twenty years ago. "MacArthur Park" was melting in the dark and all the sweet green icing was flowing down . . . I hadn't heard that one in a very long time.

I knocked with the fox's head again, then followed the line of shrubbery around the house, leaning up to peer into the darkness behind the windows. I went all the way around the house hoping to God nobody thought I was a burglar and called the cops. I heard a champagne cork popping, female squeals. Someone had left the cake out in the rain and there was doubt that the recipe could be found again . . . Then I was back at the front door.

The message I'd received had apparently been in error.

By a quarter to ten I was down by the quay, sitting on a stool in a small dark bar nursing a Bushmill's and thinking about a fool and all his errands. I felt a little like a man sent plunging down the blackness of an old well. It wasn't funny but I felt myself smiling a loser's smile into the whiskey. I was feeling very hungry.

The bartender came down to my end of the bar, the empty end. He dribbled a bit more Bushmill's into the fat, squat glass. I lifted it, proposed a toast. "Life," I said. "A very rum go, all things considered."

An American, he looked up sharply. "You can say that again, pal."

I dined in a large restaurant with gray-and-cream walls, gray vases full of flowers, a haze of cigar smoke, bottom-heavy women in print dresses with husbands yawning behind meaty fists, and a determined string quartet sawing away on a minimally elevated stage in the corner. There was a steady hum of German-sounding conversation. I had that feeling of perfect anonymity, which suited my increasingly somber mood. Poking around an empty house when you'd expected a party, a reunion, had that effect on a fellow. No Heidi. Somebody leaving a message with all the wrong information and neglecting to sign it.

A tall woman with long black hair caught my eye and then

looked away. She might have been Annie DeWinter twenty years ago. I'd been in Zurich with her once and she'd been going through one of her depressions. She'd turned to me for help and I suppose I'd failed her. Still, she hadn't killed herself. Not a complete failure, then. JC had written a song about her in those days when the bottom seemed to fall out of her desire to live, walking along the Limmat Quay wondering if she should jump, standing staring at the reflection of the full moon in the water, wondering if it was a target like a bull's-eye taunting her to jump, or rather a rippling, glowing sign of hope and life and the future. It was a wrenching ballad, "Moon in Black Water," and Annie had sung it with the band. It had been the song that started her own two-year career as a singer, but that, too, had ended when JC died. Now I smiled at the woman and she smiled back, then put her hand on her husband's sleeve and turned away from me. Of course, Annie DeWinter was twenty years older now, caught in the same squeeze as the rest of us. JC had been terribly afraid of growing old, had seemed to sense the impact of time rushing toward him—seemed to see it coming long before the rest of us. He'd sensed that the sixties represented a kind of playpen for quasi-adults, at least the sixties we lived in. While the rest of us were stumbling around thinking that it was never going to end, JC always knew it was a short-term thing, that all the beautiful birds and the kicky leaps at romance were only flashing past and then we'd all have to face reality, and reality was no picnic. He knew we were just playing while the rest of us thought the world had changed and this was the way it was going to be. JC had that sense of doom and decay that lay ahead of us and it was a curse. He hated the idea of it.

JC had written another song, back when he was a kid in his mid-twenties, which had a line in it that came to me as I was watching the girl who reminded me of Annie DeWinter. JC had known what the line meant when he wrote it, as if he'd grown old before his time. *My God, how the time slips away* . . . Just words then to the rest of us, no particular meaning, what did we know about time or any other damn thing slipping away? Now, remembering the line, the words hit me so hard I had to close my eyes and hold on to the table for a moment, until my equilibrium returned, and then I looked back at the woman who was real and so was the table, and my life, it was borderline real. That was, of course, the trouble. My life wasn't quite real and this whole crazy escapade was bringing me up too close to the nasty truths and the nastier lies . . .

"Too bad there wasn't a better view of the mountains. Perhaps tomorrow will be better."

I looked up from the tail end of my dinner, surprised. It sounded like a password from a novel by Eric Ambler. The voice was dark and thickly accented. I'd seen him on the flight from Rome. He'd been wearing a Tyrolean hat, one of those feathered green wool jobs more suitable for winter. In Rome he'd been sweating beneath the brim. He'd been listening to a small cassette player, his ears plugged with the headphones. He was staring down at me now, standing beside my table, giving the impression that he was smiling twice, once with his loose-lipped mouth and once with the rims of his jowls. He had a bald, smooth-featured face, sixtyish, built like a professional wrestler who'd let himself go a bit.

"I've been here before," I said. "I've seen the mountains many times."

"They are very beautiful," he said. "Very dangerous, but very beautiful. Like women, is it not so?"

"Would you care to join me for coffee?"

"You are too kind. I must not intrude. You were so deep in thought. You like the mountains, do you?"

"Sure, sure. They're dark, full of ogres and trolls. I like them fine."

"Mother Nature's answer to Disneyland." He didn't move away. He stood looking down as if memorizing my face for some obscure reason of his own. He could have been a phrenologist contemplating running his fingers through my hair.

"Are you a Zuricher?" I asked.

"Sometimes yes, sometimes, no." He shrugged, fingering the brim of the green hat. "Zurich, as you know, can be a dangerous place."

"Why should I know that? It's the land of cuckoo clocks."

"All that money," he said. "What else? So much money always attracts danger, don't you agree?"

"I suppose you're right."

"Mark my words. I know of what I speak." He finally began to draw slowly away from my table. "Are you staying in Zurich long?"

"No, I shouldn't think so."

"Pity. We could have taken the tram up to Uetliberg. Lovely view." He shrugged again philosophically. "But it is not to be."

"Perhaps you could tell me one thing. Is there still a place called the Moon Club? I remember it from a long time ago—"

"Oh yes, I believe such a place still exists. Much changed, however. Not, I think, the sort of place you would enjoy now. But who knows?"

"Still in the old quarter?"

"I believe so. Somewhere between the Globus Store and the water. Well, have a pleasant evening. And forgive my intrusion." He was polishing his glasses on a crumpled handkerchief he'd taken from his sleeve. Bowing slightly, he was gone.

Two strangers meet momentarily in a distant city, chance brings them together. It happens all the time, nothing more commonplace. English novelists have made an industry of such plot points. Lingering over my coffee, I saw the table where he'd been sitting. The remains of a pastry, coffee, a cognac. A salesman, perhaps.

I might have sat there another hour thinking about Annie and JC and Clive and Innis and Whitney and Heidi and Morris Fleury; my mind was turning over reluctantly, sluggishly. But it was warm in the restaurant, too warm. I forced myself to pay the bill, get my raincoat, get out. I was thinking about the Moon Club, the cellar in the old part of town across the water.

The mist was blowing in my face. It served to wake me up. I set off with the idea of walking the meal off. I wasn't really intending to visit the Moon Club, it had been a fairly idle question on my part. But Clive might still own the place, might be there. Tomorrow, I could check it all out. I wandered down a main street, looked at the arrangements of goods in the shop windows, spectacularly expensive watches and pens and binoculars displayed like jewels in fields of velvet. A few turns and I was back down by the water. I should have strolled back up toward the lights and the taxis drifting past. I should have gone back to the hotel and gone to bed. But I looked across the shiny black water at the old quarter and I had to take a look around. Old times' sake.

I crossed the void, the water lapping beneath me, sucking at the bridge pilings, and strolled along the quayside, watching the lights shining along the wet paving, dancing and flickering on the slick surface of the water. Annie DeWinter and I had spent a few nights walking there, looking into that water, and none of it had changed. Nothing but Annie and me. My God, how the time slips away.

To my left those remarkably picturesque, evocative little streets twisted uphill, all curious shadows and odd angles. I wandered in among them like a man stepping onto the set of an elaborate film. Up ahead a man in a raincoat stood whistling under a street lamp while at the end of a leash his dog relieved himself. The mist clung to the street lamps like balls of shattered crystal. It was a quiet, peaceful night in the old part of an old city, old as scary fairy tales and bad dreams. Now the Moon Club had been in there somewhere.

I made a couple of turns, had the narrow slanting streets to myself, and I knew I was bound to find the place as long as I stayed in the quarter. The paving stones shone like drenched gemstones, slick and treacherous, and I heard some music very faintly, something familiar jogging my attention, somewhere behind me, hidden in the ragged shadows. I put together stray bits and pieces of the music. I knew the singer and the song. I had heard it so many times. I had been in the studio the day JC had recorded it. He'd written two moon songs, the one for Annie and one for himself, "Zurich Moon," and they'd been released on the same single. JC's was a kind of romantic ballad, bittersweet, like "The Long and Winding Road," while Annie's had been full of pain and distanced passion. "Zurich Moon" had become a kind of city anthem. He'd sung it with a raspy, whiskey-torn voice before anybody had ever heard of Tom Waits. There were some guitar riffs that Les Paul had loved; the damn things nearly broke your heart.

Now was it just a chance song in the night? Or was it meant for me?

A wave of paranoia was washing toward me from the shadows. My stomach dropped away and I felt a tremor in my knees. I kept walking, hearing my own footsteps, straining to hear others, flinching at the sight of a fat tabby slinking through the pool of light at the corner, hugging the wall trying to stay dry.

The music was following me. Or I was following it. It was here and then it was there, hard to pin down.

I hate coincidence. I don't believe it. Now someone was somewhere behind me in the tangled cat's cradle of dark streets with JC singing, doing his thing. The music drifted this way and that. Maybe it was the breeze. I stopped and waited, trying to get a fix on it. Someone was playing games with me. Was I supposed to follow the music? Or was it following me? You never knew with a music lover.

The street behind me curved downward and out of sight and was empty. The mist had turned to rain and blew like a lace curtain in the breeze. Above the ancient rooftops the city glowed from across the Limmat. A door slammed somewhere, a man swore.

The music was coming closer as I stood waiting, trying to locate the sound more accurately. I stepped back into the shadows, a deep doorway, and tried to control the beating of my heart. Who was it, there in the dark? He had to be following me . . . maybe the sound of JC was supposed to be a signal, reassuring me, telling me he was a friend, he only wanted a word with me, maybe it was the he, she, or it who had left the message for me at the hotel . . .

Finally I heard his footsteps and from the shadows I saw the tall, bulky figure topped by the green Tyrolean hat, reminiscent of Jacques Tati as Mr. Hulot, the light reflecting for an instant in his glasses. He came into view slowly, appearing over the crest of a hill, moving steadily, head cocked slightly as if to hear the singer better. He was carrying the cassette player but he'd removed the earphones, freeing the sound to the night.

I shrank back into my hiding place, waiting for him to pass, waiting an eternity as he moved deliberately toward me. He stopped abruptly between the pools of streetlight, about twenty yards away, and looked curiously into the emptiness. Where had I gone? I could see the hesitation in his stance, the way he turned slowly to look behind him, then back in my direction as if his gaze could penetrate the gloom. He seemed to be thinking. He looked at his wristwatch. Where the hell had I gone?

At last he adjusted the volume on the cassette player, making it somewhat louder, as if that might help reel me in, and began walking toward me again. He tugged at the brim of his comic hat, shoved the other hand into his trench-coat pocket. He passed within six feet of me, head down, lost in the music, while I held my breath. Then he was past, strolling onward. I waited until the sound of his footsteps had died away, then I stepped into the street and looked after him. I could still hear the music and saw him pass into a deep shadowy overhang, waited until he came back into view, the sound of JC Tripper growing fainter.

I sighed with relief, ready to play a game of my own. I wanted to know what the hell this character was up to. I set out following him. I crossed the street at the corner and moved into the shadow he'd just vacated. The sidewalk was narrow beneath a second story that jutted out overhead. I felt a heavy cast iron railing on my right, wet, slippery.

I was leaning on the railing for a moment when it happened. I was straining to see the receding figure of the man from the restaurant . . .

There was a brief shuffling, a movement in the darkness behind me. I turned and felt a glancing blow, a heavy forearm across my back and shoulder that surprised me more than hurt me, then an immensely strong arm circled around my throat beneath my chin, yanking me backward, where we slammed into the wall. It was a big man, thick and strong, wearing an oiled sweater, his breath whistling in my ear, the arm tightening. I smelled a mint, heard him crunching it between grinding molars. I dug my elbows back into his midsection, a futile gesture as he tightened his grip, his fingers feeling for his wrist to make a vise. I was trying to cough and couldn't, felt my throat constricting, my lungs straining as he suffocated me . . . when

166

a cat screeched near us, somewhere close by, underfoot, then shot away from us out of the shadows. The man jerked away in surprise, loosening his hold for a fraction of a second, and I flexed the muscles in my shoulders, jammed my foot down hard on his instep, yanked halfway out of his grasp. I heard my trench coat rip, buttons bouncing away in the street. He reached for me again, pulling me toward him, as if determined to squeeze me to death, crush me, wring my neck, but instead of trying to escape I coiled myself and thrust back against him, driving him back with all my weight, smashed my skull into his face, felt the stitches in the top of my head ripping and popping, and suddenly everything was different, changed. He had a length of wire in one hand, I felt it lashing across my face, cutting the skin stretched tight at my cheekbone, and I reached, clawed, in a kind of scarlet anger for his face and raked my fingers across it, trying to lock into an eye socket or nostril, anything I could gouge or rip or tear off, anything but his mouth, anything but the teeth . . . Now he was the one gasping for breath, struggling to drive his knee upward into my groin, and I clubbed his chest with my poor wrecked head, feeling the strength ebbing out of him. He flailed with the wire, harmlessly beating my back, and I slammed him back into the railing, pushing, hammering at his chest, hearing him gagging as I bent him backward over the railing.

I heard him break.

It sounded like my grandfather closing the door of his Packard.

I was entirely crazy by that time. I kept pushing him, bending him backward, blood cascading down my forehead into my eyes. I kept ramming at him with stiff, extended arms, my palms flat against his shoulders, and then at his rib cage, ramming him backward in a rush of uncontrollable fear and shock and rage.

He'd been dead a long time when I finally stopped killing him.

Everything was blurred with my blood and the effect of the adrenaline rush. I was gasping and then I sagged forward, supported myself against the wall, feeling sweaty and clammy and cold, and lost my dinner. It smelled god-awful. When I

167

stepped backward I slipped on something—it must have been something I ate, heh-heh—and abruptly fell down. I felt better, just sprawled on the wet sidewalk with my legs jerking in tight little spasms, and I sat there gagging, gasping, making fish faces and trying not to faint.

Christ. Someone had been following me, I'd got that right, but I'd picked the wrong man. Or maybe they'd been working together, one setting me up for the other. I couldn't stop shaking.

The man was still hanging backward over the railing, bent the wrong way like a life-size doll cast away by a gigantic, cruel child. I tried to stand up and fell back down.

"Are you going to live, chumley?"

Someone was standing beside me. I saw crepe-soled shoes and damp down-at-heel seersucker cuffs. A hand came down and I grabbed it, felt myself being lifted upwards. "Jeez," the voice said. "You look really terrible . . ."

I couldn't see his face in the darkness where I'd killed a man, but I knew the voice.

"We'd better tidy up a bit," he said. He heaved the limp body back over the railing and it fell down into the areaway. It hit a trash can, made a hell of a loud noise. I heard a window open somewhere overhead. A woman said something angry in a language I couldn't understand. She hadn't bargained for a murder in her sleep.

"Come on, my man. Time to hasten away."

Then I saw his face, looking worried and creased and tired. Morris Fleury.

Of course.

Fifteen

The Moon Club, like so many other things in life, wasn't what it once had been. There was good news and bad news. The bad news was that the Moon Club was now in a sort of post-punk funk, which meant that it was frequented by skinheads, nutcases decked out in old Nazi regalia, and large specimens whose sexuality was in considerable doubt but might best be described as Martian. The music was earsplitting and awful, a fifth-generation parody of itself. The place was full of the ugliest people I've ever seen. The good news was that no one noticed me, dripping with blood, head split open. I fit right in. Perfect disguise. I was one of them.

Morris Fleury guided me down a dark hallway with a red light at the end and into the toilet. Two guys wearing enough chains to play Marley's Ghost paid us no attention while he dabbed at the blood. He had the corncob pipe clamped in his teeth. His suit was soaked through. It was the same seersucker suit he'd been wearing that first night I'd found him camped on my terrace. I wondered if he'd ever dried out in the meantime. I was wondering about a lot of things while I listened to him breathing heavily through his nose, felt his suprisingly light

169

touch on my scalp. He kept up a steady stream of muttered comments, the drift of which seemed to be that only a couple of stitches had pulled loose and he didn't figure there was any real cause for alarm.

"You did, however, kill a man," he mused, squeezing my head back together, "though I think we're home free on that one, too. Nothing to connect you up with the stiff."

I was staring down into the crackled, filthy sink while he kept dabbing at my head. "Why didn't you help me?"

"Got there too late. You didn't need no help no mo'."

"I don't get it," I sighed.

"No, it's all pretty confusing. This sort of thing always is. Too many details, too many angles. You just gotta let it wash over you like and check out what it leaves behind. Now lift your head real slow, don't start the bleeding again. You're gonna be just fine. What the hell happened to your head anyway? You got enough stitches up there for a sewing circle." He chuckled to himself, not really caring about the answer. "Little Heidi close her legs too fast and pop your top?"

How can I say this? It just wasn't worth telling him to shut the fuck up. So I ignored him. "You and Heidi," I said, trying to focus my eyes in the mirror. My face was right at home among the pentagrams, swastikas, and depictions of dripping penises. "The Moon Club," I sighed. There was a lot of screaming and shouting filtering down the hallway. These people were having a good time. "What are we doing here? Looking for Clive?"

"Soaking up atmosphere. Revisiting the past. Learning a lesson. Everything changes," he said. He took off his Panama and mopped his bald head with its few strands of hair crossing the top like black threads. The handkerchief was wet with my blood and left pink streaks on the wet gray expanse of his skull. He blinked at me from pouches of wrinkles. He looked tired and sixty and not very dangerous anymore. In my mind I'd turned him into something scary. The reality was looking worn out and more frightened than I. "You look like sort of a human being now," he said. "We used to say that about my uncle Verm. He was on my mother's side, the Boolers. They was always in trouble, gettin' blood on ever' damn thang." He was fanning himself with the straw hat, enjoying the dialect. "You gonna need a new shirt, sonny," he grudgingly allowed. "Otherwise . . ." He shrugged. The thing was, I looked better than he did.

When we struggled free of the Moon Club it was past midnight. The mist had thinned for the moment and the moon was shining past the shredded clouds. A wind freshened off the water. The sound of the club faded behind us. The streets were empty. The body would be found tomorrow and the cops would be up against it. My head had stopped aching. Maybe the stitches had been squeezing my brain. It felt good to walk. I felt as if someone else had killed the man in the darkness.

"I'm tired," Fleury said. "Need some java."

He led the way to a dark coffeehouse he seemed to know. We settled down at a corner table not far from the steaming, spitting espresso machine. Candles sputtered on the tables. The windows were steamed up and streaked with rain. And somebody, I kept thinking, had just died trying to kill me . . .

We got coffees on the table and I told him I wanted to know who the hell he was working for and what his role was. I told him I had seen him at Cotter Whitney's and with Heidi Dillinger in Tangier.

"Relax, chumley, you've had a tough night. You don't want to get all worked up. Ever kill anyone before?" He started spooning sugar into the thick black brew.

"Don't be ridiculous."

"Let me explain things to you. Just calm down—"

"Tell me that again and you'll be wearing your coffee."

"You're looking at the head of security for Magna. Whole shootin' match. Now I may not fit the image in your mind, but I am what I am and Mr. Whitney will tell you the same thing. I go back to the old days when Harry Mirsky ran the studio, but Whitney knew he was on to a good thing when he got me as part of the package. There's damn little I don't know about the movie and record ends of this outfit. I report directly to Whitney, you got that?"

I nodded, fumbling the pieces together in my mind, hoping the picture would eventually come clear.

"The first order of business for me these days," he went on, sucking a tooth and puffing the pipe, "is the blackmailing of

Magna. You heard about this, am I right? Okay. We've got a blackmail situation—only we're not sure who's doing it and we're not sure what they want. It's a one-way street so far. We can't contact them, so we wait to hear . . . so they keep proving things to us, telling us things they know that they shouldn't know. They've got a pipeline for information, no doubt about that—"

"Like what?"

"It has nothing to do with you, my friend. But you heard about the song we got and then Thumper Gordon's letter . . . Well, we're trying to fit that into the picture, see?"

"Not really," I said.

"Well, we'll get it all straightened out sooner or later." He noisily slurped some coffee and gave it a thorough chewing. Vivaldi was playing in the background and losing the battle with the espresso machine. Most of the patrons at the small tables seemed to be students, deep in conversation. "You and Bechtol and Sally Feinman and Miss Dillinger, you all arrived on my plate at the same time. And Bechtol's idea about a novel based on your brother coincided with the first blackmail overtures and the arrival of that damn song and the dead disc jockey and then the Feinman killing, and then Bechtol brings you into it and that goddamn Hugo Ledbetter . . ." He ran his hand over the broad bald scalp where his hair would have been. "Where to start? It's like one of those whatchamacallits . . . Möbius-strip things, like a snake twisting around and eating its own tail. What parts are hooked together? Do we have two entirely different deals going on here? Not connected at all?" He sighed, leaned back, pushed one hand down inside the top of his baggy, rumpled trousers, behind the big belt buckle with the silver longhorn on it. "I've got too damn much to do is what it comes down to. On top of trying to figure out all this craziness, Whitney tells me he sorta wants me to keep an eye on you so you don't step into any deep shit. I'm stretched too thin, that's the truth of it. He needs fuckin' Pinkertons and he throws it all in my lap . . . but he's obsessed with the idea that none of this gets out, so it's up to poor old Fleury to keep the lid on. And now Ledbetter, he's making waves and Whitney's bouncing off the walls. He hears about this little escapade of yours tonight, he'll have my hindquarters for a paperweight, I promise you." He closed his eyes and rubbed them hard. When he opened them he didn't give the impression that the view had improved.

"So what's going on with you and Heidi Dillinger? After I saw you sneaking around Whitney's place in Minnesota I asked her if she knew you and she told me she didn't. But there you were together in Tangier. What's she lying about?"

"She wasn't lying. She didn't know me from Adam until she got to Tangier and Bechtol told her over the phone who I was, that I'd be on the lookout for her and she should keep it under her hat once we connected. She's a straight shooter, Heidi is. Whitney told me I had to let her in on it so she could then report to me if she couldn't reach him or Bechtol—hell, I'm the one on the case they're watching from a sky box somewhere. And Heidi's on the Magna team, she worked for Magna before she hooked up with Bechtol . . . you, Tripper, you're a guest, more or less. She's on the inside, she's got responsibilities to the greater glory of Magna and Allan Bechtol. She's working for us, see, and you're more of an independent contractor, on board for just this one job . . . frankly, I wish I'd never heard of you or your brother. Nothing personal. Just makes my life a helluva lot more complicated." He dug a pouch of Cherry Blend tobacco from his coat pocket and filled the old corncob again, sucking it to make sure of the draw.

"Who tried to kill me? He—or one of them if they were working together—was on the plane from Rome. He checked me out at dinner, he followed me, playing one of JC's songs on his cassette player. He led me right to the guy who attacked me . . . Who are they?"

Fleury applied a match and the tobacco curled up over the rim of the bowl. He puffed, watching me through the clouds of smoke. He pushed the tobacco down with the side of the matchbook.

"Well, one of them is past tense." He grinned in the worst possible taste, gaps between his yellowed teeth. "Look, I don't know who they were . . . I wish to hell I did know." He puffed reflectively. "Somebody who doesn't want you to find JC Tripper, wouldn't you say? You must be getting too close . . ."

"How close can you get to a ghost?"

173

"Have it your way, my friend. Nobody's trying to kill me. I gotta go with what makes sense to me. Who the hell else would want to kill you? You're looking and JC is hiding—"

"All right, all right. I guess I'm the only one who thinks JC is dead."

"There's always Taillor," he said. "Maybe he knows." He yawned.

"Did you leave me a note about Taillor at the hotel?"

He shook his head. I told him of my pointless trek to Taillor's house. He kept shaking his head. Embers dribbled over the rim of the bowl, burning little black holes in his seersucker coat. "No, I'm not here to *see* Taillor. I'm investigating him from another angle altogether. Banking. I've been spending the day going through Taillor's banking records—"

"Why would he stand still for that?"

"I didn't *ask* him, Tripper." He gave me a damp, quizzical smile.

"Silly me, I was under the impression that the secrets of the Swiss banking system are more or less inviolable."

"Less. At least where clout like Magna's is involved. All our European financial dealings come through a bank here in Zurich. Which means we're a hellish large account." He nodded smugly. I couldn't bear to watch. "And Clive Taillor is a client of the same bank." He chuckled nastily in that odd way unimportant men sometimes do. "The bank does us a favor every now and then. When we want to check up on Taillor, it's not exactly something that requires board approval." His power, however third-hand it was, gave him considerable pleasure.

"Find out anything interesting?" I was trying to act as if I were only making conversation, but it was the most important question I'd asked anybody since I'd thought I was picking up Heidi on Fifth Avenue.

"Yes, Mr. Tripper, I did."

"Is is a secret?"

"Surely is." He sighed at the notion of his own importance, puffed his corncob. "But you, you're okay. You're involved— but you don't really give a shit how this comes out, one way or the other, right?"

"I can live with it. Unless somebody kills me."

"What I found out is this: *I proved JC Tripper is alive.* Hear me out. Ever since JC died, or was reported to have died, for these twenty years, Taillor's been getting a regular payoff, by wire— from here in Switzerland, or from the Bahamas, or from the United States. Just like clockwork, with cost-of-living increases, you might say . . . same amount for a year or two, once a month, then it increases for a year or two, then it increases again. So on and so forth. I ain't a rocket scientist, but I can see the evidence of my own two eyes."

"Any way to trace where these wire transfers are coming from? I mean the specific account holder?"

He massaged his chin, scraped his fingers in the stubble. "That's a little harder to do. Oh, we can do it, but Whitney's going to have to apply some personal pressure. Swiss bankers draw the line pretty quick once they start breaking rules. One rule, okay. The second rule comes harder . . . but when we do find out who's paying Taillor, who's been paying him for twenty years, I think I know what we'll find. We'll find your brother, Mr. Tripper. And I think you'd better get ready for that little reunion. You were a vegetable back there twenty years ago; he could have left Tangier in a camel caravan and it wouldn't've made no never mind to you . . . Clive Taillor faked the whole thing, that's my theory, he helped your brother disappear and he's been getting paid off ever since. And, buddy boy, I'm about to show Cotter Whitney how Morris Fleury became a legend in this business."

"Which business is that?"

"The find-out business, chumley. That's what I do better than anybody else . . . *find out.* And I'm gonna find out who's been paying Taillor off . . . and when I do we're gonna have all the answers—who's the blackmailer and where JC Tripper is these days—I'm real close. And then we'll have the big reunion, buddy boy."

"The big reunion?"

"Sure. You and your brother—who the hell else?"

"Aren't you afraid somebody might wait for you in the dark and kill you?"

"Nobody gonna kill Morris Fleury, don't worry about that."

Watching Morris Fleury have a good laugh was not the sort of thing likely to give wings to your spirits and put a smile on your face.

"Say, chumley," he said moistly, savoring what was to come, "she'd kill me if she knew I was running off at the mouth, but . . . but, man to man, I owe you, right?"

"How the hell should I know?" A man inside my head was trying to break out. All he had was a ball-peen hammer, but he was making do.

"Well, I got the idea from little things she said that our Heidi is sweet on you. Never knew her to get involved, not with any guy, ever. She's always been all business, but she gets that look when she talks about you." He chuckled. Damp, very damp. "I'd like to hear about that, if you ever get any, y'know? *Poon.* Love a good poon story."

Believe it or not, Mr. Ripley, my head got worse.

Sixteen

You heard him *break?*"

She turned toward me and I felt her warm breath on my chest. She took my hand and held it against her breast, squeezed my fingertips around her nipple, then brought the palm to her mouth, kissed.

"You poor darling," she said, "you poor, poor darling. And Fleury—*our* Morris Fleury, the phantom of the Minnesota night—repaired your head?" She kissed my hand again. "You can't be allowed out on your own again, my darling. Now we've got to get you relaxed . . . You're so stiff—"

"That's not tension, Heidi."

"I've heard it said that violent death excites some people." She giggled.

"This is serious."

"I know."

"Don't talk with your mouth full."

It was so much easier dealing with her now that I knew she wasn't one of Fleury's people. Easier, but something still bothered me. I was beginning to think Fleury might have been right about her feelings for me. That hadn't been part of the deal.

* * *

She'd been waiting for me when I'd arrived back at the hotel, after Fleury had drifted away into the night. Past two o'clock, the middle of one of life's darker nights, the mist having turned to rain, my head splitting. Really. Splitting. Morris Fleury's bank investigations twisting my brain. The sound and feeling of the man's back breaking over the railing, the memory of the wire flicking against my face. The emptiness of Clive Taillor's house, the sound of "MacArthur Park" from next door . . . Heidi Dillinger waiting for me in the lobby, curled up on a couch reading a copy of the *International Herald Tribune,* looking up sleepily, telling me she'd been wondering if I was dead or something. Then she asked me if I'd been with Clive Taillor all this time. Had I gotten her message about meeting him at his place? She'd called him from Madrid, where she'd been attending to a Spanish-rights matter for Bechtol, and then she'd called the hotel to leave word for me . . .

We made love until one of us fainted. I think it was me, which is probably the standard post-killing performance level. The little death, Hemingway—or somebody like him—called it. It helped to erase the memory of the big death a little earlier in the evening.

It also made me stop thinking about Annie DeWinter, which was probably a good thing. I didn't start thinking about Annie DeWinter again until Heidi herself brought her up later and opened the door to the final stage of our little saga. But I'll get to that shortly.

Come morning, I staggered to the shower while Heidi was already on the telephone with Bechtol or Whitney or parties unknown. She wasn't telling anyone about my previous evening's activities. She'd become very protective about me.

I stood for a long time under the hot water, feeling the steam rising around me, while I tried to put my finger on the exact nature of what was going on between Heidi and me. There was an uneasiness I couldn't shake. *We* weren't, of course, *in love.* But was she? I couldn't imagine what there was in me to love, and I hadn't loved anyone in so long I'd forgotten how one managed it. We were, I suppose, drawn to one another, but it was the kind of thing co-workers, a couple of smartasses, sometimes find themselves embroiled in almost before they know it. We climbed one another because we were there, as the mountaineers say. Still, there was more to it than that. But for me it was shallow; I'd thought it was for her, too. Maybe seeing what a mess I was, how vulnerable I could be, had touched a nerve in her. Maybe she never trusted anyone and then found herself trusting me. . . . Maybe.

I'd made no move on her. She'd been the one who got it going that night at Whitney's. Thinking about it, I was getting angry with both of us. What did she think she was doing, anyway? What was in it for her?

Heidi was a thinker. When Heidi looked at me, what was Heidi thinking?

I had no idea, not anymore.

And what was I thinking of when I looked at her?

It was time to admit it to myself.

Annie DeWinter. Like a song, a melody of the past, she kept coming back to me.

When I came out of the bathroom she was off the phone, sitting at the little desk waiting for me, tapping her front teeth with a Waterman pen, smiling crookedly. I'd seen the expression a thousand times before on the faces of countless women, and I knew it meant trouble. It was impossible to know just what kind of trouble, but I was going to be finding out right away. With emotional women, it could signal a firestorm up ahead. But Heidi wasn't emotional; she was a thinker. Something had set her thinking about me. Some women have a sense of what's going on inside your head and there's no damn point in arguing about it. When I saw her I felt guilty about my thoughts in the shower, not because I'd had them but because she *knew*. I was going to pay, now or later; the crooked smile, the sidelong appraising glance told me that.

"Well, Lee, there seems to be an increasingly popular view that you, my dear, know where JC is . . . that you may, in fact, be in cahoots with him." She was all mischief. It made me nervous. "Cahoots," she said. It sounded like a sneeze.

"Whitney and Bechtol," I said. "A pair of mental giants. Nobel winners for character judgment."

She shrugged. "I've known dumber in my time."

"So what do you think?" I was getting dressed, avoiding eye contact.

"Oh, I think you're an elusive, secretive devil. A complicated man who has spent a lifetime concealing himself. Nobody knows you. You won't allow it."

"God, how I hate cheap pop psychology." I was buttoning my shirt, making hard work of it. "Soap-opera crap."

"Apparently I hit a nerve."

"Look, I'm just a guy who had a famous brother and I can't seem to get past it. JC may not be alive but he's the un-dead, so far as I'm concerned." I was pulling my pants on, hopping about on one leg.

"You are such a liar!" She laughed. "But I like that in a man."

"Bullshit." Up with the zipper.

"But, my darling, you *are*. A liar and a scoundrel. You can't fool me. He is alive and you know it, don't you? And you've always been part of the cover-up, haven't you?"

"Socks," I said. "I must have clean socks somewhere."

"You are in love with Annie DeWinter, too, aren't you?"

Ah, the curveball at last. Set me up with the fast balls, then the slow curve from nowhere. "What a question. I have not seen the woman in twenty years. She was twenty-five. Now she's forty-five. I don't even know her, let alone love her."

"Now, don't get all petulant. But if you're not, that makes it all the more peculiar."

I found my socks and sat down on the edge of the bed to put them on. "What," I sighed, "could you possibly be babbling about?"

"You kept saying her name, 'Annie, Annie,' in your sleep. Oh, it was terrible." She was smiling very slowly. "It made me feel like a wife checking up on her husband. Or do you know some other Annie?"

Clearly, she was a witch.

There was no answer when I called Clive Taillor's house. An hour later I called again, with the same result. Heidi said she at least wanted to see the place, get some kind of feel for the man. She had rented a car at the airport, so we got directions and drove, first stopping in the old quarter to have a look at the Moon Club by daylight. It didn't look like much, but then it never had, but once it had been a kind of temple, back in the days when everybody who came to Zurich went to the Moon Club, and some came to Zurich for no other reason. Now it was tough to imagine just who wouldn't dread being there. It was locked and quiet and we headed for Clive's house. This mist clung to the city, and fog continued to shroud the mountain-tops. Uetliberg was completely obscured. The forested hillsides gleamed darkly, as if they'd been polished.

We left the car at the corner of the entry to the cul-de-sac and retraced my footsteps from the previous night. It seemed like a long time ago, probably because I'd killed a man in the meantime and gotten Morris Fleury's version of the low-down and spent a long night with Heidi. But nothing on the street seemed to have changed. It was Sunday, impressively quiet, any lingering sounds muffled by the patter of the rain in the trees and the fog.

Clearly the party next door was over, but through the foliage I glimpsed a man in a striped bathrobe kneeling with a dustpan and whisk broom disposing of the evidence. Taillor's house was quiet, streaked with damp. The pots of flowers hanging on the chalet balcony dripped steadily. I led Heidi along the route I'd followed, the door, the fox's head, the trip around the house tying to get a look through a window, and my results repro-duced themselves once again.

"Did you try this entrance?" We were standing at a heavy, scarred wooden door at the rear of the house. Two plastic trash cans were full, and empty flowerpots were stacked near a box of gardening tools, a rake, a hedge trimmer.

"No. The thought never occurred to me. The place was empty. I wasn't going in."

"Let's see if maybe Mr. Taillor is just a very sound sleeper." She depressed the catch on the handle and shoved. The door gave grudgingly, as if the insistent precipitation had swollen it against the frame. She gave it another push and it swung open into a back hallway. She reached in and turned on a light.

181

"Breaking and entering," I said.

"Just entering," she whispered. "Trespass."

"Wait a minute," I said. "Use your head—you know damn well if we go in there we're going to find a corpse. My old friend Clive Taillor will be dead. It stands to reason."

"You've seen too many movies."

"Read books, too. Don't forget books. I don't like this one damn bit."

"Be reasonable. Our coming in isn't going to affect the situation one way or another. If we find a corpse, maybe it'll be a big shock—maybe it'll be somebody else. Maybe Hugo Ledbetter will be swinging from a light fixture."

"No way. He'd pull the ceiling down." I wanted to laugh at myself and the situation, but it was a slow go. My mind flipped through the back issues, I saw myself entering Sally Feinman's loft, smelling things . . .

The house was spotless, which was pure Clive, organized and spectacularly precise in the absurdity of our rock existence. His compulsive neatness had made him indispensable to JC and me, both of us being something of a shambles. The pictures were straight, the dishes were in the cupboard, the throw rugs neat and squared with one another. The smell of lemon furniture polish hung in the stillness like a reproach to the less fastidious. The bookcases were full and arranged alphabetically, the dust jackets pristine, the ashtrays empty.

We climbed the polished wooden stairway to the second floor. It was dark because the windows were shuttered and the air was stale. Stale cigarette smoke.

Clive Taillor was tied to a high-backed wooden rocking chair in his bedroom. There was a small bullet hole in the middle of his forehead. He was wearing a white shirt with the sleeves rolled up on the forearms, black slacks, and his feet were bare. There were burns on his feet and a couple more on his forearms, which were roped to the arms of the chair. The wounds were charred, raw, blackened smudges where blood had dried. I looked down at his feet, then saw Sally Feinman's foot sticking up out of the bathtub, smelled burned flesh.

Heidi stood beside me. Her face had gone white and she kept swallowing, lips clamped tight, unable for a few moments to speak or look away or swallow. I took her arm and pulled her back out into the hallway. Her eyes were wide when she looked up at me. "Clive?" Her mouth was dry, her tongue sticking to the roof of her mouth.

I nodded. "Older, grayer, and deader. But Clive."

She was leaning against the wall. "I've got to think."

I went back into the bedroom, trying not to look at the body. Cigarettes had been stubbed out in a glass ashtray. But I wasn't looking for cigarettes. I was looking for a crust of charred tobacco knocked out of the bowl of a pipe.

I found it.

It didn't smell of cherries. It just smelled stale and burned. But it was enough for me.

Back at the hotel, with the rain beginning to drum in the streets and blow in sheets across the balcony, I started in on Morris Fleury. I told Heidi what he'd told me about how he'd gotten into this, how he'd met her in Tangier, everything he'd told me less than twenty-four hours before. I told her about the tobacco ash and I said he seemed to me to be a lethal shadow, leaving the dead in his wake. She thought I was reading way too much into things, but she was still pale.

"Come on, don't get bent out of shape about Fleury. He's just not a now kind of person. I'd say he's just somebody Rosen and Stryker foisted off on Whitney because he was good at *not seeing* some of the stuff that was going on. He's on the downhill side, just cruising on home. He's a flunky, Lee, but he goes way back, he goes all the way back to JC's days at Magna—I'm surprised you guys didn't know him, actually."

"Maybe JC met him, but Fleury hasn't said anything about it."

"Look, Fleury's a broken-down old bum—did you catch the suit he wears? I mean, have a heart . . . Whitney barely knows he's alive, but he puts up with him out of habit. He's a fixture, like an old desk somewhere they've forgotten to throw away. He's been there forever—"

"How do you know so much about him?"

"Whitney told me, he called me in Tangier to tell me this old coot was coming to make contact with me. He told me I could trust Fleury to get messages to him, Whitney, if I couldn't reach him or Allan. But really, it seems to me that you're missing the point, Lee—"

"Wouldn't surprise me, frankly. You're the researcher."

"And you're always setting me up," she said.

"The hell I am. Which point am I missing today?" I was thinking about Clive Taillor. I hated all of it. For all his decency and loyalty to JC he'd been killed. Tortured and killed. Had he told them what they wanted to know? Who were *they*? And I wondered when the police would find Taillor's corpse. When we were long gone from Zurich, I hoped. And I wondered if Fleury was in the process of having Whitney put the pressure on the bankers to find out who'd been paying Taillor all these years.

"The point is that Taillor must have known all about what happened to JC. Including where he is now if he's alive. I mean, why else torture and kill him?"

"Maybe Taillor was the one blackmailing Magna," I said. "He could have sent the goddamn song. He could be in it with Thumper Gordon." I was just talking, filling the air with words while I tried to cope with her suggestion about Taillor. What might happen if Taillor had told what he knew about my brother and, of course, about me? What ultimately had he known?

Heidi was shaking her head. "No, I don't think so. It doesn't feel that way to me. They—Magna, Whitney, Fleury—would give in to a blackmailer—and a blackmailer would have protected himself, the old in-case-of-my-death-an-envelope-will-be-opened gambit. No, I think Taillor was killed to find out something. Or"—she frowned at me—"to keep him from telling something—"

"Here we go again," I muttered, but my heart wasn't in it. It wasn't a game anymore. "Why torture him if you just want to shut him up? Anyway, I like Morris Fleury for the killer, I don't care what you think."

She kept frowning at me. Her color was coming back. She was doing something I couldn't do. She was forgetting Clive Taillor. I wanted to kill the man who'd murdered Clive. Perhaps I already had. "If Fleury killed Taillor, why?"

"I don't know," I said. "All the theories everybody is always insisting on depend on JC's being alive. And I know JC is dead."

She gave me one of those looks that said her patience was being tried. "I never know when to believe you."

"Always believe me and you'll be okay."

"If Fleury killed Taillor, two motives present themselves." She was tapping her teeth with the Waterman again. She had a faintly distracted look, as if she were programming a computer in her mind. "First, he was trying to find out where JC is . . . he tortured him to get the answer. Then, whatever he learned, he killed Taillor to shut him up, to keep him from warning JC or anyone else. Second, and I begin to like this one the more I think about it—he killed Taillor *because* Taillor knew where JC was . . . Taillor knows JC's whereabouts, let's say, and maybe he's one of only two people who know, so he's a terrible danger to JC's privacy—we don't even know *who* JC is! Time, a little nip and tuck, hair gain or loss, ditto weight—in twenty years you can become someone else. For that matter, you can do it in six months. Don't look at me like that—that's a perfectly reasonable idea!"

"One of two," I said, trying to get my feet back on firmer footing. What an imagination. "Who else knows where JC is?"

"You, of course."

I groaned. "Well, JC will always be JC."

"You mean he is alive," she crowed triumphantly.

"For God's sake," I said. "Nips and tucks, wigs and false beards and, presto, Ledbetter is actually JC! Get serious, for God's sake!"

"Oh, I am serious."

"Where do the guys–or guy, I'll never know, I guess—where do the guys who tried to kill me fit in? That was real, too. *I killed a man.* Last night!"

"I know, darling—"

"Don't soothe me!"

"It must have been terrible for you—"

"Nothing a goddamn bit funny about it!"

"I know, I'm sorry. Who were they? As above . . . they wanted to find JC or—"

"Nobody was asking me questions, may I remind you. I was getting killed, not interrogated."

"Well, what does that tell you? I don't like to be the one to tell you your brother is trying to kill you—"

"The hell you don't."

"Well, you're right, there's nothing funny about it."

"Whoever killed Clive—why torture him if all they wanted was to make sure he didn't tell anyone where JC is?"

Heidi thought about that for a moment, then said, "Maybe the killer wanted to know if Taillor told anybody else where JC is. It's possible. But more likely it's the other way—trying to find out where JC is."

Later, without quite realizing what I was saying, I remarked aloud, "I wonder if Clive told him . . ."

She looked back at me from the open door to the balcony where the rain fell steadily.

"What do you mean, Lee?" She wasn't bantering. "I thought JC was dead."

"I'm losing my mind," I said, damn near meaning it.

"A nip here, a tuck there."

"What?"

"I wasn't just making conversation before, what I was saying about a nip and a tuck, a little weight, less hair or more. JC could have become someone else."

"Sure, something only Walt Disney could love. A cartoon."

"It would explain why he's so hard to find, so determined to remain a secret."

"So would death."

She was in her slip, which was very short, her long thighs crossed, the naked flesh warm and damp. We'd made love again. Now she was painting her nails, deep in concentration, her hand utterly steady. I leaned back against the sweat-dampened pillows.

"Your Annie DeWinger is what we have left. Are you ready for that?"

"She's not *my* Annie DeWinter, and what in the world do you expect from her?"

"Look, there's no one else to go to. We don't know where Thumper Gordon is; Taillor is dead; you're here and maybe you're even telling the truth, maybe you don't know where JC is—in any case, you four were the last ones together in Tangier—"

"But Annie was gone when he died."

"You didn't see her when you were writing your book about the search for JC Tripper. I thought that was strange."

"Why open old wounds? She knew nothing about his death, she was gone. She had found the quiet life, that was what she'd always wanted . . . why make her go through it all again?"

"That was about the time her boyfriend had arrived on the scene, wasn't it?"

"I have no idea. I knew nothing about a boyfriend."

"Well, I can't imagine lovers like Annie and JC could easily get over one another."

"People die. Life does go on, Heidi."

"If he's alive, he must have gotten in touch with her. No sane man could ignore the woman he loved—not ignore her for twenty years—"

"JC could have. He always used to say that when the time came he could slam his big steel door on people and that was the end to it. When he made up his mind, the door would come down with a helluva clang. And once it came down, it could never be raised. He said it was JC's law."

"Lovely."

"Whoever was on the other side was exiled forever."

"I believe I grasp the point—"

"Maybe Annie was part of the problem, maybe he had to get free of her, she was so much a part of his old life . . . she *was* the old life . . ."

"Darling . . . you're crying." She was standing beside me. I could smell her, feel the warmth.

"Memories. I don't know . . . Christ, twenty-four hours ago I killed a man. Let's call it shock." I wiped my eyes on the corner of the sheet.

"You've begun to talk about him as if he's alive, Lee. Is he alive, Lee?"

"Dead as a fucking skunk," I said vehemently. "You suggested a hypothetical question. Now just leave it alone!"

Later she said, "We have to go to London."

187

"All right." There was no point in arguing. I knew what had to be done.

"It's Annie, Lee. We've got to exhaust the possibilities."

"Annie."

"She could be in danger."

"Not from JC," I said. "Never from JC. Fleury, maybe, if he really thinks JC's alive and she might know where—but I'm telling you, you don't need me."

"Yes, we do. You know her, she'll talk to you. And . . . I think you'll want to be there, Lee."

"She has no idea where JC is because he's—"

"I think she does, actually."

"Oh, for God's sake—"

"I think he's with her, Lee. That's the point."

She took an eleven-by-fourteen manila envelope from her bag and held it on her lap, slowly tapping it with one large, red, newly painted fingernail.

"You tried to see her, didn't you?"

I shrugged. "Not very hard."

"But you did try, right?"

"I wrote her a note, that's all, the old address. Berkeley Square."

"And?"

"I got a one-sentence reply. *Please leave me out of it.* So I did."

"That was shortly after she took up with the new boyfriend. You know about him?"

"Heidi, I don't spend much time keeping up on Annie's private life—"

"How disingenuous. Well, of course, she's nothing to you—"

"Now you're talkin'. Twenty years, Heidi, twenty big ones."

"So naturally you talk about her in your sleep."

"Heidi, you are being very tiresome."

"And you're denying the simple fact of her friend or lover, obviously, whatever he is. That is oddly amusing, Lee, but also tiresome. We have to go see her and ask some questions—I'd like you to get with the program."

I stared at her. "I didn't make you the boss, Heidi. So I'll ignore the tone of your voice; I'll forgive you. But one more

188

word of imperious bullshit from you, this boy is taking his bat and ball and going home and you can spend the rest of your fucking life looking for my poor lost brother and good luck to you."

"Aha, you add truculence to your many sins." She smiled. "I like that in a man. And now that I am properly chastened, let's give a thought or two to the man in Annie DeWinter's life. Just grit your teeth, Lee. It's no worse than a root canal—his name is Alec Truman, a financier who is very, very big and almost entirely unknown."

"So how do you know so much about him—as I assume you do?"

"Research and computers are my two specialities. Magna has an exceptionally large data base of information—there's a wholly owned subsidiary, an information-gathering firm, JQP, that never appears anywhere on any balance sheet related to Magna. But I—through Whitney—have access. Because of our search for JC—"

"He must trust the hell out of you."

"He has good reason."

"And Alec Truman is in the computer."

"Everybody is in the computer."

"JQP?"

"John Q. Public."

"Cute."

"Coy, I'd have said. But I didn't name it."

"So what's the story on Alec Truman?"

"Let me strip it down to its essentials. No family, an orphan, born and raised in Johannesburg, only the sketchiest history of his youth, adolescence, and young manhood. A very anonymous man. Until he appeared in London something over a decade ago, still shadowy but partnering with Arabs, Japanese, Germans, Greeks . . . that's when it became apparent that he has enormous wealth, leverage, and therefore power at his fingertips. Then he meets Annie DeWinter, but this, too, barely makes its way into the public forum. He pays people to keep his private life unnervingly private. He is, in short, a man with an easily faked past and an extremely anonymous present; he pays his taxes and minds his manners. Annie DeWinter is the only public event in the course of an exceedingly private life. There are almost no extant photographs of the man . . . but I have my sources; this arrived today by courier from London. I think you'd better take a look at it."

She handed me the envelope. The rain was still bouncing hard on the balcony. Night had fallen and Zurich was a glowing blur of light behind the fog and rain. I was fumbling with the clasp. I was thinking about Morris Fleury, where he might be now . . . was he always going to be just ahead of us? I thought of Clive Taillor and wondered when he'd been killed, if he'd been dead upstairs the first time I went to the house, before I'd run into Fleury in the dark street—

The envelope contained a single eight-by-ten blowup, grainy, taken from a newspaper and enlarged. It had been shot at what appeared to be a racetrack. The man wore a hacking jacket, a windowpane-plaid shirt, a dark knitted tie. He was turning toward the camera, standing at a railing, presumably overlooking the racecourse. Binoculars hung on a leather strap around his neck.

"You look like you've seen a ghost."

My throat had tightened, the muscles constricting and cutting off speech, though I can't quite imagine what I'd have said.

There was less hair, more of a dome, some gray wings over the years, a tightening under the chin, heavy glasses, but the slight grin, the flat gaze with the crinkle at the corners of the eyes, countless features, details, I knew so well.

I stared at the picture, feeling as if the ground had been cut from beneath me, feeling my feet swinging out into space.

JC Tripper twenty years later was staring back at me.

Seventeen

Magna owned several flats scattered across London. Heidi and I moved into a one-bedroom with kitchen in a massive red-brick Victorian building in Draycott Place, just a block off the King's Road, a block from Draycott Avenue. Annie DeWinter lived fifteen minutes' walk away, up from Sloane Square in the welter of expensive and elegant housing between Harrod's back door and Sloane Street. According to Heidi's sources Annie had left her Berkeley Square digs several years before and now lived in Hans Place with Alec Truman in a freehold townhouse worth, presumably, something in the neighborhood of two million pounds. Yet it was the sort of place where a multimillionaire financier who wanted to preserve his anonymity, to maintain an invisible profile, might feel safe, secure, and hardly noticed.

Although none of the original houses from the eighteenth century had survived, Hans Place had an illustrious history. It was named for Sir Hans Sloane, the father-in-law of Lord Cadogan, who'd owned all the land for blocks around. It had begun its existence as a development of comparatively modest housing that had drastically declined, was well on the road to becoming a slum by the mid-nineteenth century, when Mr. Harrod opened his store. By the latter third of the century, Harrod's had saved the neighborhood. But previous to that, in the area's first flowering, Jane Austen had lived at Number 23 with her brother, and the Prince Regent had invited her to Carlton House and allowed her to dedicate *Emma* to him. Shelley had lived at Number 1, and Lady Caroline Lamb and Fanny Kemble had attended M. Saint Quentin's school at Number 22.

This was all in my mind because I was a nervous wreck and because I had once lived in a very trendy flat in Pont Street, a cricket ball's toss away, but that had been in the sixties, in my youth. I'd learned the history of the area and, since I was sitting behind the wheel of a rented Rover across from Annie's house, waiting, I had to think of something. So I thought about Sir Hans Sloane and Jane Austen and Fanny Kemble to keep from delving too deeply into my memories of Annie and the sixties and what she and JC had meant to each other. And to keep from worrying about who was living behind Alec Truman's face . . .

The rain from Zurich had followed us to London, only it had turned to hot water on the way, and it made for a nasty, sweaty business. It was too much like New York had been at the start of all this madness. I looked through the soupy rain at the house, which wore its exterior like a face of undeniable, unassailable propriety. Solemn and old and self-assured with a staff of two or three and a Daimler and a Bentley tucked away at a discreet distance. I was waiting for Annie DeWinter because I simply couldn't call her and give her the chance to tell me once again to leave her out of it. I had to see her and I couldn't take no for an answer. I had to take her by surprise. And I had to do it alone. So Heidi Dillinger had gone off on business of her own. And I waited, worrying about Alec Truman and trying not to remember everything about Annie, all about Annie . . .

Heidi was the one doing all the thinking, and I kept turning her theories over and over in my mind, wondering how close she was coming to the truth. She was convinced that her latest brainstorm was smack on the money: namely that JC had outfoxed the world by turning into Alec Truman and returning to the love of his life, Annie DeWinter, to live more or less happily for the rest of their lives. His anonymity was the foundation of his existence and he would do anything to protect it.

Sally Feinman, she reasoned, must have somehow discovered the truth about Alec Truman and had one way or another confronted him with it. JC, knowing Fleury from the old days at Magna, had years ago engaged the dumpy, damp detective to guard his Truman identity, whatever it involved. Consequently Fleury had killed Sally after attempting to extract whatever information he could regarding whomever else she might have told. Similarly Clive Taillor became a threat and had to be silenced: when Fleury found out who had been depositing all that money in Taillor's bank account over the years, Heidi was sure it would turn out to be Alec Truman, probably by way of one of his companies. She was less sure why Shadow Flicker had been killed in Los Angeles—but it may have had something to do with drugs; how or why, she didn't know. Maybe . . . maybe his murder was a wild track, unrelated to JC.

In any case, Fleury is killing anyone who is a danger, her reasoning went, and with each killing the trail back to Truman was growing colder. But there was still one major threat, which was, of course, me. Her contention was that Fleury had hired the man or men to kill me in Zurich, which would explain his arrival on the scene. He hadn't found what he'd expected and his nerve had failed when it came to killing me himself.

It was all bullshit, I was convinced of that, but the story nevertheless had a dampening effect on my overall frame of mind. She was quick to point out that Fleury had disappeared again. What was he doing? Checking the bank records? Why? If he was working for Truman and Truman was JC, then Fleury would know perfectly well he'd been paying Taillor. And why torture someone if all you had to do was kill him? Which were only two of the flaws in Heidi's theory, as I pointed out to her. She observed that she'd never said the theory was perfect but rather a hell of a good start on the truth. Fleury was the villain. That, she informed me impatiently, was the point. Fleury was Death in a cruddy old seersucker suit.

193

I told her she was crazy. JC died twenty years ago.

She'd lost it for a moment just then. JC was the MacGuffin, she said—or maguffin, whatever it was—how could I be too stupid to see that? Alive, dead, it made no difference. He was the reason people were getting killed. He had no importance beyond that.

I asked her what happened to the big blackmail plot?

She just stared at me, angry, refusing to admit that she'd forgotten that JC and the blackmail thing had somehow merged, one becoming hopelessly entangled with the other. Finally she shut up, at least for the moment.

Twenty years ago. It could have been twenty minutes.

She came out of the front door, stood on the step looking at the rain on the trees while she fastened one of the buttons on the pale pink duster she wore. She stood with her feet apart, the long coat swirling in a gust of wind, the stance of a gunfighter in one of the spaghetti Westerns Sergio Leone had been making twenty years ago. Then she pulled a crafty little pink rain hat from her pocket and pulled it down on the familiar jet-black hair. Her long oval face with the high cheekbones and just the suggestion of squareness in the jaw seemed from across the street quite unchanged. I didn't know whether I was delighted or frightened, then reason told me she was of course changed, twenty years' worth. But standing on the step in her long, blowing pink coat and girlish, adorable little pink hat she might have been striking a pose for David Bailey or Skrebneski or Avedon, one of the men who had effectively immortalized her with their Hasselblads or Brownies or whatever.

Twenty years, and now it occurred to me that I remembered Annie herself less and the photographs of her more. One stuck in my mind, a huge head shot, an enormously wide smile that crinkled her eyes, the black bangs in dagger points across the fine pale forehead, her right arm up and the long forearm laid across the top of her head, a silly, funny moment of startling, utterly fresh, blinding beauty. I'd seen her do it a thousand times, but it was the photograph I remembered; still I heard her laughter, smelled her perfume and the shampoo in her

194

hair. Surely it all goes to show you something or other about how the time slips away, how it affects us all.

She pushed her hands into the pockets of her duster, and in her high black wellies, like a schoolgirl, she set off in the rain, her long legs kicking through the puddles. Twenty years. My God, how the time slips away.

I got out of the Rover and traipsed along behind her, from Hans Place out to Sloane Street, across Pont Street and along Cadogan Gardens, neither fast nor slow, as if she were out for a bit of exercise. She crossed back to the other side of Sloane Street and checked out some shop windows, nipped into the General Trading Company, where she moved among the Sloane Rangers and appeared on the street again with a parcel. How the hell was I going to pull this off? What exactly was I going to say? *Hi, luv . . . what you been up to these past twenty years? Give us a kiss and fill me in . . .*

She walked down to Sloane Square, crossed to the center, then crossed to the King's Road side and went into the W. H. Smith bookstore. I stood at the edge of Sloane Gardens, where I'd once had a girlfriend, and waited for her to come out. Fifteen minutes passed, then she reappeared with a bagful of books, newspapers, and magazines. She was coming toward me, had me in her sights, I thought, but no, I was mistaken. She walked by me, crossed past the tube station, stood for a moment looking at the poster at the Royal Court Theater, then turned the corner, where I watched her proceed toward an old, old pub. She went in just as thunder slapped and cracked over the Square.

That left it up to me. Really I had no choice. It was too late to worry about not having come up with a good opening or, for that matter, any real plan for how I would proceed once I was inside the outer ring of defenses.

She was sitting by herself in a booth under a leaded window depicting a large black raven perched on a tree stump. The pub, of course, was The Raven and Stump. The sound of a couple of video games boinging away on the other side of the partition clashed with the quiet, the rumble of thunder, the ancient polished wood. She was looking at the French *Vogue*, a pint and a plate of shepherd's pie steaming next to the magazine. I went to the bar, got a pint of Courage and sipped it past the foam, watching her.

Finally it was time.

She didn't look up when I went to stand by the table. She must have been lost in thought.

"Well, Annie girl," I said. My hands were shaking and I hoped the tremor didn't reach my voice.

She didn't look up for a moment but her head went rigid, her hand stopped turning the page, hung suspended in midair. "Well, I know that voice," she said. She closed the magazine. *Zap, zap, buzzz, boinggg* . . . The video game was going crazy. "Yes, I do know that voice."

"Yes, you do."

She sighed. I could almost see my reflection in the shine of her hair, smooth as ebony. "Is it really you?" She hadn't brought herself to the point of looking up yet. "What a long time . . ." Finally she looked at me. I watched her eyes tighten for a moment and then begin to search my face. I waited, like a man with a blind woman's fingertips tapping out a code on his mouth, nose, and cheekbones. "You've changed," she said softly.

"You wouldn't kid me, would you? That was the point, wasn't it? If you stayed the same after twenty years, what was the point of having lived?"

"Oh, it's you, without a doubt. But I have to tell you, I haven't really missed the corny philosophy."

"If it ain't corny, my dear, it ain't philosophy. And it wasn't quite so corny the last time I saw you."

"Times have changed, haven't they? Sit down, Trip."

Her eyes were huge and shiny and black, her face was as lean and sculpted as ever, and as a great writer once said, she was so beautiful you wanted to hit her with a hammer. That beautiful. But I didn't want to spoil it. Her face was still pale, almost unlined. Pure genetics. The black hair across the wide fore-head, then cut short at the sides and on the nape of her neck, flaring at the back of her head. Dark magenta mouth about as wide as the old Turnbury Road, eyebrows straight and black as charcoal. She wore a long black T-shirt and a very short pink skirt. The T-shirt ended low on her flat belly, just where the pleats of the skirt began, but I couldn't see that at the table. That was my memory of her walking in the rain, the duster furling in the hot wind.

"You're here at last. It's funny . . . I've always known you'd turn up one day."

"I thought I might surprise you."

"Oh, not you. You could never surprise me. I've definitely been expecting you—"

"What are you saying? You *knew* I was coming?" I wasn't getting it.

"Telltale paranoia is showing, Trip. Maybe you've only changed on the outside."

"Maybe I'm not the man you remember so well—"

"You are, amigo. Same old Trip. Twenty years, almost every day I've been on the lookout, half expecting you to come wandering into the picture not quite sure of what was going on. You're like a time traveler. Two decades out of date. Just like your brother. You were always sort of inevitable, Trip. An inevitable bastard. An absolute charlie you always were, weren't you?" She reached out and touched my face. "Now you're here, what—oh, what—are we going to do with you?"

She looked very solemn and that was the Annie I remembered, not a picture, but the real woman. A solemn expression, as if she took everything very seriously. She slowly shook her head at me. When she did, her earrings swung and I recognized them. They were twenty years old. JC had given them to her one night in New York after a recording session that broke up at four in the morning. We came out of that great old studio in what had once been a church on Thirtieth between Second and Third, we came out and piled into one of the big Caddy limos and wound up at a joint in Harlem. At about seven we were back in the street looking for a place to have breakfast, JC and the Traveling Executioner's Band, and it was about fifteen degrees with a lashing wind and it was desolate and blasted and empty with newspapers and crap blowing in the gutters. A little newsstand was just opening up and there was a fire in a trash basket, flames blowing away in shreds and tatters. And there was, honest to God, a gum-ball machine next to a rack of newspapers.

197

JC started popping nickels into the slot, bubble gum for everybody. Bubble gum and dumb little prizes, little plastic doodads, rings and cars and dice and monkeys . . . and these two little black plastic pistols. A perfect little Luger and a perfect little Smith & Wesson .38, each about an inch or so in length. Annie was dressed all in black and white; she used to say she wasn't a technicolor person. She loved the little guns but JC wouldn't give them to her. Later that day he went to a goldsmith down in the village who made 24-karat studs and turned them into earrings. JC always said he wanted to sleep with a woman carrying a gun. That night he told Annie DeWinter for the first time that he loved her.

They'd lasted a long time, those earrings.

"I almost didn't recognize you," she said, her huge eyes staring into mine, the long lashes beating slowly.

I nodded. What was there to say?

"Did you come back for me, Trip?"

"Ah, Annie . . . never one to beat about the bush. That's awfully sixties, I must say. We live in a new age of prevarication . . . lies—"

"I don't, Trip. You do, I guess, not me."

"I'm sure you're right, Annie."

"Be straight with me. Did you come back for me?"

"Jesus, Annie. Are *we* time travelers?"

"You are. I know that. Did you come back for me?"

"I don't know—you're not alone—"

"Does that sort of thing stand in your way these days?"

"Go easy, cowboy. Smile when you say that . . . I just got here. And you're the one with someone in your life—"

Her lower lip jutted out, gave her a rakish, determined look. She was forty-five. I didn't quite understand how that could be. "That didn't stop you." Her gaze softened and she patted my hand again. "What's on your mind? I'll try to do this your way. You were always into artifice. Illusions. I was never good at that. Arabesques, that was you. Complexity for its own sake." She looked down, then took a swallow of beer. "What's on your mind, Trip?"

"A lot of people are looking for JC," I said.

"Ah."

"And I'm one of them."

She laughed at that. Then she said, "Come on, let's get out and go for a walk." She caught my eye. "And you're one of them. That's grand, Trip, really grand."

The pigeons flew up in force, nervously, as the afternoon thunder cracked loudly. The crowds were tourist-thick, but we moved through them and headed off down the King's Road past the Duke of Yorks, then began angling off to the left toward the Chelsea Embankment. The rain fell steadily but it was light, more sound effects than torrents. We mooched along the way we used to when we were young. Our concerns, however, were very different now. I sketched out the situation for her but left out the scary parts. Scaring her wasn't the point. I wanted her kept out of it. It should never have touched her at all, for either of our sakes. The least I could do now was control it, move on. But Heidi had seen the picture of Alec Truman and we had to deal with it.

"So you and Truman live in London and life is good."

"And there's my nephew Chris. He's here off and on. He's not actually my nephew. My cousin and his wife were killed in a car crash years and years ago. Chris is their boy."

"But you and Truman were never married?"

"Oh, what was the point? It's not really that kind of relationship."

"But you're together."

"I suppose we each needed someone to anchor our lives. We met at the right time. It's been convenient . . . companionable. We stay very much to ourselves. I'm a London person and Alec is in the country much of the time and he travels a great deal. He's . . . dependable."

"Meaning?"

"Look, I went into a kind of prolonged shock twenty years ago. After Tangier." She looked up at me from under the little pink cap.

"I know," I said. "I really do know."

"JC was gone . . . I wasn't really surprised, he'd been slipping away from me, into his his own world, for quite a while. And then suddenly he was gone. I wasn't surprised, but that didn't make it any easier. He had turned me—nurtured me, really—from girlhood into womanhood. Does that sound too sappy? Well, it's true. A very sheltered girl is what I was. I was a model, but I was still living an English girlhood with my mother . . . JC was the first man in my life, and for a while he was so gentle—well, no point in going on about that. But then things began to go wrong, didn't they? I went to bed at night not knowing where he was, who he was with, if he'd come back to me at all—I was so afraid someone would show up to tell me he was dead . . ." Her voice was quavering, she bit back tears. "Then he was gone. I wanted to hide . . ."

"I can relate to that."

"I daresay."

We'd walked a long way and stood above Cadogan Pier, staring down at the Thames dimpling in the rain. Sad dirty tugs and barges made slow headway beneath the low gray clouds.

"So Alec Truman came along and he wanted to take care of me and I thought about it. He was . . . he reminded me of JC somehow. Minus the craziness and excesses that came later. Who came along to take care of you?"

"No one. Whatever else it is, life is a bit easier if you're on your own. And on the run, as I was."

"On the run," she echoed me. "From what exactly?"

"It's way too complicated to explain, Annie. Believe me."

We walked along the Chelsea Embankment for a long time but time didn't seem to figure in it. She was for me the incarnation of the happiest, saddest, most vivid time of my life. I wanted to hold on to her as an aging warrior might clutch a fallen talisman and believe it will return to him his youth, his strength. It seemed to transcend reality and logic as if it were a thousand times more powerful than either.

I knew she kept looking at me from the corner of her eye, much as Sasser had done in Tangier, as if I were somehow not what she expected. I knew what it was. She couldn't help it. She looked at me and she saw JC and she couldn't quite believe it. She knew JC had decided to end it all when she'd left Tangier. He'd known she wasn't coming back. She couldn't take any-more. So he had to do something. The only life he'd ever known was coming to an end. She was right, he'd been an absolute charlie, but she knew he'd loved her and she knew it was her leaving that had pushed him off the edge. He hadn't slammed his iron door against her. It had been just the other way around.

We'd passed the Royal Hospital and turned left on Chelsea Bridge Road and were walking slowly along the Ranelagh Gardens, the rain pattering on the leaves, cars with lights snapped on sliding through puddles.

"Look, this is going to sound crazy," I said, "but bear with me. Some of my associates—and they are very, very serious people—would like a word with Alec Truman. It was felt that an approach through you might be more effective . . ."

She stopped and looked out over the gardens. "You mean that's why you came here and found me?" Her voice was very quiet and strung tight as a wire. "You didn't come to see me? I just want to make sure I'm following you—this wasn't *personal*?"

"Of course it was personal. How could anything to do with you not be personal? All that matters to me in this is seeing you . . . I didn't truly realize that until I saw you standing on your front step. But I grant you, I should have known all along. I've no excuses. None, Annie. I've waited too long to come see you—"

"Enough. You *do* go on so. What do you and your associates want to see Alec about?"

"They think he's JC."

She stared at me with her mouth open, a look of real puzzlement played on her features.

I laughed a trifle self-consciously.

Then she put her arm through mine. "You never do change, do you? Always into mischief, Trip! But this one actually does take the cake . . ."

Eighteen

When I got back to the flat in Draycott Place I wasn't ready for what I found.

Heidi was sitting on the couch with one arm resting on the back, her other hand holding what was clearly a martini. She looked like an advertisement for expensive gin and the inevitably sophisticated life that could be yours if only you drank enough of the stuff. Her eyes followed me but her lips were tightly compressed. She wasn't saying anything and I knew this was going to be bad, whatever it was. What it was, however, took me entirely by surprise.

"You fucked her, didn't you?"

The remark, half question, half rhetorical statement, was particularly ugly, far beyond the five actual words. Ugly, uncalled-for, vicious, disrespectful of Annie, and me, and in a way herself.

She'd made the mistake of timing on two entirely different levels. First, she caught me when I was feeling everything from the past overwhelm me because of Annie, when I was in a sense suffering a crisis of morality, a questioning of what I had done with my life. Second, she should have waited until I'd sunk down into one of the deep chairs. On my feet it was easy to get to her.

I took two steps and slapped that perfect lovely face just about as hard as I could with my opened right hand. Contrary to kung-fu movies, it made very little sound. Her head snapped around, the point of a canine incisor bit into her lip, blood spurted from her nose, she fell sideways against the arm of the couch, and the perfect martini in its crystal container shattered against the wall. The stain on the wallpaper looked like Bolivia. The olive bounced off down the hallway, and Heidi slid off the couch to a sitting position on the Axminster.

I stared down at her, not for an instant regretting having hit her. It crossed my mind to let her have it again, this from a man who'd never dreamed of striking a woman before. Well, dreamed, maybe. But I'd never done it. She seemed to have learned the drift of my mood. She looked up, cringing slightly, just in case.

"You really do piss me off sometimes," I said. "Wipe your face." I stood in the kitchen alcove and threw her a hand towel. "The scary part is I don't regret hitting you. It's important that you know that."

She dabbed at her bloody nose. "My lip is cut."

"We're both lucky I didn't break your neck."

"Two people you'd have killed in three days. Enough to make a man want to stand up and pound his chest."

"Heidi, Heidi . . . don't push it."

"You did, didn't you—you went to bed with her, didn't you?" She was still sitting on the floor, holding the towel to her nose, feeling her lip with her tongue. "Could you possibly make me another martini? Without throwing it at me?"

"No, I didn't sleep with her." I was already pouring the Bombay Sapphire into the pitcher, splashing vermouth, stirring ice cubes. She sat on the floor, watching me. She wasn't doing a big number about my hitting her. I was shaking like a leaf, adrenaline spurting, and she just suffered the consequences of her performance and got on with it. You had to hand it to Heidi. No quarter given, none asked. Very rare attitude in women, in my experience. Willing to take her medicine, pay the price.

"Two olives, please. You're lying. It's your nature, you can't help it. Maybe I forgive you." She took the martini. "You need one yourself. Not even I—and I definitely have your number, Lee—not even I think you habitually beat up on women. Or even enjoy it."

"How generous," I said.

"But you did sleep with her. No, you fucked her—"

"*What* is the matter with you? What if I did? I didn't, I haven't seen her in twenty years, I didn't take her to bed—but what if I had?"

"Think of it, though, Lee—your brother is finally out of the way! Now's your chance. Make the most of it!" She didn't sound quite right. She was trying to mask something. Hysteria. She sounded like a woman betrayed, wronged, scorned. She sounded like a wronged wife. She'd mentioned it, when she told me about hearing me in the night, saying Annie's name in my sleep. She'd said she'd felt like a wife.

"Listen, Heidi, why don't you drink your drink and think what you're saying—"

"I've thought about it a lot." She was holding a book I hadn't noticed, an old book with a faded, tattered dust jacket. "I've thought about you, trying to get a line on you. It's just that you're not only a liar and a scoundrel and a bastard—"

"Well, that's a relief."

"—but you're such a hopeless anachronism . . . you've been on auto pilot since the sixties, you never did get over the sixties, did you? Something happened to you twenty years ago, your brother died but something went out of you too, something like life. There's an aura about you, Lee. You just don't give a damn, you just couldn't care less, you came to a halt when your brother died, when the sixties died, it's as if you somehow became someone else, insulated, self-protective, so much more remote than I am, like a dead star—you have no idea how involved in all this I am, no idea. In your soul you're still a Carnaby-Street type, Peter Max, *The Yellow Submarine,* and your poor tired old soul still wears flowered shirts and bell-bottoms. That's why I don't believe you about Annie DeWinter. She's a relic and so are you, two fossils of a lost age. The sixties might as well be the Paleolithic and you might as well be a pair of museum pieces—

it's gone and the relics are just waiting it out, waiting for the end—"

"Where are you getting all this? Why, I haven't worn my bell-bottoms in ages—"

"And all you can do is make a stupid joke. It's pathetic, I don't know why I love you!"

"Beats me, too. Let's call it perversity." Good God, now it was in the open. *Love.*

"Did she put on her old Courrèges boots? The Mary Quant mini? Does she look the same? I'll bet she does—it was her time, she'll never change, she's stuck with being a symbol—"

"Well, if it works for you, stick with it, that's what I always say." I was holding my temper in check. "Her look was better than my bell-bottoms and shoulder-length hair—I was a bit of a mess. Annie, though . . ."

"Yes?"

"She was as beautiful as anything I've ever seen. Right there with Julie Christie and Jean Shrimpton—"

"Oh, please!"

"You're right. What difference does it make?"

She opened the book to a marker and began to read aloud.

"Valerie Kipp was the girl of the moment and she had something you couldn't define, no more than you could define what you felt when you heard and saw Joe Cocker or Bob Dylan. Valerie had a way of happening to you. If she came into your orbit there was no avoiding her. Max Beerbohm would have understood. Valerie was a sister to Zuleika. She was everywhere, in every magazine and on half the billboards in London. Piccadilly, Hammersmith, the West End and Birdcage Walk and Sloane Square and Golders Green, and flying kites on Hampstead Heath and stoned out of her mind in a punt on the River Cam. Walk down Regent Street or survey the crowds in Oxford Circle or have a look at the girls on the Left Bank or Greenwich Village or Rodeo Drive or the Via Veneto and you would see a million Valeries, everywhere you looked. Gawky, big-eyed, openmouthed.

205

But those girls—all they know of Valerie, our Valerie Kipp, is on their faces. Kippy, we called her, and to do a Kip wasn't very nice. She couldn't know a man without seducing him, and when it came to girls it was all the same to our Kippy. But it wasn't sex as others knew sex. All of Valerie's sex was with herself because she was Lilith. It was her own image that she loved, the reflection of herself that she saw in the eyes and rapt faces of others, in their ejaculations and orgasms she saw her power, her own obsessions. We all thought she would die soon, never make it to thirty. She was consuming herself and others, greedily, and they were all victims of her narcissism. The question we asked ourselves was simply this: Was she worth it, worth destroying yourself? She was infinitely desirable, every gesture, every expression, each carefully guarded syllable—guarded as if she actually had something to say. She was the kind of woman who made you give up whatever you had, say the hell with everything, the future and your hope and all the rest of it, if you could get your hands on her, get within her body and feel what it was like before there was the blinding flash and empty void of darkness that sooner or later was bound to follow and envelop you and destroy you."

She closed the book, placed it on the end table and took a slow sip from her martini.

I said, "Have you got this Valerie's phone number?"

"Such an asshole," she said. "You are doomed."

"Just a joke, for God's sake." I sighed. "All right, I'll bite. What was that all about?"

"Austin Gilbert's novel, published in 1971. It was called *Gone Glimmering*. You probably weren't reading much in those days, but it's one of the first cult classics about those years. I don't know if it was even published in the United States. It was what is called a *roman à clef*, all the characters were based closely on real people—"

"No kidding? I always wondered what that meant . . .

sounds to me like Austin Gilbert ought to take two aspirin and have a nap."

"What I just read you was Gilbert's description of Annie DeWinter. Several newspapers published reader's keys to the novel, so you'd know who was who. Annie was Valerie Kippy. So, tell me, Lee, does she make you want to say the hell with everything else?" She dabbed at the dried trickle of blood beneath her nose. "Well, does she?"

"You want the truth?"

"Damn stupid question."

"Frankly, all the way back there I kept looking for a bus to run in front of for the sheer love of her. Why, I got to thinking about that blinding flash—"

"You are a cold shit, aren't you?"

"Heidi, relax, for Christ's sake."

"Tell me, did your brother treat her the way you treat me?"

"Talk about damn stupid questions."

"Why?"

"Because JC *loved* her. You and I barely know each other. I'm discovering I don't know you at all."

She threw the book at me, caught me on the side of the head. It bounced off, lay facedown on the floor.

Heidi and I made a lovely couple. We were both crazy.

Heidi had in her peculiar way discovered where Alec Truman was. He was, in fact, where he spent most of his time: sequestered away in the country, in the Cotswolds, not far from a village called Gurney Slade. She had fixed it on one of those incredibly detailed English maps which show you damn near every bush and twig. Ordnance Survey Maps, I think they call them.

"What did you tell her?"

"I told her I had associates who thought Alec Truman might be JC."

"What did she say?"

"When she stopped laughing she said she thought that was 'grand.' She told me she didn't know where he was—thought maybe he was out of the country. She didn't seem terribly involved in his daily life."

"Laughed, did she? Well, I intend to put her sense of humor to the test."

"The fellow who wrote the book obviously never met her, knew nothing about her. She has a lovely sense of humor."

"I'll bet. We'll go to Bath by train," she said, choosing not to fight it out, "and there'll be a car waiting for us. Then we'll go take your dear cuckolded brother by surprise. You'll look him in the eye. It will be what can only be described as a moment to remember."

"You're quite wrong. Alec Truman is neither my brother nor a cuckold—"

"I prefer to use Austin Gilbert as my authority, thank you. He is certainly a cuckold. Be honest, Lee. You had her twenty years ago, didn't you? When she was his girl—"

"Your dignity, once so impressive, is only a faded memory, my dear girl." It drove her crazy when I kept smiling at her. I think she preferred me in a mood to swat her one.

"I have to go see Allan's agent. Now you can go dashing off to screw your brother's girlfriend."

"Lucky me," I said.

"But don't tell her about the plan. You do understand that, don't you? Alec Truman must not be warned. Agreed?"

"Of course." She was standing by the door to the flat. We'd spent one night in London, after I'd seen Annie and we'd fought about her, and now she, Heidi, looked weary, as if she hadn't slept. "Why are you crying?"

"I'd sell my mother for a chess computer right now!" She sighed, then looked up. "You call this crying?"

Then she slammed out of the room, the door reverberating in its frame.

Twenty-four hours after seeing Annie come out of the door in her long pink duster I was back in Hans Place with the sun pouring gold across the wet rooftops, gilding the slick street. It was cool and cleansing and I'd been trying to decide what to say when I got there, when I saw her again. Maybe I just wanted to see her face and hear her voice and make sure I hadn't dreamed yesterday. But I also wanted to let her know about Heidi's surprise for Alec Truman. Annie could decide what to do about it. If she wanted to warn him it was fine with me. If she figured he could handle it on his own, that was all right too. I wanted to see Annie and I wanted her to trust me as she once had. That was all I cared about just then. The hell with everything else.

I stood on the front step in the quiet that cloaked Hans Place and rang the bell and waited. I felt like a kid on his first date. It was absurd. I thought about the novel *Gone Glimmering*. Had she ever been anything like that? I didn't think so, but what the hell did I know? I'd been pretty weird myself in those days, wrapped up in the old self. Another head case, one of so many.

The door was opened by a tall gray-haired woman with a long nose and her glasses on a chain hanging halfway down her cardigan. She regarded me neutrally. "Yes?"

I told her who I was. "Could you tell Miss DeWinter that Trip would like to see her, please?"

"I'm sorry. Miss DeWinter is not in London at present."

"But I saw her yesterday—"

"Yes, but she has left the city."

"Ah, off to Gurney Slade?"

"No, I'm sure not."

"Listen, it is important, Miss . . ."

"I am Willis, Mr. Tripper."

"Well, Willis, do you know where I might reach her?"

"This is not possible, I fear. She has gone north to see Mr. Christopher—"

"Mr. Christopher?"

"Her nephew. Mr. Christopher DeWinter. She has gone north."

"You don't know where?"

"I really cannot say, sir. Scotland, you see. Scotland has always been a bit of an abyss as far as I'm concerned." She smiled thinly. "It might as well be . . . oh, Tasmania. But if she calls as she sometimes does, I will be pleased to tell her that you called."

"When might she return?"

"She did not say. Tomorrow—or a month hence."

I stood alone in the street. It was so empty, so perfect, it might have been a movie set. I imagined I felt eyes on me, eyes behind windows gleaming gold in the sun.

I'd never been to Scotland, although I'd once been very close to a Scot. MacDonald Gordon by name, known to the world as Thumper.

Nineteen

The country road was the standard British narrow, wide enough for a vehicle-and-a-half, with a little grassy ditch on either side, then solid hedgerows high as a semitrailer truck. It—the road—was also made up of twenty-yard straightaways and seventy-five-yard corners around which there was no hope whatsoever of seeing. Every car or truck coming toward you was a complete, shit-inducing surprise, rather like all the very worst aspects of a heart attack. Such were my reflections as we struggled up a hill toward the glowing ball of sun that seemed to rest atop the hedges. A dark green lorry bolted into view, inevitably in the middle of the road, swerving and nearly toppling over as it negotiated the bend in the road, all about a foot and a half in front of us. I only had time to clamp my eyes shut and tell God I hadn't really meant any harm, at least not most of the time.

Heidi Dillinger calmly shifted down, kept the English Ford under control as the wheels on my side slid into the little ditch. The hedge's branches poked at my face through the open window and then the lorry was gone on down the road toward the village and we were trundling on up the hill, blinded by the sun. It was nine o'clock in the evening and high summer. The sun had another couple of hours to go before dark. But we were less than ten minutes from Alec Truman's country house.

We had spent an hour at a country pub munching sausage rolls and drinking beer and wondering how to proceed with the plan, such as it was, while maintaining our uneasy truce. I'd lost track of Heidi's personality, the reality of her, and couldn't find it. Her face had an emotionally bruised look, her eyes were dimmed by crying. I doubted that she cared all that much for me, but was instead mourning her ego, which had to deal with failing to bring me to heel. My concern was more with my regret at having hit her. Thank God I hadn't broken either her nose or her jaw, let alone her neck. Her lip's puffiness was gone. And she didn't seem to hold it against me. She was no crybaby. She was something special, a high-stakes gambler. All or nothing.

She was switching her focus—which had gone curiously haywire when she'd gotten jealous, of all things—back to the problems at hand. Her job, first and foremost, was to find JC Tripper if he was still alive. That was why she and I had gone to work together in the first place. Magna's blackmail problems were something different *unless* JC had somehow slipped into that mire: then it was all part of the JC problem.

The JC Problem . . .

She was worried. I won't say she was scared exactly. But she was worried about Morris Fleury. She kept coming back to him when we spoke about the job and its problems. Where was he? Was he watching us? What had he discovered about Clive Taillor's financial benefactor? Wasn't that the key to it all— who'd been paying Taillor for twenty years?

There were so many possibilities. It was a challenge to keep them clear and distinct and she had regularly reiterated a further problem. She thought I was a liar. She thought I was withholding information. She thought I knew all about JC. And I kept telling her that she was quite right, that she had my number, that I knew he was dead.

* * *

212

I'd listened to her on the train ride to Bath and I listened to her in the pub. I listened to her on the subjects of JC and Fleury, Annie and Bechtol and Magna and Whitney, how she'd gotten into computers and information gathering and storage and stockpiling, how she'd worked her way into the lucrative association with Bechtol, Ledbetter, and the rest of them. I was listening, more or less, nodding at the crucial moments, but my mind was elsewhere, thinking about what she'd said about me and the sixties.

It was all true.

The pull of the past was overwhelming me. It was my own personal twilight zone. A time warp was swallowing me, and the aspect of the process that had caught my attention was that I was an active accomplice; I wanted the time warp to do its thing, I wanted to go back. I'd spent twenty years denying it, but now I let go, I knew I'd have sold my soul for eternity, in perpetuity and throughout the universe; I'd have done it in an instant for the chance to go back and live forever in those days. Those were the days, my friend, we thought they'd never end . . . But we were wrong, we'd fucked it all up, we'd grown older and the world had slid from our grasp . . . my God, how the time slipped away . . . The sixties, they were the best thing that had ever happened to me, and my eternal soul would have been a small price to pay to go back, to stay there, but to do a few things differently. I'd been more alive then than I'd ever been again, but things had all gone so wrong, so terribly wrong . . . Given another chance, a miracle, a trick of the light and the clock, a trick of some damn kind, and I'd be back and I'd make it turn out all right, all I wanted was a second chance . . .

I never said I was profound, that I wasn't shallow. But I possess some small degree of wisdom. It is the wise man who knows his proper place in time and space. I knew where I belonged.

The full impact of the realization—you might even call it an epiphany—was the most powerful thing that had happened to me in the twenty years since it all came tumbling down.

I had outlived my era. If I was lucky, luckier than I had any

213

right to be, there might still be one way back. If not, I would forever be a stranger, an emissary from a lost world.

We left the car pulled off the road, blocking what looked to be a farmer's seldom-used gate. We were a few minutes' walk from the driveway leading to the Cotswold stone farmhouse where Alec Truman was supposed to be in residence, if not actually receiving. We hugged the vine-covered stone wall edging the field and the road. In the distance, the sun casting long shadows across the wet, black, freshly plowed acreage, a lone farmer and his tractor attended to some night work. The silence was devastating, as if the croaking of insects were being cranked up and blown at us through amplifiers. No human sounds; everything else magnified. Even the hawks wheeling against the sky seemed on the verge of deafening us. Yet it was silent.

At the mouth of the gravel driveway we stopped and Heidi said we should try to get the lay of the land. Good thinking! But what did it mean? She thought it would be ideal if I could see him, study his appearance, before confronting him personally.

"You mean window-peeping? Jesus, Heidi."

"If the opportunity arises"—she shrugged—"why not? He doesn't seem to be very security-conscious." She looked up at the trees in search of hidden television cameras. At the other end of the driveway there were only ordinary residential coach lamps illuminating the forecourt. The house itself might once have been a working farmhouse, but in the latter stages of the twentieth century it was more of a manor house, with gabled roof, heavy timbering, two or three large chimneys topping off the pile of grayish-yellow Cotswold stone. "But we'll wait for a little more darkness."

The wall beside the driveway was thickly crusted with vines. I sank down and leaned back, feeling the dampness on the seat of my pants. I watched Heidi craning her neck to see up the driveway, across the field, cataloging the property. There were two barns in addition to the main house. The driveway was perhaps a hundred yards long. My back was itching. I ignored it, then felt a leaf brushing my neck. I twitched my head but the leaf couldn't take the hint. Finally I reached wearily around behind me and there was something behind me but it sure as hell wasn't a leaf. I let out a yelp and lifted off the ground, grabbing at my back. There were three or four slowly wriggling snails on my neck and shoulders, one inside my collar. Heidi thought it was very amusing. She plucked the snails from my shirt and carefully returned them to the wall. She pulled the vines away. The wall was alive, seething with snails, tens of thousands of snails oozing among the vines, leaving the stones slick, slippery. They weren't going to hurt anyone and God knows they were minding nobody's business but their own. Still, you don't need one inside your shirt. Mother Nature, that old scamp.

Two men in suits were waiting for us in the forecourt.

"Security," I said as they stood watching us approach. Their arms were crossed but their unsmiling faces said *We have guns.* "The old-fashioned way. With guards."

"Hardly the latest technology," she sniffed.

"May we assist you in any way?" Words came out of a small round hole in the beefier man's face.

"Need to see Alec," I said.

"And are you expected, guv'nor?"

"Let's just say she's going to cry and stamp her feet if she can't see him. Me, I couldn't care less. I'd just as soon go back down the lane and play with the snails."

"I like a bit o' cabaret, Henry," the smaller man said to his companion. He was smiling.

"You should see the snail races," the large one said. He grinned with the little round mouth. "Now there's a sight, guv'nor. What do you fink, Brian? Take 'em in or send 'em on their way?"

"Flip a coin, wot?"

"Very unprofessional," Heidi muttered.

I called the flip and won.

"You're not JC Tripper!"

"I do beg your pardon?"

"You have disappointed Miss Dillinger," I explained. "She may pout. Be on your guard."

"Oh, Lee, shut up." Heidi was unhappy and she was well past trying not to show it.

"I told you he wasn't going to turn out to be JC. I've told you a thousand times JC is dead."

"And I've told you a thousand times that your saying it doesn't make it true!"

"I say, this is all terribly droll, but I'm rather in the dark." Alec Truman was about the right height, his nose was too long, his ears stuck out, and he wasn't wearing his hair. The hair was a dead giveaway. Above the gray fringe over his ears he was Mr. Cueball. His head wasn't the right shape at all, much too long. His teeth were also too long, very equine. He looked as if he might bray at any moment but he never did. So much for the camera never lying. "You, Mr. Tripper," he said, ticking things off on his fingers to keep them straight, "are the late Mr. Tripper's brother. Thus, you are an old friend of Annie's. Dear Annie. I'm on the right track thus far, am I not?" I nodded. We were sitting in a book-lined study. Through the long windows the last of the sun was turning a narrow strip across the field a vivid scarlet, fading, diminishing as I watched. Alec Truman was wearing a dressing gown, Turnbull & Asser. His bare feet were encased in monogrammed slippers.

"What are those little things?" I pointed to the floor.

"Ah, *those*. Summer brings them like a tiny plague." They were moving, thick black spots on the carpet. "Dung beetles. One of many reasons why Annie pays only brief and very infrequent visits to our little country retreat. I, on the other hand, rise above them." He was very lean, very fit, and looked like a cabinet minister. "But one must wonder why on earth you should have thought I was the late . . . well, rock star. It seems on the face of it an unlikely assumption. And why in the world would you be looking for him? Which is to say, the entire world knows he's dead. Unless memory fails me, Annie showed me a book you wrote, Mr. Tripper, which proved that beyond any reasonable doubt. I do not understand. Could you, Miss Dillinger, find your way clear to enlighten me?"

Henry had brought us lemonade in a thick crockery pitcher. It was in desperate need of sugar. Presumably our host's idea of a nightcap.

Heidi, protecting our flanks, launched into a description of Magna business that made our travails sound like a model of innocence and business-as-usual. "There are," she said in an agonizingly calm voice, "those who believe that JC may be alive. Well, we have to make sure, don't we? Who better than his brother to lead a final expedition to once and for all set the record straight. You see, there are various film, book, and recording projects which are on temporary hold . . . awaiting final word on the JC situation—"

"There must be reasons," Truman said, "to believe JC is alive. Surely Annie will find all this quite riveting—she was a very impressionable young woman when she knew your brother, and you too, of course. It was a very long time ago. But I know her well and I believe JC left his mark on her forever. I don't mean a bad mark . . . I just mean she never quite got over him. Or wanted to, if it comes to that. One can hardly blame her, can one? I've often thought how large he must have loomed in her life." He sighed, staring either at the pattern in the carpet or the dung beetles. "But surely, if he were alive, he'd have been in touch with Annie—"

"Who knows? It's possible he has been," Heidi said.

"Ahhh." He frowned. "The thought never crossed my mind. But, of course, you're right. She needn't have told me."

"Well," I said, "we have to put the whole issue to rest."

"Yes, I quite see that. You're an interested party." He smiled slightly, rubbed his palm over his smooth, shiny cranium. "And I am, too." He was thinking aloud, very softly. "If she were to meet JC Tripper now· . . . well, who can predict the consequences?"

"I'm quite sure my brother has been dead these twenty years."

"Yes," he said abruptly, pulling himself back from the void of speculation. He was switching gears, trying to ease free of his thoughts and fears about Annie. "Yes, that's certainly the odds-on bet. Well, it all sounds a bit nonsensical, doesn't it? Comic opera. But you and your masters must know what you're doing."

"Not necessarily," I said. "It's a big assumption."

217

"Well, allow me one more assumption—I take it that Mr. Fleury is a colleague of yours, am I right?"

Heidi's bullshit and double-talk trailed off and turned into a puzzled silence. She looked from Truman to me as if I might have caught some hint she'd missed.

"No kidding? Old Morris is in on this one, too?" I did everything but smite my forehead in amusement over this happy occurrence. "Just goes to show you. Magna's so huge nowadays, the left hand never knows what the right is doing. Fleury's been on to you about this?" I shook my head, overdoing it. Next I'd be picking straw out of my hair. "What a character! Really a throwback." I felt like a graduate with honors from the Monty Python School for Village Idiots.

"Yes, the man's a corker! You've got him precisely—a character. But an interesting character, one must allow him that. And he talked rather a lot of sense once he got under full sail."

"Perhaps you could fill us in." Had Fleury finished with the bankers in Zurich? Did he know who'd been making all those payments to Clive Taillor? "When did Fleury make contact with you?"

He rubbed his long nose. "Week ago. The man had very good information. Knew where I was, called me from Gurney Slade, said he'd come all the way from Los Angeles—in short, his bona fides were all very much in order. And—let me be quite candid—I am always in the market for smallish investments. There are tax situations, there are losses and profits, there are cash positions which can be useful, there are stock arrangements—but that's all quite irrelevant to our discussion, I suppose. At least to you. But Mr. Fleury had an interesting proposition."

"He often does," I said.

"It was the film you mentioned, Miss Dillinger. The film about JC. He was offering me what amounted to a limited partnership—he knew about the production company I own here in the UK." He tossed that little gem off in the airy manner of the highly diversified plutocrat who can barely keep track of his affairs. "Film to be made here and he made it clear that it was my firm or it would go to Handmade Films and, frankly, Handmade is getting so many of the goodies these days, I reckoned this might be my turn. Magna could guarantee distribution worldwide, my exposure would amount to fifteen million and I could have another of my companies handling the completion bond. Frankly, I was intrigued. I gave him some first-stage encouragement and we spoke about a few details. He was having the screenplay sent to me—odd how they always believe the money people want to feel included on the creative side." He laughed quickly. "What do I know or care about screenplays? From what I gather, the more illiterate they are, the greater the chance of success, though I could be wrong. The last film I really liked was *The Man Who Would Be King*."

"What were some of the details?"

He shrugged. "He mentioned some involvement for Annie if she was interested and I told him I thought it would be wonderful for her but he might have a tough job convincing her. And, let's see . . . oh yes, Mr. Gordon, the drummer. Thumper Gordon. He was most interested in getting hold of him—said he was having the very devil of a time. Said the man had gone to ground. He said Mr. Gordon would be the perfect technical adviser. He said all the band members were scattered across the planet, selling real estate or cadging drinks in exchange for anecdotes about the old days . . . or just plain dead, drug overdoses and so on. No, Thumper Gordon was the only one who would do . . . He thought Annie or I might know his whereabouts—" He caught Heidi's eye and smiled at her intent expression.

"And?" She nodded at him to get on with it.

"Well, it was all utterly aboveboard, of course. Frankly, I *am* interested. It works for me in so many ways. So I told him that while I barely knew Thumper Gordon, he belongs to Annie's other life, her old life. Annie and I had once visited him on that island of his." He smiled, then yawned. It was getting late.

"Don't tell me he's still got that place in the Channel Islands— what was it, the Isle of Wight?" I visibly racked my brain. Thumper had never mentioned any island to me.

"Ah, that must have been in the days of your youth," Truman said, "days gone by. This island is way to hell and gone in the Outer Hebrides. My God, what a lonely, blasted, forgotten place!"

219

Twenty

"This is utterly unconscionable. My well-known mask of geniality is shattered." The voice of Hugo Ledbetter was heard in the land and one or two of the leaded casement windows were left intact. We were gathered at Magna's London headquarters, a penthouse in Greek Street overlooking Soho Square and the ceaseless bustle of Oxford Street beyond. As was his custom, Ledbetter was surveying the view, leaving the rest of us to survey several square miles of navy-blue chalk-stripe on his back. The sun shone brilliantly and London was in for what was for them a scorcher. "I must say, Cotter, this is an appalling situation. The man is running amok. He's gone bloody rogue is what he's done. Awful man." He coughed softly into his gigantic fist, then ran his fingers down through his beard as if lackadaisically searching for survivors. Maybe it was more like raking the rough at St. Andrews. He was a man who tested your mettle when it came to the apt simile. "Forgive me, I get terribly English over here, every other word turns out to be either 'bloody' or 'rum' or 'quite.' But mark my other words . . . I'll be damned if I'm putting my publishing house into the hands of people who find it impossible to control a nitwit like Morris Fleury."

"Now come on," Sam Innis said, "relax. Don't screw up a deal that's mutual 'on bofe sahds,' as my old colored nanny used to say."

"You never," Ledbetter rumbled, "had a nanny of any color whatsoever. The very idea is absurd."

Innis was slouched in a deep chair with his feet on a coffee table. He wore desert boots and what appeared to be a faded tan uniform from the North African Campaign. He was smoking a fat cigar. Heidi Dillinger was looking cool in gabardine slacks and a teal silk blouse and a flat-brimmed straw hat. She was leaning, arms crossed on her chest, against a glass-fronted bookcase. Cotter Whitney was sitting behind his desk, his cherubic face somewhat crestfallen, like a boy who'd been passed over for the cheerleading squad. He wore an immaculate white suit, a French-blue chambray shirt, a cream-colored tie. We were a curious lot and doomed to get even curiouser before we were done. It reminded me of a reunion of the hapless scoundrels last glimpsed in *Beat the Devil.*

"Well," Cotter Whitney said, twisting his University of Minnesota class ring around his finger, "I'm in the dark on all of this." He seemed poised to suck his thumb.

"That would seem to be the problem, wouldn't it?" Ledbetter stood at the edge of the desk and must have looked to Whitney rather like a displeased Jehovah contemplating payback. "You have this employee, this *insect,* running across the English countryside badgering a man the substance of Alec Truman, *lying* to him . . . and according to Miss Dillinger and Mr. Tripper, he has also indulged in a program of mass murder. The mind—*my* mind—reels, boggles, does nip-ups and falls in a heap." He turned to Innis. "We have a major problem here. The inmates are running the bin."

"Why don't you take a load off your feet, Hugo? You're forgetting the larger dimensions of our project. I want to do a book based on JC's life . . . and Magna *is* JC in a very real way. And besides, Lee here is into me, us, for a fair country piece of change—"

"This is a perfect example of your problem," Ledbetter said.

221

"You attempt to think. Writers should write, not think. I've told you that acting as your own agent is penny-wise and pound-foolish—you see, there I go, jabbering like a Brit! It is not the wisest path. You insist. Fine. But if you had an agent, he or she would tell you that your book—indeed, *you*—is equally as valuable to a dozen publishers without our having to put one foot inside this enchanting combination zoo-and-morgue Whitney is running."

"But I like him, Hugo. He's a spud, God knows, but I like him. I like Magna. Connecting with Magna is the beauty part of the project. You may recall that I am famed for my research—"

"You are famed," Heidi said coolly, "for my research."

"Don't quibble," Innis snapped. "Heidi is plugged into Magna. It works. That's the point." Whitney had decided to fill Ledbetter's place at the window. I went and stood beside him. I found myself looking down through someone else's skylight where a large woman in a white T-shirt and sweatpants was professionally kneading and massaging a naked woman who lay facedown on a table. Whitney turned to me as if he'd missed the show completely and said, "He's trying to raise money from Alec Truman? You have Truman's word on this?"

"Why would he make up such a story?"

"I suppose. Still . . . Fleury in his seersucker suit?" Disbelief trudged across his round face.

"Truman didn't actually comment on his tailoring."

Heidi Dillinger said impatiently, "To the point, is Magna actually interested in raising money from Alec Truman?"

"Good Lord, no! The thought is deranged."

"Well, Truman was interested," she said. "Fleury was offering the moon and the stars, of course."

"Well, I did not send him to Alec Truman, period. Magna has no interest in Truman. It would be like an interest in Kirk Kerkorian or Boone Pickens or Marvin Davis. One day you'd wake up and discover you'd been lunch. No, Fleury's off on his own. Perhaps he's lost his mind." He put his hands in his pockets and his round shoulders slumped.

"Did he find out who was putting the money in Taillor's bank account? He said you were going to have to exert some personal pressure on the big boys at your Swiss bank."

"I haven't the vaguest idea what you're talking about, old sock. Don't you understand, the man is acting on his own. Hugo is absolutely correct . . . could happen in any large corporation. Or small, for that matter." He turned to the bearded, shaggy-browed giant. "That's what you've got to understand, Hugo. There's no point in rushing to judgment. There are problems that can be fixed like any other problems—"

"Problems," Ledbetter muttered. "The man is a master of understatement. Murder is, indeed, my idea of a problem. We are in agreement." He plunged his hands into the pockets of his suit coat, straining the buttons. "Blackmail, rock music, drugs—"

"Now, Hugo!"

"Oh, stop fussing. It's a great steaming mess."

I said, "But seriously, folks, is it too late to just back out of the whole thing? Let bygones be bygones, we could all turn over a new leaf—"

"Yes, Tripper," Whitney said sadly, "it is too late. We're going to find your brother if he's still alive. And I know darned well he is—"

"Why," Ledbetter asked weightily, "is it we think JC Tripper is alive? I lose track of things."

Heidi said, "Because people who knew him very well are being murdered. Shadow Flicker, Sally Feinman, Clive Taillor. What they have in common is knowing our man intimately enough that they might know if he's alive. Sally didn't know him personally, but she'd done a great deal of digging into the subject . . . Yet Lee here, who knew him best of all, as only a brother can know a brother, hasn't been harmed, tortured, strong-armed, or even approached on the subject of JC's whereabouts—which could be for the simple reason that JC in his hideout, in his new life, doesn't wish Lee any harm."

"Hold on," I said. "I know my brother is dead, but I can't help wondering who sent the goons to kill me in Zurich?"

Whitney's head jerked up. "What goons in Zurich?"

"One was the goon I killed."

Whitney's mouth dropped open. "You *what?*"

"I killed a man who tried to kill me with a length of piano wire. I broke his back over a railing—"

"When? Who? Miss Dillinger—Heidi, I mean—what do you know of this? What's going on here?"

"In the dark. In the street. In Zurich. And he was a stranger."

"Good God!"

A bit of explanatory babble ensued before Heidi regained the floor with her explanation for Ledbetter of why we—they—thought JC might be alive. "We also have the song purportedly sent by Thumper Gordon. It could be old but it could be new—JC's way of getting back into the game. And there are the monthly payoffs to Taillor ever since JC's death. Taillor was in a position to know if JC had agreed to pay him for helping JC fake his death and start a new life . . . It adds up," she concluded, "but we don't quite know to what—"

"Tell me," I said, ever the searcher for truth, "are we looking for a killer or a blackmailer?"

Sam Innis said, "We're looking for JC Tripper." He stretched, as if rousing himself to eventual action that he was regretfully beginning to contemplate. "There's a trail to follow here, just like one of my books. It isn't hard to follow, my fellow morons. Thumper Gordon on his island. It's obvious. That's the one reason, the sole reason Fleury went through his fancy dress with Alec Truman . . . to find out where the hell Gordon was. Now he knows." Innis stood up, wearing his through-hell-and-high-water face. He was getting ready to go after both Stanley and Livingstone. "For all we know, Gordon's dead out there in the Hebrides and, depending on who Fleury's working for, JC is maybe safely out of our reach forever and having a good laugh with Fleury . . . or Fleury is his nemesis and may have tortured the truth out of him and now Fleury knows for his own reasons where JC is—"

"There are," I said, "other possibilities."

"None that really matters," Heidi said.

Sam Innis went on, "Who says JC isn't out there on the island with Thumper? In fact, nobody's seen Thumper for years—who says JC didn't *become* Thumper? We've got to climb on our horses and get going. Never let it be said Sam Innis doesn't want to be in at the kill!"

224

Twenty-One

I felt like one of the sadder specimens manning a Winslow Homer fishing boat in a high gale, dwarfed by waves that would have blotted out the sun had there been one, huddled in a ratty old slicker that came with the boat, blinded by wind-driven winter-cold rain blowing angrily, as if the North Atlantic had something very specific against Scotland and the Scots as a people. Somewhere up ahead, infrequently glimpsed through the fog, was a small nubbin of rock, gorse, and discomfort that as far as we knew had never been singled out as deserving a name. About a hundred and fifty yards separated the large Isle of Lewis from the boulder where Thumper Gordon lived his lonely existence. I mean, it had to be pretty lonely out there. That was the Outer Hebrides for you, last stop before you reached North America, which was a hell of a lot of water away.

I felt it coming again and got myself draped over the side of our little craft and threw up. This was not a good thing. This was a man out of his element was what it was. Heidi Dillinger sat in the back of the boat—aft? fore? stern? Could anyone possibly care? It was back near this hellacious noisy motor. She was clutching her huge leather shoulder bag as if it were a new baby. She wore an oilskin hat that matched her torn slicker; her blond hair was plastered across her forehead. Cotter Whitney crouched beside me, trying very hard not to notice what I kept doing over the side. I told him if any of it got on him, the rain and the sea pouring down on us would wash it right off. He may have been bailing too hard to take notice. He was looking pretty green around the gills himself, as if the power of suggestion might do him in.

Ledbetter seemed impervious to the weather or any attendant discomfort. He sat quiet and unmoving, arms folded across his chest. Thus, in a manner of speaking, must the great stones have been ferried to Salisbury Plain for the building of Stonehenge. Sam Innis, writer in residence and self-appointed captain, sat by the motor, steered our hapless, rented vessel, and inspired—at least in me—the absolute minimum of confidence.

The rain was everywhere, from every direction, like random machine-gun fire. Thick, pulpy fog shrouded both Lewis behind us and the lump toward which we were slowly making our way. It was awful. Up, slammed down, rammed sideways, shoved wildly upward, only to be half-drowned. It went on and on. We were out in the gap, in no-man's-land, suspended in the last minutes of the old world I'd created for myself twenty years ago. In the gap, waiting for it all to explode in my face. Once we reached Thumper Gordon's island, everything would change forever . . .

We had flown from London to Inverness, landing in a gathering fog that grabbed us as we slipped down out of a watery sun. The fog kept getting worse as we stood in the airport waiting room. In the end we got seats on the last plane out to Stornoway, the town on the Isle of Lewis in the Outer Hebrides. It was a two-engine job of great age and remembered dignity, one of those planes that would give a determined struggle before descending into the drink. The wind kept trying to blow us back to Inverness. We strained against our seat belts, and the smell of people being sick in little brown bags slowly filled the cabin. It was damp and cold and clammy. We kept nosing into the fog seeking holes, tunnels. It was, somebody said, a typical summer day in the north. The man sitting next to me said, "You've never known cold until you've spent a fine July day out on Loch Ness."

We landed like a load of coal in Stornoway, which was reputed to be a town but could barely be seen at all under the gray shroud. At an all-purpose garage we rented an old Dodge four-door from 1955 and a motorboat of an age that made a query impolite. Innis and I engaged the garageman in conversation about exactly where Thumper's island might be and got squared away with directions, landmarks, distances, where we might launch our little craft.

I drove and Innis navigated. He kept talking about how the three of us—JC, Innis, and yours truly—had once driven through fog and rain to the Cape, Provincetown, and I nodded. But I had no memory of such an event. This road wound and dipped through fields of peat that were in some places cut six or eight feet deep. You had the feeling you had landed on a vast chocolate cake with mint frosting and somebody was carving big chunks from it. Most folks used the peat to heat their homes and you could smell it, smoky, like single malt Scotch, a shot of which would have come in handy just then. . . .

We found the point described by the garageman and wrestled the boat down the rocky slope to the narrow gravel shingle. The wind roared off the sea and the rain screamed around us and I suggested that anybody with an ounce of sense would wait until the storm blew itself out. Sam Innis gave me a hard look and told me we weren't racing the storm, we were racing Morris Fleury. "It's *your* brother," he said accusingly.

"My brother," I said as carefully and distinctly as I could, "is dead."

The tiny island took shape in the fog, brown and green and gray and wet. There wasn't much time left now. It was almost over. I wondered what was about to happen. What if Fleury was on the island? Was he actually a killer? It seemed a strange idea, now that I thought about it in the last moment. Morris Fleury sitting sound asleep on my terrace in New York a thousand years ago didn't seem like a murderer . . . Still, he'd had a

227

gun. He'd known all about Sally Feinman, he'd been there. Well, you never knew. I suddenly wished I'd had a gun to bring with me now. My God, were we about to go to battle unarmed?

Suddenly the choppy, malevolent channel sea was hurling us toward the rock-strewn beach that was more accurately a gravel-and-stone-slab ledge. The wind cut like a frozen knife and our little boat seemed out of control now, pitching and jerking, thrusting nearer and nearer the rocks where it would surely be smashed to pieces. But at the last moment we slid between outcroppings of stone that jutted like bookends into the sea and gave cover from the wind. Sea foam sprayed us as we settled with a heavy bone-jarring crash on the gravelly ledge, but there was no splintering of wood, no outright destruction. Sam Innis sagged across the motor and tried to wipe the seawater out of his eyes. He looked spent. "Jesus and the horse he rode in on," he said, but I barely heard him. The waves crashed like cannon fire, artillery blasting away at the island.

There was a steep escarpment to negotiate and it was slippery, dark, and wet, with running water coursing down on us. The fog clung to the top of the rock face, but dogs were barking, welcoming us. We climbed the steps, which had long ago been hewn from the cliff. I helped Heidi, who was struggling with her bag. Ledbetter followed, then Whitney, Innis last.

Two hounds dashed back and forth, yapping, when we reached the top. I was out of breath, sweating hard. The rain slanted across the bleak landscape, but the early-evening sky was lightening a bit behind the fog and clouds. Or I was indulging in wishful thinking. When had I last been warm and dry and comfortable? I couldn't actually remember. It had been hot and humid the day I met Heidi, and it had been absolute hell ever since. My head was aching and hurt from the beating I'd given that wall in Tangier. Show me a fist and I could attack it with my nose every time.

There were a couple of falling-down stone huts from years ago, from the days of the crofters. The dogs were muddy and apparently perfectly delighted by our arrival. A brown, muddy trail lay ahead of us. Not far away it disappeared in the fog. But clearly there was nowhere else to go.

Ledbetter was leaning forward with his hands on his knees, trying to catch his breath. Whitney was petting one of the dogs. Innis was talking to Heidi. The wind and the waves were deafening. Whitney was watching the two of them while he fiddled with the dog. I finally set off up the track because there was no way to go back and forget the whole thing. I heard them fall in behind me.

No damn good was going to come of this.

Eventually something appeared before me.

It was a man coming out of the fog and all I could see was the shape. He wore a slouched fedora and a long trench coat with the collar turned up. The rain came relentlessly from the low gray clouds. It stung. He was cradling a shotgun in the crook of his arm. He was about the right size.

"Thumper," I called into the wind. The man waved his hand.

"Thumper," I called again. There was something I wanted to ask him I didn't want the others to hear.

Then he raised his face from behind the protective collar.

"Sorry to disappoint you, Tripper. Thumper is waiting back at the house."

I felt a long sigh escape me. It was all so inevitable.

It was goddamn Morris Fleury again.

Twenty-Two

Smoke rose from the farmhouse chimney and you could smell the distinctive burning peat as we approached. There were a couple of outbuildings, a generator to take care of what seemed to be extravagant electrical needs, a battered old truck that could only be used for hauling provisions brought over by boat. Morris Fleury wasn't really holding the gun on us. Our roles were not so clearly defined. He walked with Cotter Whitney, their heads bent against the wind as they talked. Employer and employee. But what, I wondered, was really going on?

As we reached the house the weather-beaten door creaked open and Thumper Gordon stood there looking at me. It had been twenty years since we'd last seen one another, but as he peered through thick glasses at me, the penny dropped, his face slowly broke into a broad smile behind a beard that was now all gray. He wore a heavy blue sweater and jeans faded and worn threadbare in spots. He stretched his arms out toward me, a welcoming elf, and I ran the last few steps, threw my arms around him. Tears mingled with the rain on my face. I couldn't help it. My God, how the time slips away.

We held each other at arm's length then, adding up the years, accounting for the changes. Slowly he winked at me. "Well, I'll be a monkey's uncle," he said. "I never thought I'd see you again."

"Oh, hell, I knew it was bound to happen, sometime, someplace."

"Well, it seems we've got ourselves a situation here." He looked at our bedraggled faces and shook his head. "Man with the gun calls the shots. Come on in, folks."

We were sitting at the kitchen table. The main floor of the two-story building was one big room. There were thousands of books and records, which must have been a laff riot to transport to the island, comfortable couches and chairs, a smoky fire of peat in the stone fireplace, several oil lamps—presumably in order to conserve electricity—heavy hooked rugs. The kitchen table was round and could have seated a dozen people and must have weighed two hundred pounds. Thumper had hot coffee and brandy and single malt Scotch at the ready as we all sank tiredly onto chairs at the table.

Once everybody was clear on who was who, Sam Innis bubbled over, slammed his fist down on the table, and let his frustration hang out. His thin voice was shaking with fatigue and anger.

"We've gone about as far as we can go on this one, fans. Three people have been killed—no, make that four, some asshole tried to kill Lee here in Zurich and I am exceedingly glad to report"—he was breathing hard, veins in his neck protruding—"that Lee punched his lights all the way out . . . I have spent a helluva lot of money, we've got people running all over hell's half-acre, we've got people blackmailing Magna—among them, you, Mr. Gordon—"

"Whoever you may be," Thumper said in his soft raspy voice, "I suggest you go off somewhere by yourself and shove it up your ass. I don't even know you, man, and I'm real tired of you." He smiled, ever the elf.

Only Morris Fleury had remained standing, leaning against a hutch containing plates, mugs, bowls, crystal. He'd shed the trench coat to reveal drooping corduroys, a ratty old cardigan, and he still held the double-barreled shotgun.

Sam Innis went on as if Thumper's comment hadn't registered at all. "Now I want to know the answer to the question that started the whole damn thing—we have no place else to look. Is Joseph Christian Tripper alive? Is he on this godforsaken shit pile of an island right now?" He was trembling, staring at Thumper Gordon.

Thumper grinned. "JC? You lookin' for JC? Well, sure, he's here. Of course. You don't mean to tell me you came all this way without bein' sure? What a bunch of intrepid guys. And one intrepid lady. I haven't had this many people out here at one time in an age. I came here . . . to get away from my fellow man."

Innis shouted in his comic reedy voice; "Alive, goddamn you! I mean is JC Tripper alive?—don't play games with us, my little friend. Whatever else we may be, we are desperate men indeed. We didn't come this far to play games—"

"Games?" Thumper looked at him contemptuously. "I'm not playing games. Yes, alive, of course. You think I've got him stuffed and standing in a corner for old times' sake? Yes, certainly, Joe—JC—he's alive, you great red-faced git."

Maybe it was so unexpected an exchange that we were all dumbstruck. I sure as hell couldn't think of anything to say. Everybody was staring at Thumper. The wind gusted outside and blew down the chimney, puffing peat smoke into the room, then sucked it back up.

I looked up and saw Fleury watching me. He alone didn't seem interested in what Thumper had said. Maybe he already knew the truth.

I broke the terrible silence. "Tell me, Fleury, did you ever find out who was paying Clive Taillor all these years?"

"Yes. I did, Mr. Tripper."

"And do you know where JC is?"

"Yes, I do." Fleury stared at me impassively.

"Do you actually know what's going on here?"

He gave me that gray-faced look, his hair plastered across his cement-colored skull, jowls wobbling. But he wasn't funny or pathetic anymore. "Yes, I do. That's why I'm the one with the gun. I have every intention of getting out of this room alive."

"Are you going to tell us, pal?" There was the sense of our breath, collectively held.

"That is exactly what I'm going to do, Mr. Tripper."

He managed to fill and light his corncob pipe, adding to the smoky fug the dread smell of the sweet cherries, without setting the gun down or having it go off and kill somebody. He didn't look like a dangerous man. He looked tired and sad and depressed but willing to see it through. He did, however, look like a man who was sorry he'd ever started whatever the hell he was up to. He kept licking his cement-colored lips with a matching gob of tongue. He made a sound, then cleared his throat as if he was still doubtful as to where to begin. He clearly wasn't accustomed to having such close attention paid to his each and every word.

"Well, lookee here, folks . . . mighty nice you could all drop by this way." He either coughed or laughed, impossible to tell. "I do know what's going on here. It wasn't easy to get it all straight, but, what the hell, I do this for a living. Never had one like this before, but, but . . ." He couldn't seem to think but what. "Anyways, forgive the blunderbuss, but my momma didn't raise no idiots, as they say. If anybody dies here—and I'm not saying anybody will, for sure—I damn sure don't want it to be me. So, remember the gun, it's all loaded and ready to blow pieces of you all the way back to Inverness—"

"Look," I said, "I hate to interrupt a man's threat, but frankly, the suspense is killing me."

"Right, right, I'll get on with it. Right you are . . . now"— puff, puff—"where the hell am I gonna start?" He looked around the table, face-to-face-to-face. "All began with Cotter Whitney here." He smiled moistly. "I'm Security Director of Magna, you all know that—well, if you go far enough up, you could say Mr. Whitney's my boss, one of my bosses. Freddie Rosen's another boss of mine. My bosses make jokes about me sometimes, hell, that don't bother me, I'm that kind of guy— people make jokes about me, always have. Well, that's okay. I use it. Somebody rates me low, underestimates me, fine, I use it. I may look kinda funny, my taste in clothes is not exactly Ralph

Lauren or somebody . . . but I am one tough old motherfuck, as they say.

"So Whitney knows when it's time to cut the crap, skip the jokes, and get down to cases. He knows when Fleury's the answer to his problems . . . so what, coupla months ago, Cotter calls me back to Minneapolis there, takes me for a walk around that swell house and yard of his and the fact is he was outta sorts." Cotter Whitney was staring at his hands, folded on the table before him. "And I sat Cotter down and listened to his story and first thing I told him was 'Cotter, don't get your hair in the butter' . . ."

"He did, too," Whitney murmured. "Don't get your hair in the butter. That was a new one on me." His fingers began interlocking, intertwining, unlocking.

"Cotter had problems. Somebody was beginning to put the fire to the feet, and Cotter, Rosen, some of the other top boys, they was beginning to scream like something was chewin' on 'em. Someone, maybe someone inside Magna, was setting out as a free-lance information broker . . . someone was building a series of dossiers tracing the big-time narcotics traffic that Magna had once been involved in—oh, starting way back in the fifties and early sixties, when rock hit, drugs hit, the two went together like lox and cream cheese. You know what an information broker is? A blackmailer, a spy . . . a very dangerous person. And in a deal like this one, a very smart person— someone starting something big and not wanting to blow it and willing to preserve it. What's involved? Money, power, the works."

Ledbetter said, "What did the blackmailer want?"

"Wouldn't say. Just kept letting us know how much he knew. Little dribs and drabs of very, very privileged information. That was the question, what the hell was he after? But he kept us in suspense . . . Now the men at the top who were deep in all that shit back then, they're all long gone from Magna . . . Roarke, Bernstein, D'Allessandro, Levitsky, all gone. All dead but D'Allessandro, who's got the Alzheimer's, thinks his dick is his old schnauzer Otto, keeps petting it and sticking it in the dog's dish—sad, sad—D'Ally was very well connected, y'know what I mean? But gone is not necessarily forgotten. What they did could make Magna look like something you step in, even today. The spotlight on Magna today might pick out a whole lotta zits . . . for instance, Cotter's daughter and the All-American Stryker kid; there's dope there, it's not big, but it's jail time anybody starts looking too close—"

"Enough," Whitney said. "Leave them out of it."

"Right. Enough. My master speaks. But the blackmailer wasn't done. He played the Murder Card. Subtle indications that he knew about a murder in Magna's past—a very *big* murder . . ." He nodded smugly.

"And how, pray tell, did he convey this?"

"Ah, Miss Dillinger—he really had the inside dope on that one. One word was all he had to send them. *Bellerophon.* A bit of Greek mythology. In this case it was a code name and our blackmailer knew it. The word arrived, Cotter called me, asked me if I knew anything about it—he knew, he'd known for years, and I knew some of it . . . which brings us to the fella who named it and saw to it that it was carried out. Fella by the name of Martin Bjorklund, nicest fella you'd ever wanta know. Pardon me, folks, but I mist up a little when I think of Marty Bjorklund—he died not long ago, six weeks. Marty—old son of a gun hired me at Magna twenty-five, thirty long years ago, taught me what the hell I was getting into . . .

"Well, I went looking for Marty when we got the Bellerophon notice. I was thinking about lookin' him up anyways, about the blackmail thing in general, but I'd lost track once he retired. Finally tracked him down up near Seattle, in a hospice, with his daughter living nearby. Four packs of Luckies a day for fifty years—well, I hope he'd enjoyed 'em 'cause he was payin' a helluva price by the time I got to him. Emphysema, cancer, but he was still pretty alert. I told him the story, and when I got to Bellerophon, old Marty came to life, so to speak. Spit the bit. He starts to wheeze and cough and sputter, I think he's gonna croak on the spot. But he gets calmed down and tells me the whole story . . . and it's a murder story okay, a real stunner. But I'll get to that in a second. I was more interested in exactly how the blackmailer hooked into Bellerophon. It wasn't exactly in the company history, y'know what I mean? So how'd he know? I figured it was the key to identifying him. After all, how many guys could know? So Marty says no, it ain't exactly in the company history, but in another way *it is* . . . Marty knew his job, he did what he was told and that covered some very hairy operations, but he always sat in the gunfighter's chair, back to the wall. Old Marty liked to cover his ass in case any of the big boys decided to sell him out, let him take the fall for some blown deal . . . y'see, old Marty used to be a rumrunner, Catalina to San Pedro, routes like that, up from Mexico, used to tell me about the flyin' fish, and he supplied dope for one of the big studios back in the thirties when he was a young fella, had to waste a movie star once who was being uncooperative, and in the sixties he was Magna's drug overseer to the stars." He looked at me, frog's eyes blinking heavily, slowly, tip of tongue between his lips. "Why, you musta known Marty Bjorklund pretty good, now I think of it."

"That's right," I said, "I knew Marty pretty good." I had that sick, sinking feeling in the pit of my stomach.

"Y'know, now I think of it, didn't old Marty say he passed through Tangier there when you fellas were making your last stand?"

"Why, yes, I believe he did. Of course, I was pretty groggy. It could have been another guy in some other town." I shrugged. "My memory's pretty hazy about Tangier."

"Everything's hazy in Tangier, right, Mr. Tripper?"

"Couldn't have put it better myself."

"Come on, snap out of it, you two." Innis sounded pissed off. "Where is this heading?"

"Oh, why don't you shut your yap? I'm getting there, never you fear. Once Cotter here knew how deep the blackmailer was into all this stuff—"

"Wait a minute," I said. "Let's go back to Marty covering his ass on Bellerophon . . . murder . . . how'd he do that?"

"Ah, yes. Well, a coupla ways. For one thing, he held on to the key evidence in the Bellerophon murder. Which meant the killer was on the hook to Magna ever after 'cause they could nail him anytime . . . and before he left Magna, which was about five years ago, Marty succeeded in having the facts of Bellerophon inserted into Magna's computer system. Not in one place, mind you, but bits and pieces in four or five different places—

find them all, you'd have the whole story. Smart, smart cookie. Marty held on to the access codes, one each for the various entries. Anybody rattles Marty's chain, Marty can rattle right back—that's how he covered his ass, got it?"

"Got it," I nodded.

"So, once Cotter here and his fellow bosses realized that somebody inside was looting the computer files, collecting all the old garbage, once they knew just how fat the blackmailer's dossiers were getting, once they knew he was on to the Bellerophon stuff—well, you can imagine how scared they were. This was bad stuff, it sure as hell couldn't come out. I mean, it had almost come out twenty years ago. They were—excuse my French—shitting bricks."

Ledbetter was shaking his massive head and running his fingers through the tangle of his beard. "I seem to be missing something here, my man. Now correct me if I'm wrong, but weren't we supposed to be looking for JC Tripper? Wasn't that the point of the exercise? You talk about blackmailers and murderers and ancient rumrunners, but not a word do I hear of Mr. JC Tripper—"

"—Who's supposed to be alive on this fucking island?" Innis shouted.

"What, may I ask," Ledbetter continued, "has any of this admittedly thrilling material to do with JC Tripper and the Allan Bechtol novel the world is waiting for?"

Morris Fleury was tamping at the ash in the bowl of his pipe. "Well, let me try to put this in . . . context, as they say. JC Tripper is very much a part of all this. You see, Mr. Ledbetter, twenty years ago, JC Tripper had had a bellyful of the life of a rock star, the drugs, the waste, and the bullshit and the endless hype . . . and, yes, the drugs, I said that, didn't I? The drugs. JC was a powerful man but not perhaps as powerful as he liked to think he was. They were prey to that, the excess of ego, the rock stars. JC . . . miscalculated. Rather seriously. JC threatened to blow the whistle on the Magna drug operation and record kickbacks and payoffs and who knows what else. He and his brother were hooked on pills, injections, that's all quite true, but JC was going public or to the police in Los Angeles . . . they could either try to keep him on the Magna team or they could try to shut him up, exercise some of their leverage one way or another . . .

"They brought Marty Bjorklund in on their final plan. Maybe they could frame him—child molestation, statutory rape, something to get him under their thumbs. What to do? Then Henry Bernstein spoke up and spoke sense to the group . . . and Bellerophon was born—"

Ledbetter interrupted excitedly. "Bellerophon! I've got it—they decided to frame JC Tripper for murder and hold it over his head to keep him in line! By God, how devilish!"

"Not exactly. Devilish? Yes. But not exactly a frame-up."

"How do you mean?" Innis said.

"It was JC Tripper who was murdered . . . Bellerophon was the plan to murder JC Tripper . . ."

Twenty-Three

Fleury blinked at the upturned faces, obviously feeling rather pleased with himself but hardly daring to enjoy it. I shrank away from the whole business. He was so close to the heart of it now, so close. Heidi Dillinger tensed in her chair, watching Fleury for any hints of what was to come. She was sizing him up, her arms wrapped around the leather bag in her lap. The way she stared at him made me feel she had a kind of X-ray vision that tested the truth of everything he said, or the lie. She turned to me, slowly raised her eyebrows inquiringly. *Bellerophon was the plan to murder JC . . . so how much did you know?* I avoided her penetrating eyes.

Sam Innis made a sour face, his little mouth drawn tight. "That's all well and good, pal, but this one here"—he nodded at Thumper Gordon, "he says JC is alive, here on this island. Now somebody's got the wrong end of the stick—"

Morris Fleury had laid the gun on the mantelpiece above the kitchen fireplace and was knocking the corncob against the blackened brick facing, sprinkling ashes. He tucked the corncob into the tobacco pouch and pushed the cherry tobacco into the bowl. "You're not listening to me," he said. "I said there was a plan." He struck a match on the brick and sucked the flame down into the bowl. "I didn't say it worked." Slowly he grinned at Innis. "Or maybe it only sort of worked . . ."

Sam winced, shook his head. "Oh, come on—what's that supposed to mean? Who was supposed to kill him?" He jerked his face around toward me. "Why so quiet, Lee? Where the hell were you? You keep telling us your brother's dead, so what's your story? You were there—you saw it all, right? Lee, we're up to our assholes in manure here and I think maybe you should be the one to start shoveling—"

"Sam," I said, "you get on my nerves, you know that?"

Fleury took the gun from the mantelpiece and swung the muzzle in an arc taking us all in. "Maybe we could let me carry on with my story. Trust me. You'll see things fall into place. At least most things. Let's go back to Cotter here and me, what he wanted me to do for the team. It was this blackmailer that was workin' on him—the blackmailer who'd found out everything, who'd somehow uncovered the secret of Bellerophon Marty Bjorklund had hidden in the computer. The blackmailer had Magna twisting in the wind . . . and they kept trying to figure out who this guy might be . . . and hell, nobody from Magna had ever *seen* JC Tripper dead—"

"What about the killer they sent?" That was Thumper Gordon, caught up in the puzzle.

"Let's say the killer they sent to do for JC wasn't exactly trustworthy," Fleury said. "So they—Cotter here and Rosen and some of the boys—began to wonder, could JC be alive? Maybe the killer hadn't gotten him—but no, they couldn't believe that! It was ridiculous . . . Well, think about that while we move along—now what did the good folks at Magna want me to do? It ain't too tough to figure out when you think what's at stake—they wanted me to find the blackmailer and kill him. I was now stepping into Marty Bjorklund's shoes, I was now Cotter Whitney's Marty Bjorklund . . .

"But before they sent me out to kill somebody, they decided they had to know whether or not JC was dead or alive. If they knocked off the blackmailer and JC was actually alive, they might still have big trouble on their hands—I mean, let's face it, JC had wanted to nail Magna twenty years ago, and if he was still alive, he was still a danger, if he was alive and clean and deciding it was time to get even for what they tried to do to him—see, it was one of those awful what-if deals, what if, what if. People with things to hide or fear are always saying 'What if somebody finds out, then I'll be in the dumper,' and that's where guys like me come in.

"JC Tripper alive was a time bomb, he could blow Magna into a million crispy, bite-sized pieces. He could dig up drugs and murder and mob connections and wreck the present, beat it to death with the past, he was sitting on a scandal that could wreck Magna and Cotter, and the boys were sitting right beside him. So I had two jobs: find the free lance and find JC if he was alive . . . and kill them both. If JC was the blackmailer, I'd only have to kill one person." He looked up with the open-mouthed grin full of bad teeth, gray, gapped teeth. "Right, Cotter? Wasn't that my job?"

Cotter Whitney said nothing. He didn't seem to have heard.

Fleury sipped noisily at a fresh cup of steaming coffee. Thumper laced it with a single malt while Fleury watched. Then Fleury began talking again. "It was then that Allan Bechtol, or Sam Innis, as you call him, Mr. Tripper—Bechtol and Ledbetter came to Magna with this crazy idea for a book, the novel based on the JC Tripper story. So there's all this to-ing and fro-ing with Magna and Purvis and Ledbetter, Magna wanting to pick up a publisher—this is not my area of expertise, y'unnerstan'. The part that concerned me was what Cotter and I decided right away—could this be a coincidence? Or is JC alive and behind it? And if it is a coincidence, does it mean that Bechtol knows something about JC? Namely that he's alive? Hell's bells, we figured Bechtol was a good bet to be working hand-in-glove with JC . . . or with the blackmailer. I sorta liked that . . . Innis/Bechtol in league with the blackmailer. Whichever, he seemed like a good source for us to use, being an old pal of JC's from Harvard days. And then Bechtol says he can sign up JC's brother Lee too, another big plus, right? So we figured why not get in on the play ourselves? Made good sense. It couldn't hurt and, anyway, did we have a better way to go? We'd been trying and we weren't coming up with much . . . and things were beginning to heat up."

241

Heidi Dillinger interrupted the flow of Fleury's story. She'd been thinking. "I want to get back to this plot to kill JC Tripper. Are you saying you *know* he survived? Or were you just speculating?"

"Oh, my goodness, just speculating, Miss Dillinger. Just playing the cards we were dealt. *What if.* That's the name of our game. Course, Mr. Gordon here says—"

"I know what Mr. Gordon here says," she snapped. "Mr. Gordon's brain was probably done sunnyside up in 1969—I believe what I see and I have yet to see JC Tripper on this island. What I want to know is, why didn't they kill Lee, too? I mean, why leave Lee to run loose and maybe tell what happened to JC—"

"I was in pretty rotten shape," I said.

"Yes, yes, we've heard all that before. But then you're a bit of a joke, aren't you, Lee?"

Fleury said, "There's a good reason why they didn't plan to kill Lee—ain't that right, Lee?" He was looking at me. I felt like a guy in a jail break standing in the glare of the spotlight.

"You're the man with the answers," I said. "Get on with your story."

"Well, things were heating up, like I said. Somebody had knocked off the deejay, Shadow Flicker—he'd been close to JC, see. Drug runner, distributor, big Magna kickback guy, made him rich at one time, slipping bad in later years—I was a little slow to realize why he had to die, but once the blackmailer was through with him—and he hadn't learned if JC was alive or dead—he had to die to protect the identity of the blackmailer. Real simple."

"Pardon me for being so dense once again," Hugo Ledbetter rumbled, "but why was this blackmailer of yours so interested in finding JC? What did JC have to do with his blackmail scheme?"

"The blackmailer wanted to up the ante, to strengthen his hand—JC could deliver all the details about the murder plan and all the rest of the dirt . . . They were natural allies, weren't they? They both had it in for Magna—imagine, JC Tripper back from the dead twenty years later with a hell of a story to tell—jeez, think of it." Fleury smiled one of his sour smiles primarily to himself. "And if JC didn't want to team up, then our blackmailer could kill him without the slightest qualm. That's why, Mr. Ledbetter." He sighed, remembering where he was in the story. "So Shadow Flicker was a discarded back issue—probably didn't know a damn thing. And when I got on to Sally Feinman and all of her ideas—I was just getting her confidence, she was gonna tell me her own theories about the Brothers Tripper—somebody bumped her off, too. Not just murders but torture murders—somebody was trying to find out *something* . . . and the more I thought about it, the more it looked like it had to be the whereabouts of JC Tripper. Later on, the same thing held true in the case of Clive Taillor, but I found out somebody had been paying Taillor off for twenty years. For his silence, I presumed. Reasonable, right?

"I had a lot of time to think and I've got me a nasty little turn of mind. I fussed around with the whole Bellerophon thing, how they were going to polish off JC to save their asses—how they were gonna keep Lee Tripper here from raising hell without having to kill him, too . . . and I began to see how Bellerophon worked and I remembered something Marty Bjorklund said at the end, the day before his lights went out for good. He kept telling me I had to see Lee. I thought he was rambling and babbling in a kind of delirium, that he was talking about Leo Roarke, one of the guys who ran Magna with D'Allessandro and Bernstein and that bunch. I thought he was thinking Leo was still alive, he kept saying Lee knew it all, and he'd laugh and it was one gruesome sight, I kid you not . . .

"Then I had me a brain wave. It was Lee Tripper he was talkin' about, not old Leo Roarke. He said old Lee knew it all . . . now what did he mean? Then my deceitful, bent mind began figuring it out. Do you know what he meant, Mr. Tripper?"

Forever crept past. Whitney said, "Answer the man."

"Yes," I said, "I know exactly what Marty Bjorklund meant." I heard my voice from a million miles away.

"Your memory freshening up a bit?" Fleury grinned wetly, licked his lips.

"I'm still listening," I said. "Go on, go on." I was trying hard to think about my options, the cards I'd been dealt so long ago.

"I knew Lee was deep in it," Fleury said, enjoying all the

insinuations, "but I didn't know how. Damned if I knew how. But in Zurich I found out how Clive Taillor had been getting those regular payments, twenty years of them. *Hush money*." He relished those two words as if he were an actor in the last moments of a thriller, had been waiting for his favorite lines. "I couldn't get any answers from the bankers in Zurich, they wouldn't let me in on where that money had come from. Then . . . then I saw I could come at it from the other end. Who might have paid him off? I made a list . . . and at the top of the list was *the brother*. Lee, old pal, I gotta tell you, you're one for the books, you are."

"I'm glad to hear it," I said. Everything at the table was changing. Everybody was turning toward me, everyone but Thumper, who was sipping Scotch, watching.

"I've been a security man for a helluva long time. I've got some damn fine connections. Professional courtesy. I had a man back in New York give your banking records a once-over. I didn't have him go back twenty years, Lee, I didn't need to." He puffed out his cheeks and blew out a long sigh. "Lee, you're the guy who's been paying Clive Taillor. Lee, you've been naughty, haven't you?"

"Naughty?" I shrugged. "I have been paying Clive Taillor. I was hoping you wouldn't find out."

"For Christ's sake!" Innis was looking at me hard. None of them knew quite what to make of it or me.

"You're not going to stop now," I said, "not when you're on such a roll, surely."

"Don't call me Shirley, Lee." Fleury grinned. "Shall I explain how Bellerophon worked, Lee?"

"Give it your best shot," I said.

"I looked up the word 'Bellerophon.'" Fleury was still grinning at his own cleverness. "My mythology was always a little weak. But you know who old Bellerophon was? I'll tell you. He was the fella, along with the flying horse Pegasus—remember the old gas stations, the flying red horse? Well, Bellerophon was the fella who slew the horrible monster Chimera. Bellerophon killed Chimera . . . Now it don't take your rocket scientist to know who played the Chimera—JC Tripper was Magna's Chimera, the monster who had to be slain." He waited, his

244

moist little eyes darting from face to face. He'd probably never been happier. "Now, who best to slay JC Tripper? Who could play Bellerophon?" He waited. Heidi Dillinger had gotten the idea. But she didn't know what to think. She was in an odd position, thanks to me. Each of us was in an odd position and it was going to get odder. The whole thing was out of control. Fleury spoke softly, slowly. "Who would you say, Lee?"

"Oh, Morris. What a guy you turned out to be."

"Thank you, Lee. High praise from you—"

"Marty Bjorklund," I began, "turned up in Tangier. Out of the blue. He was a very pleasant fellow, really. Family man. Nice little wife. We both always liked Marty. But he was up against the wall that time. JC was making trouble, just the way Fleury says." I remembered the day as if it were yesterday. "JC had to go. JC was about to ruin all our lives . . . JC had gone off the deep end, JC had to die. Marty didn't want to kill both of us. Hell, Marty didn't want to kill anybody. But JC had to die, no two ways about it. If Marty had killed him, then Lee would know . . . and then Lee would have to be killed, too. You see the way his mind was working? It was pointless—why did both of us have to die? But . . . if one of us killed the other and Marty held on to the proof of the murderer's identity, then we'd all be safe and JC would have gone to rock-star heaven . . . Makes a crazy kind of sense, doesn't it?" My mouth was dry. What a mess. My God, how the time slips away . . .

Fleury couldn't wait.

"You, Lee Tripper, were Bellerophon. You, Lee Tripper, killed your brother!"

"Well, you funny little man," I said, "you finally figured it out."

Twenty-Four

Heidi Dillinger was looking at me through eyes narrowed to slits. I'd turned out to be just what she'd said, a lying scoundrel, but maybe more so than she'd bargained for. I wondered what she was really thinking. Was she remembering how jealous she'd been of Annie? Did she care anymore? Her face was unreadable. Sam Innis wasn't having quite such a complex reaction to my perfidious behavior.

"Why, you miserable son of a bitch!" He was starting to rise but sank back when Fleury twitched the shotgun in his direction. "JC was worth ten of you, creep! And you killed him . . . killed your own brother . . . Christ! All this time you knew he was dead—"

"I always told you my brother was dead, Sam. I told everybody. But nobody would believe me. Is that my fault? It was Marty's plan. Bellerophon. Old Lee was supposed to waste JC . . . that was the plan, all right. I was Bellerophon."

"Good Lord," Ledbetter murmured, rumbling. "Some stories you just don't expect. I'd not have thought it of you, Mr. Tripper."

Fleury cleared his throat. "You all got your outrage and

righteous moral indignation outta the way now? Fine, then let's get back to bidness here. I'm still working for Magna and the meter's running—"

"But where does the killer of Sally Feinman and Mr. Flicker and Clive Taillor, where does he surface?" This was Cotter Whitney, who hadn't seemed unduly moved by the news that I was Bellerophon. Of course, he hadn't heard the whole story yet. None of them had.

"I'm comin' to that. Finding out that Lee here was a killer, that he'd killed his brother, only made Lee a monster. Nothin' personal, Lee."

"Of course not, Morris," I said.

"But my problem wasn't solved. I knew JC was truly dead . . . but who was the blackmailer? Who had killed all those people? Well, hell . . . I got to think about how I'd put old Lee here under surveillance in the first place. I knew I'd have to talk with him eventually, so I thought I'd have a look at him in his natural habitat, as they say. I had an appointment . . . well, not an appointment, actually, but I'd planned to see Sally Feinman. But first I was going to have a look at this Lee Tripper character. So I watched Heidi Dillinger pick him up that day on Fifth Avenue . . . Lee Tripper, this Bechtol/Innis character with his two names—his secret identity, all the bullshit, as if he was important or some damn thing—and his right-hand man Heidi Dillinger. Lots of possibilities in these three, I said to myself . . . I'd done some checking on the three of them before I went to work, dontcha see? And this Heidi Dillinger, she was the smartest of the three by a longshot. Stuck out like a green thumb, as they say—"

"Sore thumb," Heidi said.

"What?"

"Forget it."

"Well, she had all the brains, all right. Innis was an eccentric egomaniac who seemed to think the world existed only to provide backgrounds for his books—in other words, Innis was a Section Eight, a head case—"

"You asshole!" Sam again. Once he got mad, he stayed mad. "You insufferable little turd! Who are you to call me a head case?"

"You are also a bad writer," Fleury said. "But that's not punishable by law. You just don't have the brains for anything really interesting—I got that from reading your books."

"Everybody's a critic," Innis muttered.

"Heidi," Fleury said, "she was the smarty-pants. Maybe Innis didn't have the idea to do a book based on the search for JC Tripper. Maybe Innis didn't have the idea to bring Lee Tripper in on it. Maybe the whole damn thing was Heidi Dillinger's idea. Now that made sense to me. You get used to doing these little double-thinks in my business, everybody's always using somebody. As soon as you take a look at things, you can be damn sure that nothing is what it seems to be. So you start trying different scenarios. And I was thinking about Heidi, our pretty Heidi. So I began to dig a little more into our Heidi . . ."

"I rather resent this," Heidi said softly, shifting the weight of her big leather bag.

"Well, I'm mighty sorry about that, but it's an interesting story. You're all gonna enjoy it, I promise you. Just bear with me, Heidi . . . guess what I found out about Heidi . . . ? Heidi had started out as a researcher and computer programmer at Magna-mation, our data-processing and credit-information wing . . . that's where we know everything about everybody." He chuckled, indulging himself. "You gotta know how to retrieve the information. And our Heidi played with things, began finding out things. She worked in London for us, then at the San Diego computer center. Well, a while back, before all this began, Heidi did a workup on publishing companies 'cause Magna was interested in acquisitions. And she found Purvis and Ledbetter particularly fascinating, she suggested a closer interest be shown—am I right so far, darlin'? What was the focus of interest? What made P and L valuable? Allan Bechtol, or, as she already knew him to be, Sam Innis. He was the lure. She left Magna, she presented herself to Innis—and he's only human, he couldn't resist. She was *his*. She was indispensable, she did everything she was asked to do and more, lots more—she was . . . magic word—*creative!* She was worth her weight in gold—"

Sam Innis, red-faced, began yelling again. "What is the point of this? Is this going somewhere?"

"And then, God love her, I'll bet the farm the idea for the JC Tripper book was Heidi's, wasn't it, Mr. Innis?"

"Well . . . I probably thought of it, she saw it was a good idea. Sure. Yeah, she was behind it all the way." Sam Innis's voice trailed off as he turned to Heidi. "It was your idea, I guess, wasn't it, kid? You came to me . . ."

"She'd been thinking about it for a long time," Fleury said. "It all hatched in her mind at Magnamation when she discovered that Allan Bechtol was Sam Innis and Sam Innis had been a schoolmate and pal of JC and Lee Tripper." He shook his head, smiling faintly at Heidi Dillinger. "You've got to hand it to Heidi, everybody. She's what we used to call one smart cookie. I figure it was her plan all along—but what was the point? Just money? Not our pretty Heidi. What she wanted was to leverage herself into some real power at Magna by using the JC Tripper story, the Bellerophon plot, all the narcotics dossiers she was building . . . Jesus, it was a thing of beauty! She was even able to turn all those fuckin' computers at Magnamation against the great mother company itself.

"Finding JC Tripper if he was still alive—somehow she'd got it into her head that Bellerophon had gone wrong, had come apart—would be the frosting on the cake. The perfect partner for her. But she had to find him . . . and she didn't know if Lee here knew where JC was or not, and Lee kept telling her and everybody else that JC was dead . . . so she had to start killing people." His eyes rolled wetly toward Heidi. I didn't know if he was expecting a round of applause or a denial or what.

Sam Innis shook his head. "I simply don't believe it, Fleury. You're trying to shift the blame away from yourself. Oldest trick in the world."

"You'd better believe it." Fleury was frowning. Was he having doubts? "Oh, she didn't kill them and torture them first, not Heidi herself. God's love, no. She was there, mind you, she asked the questions—didn't you, Heidi? But you had muscle on hand . . . for the heavy lifting, as they used to say in the old days. You know, Lee, the fella you killed in Zurich? One of Heidi's little persuaders, probably the same guy who killed Clive Taillor . . . oh no, she didn't want to *kill* you, Lee. She wanted to scare you, make you think that JC, if he was still alive and you knew it, was turning against you, killing people, even you, to protect his hiding place . . . turned out you killed the guy. Damn fine piece of work, by the way. You're a tough customer, Lee—" He broke off and turned back to Heidi. "So, young lady, you're the blackmailer . . . and you're the killer. Whattaya say, pretty Heidi?"

"Madness," Ledbetter muttered.

"You can say that again," Innis said. "And you, Lee, are the world's prize son of a bitch . . . goddamn killer, bastard, fratricide, fucker—" He stood up, knocking the chair over backward. He was, I think, coming after me, though I never found out.

"I'm a lot of things, Sam," I said, "but one thing I'm not. I'm not Lee Tripper."

Twenty-Five

I'd been waiting a long time for the inevitable and there it was at last.

I'm not Lee Tripper . . .

Then everything happened very quickly, too fast to follow clearly, but looking back at it you can slow it down, slower and slower, until you can see the full shock of it, particle by particle.

No one quite knew what it meant when I said I wasn't Lee Tripper. Thumper gave one of his characteristic soft, high-pitched laughs, thumping the table before him with both hands like the old drummer he was. Ledbetter turned in his chair, rumbled, "Come again?" Cotter Whitney peered at me as if he might, if he really strained, see the truth. His mouth made a circle and he was in his mind hearing the other shoe drop.

Fleury was licking his heavy, trembling lower lip, his eyes showing an animal mixture of fear and confusion. "You're not? You're not Lee Tripper?" Then his gray face paled and he said, "Oh my God, I never thought of—"

Heidi Dillinger didn't do any talking. I'll never know what she was thinking, what she had figured out and what was still a mystery to her. She was fighting for her life and I'm sure she

251

was disgusted by the irony in being brought to grief by a creep like Morris Fleury. It must have galled her. She was so bright and so determined and so able. Why did she ever decide she needed to kill people . . . was it just to hurry the process along, get there faster? Yuppiedom gone wildly awry? Or was it the love of the game? The delight in plotting a course and then sticking to it, whatever it took? Maybe that was it. I like to think she hadn't started with the intention of hurting anyone, let alone killing them . . . but then the game had begun to run out of control, taking her with it. Destroying her . . .

She quickly—I didn't see it happen, it just *happened*—she quickly had a gun in her hand. No wonder she'd held on to that bag for dear life. Was it stupid for her to go for the gun? Christ, I don't know—what did she think she was going to do after using it? She'd just had it, I guess. Fleury had figured it all out and she was a goner one way or another. It was a terrible mess. What was she supposed to do? Sit there and take it? Have all her dreams crash down on her and leave one trampled yuppie?

She had the gun out, pointing it at Fleury, but guns weren't really her thing, were they?

When I saw her with the gun in her hand I thought about the time we'd spent together. I saw her whipping Mellow Yellow's ass on Fifth Avenue, I saw her head on the pillow the first time we made love, I saw her happy and angry and—

Fleury wasn't thinking at all. He didn't blink an eye. You had the feeling he was finally playing in his own ballpark.

He gave her both barrels in a fraction of a second and I saw most of her beautiful face disappear in a cascade of blood, bone, tissue, and hair.

It blew her back out of the chair, ass over appetite, left her body jerking spasmodically on the floor. The noise was deafening and the smell was everywhere.

Cotter Whitney let out a scream. At least I think it was a scream and I think it was Whitney. There was a lot of noise. He half-stood, tripped, fell backward over his chair onto the floor. I thought he'd cracked and was trying to escape. It was all happening so fast.

Innis and Ledbetter were shouting and I was trying not to

look at the remains of Heidi Dillinger and Fleury was yelling at everybody to calm down.

Cotter Whitney wasn't trying to escape.

He was trying to get to Heidi's gun.

Fleury wasn't really paying attention. And anyway he'd have to reload.

Whitney got to the gun, I saw him out of the corner of my eye, saw him bringing it up.

Fleury saw him, too, turned, and pulled the triggers on the empty chambers. Then he smiled the thin smile of the pessimist who has had his pessimism confirmed. He's right but he wishes he weren't. It was funny, how much class he had at the end.

Cotter Whitney shot him three times. Once for being too zealous an employee, once for talking too goddamn much, and once for shooting a lady. All three rounds went into Fleury's chest, making quite a mess of his cardiovascular system. One got him right in the pump. As they say. He went back against the wall next to the fireplace. The shotgun clattered to the floor. He sat down and by the time he came to rest he was dead. Eyes open, floating off into infinity. Maybe he'd just joined up with Heidi Dillinger, two of a kind, a couple of escape artists on the journey of a lifetime. As they say.

Cotter Whitney was not your ordinary fool.

Whatever Heidi Dillinger had plundered from the Magna computers and whatever other sources she'd developed—it was all gone now. Fleury had erased her, her sharp brittle mind, all the information she'd collected. Erased.

And Cotter Whitney was no fool.

Morris Fleury was the only other wound from which Magna's lifeblood was draining. Cotter Whitney had just stopped the bleeding.

Whitney stood stock-still, staring at Heidi's body.

Maybe I was wrong about the way his mind was working.

Maybe he was just fed up. Maybe he was being gallant, making a gesture.

But I don't think so. I think he knew exactly what he was doing.

Finally Thumper said, "Okay, mates. The show's over, our revels now are ended." He took the gun from Whitney. "None of this ever happened, see? I'm going to take the remains of these two people, whoever the hell they are, I'm going to take them out in my boat, all weighted down with stones, and I'm gonna feed the bleeding fishies with them. Lost when your little craft capsized getting across from Lewis. End of story. Lost at sea. Nobody's gonna argue." He turned to Whitney, then to Innis and Ledbetter. "Hearing no objections, the motion is carried."

Then Thumper came to me and we looked at each other a long time. Then he said, "Jesus, you're a sight for sore eyes . . . twenty years, man. I didn't think I'd be seeing you again, JC." He put his arms around me. I felt as if I'd come home.

Innis was trying to get it all straight. He kept falling farther and farther behind. "Who the hell are you?"

"Ah, Sam, for God's sake, use your head. It's me. JC."

He just stared at me, eyes wide, mouth open.

"Thumper knew me," I said.

"Well, not for sure," Thumper said. "You're twenty years older, you're fifty pounds heavier—hell, seventy pounds heavier than you were there at the end. You musta been down to one-fifty. You got a whole lot less hair. And you've had a bit of work done, around the eyes, around the nose." He grinned at me. "I'm not sure I'd have recognized you. On my own, I mean."

"What do you mean—on your own?"

"I was told you were alive, that you'd be paying me a visit."

"What the hell are you talking—"

"Annie, Trip. Annie told me—"

"Of course," I said.

"She knew right away, said you came up to her in a pub in Sloane Square—she knew you before she saw your face. It was your voice."

"Yes. It would be."

"She's here now."

"What do you mean?"

"She's out in the recording studio. One of the barns, I've fixed it up. Deluxe, actually. She comes to see Chris—he's studying composition with me. Gifted kid. Real future. They're

254

out there." He pointed out the window to a stone barn, whitewashed. "It's soundproof. No windows." He looked around the room. "Why don't you go out and see Annie . . . these three catatonic specimens can help me clean up the mess."

"No, no, I'll help—"

"Trip, listen to me. You sound like you're insisting on helping with the dishes. Now just listen. I was always the brains of the operation, right? You were the talent. I was the brains. Try to remember that. You're entering a whole new world . . . you won't know it for a while, but the first step is to go out to the studio. Listen to Thumper. Leave this to me."

"One thing, Thump," I said.

"Sure."

"Bellerophon. They set up Lee to kill me—"

"I figured that, just listening to all this—"

"But you know how Lee was. He was a head case, he was drugged to pieces thanks to Magna, all their Dr. Feelgoods, he couldn't handle any of it . . . The night he was supposed to kill me, he couldn't do it, he just couldn't do it, he could not kill old JC . . . But he was in deep, he knew they'd kill us both if he didn't kill me, he knew he wasn't going to last much longer anyway . . . So he had a plan, he told me I should kill him and switch our roles . . . then JC would be dead, I would become Lee, I could go the hell away, he was almost out of his mind, he was shot up with shit . . . I told him no, we'd figure out something else, I didn't want to believe he was in the shape he was in, that he was too far gone ever to get back . . . I wouldn't go for it . . . So my brother Lee put a gun to his head and did it for me . . . and I carried out his plan. I photographed the body, lousy light, head shot to pieces, and I sent the gun with Lee's prints on it to Marty Bjorklund. I followed all the instructions Marty had given Lee to prove he'd done it . . . and I became Lee Tripper. You see, I had to keep Annie out of it. Magna felt safe, they had all the proof that I, Lee, had killed JC, and even if I went public as JC they'd say I was mad, had killed my brother . . . or they'd just kill me. And if I'd dragged Annie into it—well, she'd have been at risk, too. So . . . I just had to disappear."

Thumper had opened the door to the outside. "Go on, Trip. Seems to me you owe Annie one hell of an explanation." He smiled raggedly behind the beard. "Come on, you've come all this way. Take the last step."

"All right," I said.

"You'll find Annie has a story for you, too."

And Thump was right about that.

Annie listened to my tale of woe and held my hand and kissed me when it was over.

And then she introduced me to Chris.

My son.